Lesson number one . . .

The civilian recruit snarled, "I'm not in your army. I'm a damned civilian, and there's been one giant screwup here, see? So you can take your uniform and cram it. I'm leaving."

Peach stayed perfectly calm and stood up, blocking the light. "Not yet, sport. Just do what you're told."

The civilian, shorter than Peach but with huge shoulders, showed no fear. He reached into his pocket, casually drew a long switchblade and flicked it open. "Last chance to back off, soldier." He was cool, confident, and held the knife like he knew how to use it.

Peach grinned. "Well, knife-fighting wasn't on the schedule for today, but since you offered . . ."

The shorter man moved forward at Peach with surprising speed and whipped the knife in front of him. Peach caught the man's wrist in midslash and twisted hard, almost to the point of breaking. The knife dropped to the floor, immediately followed by the civilian, howling in pain.

Peach eyed the recruits coldly. "Commander Getts will be here in a few days. Before he comes, you *will* be in uniform. You *will* perform as ordered. Or I *will* punch your ticket straight to hell. Any questions?"

No one even breathed.

NAVY SEALS
BLACKLIGHT

Mike Murray

A SIGNET BOOK

SIGNET
Published by New American Library, a division of
Penguin Putnam Inc., 375 Hudson Street,
New York, New York 10014, U.S.A.
Penguin Books Ltd, 27 Wrights Lane,
London W8 5TZ, England
Penguin Books Australia Ltd, Ringwood,
Victoria, Australia
Penguin Books Canada Ltd, 10 Alcorn Avenue,
Toronto, Ontario, Canada M4V 3B2
Penguin Books (N.Z.) Ltd, 182–190 Wairau Road,
Auckland 10, New Zealand

Penguin Books Ltd, Registered Offices:
Harmondsworth, Middlesex, England

First published by Signet, an imprint of New American Library,
a division of Penguin Putnam Inc.

First Printing, April 2000
10   9   8   7   6   5   4   3   2   1

Chapter One

Ancient mountains, burned bare of vegetation by too much sun and too little water, despoiled by spilt blood from eons of warring tribesmen, appeared to be the fractured remains of God's hammer blows from the time when Jehovah forged this earth. The mountains were jumbled, jagged, twisted rocks and sand that only goats and dedicated men chose to traverse.

Muted sounds and blurred motions in the darkness were sensed along narrow paths made by wild animals. Sounds of grunting punctuated the inky blackness as climbers passed with difficulty from rock to rock, lowering themselves from one hand perch to another. They were nine in number, their figures contrasting in size: four were children, the other five were men. The first rays of the dawn's orange-yellow light streaking across the sky revealed that the group all wore desert camouflage clothing, including balaclava scarves that covered their faces. Each carried a heavy load for his size. A good part of their loads consisted of new, freshly oiled guns.

The larger men occasionally helped their smaller counterparts as they hurried to beat the early morning sun. When they spoke, which was rarely, it was in whispers; and each responded at once to hand signals from their leader, a man called Conrad. Conrad was no taller than the other men in the group, but his hair was brown rather than black, the sun having lightened its ends to a rusty hue. Conrad's face was smooth, unlike those of his adult companions, two of whom had mustachioed faces scored by pockmarks.

They had almost reached the end of the first leg of a difficult journey. Below them in the valley, appearing blacker than the shadows of the mountains, was a thin strip of asphalt highway. Conrad removed field glasses from a

leather case slung around his neck and surveyed their position. Satisfied for the moment, he signaled to his eight-man
force to rest. He was pleased that none of them removed
their packs as they slid silently to the ground. One young-
ster removed his balaclava to cool his face. He could not
have been twelve years of age.

A Mercedes-Benz touring bus was grinding its way up a
steep grade through the upheaval of the Taurus Mountains.
At a crest, the driver shifted into a higher-ratio gear, and
the bus picked up speed. That particular stretch of road
was more than one hundred kilometers north of the Sea of
Galilee, below the town of En Hor near the Syrian-Israel
border. In the background, competing with the noise of the
bus's howling engine, was the sound of children's voices
singing.

> *You are my sunshine, my only sunshine,*
> *you make me happy when skies are gray . . .*

Inside the bus were twenty children ages ten through
thirteen, plus a teenaged girl, Linda, who acted as an aide
to the adult chaperons, Gerry Scarborough, Genevieve
Wheatley, Shirley Kerwin, and Doris Bradburn. Their
driver was Israeli. Mrs. Wheatley had noticed that the
driver had what appeared to be an automatic weapon
placed inconspicuously against the inside wall of the bus
near his left leg. That the weapon might actually be used
never occurred to her.

Not all of the children sang. A few slept, some pored
over comic books smuggled aboard the bus despite Mrs.
Scarborough's threats, which included an embargo on bub-
ble gum and candy bars. This was to be an enjoyable excur-
sion, but foremost an educational experience. "Nelson,"
she said to one of the current thorns in her side, "are you
writing on the back of Barbara's collar? Give me that."
She collected the stylus from the boy's pudgy fingers and
noted with relief that it was a pencil and not a ballpoint
pen.

Shirley Kerwin's head kept nodding forward as she bat-
tled against sleep caused by her oldest enemy since gram-
mar school, rising early from bed. Richard Miller, one-third
of Mrs. Kerwin's thirty years, tantalized himself as well as

his male buddies by trying to stick a finger into her open mouth and withdrawing it before she snapped closed her sagging jaws.

you'll never know, dear, how much I love you,
please don't take my sunshine . . .

The impromptu chorus trilled on.

"Charles," said Mrs. Wheatley, "please put your comic book away and watch the countryside. You're going to miss the Sea of Galilee."

"I have to go to the bathroom," bleated a nine-year-old.

"Are you sure, Gary? You just went." *Of course he is sure,* Mrs. Scarborough said to herself. After all, they had been on the road for two hours since leaving Anshier, and the children had been drinking water and tea. The sun was now fully up. Mrs. Scarborough suddenly felt thirsty. "We'll stop soon," she promised.

"Having fun?" grinned Doris Bradburn.

"Next time Alan sponsors an educational trip, he can go, and I'll stay home to fill out his foursome at the club," Mrs. Scarborough returned with level sincerity.

"Come on. You'd do it again. Haven't we had a good time?"

Just then, the tires on the bus seemed to explode.

From the outside, it looked as though they had been shredded. Even extra-heavy-duty bus tires could not overcome the devastating effect of military tire rippers placed strategically in the path of the motorized coach. The bus lurched and ground to a rapid halt. For a long moment, there was silence from within while the American children and their chaperons sat stunned and confused.

Ehlel Herzog, however, was not confused. The driver had fought in two desert wars. Even before the bus's engine coughed and stopped, he was reaching for his nearby assault weapon. He had twisted the weapon from its restraining clips and turned toward the door of the bus. The door contained a window lower than all others on the passenger vehicle, and Herzog instinctively focused on his most vulnerable flank. He was thus unprepared for the burst of autofire from the road on the driver's side that caught him in the back of the head and propelled his forehead and the upper half of his face across the bus leaving an unrecognizable congealed mass of flesh clinging to the far wall of the bus.

The children began screaming. The bus door flew inward and Conrad's form filled the opening, his balaclava scarf fastened closed so that his victims might not see the face that would cause them so much pain.

"Out!" he barked. "Everybody out! Quickly, get out of the bus!" His authoritative demand was supported by loud, urgent shouts from his comrades, who broke windows, pulled open the bus's emergency rear door, and climbed inside.

Conrad's young commandos, still wearing petite-sized military camouflage, fired rifles through the roof of the bus and out of its windows, while screeching at children their own age to do as their leader ordered.

"Out of the bus!" they yelled, seeming to enjoy the terror visited upon children of their own age.

The Americans were roughly herded into a nearby cul-de-sac of rocks. One of Conrad's men sprang into the bus, then kicked the dead driver onto the sun-baked side of the road. He slammed the bus into gear, harshly revving the engine so that despite its ten shredded tires, it rolled slowly over the brow of the sheer side of the road. The terrorist jumped clear of the bus as it plunged over the lip. For a long moment, everyone was mesmerized by the huge vehicle floating through space, bouncing once, then twice, before striking large rocks far below.

"You . . . you . . . and you . . . over there. Stand there by that boy. Move!" Conrad barked to the adults, including Linda.

"Good God," began Mrs. Bradburn. "I don't think you understand who we are. We're not Israelis, we're Americans."

"Shut your mouth," Conrad said evenly.

"I will not shut my mouth. We are . . ."

Conrad struck her on the jaw with closed fist. Mrs. Bradburn fell to the ground, dazed. She pulled herself to one knee and willed herself to rise and stand erect. The children began to cry anew as Linda rushed to Mrs. Bradburn's side.

"I'm all right," Mrs. Bradburn said.

Mrs. Kerwin stepped forward. She controlled her fear

only with great effort. She reached inside her handbag to come up with a wallet. "We all have money. Here. And we have traveler's checks." She handed them toward Conrad, who calmly raised a pistol, pointed it at Mrs. Kerwin's head, and pulled the trigger.

Mrs. Kerwin was blown backward by the force of the parabellum round, cross-filed to expand upon impact with flesh. Hysterical children shrieked in horror. Some covered their eyes and made no sounds. Still others were shocked into total immobility.

Conrad's four adult colleagues made the American women kneel while their hands were tied behind their backs. This done, the children's hands were easily tied as well. They were made to face large rocks in the cul-de-sac. All had soiled their pants, most cried, and some were too terrified to move or look.

"Lafi," Conrad said to one of his adult men, "watch closely. After today, I have other missions to accomplish. You will be on your own. Do you understand?"

"Yes, Conrad. We are ready," Lafi said.

Lafi had positioned the small, uniformed apprentice terrorists behind the back of each woman. Each boy held a gun that he carried in a webbed holster. The first, a boy named Rashef, stood behind Mrs. Bradburn, whose eyes were locked on some distant point far off on the horizon. But it was Rashef's eyes that suddenly filled with tears.

Conrad spoke to him in an understanding, even sympathetic way. "You are a warrior, Rashef. A soldier for Mohammed. Remember how Mohammed had to fight the enemies of Allah? You must do no less." Conrad reached out to touch the boys head, almost caressing his hair. "Do it now, Rashef. You understand. Do it."

Rashef pulled the trigger. The 9mm pistol bucked in his small hand, and he watched in fascination while Mrs. Bradburn, shot through the neck and the larynx, bled out slowly onto rocks already warming under Middle Eastern sun.

"Good, Rashef," Conrad congratulated the boy. "Very well done. Now, we have more to do. Let's help the others." Conrad put his arm around Rashef, who, shaking, obeyed without speaking. For fifteen minutes, Conrad and his cadre coaxed, threatened, and always praised, while children killed children.

At another of Conrad's commands, the small servants of the same Allah who blesses the Eastern *jihad* against the Western Satan, picked up their gear, lightened now by spent ammunition, and prepared to move out, back into the mountains whence they came. Conrad was the last to leave the killing grounds.

He turned to one of four remaining American souls. Kneeling slowly, gracefully, he spoke into her ear: "Listen to me carefully, Mrs. Scarborough," he said evenly in a clear European accent. "Salvage divers will bring up pieces of Flight Two-Eight-Zero, which will have been blown up with explosives. Tell the experts to examine the area behind seat number 48A. Can you remember that, Mrs. Scarborough? Seat 48A. And tell them that more American airplanes will go down. Many more. Now walk, Mrs. Scarborough. Take your children and walk, while you can."

Chapter Two

Fourth Officer Jon Ewing stood at the ship's rail, lowering his head and squinting one eye against the arctic winds and the whipping spume from the caps of six-foot heaving seas. He was turning back toward the bridge of the twenty-thousand-ton freighter *Rensblume* when a small flash against a black horizon caught his attention. He looked briefly into the sky off the starboard quarter but saw nothing more. He started to turn away again when he heard distant noise, like far-off thunder. Concluding that a thunderstorm was brewing from the north, Ewing resolved to check the weather radar when he reached the bridge. It was then that he saw sudden tendrils of fire illuminating the night, like fizzled fireworks trickling downward from the heavy slate clouds. Before the first burning fingers of flame reached the sea, Ewing realized with horror what it was. He raced toward the bridge, climbing ladders with the drive of a charging animal.

Very quickly, Thor Geppshell, captain of the *Rensblume,* ordered fifteen degrees right rudder, swinging the bow of his ship off its course for Bergen, Norway, toward the site of what his fourth officer predicted would be aircraft wreckage. The captain did not order an increase in engine revolutions because he knew he would lose stoppage at the wreck site. The huge ship should even now be slowing from its current speed of sixteen knots. He used a ship's telephone to dictate a message to the radio room to be sent over international emergency frequencies.

Her Majesty's Coast Guard Station at Mizen Head, Ireland, received a distress transmission, as did two other Coast Guard stations: one at the Faeroe Islands, another at Stornaway in the Hebrides. Each dispatched rescue cutters. Search and rescue aircrews from England, Scotland, and the Faeroes were alerted, and assigned search areas near the coordinates of 17° 22' west longitude; 58° 10' north latitude. Winds were approaching Force Seven, and the outlook for clearing was not good.

Les Havil, vice president in charge of aviation operations for United Airlines in the UK, was roused from a deep sleep in the early morning hours. It was with a certain amount of dread that he lifted the receiver from the hook. He had learned long ago that good news never came at this time of the morning and rarely by telephone.

"Yes?" he rasped, propping an elbow under himself to better draw a breath of air. He promised himself once again that today was the day he would quit smoking.

"Mr. Havil, sir? Tony Barger here, acting supervisor for UK Air Traffic Control, western approaches." The voice hesitated to allow Havil to respond. Havil had no idea who Barger was, but that was no matter.

"Yes, Mr. Barger. What is it?" Havil said, a black fog of foreboding beginning to crawl across his brow.

"Seems that we lost contact with your Flight Two-Eight-Zero out of Kennedy . . ."

Fingers of ice clutched at Havil's entire central nervous system. In twenty-eight years of service in almost every level of management with United—from cleaning aircraft while attending university at Wisconsin, to selling tickets, to advertising and promotions, finally reaching the lofty upper echelons of directing one of the world's largest commercial air fleets—he had never lost an aircraft. He had begun to believe he never would. "How long ago?"

"About . . ." the voice hesitated again, as though Barger were referring to a timepiece ". . . a half hour, it's been now."

"A half hour?" Havil was already getting out of bed, his face feeling flushed from instant anger. "Why wasn't I notified immediately?" The words had hardly escaped his lips than he wished they could be recalled and replaced by calmer, more constructive instructions. He reached for his cigarettes on the nightstand.

"The controller handling Two-Eight-Zero was not certain that the aircraft commander had finished his transmission, Mr. Havil. It was a routine altitude change advisement. Transmissions have been chunky in tonight's atmospherics, too."

The excuse sounded weak, Havil thought, but traffic controlling was never an easy task, even for the sharpest observers. "All right, go ahead."

"The transponder faded from radar, sir. We were running up our emergency location procedure when a Norwegian freighter reported a flash in the sky at about the correct location for your aircraft, I'm afraid."

"Oh, God," Havil murmured.

"I'm very sorry, Mr. Havil."

Havil obtained a dial tone and dialed an international number from memory, connecting with UA's corporate headquarters in Chicago. Noting the early time and the grim circumstances, he stabbed the receiver back into its cradle and rummaged through his nightstand for a small leather book containing telephone numbers to call for exactly this kind of disaster.

President and chief executive officer of United Airlines, Herman Castanza, was in Miami, Florida, where he was scheduled to address an assembly of the International Brotherhood of Machinists. Castanza ordered that the National Transportation Safety Board and the Federal Aeronautics Administration be notified of the disaster. The NTSB, located in Washington, D.C., was alerted via an emergency hotline, as was the FAA division in Oklahoma City in charge of European and Atlantic operations. A team of expert crash investigators were awakened shortly after midnight and within the hour were boarding a chartered aircraft from Dulles. They would be joined shortly by a member of the permanent Technical Investigation team and then begin their flight plan to Glasgow, Scotland.

Before noon the following day, United Airlines, in cooperation with the British Air Ministry, had chartered the services of Argos Oceanic, an experienced commercial salvage company. Argos Oceanic dispatched an engineering ship, a diving barge, and a tender along with two crews of highly trained deep-water divers. Simultaneously, two crews of American divers and their equipment would leave that afternoon from Boston by a United Airlines cargo 747 aircraft.

There was, everyone knew, no hope for the survival of any passengers aboard Flight 280.

Reuters News Service was first to break the "Disappearance of Flight 280." Morning newspapers and television stations all over the world carried the story as its lead, many with a picture of a wide-body jet to set the tone of the disaster. The media were confident in reporting the unlikelihood of survivors being found in the frigid waters of the North Atlantic.

There had been articulate, carefully phrased speculations about the cause of Flight 280's fateful plunge into the ocean since the time it was witnessed from the deck of the *Rensblume* almost twenty-four hours prior. Television oracles were certain that there had been an explosion. Security experts speculated on sabotage, explaining that not enough money and too little manpower was spent in securing sophisticated detection equipment that could prevent just such a calamity.

"Does this mean that the United States has been singled out for airborne terrorism?" every talking head asked every media sage.

No one was willing to directly attribute the death of Flight 280's three hundred plus souls to sabotage or a calculated assault on America's air fleets. Not even after the appearance on network and cable newscasts of Mrs. Gerry

Scarborough's horrifying account of the tour bus of American children and their chaperons brutally murdered by terrorists, led by a man who not only claimed credit for downing Flight 280 but promised more air disasters to come. After all, there had been numerous claims to having sponsored Flight 280's crash from every crackpot militia and fanatical group.

But when scientific tests proved incontrovertibly that UA's aircraft had been destroyed by a sophisticated explosive device and when it could be demonstrated that the explosion had occurred at or near seat 48A as the man who called himself Conrad had prophesied, a number of conclusions were inescapable.

The first and most obvious was that further attacks might be made against United States commercial flights. The second deduction was that it was indeed Conrad, whoever he might be, who had masterminded the event.

These facts instantly filled newspaper space and television news and talk shows, running endless days on radio call-in programs. It was no longer speculation, averred one think-tank security consultant. America was finally a specific target of terrorism, and its object was the isolation of North America from the rest of the world. Just as Conrad warned via Mrs. Scarborough, Desert Storm in the Middle East was not yet won, America had been notified that their military personnel desecrated holy ground in Saudi Arabia and warned that their satanic influences around the world must end at once.

Security measures in and around all international airports were elevated to an extremely high level, as civil and government officials issued official addresses to reassure the general public. Employment of hitherto secret explosive detection devices were alluded to, some real, some exaggerations meant to discourage would-be bombers. Copycat killers and hysteria at home were regarded as more serious threats than groups of so-called terrorists abroad, the government and gratuitous security experts opined.

In the cacophony that followed publication of the preliminary findings of the downing of Flight 280, the American public deserted airlines in favor of any other form of transportation. Despite professional soothsayers, international terminals began to resemble empty warehouses. Carriers, however, swallowed their losses until, gradually, early signs of travelers' panic subsided among PR claims that new security procedures had all but eliminated the risk of further bombings. Passengers began gingerly reboarding overseas flights.

In passing weeks, the loss of Flight 280 became recalled as an isolated, albeit intentional, victory for the fanatic supporters of foreign madmen.

While public relations campaigns and short memories blurred that air disaster, as other lives were lost to famine, earthquakes, and volcanoes, those at the highest levels of government were not so sanguine.

In a rural area of Virginia was an estate that had once been a horse farm. A ten-foot spiked iron fence surrounded many acres of property, most of it concealed by smilax, or catbrier, a European hedge of exceptional density. On a brick post at the front gate, a brass plaque announced with subdued distinction the home of the H. P. Carlisle Foundation.

One half of a great steel bar gate was attached to the same brick post; on the opposite side of a driveway, the other half of the gate was anchored firmly. Not even the smilax hedge could entirely obscure the large manor house situated beyond a long, gently sweeping driveway. A middle-aged gardener was at work nearby.

The gardener was first among his several assistants to hear the Mercedes approach down the county road, turning toward the gate and then stopping. The car was an old model 300S and was driven by Mr. Bradley Wallis. Wallis was as trim as the car was spiffy, his silver hair neat, his patrician nose held in just the correct position to assert his lofty place in society. The automobile coughed, then lurched a second time when Wallis pumped the gas pedal.

The gardener, Mr. Bucks, moved from a row of flowers to listen more closely to the hacking engine. "Morning," he called out to Mr. Wallis without looking at him, his attention drawn toward the rough engine. "Lovely day."

"Morning, Mr. Bucks," Wallis managed through gritted teeth. "I hadn't noticed that it was so beautiful. It's cloudy. And chilly. Only a gardener could find beauty in a day like this." Mr. Wallis pumped the gas pedal again, and the 300S engine roared back in complaint.

"Growing weather. We're putting in some gypsy queen and some idesia," Mr. Bucks said. "Fuel pump."

"I know it's my fuel pump, Mr. Bucks. It's dying. I've tried to find one everywhere." Mr. Wallis's head seemed to shrink deeper into the Scottish tweed jacket he wore.

"We'll have to be careful with the idesia. They're fragile." As Mr. Bucks spoke, he glanced into the backseat of the Mercedes, never quite losing his tight-lipped smile of typical old New Englanders. Removing his head from Wallis's proximity, Mr. Bucks nodded slightly toward another "gardener" on the other side of the fence. The gate silently began to swing inward.

"Have a nice day, Mr. Wallis," Mr. Bucks said, though doubtful that a nice day for his employer was possible.

Having forgotten his keys, Wallis knocked at the front door of the huge, two-hundred-year-old estate. He waited only a few seconds until it was answered by his butler, Cletis. "Good morning, Mr. Wallis."

"So I've been told," Wallis snapped.

"Will you have breakfast, sir?" Cletis asked, oblivious of Wallis's irritation.

"Just tea. And a muffin. But I'll go downstairs, first." Wallis allowed Cletis to take his coat and hat.

"Very good, sir." The butler cleared his throat. "I heard the Mercedes coming up the drive. It didn't sound quite right."

"It doesn't sound right because it isn't right," Wallis huffed. "The damned fuel pump is going out." Wallis moved into a small, old, scissor-gate elevator, and punched the Down button.

"Shall I call your garage, sir?" Cletis called gently over the older man's disappearing head.

"It may surprise you to know that I've already thought of that, Cletis. They can't find a replacement."

The elevator descended into the basement and subbasements of the house. The lighting became increasingly dim as the walls surrounding the elevator changed from wood panel to concrete. The elevator continued downward several floors before finally coming to a stop. Wallis stepped out.

Almost immediately in front of him was a door made of tool steel. At either side were cameras that functioned continuously. Near the entrance was a slot, which, when Wallis inserted a plastic card, activated a voice, piped via electronic oscillator, that greeted him.

"Good morning, Mr. Wallis," the device said unctuously.

Wallis did not respond at once, angry at having to be inspected by a camera and specially piqued at being forced to respond to an electronic host. Rather than speak, he chewed on the stem of his ancient pipe. The door remained motionless, soundless. Then, almost wincing in pain, he muttered, "Damn."

The door opened.

Wallis snatched his coded plastic card from its slot and entered the room. Indirect lighting allowed only enough illumination to reveal a covey of mostly young men and women peering into blue, gray, or black screens. They might have been visitors to an aquarium, gazing raptly into fish tanks. Wallis could not help but peek over the shoulders of the operators as he shuffled slowly on his rounds of the Collection Room.

Wallis was soon joined by Colonel Adrian Barnes, 36, bursting from civilian clothing that he had always worn awkwardly. Barnes carried a clipboard under one arm like a riding crop and moved with military precision. Wallis nodded to him without altering his step as he continued to circulate through the room.

"Good morning, Mr. Wallis," Colonel Barnes said.

"Hmmm. I want you to get rid of that swinish voice at the door."

"Is there something wrong with it, sir?"

"Yes. It isn't real."

"It's necessary for voiceprint identification, Mr. Wallis," the colonel replied.

"Then have it say something else," Wallis snapped, stopping at a table covered with black and white photographic prints.

"What would you have it say, sir?"

Wallis turned to the army officer, lowering his voice, allowing a trace of menace to creep in. "I don't care. I just don't want it to say 'good morning' to me. It isn't human, and I don't want it pretending that it is."

"Very well, sir," Colonel Barnes said, making a brief notation on his clipboard.

As Wallis continued his tour around the ELINT floor, Barnes began the morning summation. Despite the apparent end of the Cold War, it would be politically and militarily naive to shut down America's electronic and HUMINT sources of intelligence regarding Russia. Until he received orders to the contrary, Wallis would continue to hear of briefings similar to this one for many months more.

"We have some interesting data from Keyhole, sir. They're on visible light and infrared almost around the clock. Garbage report shows the Russians have launched what is obviously a recon COSMOS from Plestek at 0423 Zulu—"

"Didn't they pass that track to us three weeks ago?" Wallis interrupted.

"It isn't in our logs, Mr. Wallis." The colonel replied as he flipped through the paper on his clipboard.

"All right. What else?"

"They also launched an ASAT type test vehicle from Tyuratam at 0945 Zulu," Colonel Barnes continued. "Teal Ruby got a burst of big time infrared laser from Sharyshagen yesterday. It's showing a decimal zero five degradation. That seems normal to us. The *Kiev* had a fire on board while in port. No details yet but it's going to be out of business for a few weeks. . . ."

"Did you interview the *Kiev*'s Damage Control Officer?" Wallis asked.

"No, sir, but we were able to assess the BTU emissions on DEFSMAC satellite. We figured at the rate of 23,000 units per ten minutes of burn, the fire source was aviation fuel. We've got a bank of machines at ONI that traced out more than twelve miles of fuel lines and electronic cables that will have to be replaced. That estimate is the low end, Mr. Wallis."

"Incredible," the elderly man said, squarely facing his younger aide, his amazement quite genuine.

"Would you like the high end, sir?" the colonel asked, proudly aware that his carefully researched report was appreciated.

"No. I'd like a cup of tea."

Barnes's face momentarily reflected confusion. "Sir, we have information on a Spetsnaz unit moving south—"

"I don't care what the Russians are doing, Barnes," Wallis said, his chest heaving in exasperation. "I want information on the butchers who murdered the women and children in the Taurus Mountains."

The colonel's eyebrows knit together. "We don't have that assignment, sir."

"We're going to get it," Wallis said without a trace of doubt.

"Yes, sir, but A-5 will have to get it first, and then they'll probably have a target for us. Or maybe more than one."

Wallis fixed Barnes with a long, intolerant stare. But then he reminded himself to keep patient with Barnes, who was, after all, a remarkably capable staff officer. Nor was he bloodless. Barnes was kind and considerate, and cared about the men and women who labored long and often thankless hours in what Wallis referred to as a special kind of sensory deprivation chamber. God, how he was tired of concrete walls. "They are not going to have a target until we give them one. Have we heard anything from our assets in Benghazi?"

"Nothing, sir. But there's talk about Khail Arum. And he is definitely moving."

"It wasn't him," Wallis said with finality.

"Would you like to review the trimester reports?"

"I suppose so," said the elderly intelligence officer. "But I think this is a new man." Wallis passed through the main entrance and began to walk toward the elevator that led to his personal working space within the mansion.

"I think we shouldn't scratch Khail Arum," the colonel said, causing Wallis to pause inside the sliding elevator door. Wallis waited while Barnes continued. "Arum has three personnel carriers assigned to him by Colonel Khadafy. None of them has moved in two days. His car hasn't been washed in the same period of time."

Wallis considered for a moment. Arum lavished attention on the American Chrysler given to him by a grateful sponsor of terrorism. If it was not washed, it was because he was not there to see the dirt upon its otherwise meticulously waxed paint. Wallis liked Colonel Barnes's assumption.

"Hmm. Khail loves that car." Even though Wallis had doubts that Arum was the Taurus killer, he deserved attention. "All right," the frosty-haired spy nodded, "ask Eli Reveler to go there." Reveler was a Jew, and if a Jew was caught near Arum's lair he would have his head displayed to the world atop a pike at the gates of Mizdah. What, he asked himself rhetorically, have these wretched people, the Khadafys, the Saddams, offered to world civilization in six thousand years? Wallis stepped into the elevator. Maybe it was time he communicated with the Mossad. "Colonel Barnes," Wallis called as the old elevator doors began to close.

"Yes, sir?"

"Set up a meeting with Rabbi."

A man in his mid to late thirties sat cooling his heels in one of the White House's many meeting rooms. When you got this far down in the basement, there weren't any historical frills left behind by Thomas Jefferson or Abraham Lincoln. There were no windows, and the furnishings were spartan.

At one end of a medium-sized conference table, there was a spread of food: two bottles of French red wines and a pair of ice buckets containing Chardonnay. There was also what appeared to be a liver pâté, which he loathed, an assortment of gourmet crackers, fresh bread, chilled salmon, roast beef, barbecued sliced chicken breast, artichoke salad, capers, and assorted condiments. He began to pile salmon and pickle spears on a slice of Italian bread.

His mouth watered briefly at the sight of his ad hoc salmon sandwich before he took a big bite. In one long, continuous swallow, he downed almost an entire glass of ice cold chardonnay before taking another mouthful of the sandwich. He didn't know for whom the food was set out, but, what the hell, he was ordered to be here, wasn't he?

A woman in her late forties entered the room, a leather folder in her hand. Her hair had once been black, but was losing ground to gray. Her face was almost entirely unlined, as though it had been carefully protected from the sun. Her body was the shape of the box her clothes came in. Her eyes were blue and so bright they reminded the man of cat's eye marbles.

She took a chair without arms, managing to give the impression that she was perched rather than seated, her knees touching as though held together by twin magnets, her hemline discreetly settling at the patella. She placed her writing folio sedately on her lap and busied herself for several minutes studying the wall thirty feet away. She wanted to turn her head to look at the man more thoroughly. He was startling, she thought. It was something about his eyes. She had no way of knowing that his boyish face had been repaired by a series of plastic surgeons, both military and civilian, who had rebuilt most of his nasal passageways. The once smashed and splintered bones that comprised his cheeks, the result of a LALO jump in which his chute did not fully open, were now masterpieces of molded plastic bonded with resident bones sculpted back into their original shapes. His right ear, torn and cauliflowered from hand-to-hand fighting in Afghanistan, had been remodeled using pig cartilage and skin harvested from his feet. The outsides of each ear looked much better than the inside part functioned. His brief smile raised his entire mouth, not just the edges, like the curtain going up in a school play. He looked much younger than she had imagined him.

The man dug into the mustard, which he spread on a second piece of bread, then piled still more salmon on top. He remembered the salmon he and his father had often caught near the Columbia River in the years before spawning rivers were gutted by development and the fish became scarce. This salmon was probably the product of a hatchery, its meat a paler version of the real ocean species.

The woman wanted to exchange small talk with the man but decided not to.

The other people were late. If someone didn't show up soon, he would leave. Fuck 'em.

He considered a third glass of wine but reluctantly shut himself off from the delicious drink. He did not fear the others would notice, when they arrived, whether he had anything to drink or not, but he would know. He flicked at crumbs on his tie. It was quiet in the room except for the almost imperceptible movement of air that was delivered, filtered and heated, through ducts in the upper walls. He had not examined the physical setup himself, but he had no doubt that the White House security personnel were the best and their methods state of the art.

He looked at his watch. Now that he had eaten his fill,

he was aware that he had work to do. When he had first arrived at the National Security Council offices eighteen months before, he was not given a job description either orally or written. His boss, David Magazine, Ph.D., had said he was to mull over the things he had encountered in the field and consider how to improve existing policies of universal antiterrorism. He had asked for more specifics, but Magazine, whom he saw approximately once per month, said that if he could be more specific then he would not need his input. He wasn't active duty anymore, and for the first year of work at NSC he reflected, read, and wrote at length about his experiences in the field. His time at Stanford's Graduate School of Psychology was reflected in rather well formed reportage, properly annotated and footnoted, and promptly, he believed, tossed into the trash.

He faithfully followed his boss from meeting to meeting, conference to seminar, in ever-decreasing concentric patterns of futility until it hardly mattered whether he was there or not. He was not often consulted, was, in fact, kept at sufficient distances that he could do no harm. If his colleagues at NSC had little use for him, he gradually found none for them, either, and he retreated into a more eclectic form of research, i.e., reading things he enjoyed. Requests for his essays and findings, never many, dried up completely and so did his interest in preparing them. Instead, he read his way through everything Elmore Leonard had written, most of Robert B. Parker's stuff, and picked gingerly through Scott Turow. He even nourished his brain with some light history, Tuchman's *March of Folly* and *Origin of the American Revolution: 1759–1766* by Bernhard Knollenberg. He now believed that the comic strip was the most important section of any newspaper.

The President, when he strode into the room, his footfalls entirely muffled on heavy carpet, was unaccompanied by aides. The man could see that Secret Service agents waited outside the conference room door and closed it behind their boss after he entered. The President was tall, at least four inches higher than his own 5' 10", but had much more disposable weight. Where he had a spare four percent body fat, the President carried around the results of high living, compliments of the taxpayer. He wondered if it was true that the President had never had a job in his life outside of the public dole. The President extended his hand. He took it. "Commander, thanks for coming. I appreciate it."

The man wondered if the President was aware that he had been summoned by order, arrived in total ignorance, and was obliged to remain until dismissed. This was the nearest in proximity he had ever gotten to the President. The chief executive officer of America was only fifteen years his senior but looked older. His once blond hair had begun to gray, giving him a decadent, washed-out appearance with rheumy eyes. His teeth were well tended but, he thought, so were his, also compliments of the taxpayer and dedicated orthodontists and oral surgeons. The President had a cold sore on the left side of his lower lip that had been touched up with an application of makeup. His handshake was stronger than he expected.

"I read your essays on terrorism," the President said after sitting down and motioning the man to a nearby chair. His easy southern drawl and boyish grin made everything he said sound like a compliment to the listener. " 'Do Unto Others,' I think was the title of one." The President put his head back. "In fact, I read them all."

"I didn't think anybody read them," the man said.

"Well, I did. And you're going back on active duty."

"Sorry, Mr. President. I'm out," the man said.

"Read your commission. If the President tells you that you're back on active duty, by God, you're back."

The man did not respond. The President nodded his head knowingly. "I know what happened to you and your men. It won't happen again. My word on that."

The man insulted the President by chuckling softly.

The President turned to his personal secretary. "Mary Ellen, cut the orders I gave you. Two copies. One for me, one for the commander, here." The President turned back to the "commander." "I'm giving you a blank check. What do I write on it?"

The man thought for a long moment before answering. "Nobody knows who I am. Nobody. My real name is between you and me. Same for my men. That's for openers. Sir."

"You have it. What else?"

For the next two hours the man sat down and dictated his needs to the President and his secretary.

*   *   *

It was late in the day when Wallis arrived for his meeting with Rabbi. The sky was cloudy, and the threat of rain was in the air of this, one of the many seaside communities on the coast that seems to exist not because of but in spite of its seclusion from a city. There were no parking meters in the town, no hard industry that Wallis could see, and most stores were locally owned. Tourism would provide some income to the town's purse, but he imagined that hardy, self-reliant citizens eked out their livelihood independent of the seasonal influx.

He entered Ernie's Cafe through a screen door whose hinges were corroded from sea air. The heavier main door had swelled against its frame for the same reason. Ernie's Cafe would have been called a greasy spoon in the city, but to this community, and to Wallis, it comfortably reeked of humanity. Warmth came from a grill never shut off, deep-fry oil kept at 375°, and walls so close together that no customer's body heat ever escaped to the outside. Wallis breathed deep with satisfaction as he straddled a stool at the counter. As he perused a menu he could see dishes, still dirty from lunch, stashed under the counter waiting for a more opportune time to be washed. The fry cook splashed oil atop hash brown potatoes sizzling inches from a hamburger steak on the grill, while white bread, turned near black, popped out of a toaster. The fry cook doused these, as well, with the yellowish oil, possibly butter. "What'll it be?" the cook asked Wallis.

"Tea, and . . ." Wallis almost asked for toast, but while he admired the atmosphere of the cafe, could not imagine himself swallowing all that butter. Times had treated him too well in recent years. "A doughnut," he finished.

"Try the coffee," a European voice next to him said. "It will clean you out."

"I've already had the pleasure of moving my bowels," Wallis said to Rabbi. Wallis removed his gloves with deliberate care and placed them in a pocket. "It's good to see you," he said to the man. "Are you well?"

"Of course I am," Rabbi said, draining his cup of heavily creamed coffee. He motioned to the fry cook for a refill. "All of God's chosen people are well, no matter how we feel. How's business?"

"I don't like electronics. I'd rather deal with people."

Wallis regarded his tea bag with distaste, wringing surplus water from it by wrapping its string around a spoon. "I'm old-fashioned that way."

Rabbi smiled. "I've been telling you that you need to diversify. Have you given it any thought?"

"Yes, indeed," Wallis said. "We're putting together a group of people very soon."

Wallis looked once more around the room. There were four tables in addition to the linoleum and chrome counter where they sat. There were two other people in the restaurant. One was a woman in her early twenties, the other a man older than both Wallis and Rabbi's sixty-plus years. He seemed deeply absorbed in his newspaper, peering at it intently through thick glasses. Wallis was not concerned that they could be overheard.

"That's good to hear, my friend. We have always believed in having the right people in place whenever they are needed. Tell me, do you need help with leadership? We have people with that specialized experience."

"Thank you, but no," Wallis answered. "We believe we have the right man."

"Ah, yes. Well, you have resources that even we don't have."

"If you would accept Jesus Christ as your savior, you wouldn't have to borrow money."

Rabbi laughed heartily, his body shaking as Wallis enjoyed his own humor with a smug grin.

"I need to know who did the bus," Wallis continued, his mouth still smiling but his eyes cold. "I understand you have an outstanding asset."

Rabbi's eyebrows twitched slightly. "Is that so? Who?"

Ah, the little game, Wallis thought. "The defector. What is his name?"

"How do you know about him?" Rabbi asked, annoyed.

"Our people put up the reward money, that's how," Wallis stated simply.

Rabbi reached for sugar near Wallis. He remained inches away from Wallis as he spoke. "That is the trouble with paying rewards to defectors. Everybody has product for sale. Even if he has to make it up."

"And is that what this one is doing? You've determined

that, have you?" Wallis said patiently, knowing exactly where he was going.

Rabbi shrugged. "This one, he claims to know who did the bus. And he says it was the same people who brought down Flight Two-Eight-Zero."

Excitement bolted through Wallis, as though a mild shock had been administered to all parts of his body simultaneously. His outward demeanor did not change, however, having had years of discipline against betraying a secret through body language. A good spy must first be a great liar. And, in point of fact, a decision for the project that Rabbi urged upon Wallis had already been made at the highest level of government. It was not made to benefit Israel, or any other particular nation, but the United States itself. Wallis felt no need to divulge his part, intelligence support for the newly authorized unit, so easily to even a friendly nation.

"You don't believe him?" Wallis asked after judging Rabbi's enthusiasm to be low.

"Every terrorist in the world is claiming responsibility for that one," Rabbi said in a guarded tone.

"You know about the message that he gave to Mrs. Scarborough?" Wallis asked.

"Seat 48A? We'll see," Rabbi said. "We don't know why the plane came down, whether it was an accident or not."

"You think we should wait for a black box?" Wallis framed the question rhetorically. "A single aircraft disappears from radar at almost thirty thousand feet in the middle of a wireless transmission," Wallis pointed out. "It does not declare an emergency, it does not report fire on board. An explosion, Rabbi. Nothing else."

Rabbi chuckled softly. "Nobody refers to radio as wireless anymore, Bradley."

Wallis remained silent, thus putting pressure on Rabbi for a response. "I am not willing to stipulate for the defector," Rabbi said.

"Of course not," Wallis agreed.

"Well, we've had him a week. He said he was close to Colonel Khadafy. We know that for certain," the Jew said with resignation.

Wallis swallowed a mulched piece of doughnut. "I want to see him."

"All right. Will you do the interrogation? I am responsible for him." Rabbi said.

"That decision is not all mine," Wallis said.

"Then who?"

"When the time comes, the man who will form our group will also question your defector. His name is Getts. Commander Bob Getts."

"Intelligence officer?" Rabbi said.

"Not exactly. Commander Getts is putting together a very unusual unit. . . ." Wallis hesitated. The need-to-know axiom ruled all military and intelligence affairs. But Rabbi was certainly one who needed to know. "They are a black organization. Antiterrorist."

Rabbi smiled. "There are antiterrorist groups and there are *antiterrorist* groups, my friend."

"You'll have to judge this one for yourself," Wallis said.

An army officer in a captain's dress uniform waited at the quaint airport terminal building at Santa Barbara, California. His bearing was professional, the many ribbons adorning his chest included army aviation wings, a Ranger patch, and decorations won in Desert Storm. Under his arm, he carried a simple briefcase. He paced as he alternately gazed out of large windows toward the end of Runway 26 and his chronograph watch. Eventually, a civilian Boeing 737 aircraft with Horizon Charters marked on its fuselage landed and taxied back toward the terminal. The army officer watched as the 737 stopped well away from the terminal and lowered its boarding stairs. The captain exited the terminal through a side door, walking toward the aircraft and ascending the stairs.

While the 737 is not large as far as Boeing products go, the captain was impressed by the number of other passengers on board. There were seven altogether.

"Sit anywhere you like, Captain," a civilian steward offered.

The captain hesitated slightly, then turned to the steward. "Where are we going?" he said.

"I don't know, sir," the steward replied.

The captain found a seat and strapped himself in. The pilot, unseen by passengers, spooled up the jet's engines and, upon receiving clearance from the tower, taxied into position short of Runway 26. After waiting a scant twenty seconds, the plane turned onto the runway and accelerated,

All aboard watched with varying degrees of interest as the Santa Barbara mountains receded below, the aircraft then banking starboard to pick up an easterly heading.

There were three other army men aboard, enlisted men who wore class A uniforms, one without ribbons, badges, or stripes on his sleeve. There was also a sailor, a marine, a civilian, and a female air force lieutenant. None sat in adjoining seats. It was clear to the army captain that no one aboard knew anyone else. Well, that was fine with him. He had no reason to consort. Except, maybe, with the lieutenant. Black hair, Asian eyes, olive skin. She was a knockout. But he kept that to himself.

The flight steward passed out soft drinks, tea, and coffee. No alcohol was aboard the aircraft, he apologized. In-flight box lunches would be distributed in about two hours.

As the aircraft hissed its way through flight level 280, one of the army men looked across the aisle at the lone civilian. Like the soldier, the civilian seemed to be in his middle twenties, but unlike the soldier, was immaculately dressed in an expensive suit and tie. His shoes were brown and white, made of reptile leather of some kind.

"Feel kind of out of place?" the soldier asked him. The civilian did not answer at once but seemed to study the soldier with interest, then turned his head away dismissively.

"Why? Do you?" he said.

"No. We're wearing uniforms, but you're not. How come?"

The civilian regarded the soldier again for a moment before responding. "Because I went to my fucking closet this morning, and guess what? No uniform."

The soldier was abashed only for a short time before saying, "What do you do? I mean, you work for the government or something?"

"Retired," the civilian said and turned toward his window.

The soldier had finally been insulted. His friendly manner diminished. "Hey, I was trying to be friendly, man, but you got some kind of problem with me, don't hesitate. Know what I mean?" When the civilian did not respond, the soldier turned away. "Fucking asshole."

The marine watched the exchange. He seemed disappointed that it had ended without violence. "Hey, ground pounder," he said to the soldier. "I got a little something in case you need help." He slowly removed a lock-blade combat knife from his waistband, and smiled viciously. "No metal detectors where I came on board."

"I don't need that," the soldier said.

"Never know," the marine replied. "Somebody fucks with me, they're going to end up more or less dead. I let 'em know up front." The marine was smugly confident as he relaxed against his seat.

"How come you're on the plane?" the soldier wanted to know.

"Because I'd rather be here than . . ." He stopped himself. "How come you're on it?" he said instead.

"I'm a volunteer. This is a tough outfit. I like that. I guess you'd say I'm kind of a thrill seeker. I used to do all kinds of crazy things in civvy life. Scared the hell out of everyone. My folks, girlfriend. I'd play chicken with cars at 70 miles an hour. Sky diving. Bungee jumping. Walked hand over hand once on a power line near a dam. Hell, I'd do anything. I'm just crazy, they tell me."

"You Indian?" the marine said.

"Yeah. Numash. Ever hear of my tribe?"

The marine looked at the soldier, shook his head almost imperceptibly. Then he closed his eyes without comment.

Another soldier wearing jump wings and sergeant's stripes heard part of his conversation. "Hear that? Lying his ass off. Bet he'd run if somebody pointed a gun at his nose." He took a sip from a soft drink can.

"Sometimes those guys surprise you," the sailor said as he looked down toward the ground.

"You ever jump? I mean, I have. I'm Airborne. Was, anyway," he said, pointing to his jump wings.

The Navy man nodded. "Yeah. I was a SEAL."

The soldier whistled softly. "I guess you did. It's okay if we talk about it, right?"

The Navy man shrugged. The soldier pursued the subject. "How come you don't wear jump wings?"

"Long story. How come you're here?" the sailor asked.

"I got invited," he said.

"To what?" the sailor asked.

"To kill somebody. That's why you're here, too."

The female air force lieutenant did not engage others in either eye contact or conversation.

* * *

Almost five hours later in the dark of night, the *Horizon* jet landed at a U.S. Army post. Ground transportation awaited them. They were driven through a gate guarded by four security service personnel then along a road sided by pine trees for about two miles. They passed through another secure gate that said simply *WEST GARRISON* and continued to a small company area. A sign read *Echo Company, 344th Theater Group, United States Army.*

The drivers of the vehicles wore fatigues and cryptic name tags. One driver's stenciled identification was "Bartender," a second was "Busboy." Bartender and Busboy showed the new arrivals to a building which, like most of the others on the post, dated from World War II. The building into which they were escorted had bars on the outside of the windows. Inside, it appeared to be exactly what it was—a supply room. Bartender and Busboy moved behind a long counter and retrieved fully loaded barracks bags. They were passed over a counter to the new arrivals. "Orders are to change into fatigue uniforms contained in these bags. Your quarters are across the walk in building T-12. The lady's building is next door, T-14. Assemble in twenty minutes at Echo Company day room."

"Just a minute . . ." the captain said. "What's your rank?"

"Rank?" Bartender asked.

"Yes, rank. How do I address you?" the captain said in his best military manner.

"Just call me Bartender."

"Well, Bartender, in case you hadn't realized it before, I am an officer. Captain. I don't take orders from enlisted men, and I certainly do not accept billeting assignments with them. Who is the commanding officer here?" he demanded.

"His name is Commander Robert Getts, U.S. Navy," a voice came from behind the group. All turned to see Chief Gunner's Mate Glenn Crosley, known to his swim buddies as "Peach." Peach stood six feet three inches, with broad shoulders, narrow hips, dark hair and eyes. He spoke softly and moved with a dancer's agility. Peach carried his head held almost unnaturally high, his muscled back a complement to his grace and balance. He emitted the aura of a warrior, a man who could project violence. He was ruggedly handsome, though his face and hands were scarred from the hundreds of fights he had been in, both on duty and off. He smiled at the group.

"And who the hell are you?" the army captain wanted to know.

"I'm Peach." He pointed to his name stitched above his right pocket, his smile widening as though he were part of a great game. "Just call me Peach."

"If you're an NCO, where are your stripes?" the captain demanded.

"We're informal around here. Now, people, go change uniforms."

"Hey, Peachy, or whatever the fuck you like to call yourself," the civilian said.

"Peachy is just fine," Peach said, his easy smile revealing pearly teeth.

"Yeah, well, Peachy, you might see here that I'm not in your fucking army. Not in anybody's military. I'm a goddamn civilian, and there is one giant fuck-up going on around here. See? So I ain't changing into anything. I'm calling me a cab and getting the hell out of here."

"Not yet, sporty. Just do what you're told," Peach said, his voice barely audible but as hard and threatening as the blue tint of gun metal.

The civilian, substantially shorter than Peach but with a broad, fit build, showed not the slightest bit of fear. He merely reached into his pocket and came up with a fourteen-inch switchblade. "Hey, I carve up pieces of shit like you and leave 'em in the street. Last chance to back off, soldier." The civilian was cool, confident, and knew how to hold a knife to be effective. He moved toward Peach on the balls of his feet, keeping them apart, never putting himself in danger of tripping. He held the knife low in a thrusting position.

"Knife-fighting 101 wasn't on the schedule for today," Peach said to the other arrivals, "but we might as well get our first demonstration under way. First, notice that my weight is centered, and I am on the balls of my feet, one foot leading, the other back."

Peach's eyes narrowed, his concentration focused as he assumed his own fighting stance. His posture was straight, arms low. His entire body moved in rhythm. He waited for the civilian's attack, and when it came it was low, in a

sweeping motion. Peach had seen the move a thousand
times. He used a classic Aikido move to defend the attack.
Peach's left hand circled behind the civilian's knife hand,
catching it at the wrist before the knife could complete his
arc. Using the civilian's momentum, Peach twisted the
man's knife hand. The civilian howled in pain. Peach moved
his feet slightly, then made a small circular motion with
both of his hands, and the civilian's feet leapt from the
floor, and the man landed hard on his back.

"Hurts, doesn't it?" Peach said, twisting the civilian's
wrist even more.

"Uhnnn . . ." the civilian grunted, doubled over in pain,
unable to speak.

Peach eased the pressure and released the man's hand.
He spoke again to the group. "In fifteen minutes, we go
on a five-mile run. Tomorrow, we kick it up a bit to seven.
Your commanding officer will be here in a couple of days.
Before he arrives you'll be in uniform as ordered. You'll
perform as ordered. Or I'll be your ticket straight to hell."

Peach turned on his heel and walked out of the supply
room.

Chapter Three

Above a military gatepost a sign read:

Welcome
to
CAMP McREYNOLDS
United States Army
Authorized Personnel Only

Two military policemen wearing berets and dressed in
camouflage fatigues vigilantly examined automobiles and
their passengers before allowing access to the base.

The verdant silence of the tall pine trees on the sides of the rural road leading to Camp McReynolds was shattered by the sound of the engine of a Harley-Davidson chopper as it approached the main gate. The faces of the two uniformed guards turned even darker, the edges of their mouths sagging downward as they realized that the road bike was about to enter their realm of control.

As the motorcycle braked to a halt, they could see that it was filthy—layers of mud were caked everywhere, dirt atop dirt, dust covering everything including a bedroll tied behind the seat. The rider was as filthy as the machine he rode. His denim vest, the only clothes he wore on his torso, had no sleeves. A red bandanna was tied above his dark glasses, and an earring dangled from one side of his head.

An MP raised his hands for the motorcycle rider to stop, hoping that he would not. "Hold it right there, fella. Where do you think you're going?" the security man demanded.

"Through the gate," the rider answered. "I'm supposed to report here for duty."

The two guards exchanged quick glances. "You in the army?" one of them asked incredulously.

"Sure am," the biker replied.

"*American* army?"

The biker laughed in appreciation for a joke he might very well have cracked himself. He patted his pockets. "Well, navy, really. Got some I.D. here, somewhere."

The first MP let his hand slide down to the butt of his pistol. "Okay, what's your name and rank, soldier?" he asked.

"Getts, Robert. Commander, United States Navy," the biker responded.

"Bullshit," the first guard blurted out.

"Here it is," Getts said, offering him a plastic laminated card.

The second guard read the card over a shoulder of the first. "I'll be damned."

"Great countryside," Getts said, glancing around. "Think I'm going to like the place." Getts patted his motorcycle while the security men continued to study the plastic card.

"It's a DD-2 card, all right. Picture's on there, too," one of them confirmed.

His partner pulled him out of Getts's earshot. "Check it out, Richie. Son of a bitch coulda stole it," he said.

"Yeah," he answered. Turning back to Getts he said, "Stay right there." Then, in the unlikely event the card had not been stolen, the soldier added, "Sir."

"Call Chief Gunner's Mate Peach, Theater Group One," Getts suggested.

The guard nodded his head, stepped inside the gate house, and dialed a number that connected him with a base operator. "This is Ryan, Main Gate. You got a Chief Gunner's Mate Peach on post? Yeah. Naw, just ring it." The MP waited for several moments then spoke again into the telephone. "Chief Peach? Sergeant Ryan, Main Gate. We got a . . . man . . . here at the gate says he's an officer. Name of Getts. But you oughta see this piece o' . . ." The MP turned toward Getts, then spoke again into the telephone. "That's right. Hangin' from his ear."

Ryan listened for several more seconds before hanging up the telephone without further acknowledgment. He turned, regarding Getts for a long moment. Standing near Getts, Sergeant Ryan drew his shoulders back, returned Getts's I.D. card, took one step backward, and saluted crisply. "You may proceed, sir."

Getts pocketed the card, fired up his Harley, lifted his right hand in an uninspired salute, and, still smiling, roared away from the guard post. The two MPs continued to watch as Getts faded into the distance.

"I think we shoulda shot him."

"Theater Group," Sergeant Ryan said. "Bunch of bed wetters."

Camp McReynolds had been built hurriedly in 1940 as a temporary post to help train an overflow of America's conscripted army. Almost sixty years later, many buildings that were designed to stand ten years or less were still being used. There were improvements made, however. Concrete revetments protected the infantry's close support aircraft, tank repair was at subground level, and only a few of the heavy armored vehicles and their personnel could be seen during daylight hours. The post had been modified to accommodate special warfare tactics and operations with an emphasis on night fighting. Virtually every piece of rolling stock and most operational personnel carried ambient light equipment. Aircraft along McReynold's flight line, most medium lift, capable of transporting troops and their supplies, were covered with camouflage netting. Outlying buildings and blockhouses were camouflaged in the spirit of reminding trainees that here is where the training war goes on twenty-four hours every day.

As Getts drove his Harley down macadam roads, he noted that the post looked practically deserted. He was pleased. He leaned his bike toward a group of barracks buildings set apart from the others by multiple rolls of concertina wire. Two men in camouflage fatigues holding automatic weapons stood near a crudely built but effective gate through the wire. Getts halted at their upraised hands to show his access papers.

The headquarters building was also old but made of river stone, its roof painted bright red with white window trim. A small, well manicured lawn graced the front of the structure. Chief Gunner's Mate Peach, carrying himself as stiffly erect as the starch in his uniform, strode through the rear door and into the barracks beyond. They were newer, more comfortable than most and always kept neat and clean.

Peach widened the stance of his highly polished parachute jump boots, allowing his beret to rest at a rakish angle on his head as he faced a group of soldiers in fatigues lounging around in various positions of rest. They were, without exception, fit, muscular, their hair cropped short—all hard of eye.

"All right, troopers, listen up," Peach said. "Commander Getts just passed through the main gate. Fall out in platoon formation. Let's move."

Murmurs came from the group as they moved without hesitation to adjust uniforms and take their places.

"About time . . ."

"Anybody know the CO?"

"Yeah, he's a bad-ass . . ."

"I hear he worked for General Case in the desert . . ."

"He's an actor?"

The men—and a single woman—fell in quickly and expertly. Their uniforms were fresh, from their spit-shined boots and bloused fatigues to their red berets. Above every left pocket, jump wings gleamed. Missing, however, were any insignia of rank and regulation name tags. Peach watched carefully as his new group formed up. He showed little emotion but appeared to be satisfied with the discipline and pride in their wordless movements.

"Dress right, *dress*!" Peach barked.

Forty arms moved into the air as one, touching the shoulders of the person next to them. Men in the first positions looked ahead, all others looked right.

"Ready, *front*!" he ordered.

Arms snapped down, heads swiveled straight.

"Open ranks, *harch*!" Peach commanded.

Again, the movement was executed with precision, each rank opening the same distance apart from the man before them.

The troops stood for several minutes until the sound of a rattling motorcycle engine split an otherwise tranquil day. Peach watched the eyes of his men as the sound grew louder. He was pleased to note that not a single eyeball drifted toward Getts's chopper.

Getts stopped his bike within a few yards of the formation, dismounted, and slouched forward toward his chief gunner's mate. Peach threw a stiff salute which was languidly returned by Getts. "Hi, Peach. Good to see you again."

"Thank you, sir." Peach responded properly. "Good to see you, too."

"How was your leave? Family okay?" Getts asked, conversationally.

"Yessir. Everything is just fine, sir."

"These our people?" Getts turned his attention to the ramrod straight formation.

"Yes, sir. Would you care to inspect the troops, Commander?" Peach queried.

"Let's do it."

To the great credit of the men in the ranks, despite the ratty appearance of their commanding officer, no soldier rolled up his eyes or his nose, nor did any betray surprise. Getts, with Peach at his side and one-half step behind, inspected the troops carefully. Getts hoped these people had the mental toughness required to go along with their outstanding physical appearance. He imagined that there was not thirty pounds of excess weight in the entire assemblage.

"Have the platoon stand at ease," he said to Peach.

"Platoon," Peach said, "hat-*eeze!*" Peach did another about-face, the platoon now at his back as he faced Getts. The platoon did not stand at ease in the strict military sense of the word, but assumed a position of parade rest, a form of attention with hands behind the back and legs spread apart. Their concentration on their commanding officer was total.

"Gentlemen, and ladies," he began without a trace of irony, "I'm already proud to be your commanding officer. I say that because I picked every one of you myself from your records . . . and from other resources. I know your backgrounds better than you know your own. I know what other people think about you. I even know what you think about yourselves." He paused to survey each individual. "I need to know your language specialties and how fluent you are. I'll want to talk to all of you who know a foreign language tomorrow at 2000 hours." Heads moved slightly, eyebrows raising among the troops.

"Some of you are officers, and some are noncommissioned officers. That's what it says in your pay records, but in the Blacklight you are just a trooper. Peach and I are Navy SEALs. You people come from Rangers, Force Recon, SEALs, and airborne units. But that doesn't matter anymore. We're not conscious of prior assignments or rank here. We're going to be unit-oriented, mission-oriented. You take orders from whoever is in position to give one. You may lead one part of a mission, you may follow on another part of the same mission, then resume leading it on the last lap. So we're not going to get hung up on who's got bars, stars, or stripes. Right now you're wondering if you haven't made a mistake volunteering for this one."

There were strained, sometimes startled expressions among the troopers. "Okay, so you didn't volunteer. You were grabbed out of your units or pulled off of the street. But you can get out. Just show me that you can't hack it, and believe me, you'll be out of here."

Getts looked carefully at the formation in front of him. "Our mission is to deal with our enemy at a primary level. People who do harm to the United States of America are people that we will seek out and lay hands upon. Our enemies are extremely lethal people. They are dedicated to

your death. We have to be more deadly, in better physical
shape, and much smarter. You are cautioned that from this
very minute, you may show up on their target list. You or
your family may be singled out for torture and execution,
now or in the future. Training for Blacklight will be hard
and often dangerous. It will be a psychological nightmare.
Think about it. Blacklight is an elite organization of extreme fighting men and women. You will have the world's
most advanced field equipment with which to wage war,
and under our optimum plans the enemy will never know
we are there until after they are dead." Getts paused to
look each trooper in the eye. "Blacklight owns the night.
It is as much our friend as it is terrifying to our enemies."

"You may choose to withdraw from this unit. I will discuss that issue with each and every one of you tomorrow
morning at 0700 hours." Getts waited for a reaction from
the platoon. When none came, Getts turned toward Peach.

"Peach, pass out the name tags," he said.

Peach reached into a box and withdrew a handful of
plastic name tags. He handed several to each of the first
men in line, who each took one and passed the others down
the line. Marker pens were handed along the same way.

"Write a name on the tag, then pin it onto your blouse.
I don't care what the name is as long as it isn't your real
name. From this moment on, as long as you're attached to
this unit, do not divulge your real name, neither to me, nor
to your comrades in the unit, nor to any civilian. Nobody.
There are only two names that are off limits. Dopey and
Grumpy. All others are yours for the choosing."

One of the men in ranks could not contain his incredu-
lity. "Sir, you mean any name? We should write *any* name
at all?"

"I don't care if you call yourself Donald Duck, trooper.
And don't call me 'sir' again. Call me Bob." Getts stole a
glance at Peach, who, attempting to suppress a grin,
winked.

The troops looked at each other as they quickly printed
names onto the cards and, as ordered, pinned the tags to
their uniform blouses. Getts walked along looking at the
new appellations.

In the front rank was a woman. She was in her early

twenties, barely over five feet in height even in her jump boots, with Asian features. Her affixed name was "Toni."

Getts stopped in front of her and smiled. "Hi there, Toni," he said.

"Hello," she responded, then added, "Bob."

"Toni," Getts said again, a slight smile playing at the corners of his mouth. "I like that name. You came here from the Air Force Academy. What's your real name and rank?"

"Gurwell, sir, Rita B., First Lieutenant," she responded.

Getts stood for an eternal moment staring deeply into Toni's eyes. The smile vanished from his face. As his face set into a block of ice, Toni realized that she had just disobeyed what was literally her first order. With all of her physical strength, she forced herself not to shrink before his withering gaze.

"An order I gave two minutes ago is too tough for you to understand, huh?" Getts said.

"Toni" did not respond. Getts positioned himself more directly in line with her eyes. "Well, honey, what should we *really* call you? How about sweetheart? I mean, you sure are a good lookin' little lady." Getts leered openly. He watched as her face turned white, her lips compressed as she spoke.

"Toni will do, Bob," the woman replied.

Getts liked that. If her face had reddened, it would have revealed bluster. Whitening of the skin is a different signal from the body's central nervous system. When combat is imminent, the body drains blood from surface vessels to minimize the effects of a bleeding wound. A red-faced animal, or human, is no threat. When a face turns white, one should tread light or prepare to fight.

"Well," Getts drawled, "we're going to be doing man's work here, Trooper Toni, so there won't be any hard feelings if you want to catch the first bus heading off post."

"I'll stay, Bob," she said.

Getts nodded his head as he walked back to the front of the platoon.

"Okay. That's fine. Remember, nobody knows who you really are. Anybody asks you about your job here at Camp McReynolds, tell them you're in the First Army Division Theater Group. You tell that same story to your friends and families." He surveyed the group one more time before allowing a slight smile. "Now, I know you men and ladies have been sitting around these barracks waiting for something to happen . . ." Getts could hear an undertone of agreement. "You're bored. I also know that most of you have been through rough training programs and refresher courses at other bases. I know that Peach has been working you hard for the last couple of days. You feel strained . . ." Getts glanced at faces that visibly relaxed, heads nodding in agreement. "Hey, don't be too proud to admit you could use some relaxation. Me, too."

The platoon looked at each other, most smiling in their tacit agreement.

"Peach," Getts said to his chief gunner's mate, "did you make arrangements at the slop chute?"

"Sure did, Bobby," Peach smiled.

Getts turned back to the platoon. "We've got a lot to do, but we don't have to start right away. Folks need to kick back when they can. We're going to do that tonight. Get to know each other a little bit. Okay, Peach, let's hit the suds." Getts and Peach did not exchange salutes this time. Nor would they again.

"Men," he said, "all the beer you can drink is on Bobby. If you don't like beer, just order whatever you want. Fall out and fall in at the Garden."

The Garden had originally been a barracks but had been wainscotted on the outside with red brick. Inside, a circular fireplace had been built in the center of the main room. An indoor/outdoor carpet was laid over linoleum, and a twenty-five foot bar faced numerous tables and chairs. There were no booths and no stools there so that anyone who chose to drink at the bar had to stand. A jukebox played for dimes, the proceeds used to buy new records, according to a sign affixed to the machine.

Hours past sunset, the once neatly uniformed professional soldiers more resembled professional drunks. Their blouses were unbuttoned, sleeves were rolled up or removed, boots scuffed carelessly. Beer had been poured into yawning mouths directly from service pitchers, and whiskey filled water glasses. Troopers were taking turns in tests of strength and endurance. A half circle had formed around a man who hopped from the floor to a wooden chair, down again, then up. Bets were made, paid, collected. Others took their turns. Some troopers fell down, others staggered. Arm pinning was a major attraction. Several troopers danced with two cocktail waitresses who obliged only because their customers insisted. One man was slumped in his chair, passed out, a mug of beer slopped onto his crotch.

A young man in a white coat, wearing a name tag identifying him as Busboy, worked hard at sweeping butts from the floor, clearing away beer bottles, dirty mugs, and glasses, and bringing ice for Bartender.

In the middle of this cacophony, Getts appeared to be having a wonderful time. Men sat or stood around him, one draping his arm over his CO's shoulders, pulling him by the neck to stress a point. His name tag identified him as Sneezy.

"Hey, Bob. Bobby," Sneezy slurred. "Know what, Bobby? Huh? I like you. No shit. Like your style, Bobby Baby. 'Bout time officers were like us, you know? Hell, man, we all catch rounds that got names on 'em. Rounds hit you in the eyeball don't care if you're a colonel or a fucking sergeant. Right? Hell, I love this outfit already."

Sneezy took a long drink from his mug, draining its contents while Getts watched with interest. He took only a sip of his own beer.

Another trooper—Huck Finn—staggered forward, fumbling with a cigarette and soggy match. He spoke to Peach. "What's all this secret stuff, Chief Gunner's Mate Peach? Hmm?"

"Who we are is nobody's business. Not even the name of the unit," Peach answered.

"Suits the duck shit out of me," Huck Finn said. "You know where I was going when I got orders to report here?"

"Yeah, I do. U.S. Army Hospital Fort Russel, psychiatric ward," Peach replied.

Huck Finn closed his eyes as he started giggling. "That's right. You got it, Peachy. Did you fuck up or what?" It was a statement, not a question. He looked up at Peach's sober face and laughed even harder until he was forced to sit down from the exertion.

"No fuck-up, Huck Finn, but you might soon wish it was." Peach smiled with assurance.

"Hey, not me, baby. Packin' a rifle is better than . . ." Huck Finn could not find the words.

"Sitting in a cell? Electroshock treatments? Or maybe they'd just let you walk. Out of the service and down the street. Might happen," Peach said.

Huck Finn's eyes narrowed. "But not likely," he said.

One of the waitresses wore a name tag that read "Carla." She wore no bra under a low-cut peasant lace blouse. She was young, blonde, and built like a college cheerleader. Carla had trouble moving among drunken troopers who breathed closely down her neck as she attempted to deliver beers and whiskey, trying to keep a dazzling smile on her face. She appeared to be enjoying herself as much as her customers.

As she walked by a trooper's outstretched arm, he slid his hand underneath her short skirt and onto her backside. Without raising alarm in the least, Carla turned and, using one hand while the other balanced drinks on her tray, placed an index finger under the trooper's nose and pushed sharply upward in a deliberate, practiced, movement. The trooper, named Lurch, reacted the only way he could to a painful thrust. He fell over backward in his chair to the howling delight of his fellow soldiers.

"Hey, Carla," Razorback said. "Fine move. Where'd you learn that?"

"On my first date."

"Did she break my nose?" asked Lurch from the floor. "I gotta take care of my good fucking looks, man."

"Valentino," the stocky civilian on the airplane days before moved close to Getts at the end of the bar. "Bob. Bobby Getts. That's what you want us to call you?"

"That's it. Valentino. That's a good name for an Italian," Getts said. "Do you have a little Spanish blood in you?"

"Hell, who knows? Fact is I don't intend to be here very fucking long, Bobby. See, I'm not in the army anymore. That was then, this is now. I'm a civilian. So there's been a big-ass mistake, and I'm getting outta here." Valentino motioned to the bartender to refill his glass of whiskey.

"You can walk out tomorrow, if you want," Getts said.

"Bet your ass." Valentino knocked down the drink, feeling better as he smiled at Getts.

"Have another one," Getts said.

"Don't mind if I do," Valentino said. Bartender refilled his glass. "I shouldn't tell you this, but you look like somebody who can keep their mouth shut. Am I right, Bobby? Huh?"

"I'm in the business of keeping secrets," Getts said as he sipped his beer.

"Well, you know who you got your delicate little hands on, here? You know my real name?"

"Yes, I do." Getts said.

"No, you don't. It ain't Valentino, for sure. And it ain't Vic Palermo, neither. Hey, I look familiar? Ever see my face before? Maybe in the newspapers? I'm Nick Gambono. Huh? They call me the bull. Am I ringing your bells yet, Bobby?"

"You set up boss Rocky Vanzano." Getts said.

"Yeah. You got it. That's me," Valentino said finishing his whiskey.

"You officially killed fourteen men for the mob. Maybe more, but you only confessed to fourteen to avoid death row," Getts said.

Valentino's smile slowly faded, his mood turning dark. "Okay. So you know I'm in the witness protection program. Understand? The fucking U.S. Marshals made a mistake, man. The plane I want on doesn't go to no fucking army post. They're supposed to hide me. That was the deal. Capiche?"

"No mistake. The U.S. Marshals put you here because I wanted you here. You have military experience that I need. I need your civilian experience, too. So it's either work for me, or go back to New York to tell your old gang that you made a mistake and you're sorry. You didn't mean to rat on Vanzano. Maybe they'll understand," Getts said.

"The fuck are you talking about, Getts? You trying to be funny or something? You know I can't go back there, you prick son of a bitch." Valentino's eyes flashed darkly, his lips turning white with rage.

"I'm going to forget you said that just this once. You're back in the military now, and I have my own way of handling insubordination. Show me disrespect, and I'll teach you something you didn't know about pain." Getts moved away from Valentino and mingled with the group.

Bartender was not amused by drunken antics, maybe because of his proprietary nature, and affected the face of a basset hound. He glanced at an electric clock. The clock read ten minutes to midnight.

An overdosed trooper, a black man whose name identified him as Crush, dropped a five dollar bill on the bar. "Beers," he said to Bartender.

"Bob's paying for the drinks," Bartender said, pushing back the trooper's money.

Crush retrieved two more bills from his pocket and placed them on the bar. "I'm buyin' two beers and another one for Bob and another one for you."

"Thanks, but I don't drink."

Crush's voice turned ominous. Other Blacklight personnel began to listen to the exchange. "Bartender, by the time I finish this beer you better be halfway through one of your own."

After a moment of hesitation, Bartender placed a glass under a beer spigot and filled it to the top. Then he held it up as a salute to the buyer and took a large drink.

Crush smiled. "There. Isn't that a hell of a lot more fun?" Crush placed another bill on the bar. "Buy that kid there a beer. The busboy."

Bartender filled another glass with beer. As Crush looked back at the party, Bartender caught Busboy's eye. Busboy turned back toward his cleaning; Bartender poured the beer into a sink.

Bartender looked again at the wall clock which now read 11:55. He raised his voice above the noise of the party. "Gentlemen . . . gentlemen, ladies, please. We close in five minutes. Post regulations, the bar has to close at 2400 hours."

Hearing that, Crush reached into his jump boot and came up with a commando throwing knife. Fluidly, he brought his arm to his ear then let the knife go. The blade not only penetrated the clock's plexiglass covering, but pierced the case and lodged against one of its hands.

"Clock ain't gonna stop this fuckin' party, Bartender. Keep on pouring, man."

Troopers applauded, cheered, whistled, and produced

knives of their own. The air was suddenly full of flying metal, several knives sticking into the face of the now-shattered clock. Bets were made, knives retrieved, and soon a target was chalked into an upended table for all to throw at.

"I'll put fifty bucks on Crush," the Numash Indian who now called himself Redskin said.

"Make it a hundred," Huck Finn said, "and I'll take him myself."

"Covered," Sneezy said. "Got another fifty. Who wants it?"

"Hey, Bobby," Razorback yelled at Getts as he fumbled with a wad of cash from his own pocket, "you're going to have to get a haircut, man. Look like a fucking hippie."

Getts smiled thinly. "You're going to have to let yours grow." Getts handed Razorback a cigar.

"Commander," Razorback began.

"Bob."

Razorback smiled. "Okay, Bob. You know I'm an officer, right? When do we get our rank back?"

"When you leave Blacklight," Getts said.

"What you're going to have here, Bob, is a mob. You need officers and NCOs to make a unit run. I'm Ranger qualified."

"I know you are, Razorback. That's one reason you're here. I also know that you were facing a court martial for blowing up a tank full of our own men because you were too lazy to preflight your Apache before an exercise. You'll get your bars back when we're through with our mission—if you work your ass off. And if you're still alive." Getts said.

"I made a mistake. I can handle anything this outfit has to do."

"Handling in Blacklight means doing it without mistakes," Getts said. Getts glanced at Bartender as the knife throwing contest got well under way. An imperceptible nod was returned. Getts made eye contact with Carla, then with Peach. Getts rose and crossed the room to stand by Peach.

"I'm going out for some air," he said.

Peach placed a cigar in his mouth as Getts continued toward the latrine near the Garden's rear door. Making sure he was not being watched, Getts let himself through the exit. One step behind him was Busboy.

Once outside, Getts and Busboy moved to quietly close

all the Garden's windows, securing them with steel latch mechanisms. The window shutters were made of quarter-inch plate steel. They would not be forced. Getts and Busboy then walked into the blackness of surrounding trees.

Inside the Garden, Peach made his way slowly toward the bar, leaning on it. Without exchanging a word, Bartender laid three gas masks on the bar. Carla slipped on hers as did Peach and Bartender. Peach vaulted lightly over the bar, dipped into a bin full of canisters underneath its shiny surface, and placed a number of gas grenades on the bar top. As Carla began pulling pins, Bartender and Peach rolled them into the drunken crowd of knife-throwing troopers. Within seconds, clouds of thick, billowing tear gas filled the room. In addition, flash-bang percussion grenades were lobbed into the drunken group, creating a chaotic melee.

Peach knew that people exposed to undiluted tear gas want nothing more in life than to get away from it. It is designed to be debilitating in the extreme. It can cause panic in the most steel-nerved individuals in the world, even those who have experienced it before. It did not make it easier to take when one's eyes, throat, and nose burned like fire, water running from tear ducts and skin pores. Escape became imperative. Peach was ready, then, when Razorback whirled and made a grab for his gas mask. Peach put up a defensive forearm, but Razorback was determined. He aimed a knockout kick at Peach's solar plexus. Peach easily moved inside the blow and placed the edge of his jump boot against Razorback's pivot foot. The aspiring Blacklight trooper went down hard, then crawled toward a door.

It was locked.

So were the windows into which chairs and tables were vainly thrown.

For several minutes, Peach, Carla, and Bartender listened to the sounds of wracking sobs as grown men cried uncontrollably, vomiting, and retching as each puked up his considerable libation. Determined that she would not violate another order, in this case the base's ban against booze, Toni had touched nothing from the spigots of the Garden. She was thus more capable than the others of finding a way out. Instead of hammering against the steel-shuttered windows, Toni crawled, staying as low as possible to the floor, where there was a layer of fresh air. She slipped the thin blade of a throwing knife between the steel shutters, then pulled sharply upward. As the outer latch fell free, the window opened and cool night air rushed inside. The effect was like a bright moon on the open sea. Every man surged after Toni through the opening and collapsed on the ground, continuing to retch and to cry.

A ring of trucks, each equipped with halogen head lamps, was parked in a semicircle around the Garden. Moments later, the furies of hell itself seemed to explode when a wall of automatic rifle and machine gun fire slammed into the sides of the Garden and around the milling crowd of confused soldiers. Live bullets kicked up turf around them.

In addition to bright lights and explosive gunfire, fanatical screaming, and yelling rose hysterically from somewhere in the darkness around the already bewildered troopers. Then, suddenly above the roar, was the voice of Chief Gunner's Mate Peach firmly directing the men.

"This way. Move! Move! Move it out. This way. Get up and run! Double time, move, move . . ."

Troopers pulled themselves off the ground and began to run, falling and staggering in the direction ordered, following on the heels of their chief gunner's mate. As the last trooper stumbled forward to keep up with those in front, truck engines fired into life, clutches were popped and the trucks drove slowly alongside the Blacklight platoon. Tarpaulins on the trucks were pulled back, and men inside began throwing equipment down to those on the ground.

"Take your equipment," mysterious voices out of the night commanded. "Get your packs on and run! Run, goddamn it! Don't stop to look around, or you die." As if to punctuate the reality of their situation, bullets cut up brush near them in withering bursts of live automatic gunfire.

Blacklight personnel plunged into protective darkness of the forest.

There was confusion among the uniformed drunks who attempted to regain sobriety in split seconds. "You're at position Alpha," a voice shouted out from the darkness. "You have two hours to reach position Foxtrot on your map. Buddy up. Find someone to take with you. Don't get captured. Start now."

Then the voice faded back into the trees, becoming one with the shadows. While the Blacklight troopers ran, other voices harassed them. These people were dressed in terrorist clothing, including balaclava scarves that masked their visages.

Anxious to escape the frenzy of Alpha, Sneezy lit out on his own. He picked his way through the woods, arriving at a narrow footbridge. He paused momentarily, considering the cost of passing over the stream via the bridge. Surely, it would be booby-trapped. He stepped cautiously to one side and, moving clear of the bridge, leaped from one side of the stream to the other.

As his foot touched the ground on the far side of the water, it hit a trip wire. At once, a snare closed around his foot, and he was snatched into the air dangling by one leg.

Chapter Four

Valentino and Redskin moved together, watching each other's flanks. They referred continually to the map Valentino carried. When he arrived at the creek, Redskin washed vomit from his blouse.

"We need a bearing," he said.

"Should be a paved road to the west, couple hundred meters," Valentino said.

"Fuck the roads. They'll be covered like a blanket."

"Okay," Valentino agreed, "there's a meadow up ahead. We sprint it."

"Mines. It's gonna be mined."

"Who gives a shit? Think they're gonna kill us? It's only a training exercise, man," Valentino argued.

Redskin considered for a moment, then nodded his head. "Right. We can save ten minutes."

The two men moved off, barely discernible in the pitch-black night.

Crouched near an outer perimeter of the meadow, the two men looked in all directions for the "enemy." None could be seen.

"Ready?" Valentino said.

"Yeah."

The two men leaped to their feet and began running as fast as possible through waist-high grass. Their breathless progress was good. Suddenly, there were sounds of mortar shells being launched, and night was turned into day. The two men were silhouetted within the blazing light of a star shell.

"Freeze," Redskin whispered. "They can't see us. Don't move."

While the two troopers stood indistinct among tall grass, reeds, and scrub trees, mortar rounds began to fall in front of them walking inexorably in their direction. The mortars were of large caliber, and their explosions shook the ground.

"Fuck," Valentino said incredulously. "Hot rounds!"

"Let's split."

The two troopers ran whence they had come, moving fast. Before they could make the safety of the tree line, the trunks themselves seemed to come alive, materializing into men dressed in black. There was no need for gunfire; the terrorists bludgeoned their victims efficiently in the body and back of the neck.

The terrorists carried their prisoners the way natives carry slaughtered carcasses of animals: tied and strung under poles. This method of transportation was extremely painful. The entrance to a ground-level hut was opened, and the prisoners were taken inside.

The hut inside was dimly lit with candles. Its walls were bloody, rusted, primitive. There was one metal table and three chairs.

Huck Finn was strung up by his thumbs, his toes barely touching the floor. He was in pain but refused to speak or cry out. Sneezy, Lurch, and Crush were lashed, hands behind their backs, bamboo sticks between their legs under their knees. They could neither stand nor sit without great pain.

Two terrorists walked toward Valentino. Their eyes, as Valentino looked into them, were cold. They held Valentino as another drew a knife from a belt, placing the point over his crotch, then ripping quickly downward.

Valentino screamed.

"Shut your filthy mouth, you pig," the terrorist spat. Valentino was shocked to hear it was a woman's voice. "You still have your little penis. Before the sun rises, I'm going to cut it off."

Valentino looked down to see that he had been grazed but not cut deeply by the knife, his genitalia intact.

He then heard two voices speaking in an Arabic tongue. A door opened and the two men entered. Like the other terrorists, they wore black clothing and carried automatic weapons. What the prisoners did not know, however, was that it was Peach and Getts. Peach stepped in front of Valentino, saw his ripped pants and bloody flesh and broke into laughter. He was so amused that he could not stop laughing.

"When I get out of here, I'm going to ram your goddamn tongue up your own ass," Valentino hissed at Peach.

Peach's laugh slowly lost its humor, his eyes taking on the coloring of a storm cloud. He savagely smashed Valentino on the jaw, knocking him to the floor. "Shut up your filthy hole, you son of a whore," Peach shouted into the Blacklight trooper's face.

"Listen to me, all of you," Getts said. "This is not what you think. You think this is a test. That you are being trained." Getts's voice had taken on a distinctive Middle Eastern accent. "You are wrong. If you answer questions, you will live. If you do not answer questions, you die. My name is Yaral. These are my people. Do you understand?" As if to emphasize his point, he kicked Lurch in the stomach. The trooper doubled over, gasping in pain.

But from within his suffering body, there came a laugh. Forced. Hurt. But a laugh nonetheless.

Getts motioned briskly with the barrel of his automatic rifle. Peach stepped forward, and used a knife to cut Lurch's bonds before stepping back. Getts tore off his balaclava and revealed his face to the prisoners. Their eyes widened in surprise but it was nothing compared to what they felt next as Getts fired a burst of rounds into the scoffing soldier. Bullets tore into Lurch's battle jacket as he grasped his guts, his face betraying ultimate surprise.

"Oh, God, no . . ."

His pirouette of death carried him to the far wall of the hut where, blood seeping rapidly through newly stitched holes in his uniform, he died.

"You people are so easy to fool. I came to you with an army card that a child could duplicate. You follow like sheep," Getts said, maintaining his accent. He stared for several moments at his confused and terrified prisoners, then turned on his heel and walked to a dimly lit corner of the hut. There was a pile of dirty rags and an oil tarpaulin. He threw off the tarp and rags, and reached down and grasped on to a human form of what had once been a man. He pulled the body toward the middle of the room. The body was obviously dead and horribly mutilated. The teeth of the corpse were smashed, deep knife gashes criss-crossed the body's chest, back, and arms. An eye had been crudely gouged out.

"Here is your Commander Getts. The *real* one. Now, quickly, we have little time."

Getts moved to Razorback, a one-time University of Arkansas football player. "For whom do you work?" Getts demanded.

"I'm a volunteer," Razorback said through pain and gritted teeth.

"For what mission?"

"I don't know. They haven't told us yet."

"The code word, Blacklight. What does it mean? What kind of mission? Where will you be sent?" Getts demanded in rapid fire.

"We're supposed to find that out later," Razorback said, choking on his own spit. "We're supposed to go to the Middle East. We only know that."

"But where? Where in the Middle East? *Speak!*" Getts raised the muzzle of his automatic weapon and placed it against Razorback's mouth.

"Syria. I think. Lebanon, too. Yeah, Lebanon," Razorback blurted.

Getts stepped forward and delivered a stinging blow to Razorback's face, succeeding in making the former Arkansas athlete wince, bowing his head to hide his pain and intense anger. Getts motioned again toward Peach, who,

along with Busboy, stepped forward and dragged Razorback toward the door.

Getts called after him. "In fifteen minutes, you will beg
to tell me the information I want to know. In twenty minutes, it will not matter because you will be dead."

Outside of the hut, a hole had been dug in the rough
shape of a grave. Also near the grave was a wall locker,
the kind found in any barracks on any military reservation.
Still bound, Razorback was roughly stuffed into the locker.

"No, don't do it! I don't know anything," he struggled
to be believed. "I'd tell you if I did."

Without speaking, Peach and Busboy slammed the lid of
the locker closed, pushed it into the hole, and quickly
began covering it. Muted moans came from within the
metal box.

Back inside the hut, Getts was still working on the prisoners as Peach and Busboy returned to take up their stations. Getts had singled out Sneezy for questioning.

"You are a counterterrorist group. Isn't that so?" he
asked.

Sneezy did not answer.

Getts, impatient, inhaled deeply. "It is funny. Do you
know why? Because you have no cause. America eats ham-
burgers. That is all. We do what is impossible because we
are willing to die. If we live, we build a better world, and
if we die we are martyrs. Either way is fine. Is that fine
with you, Mr. Sneezy?"

Again, Sneezy offered no response.

"Well," Getts said, pointing his assault rifle at Sneezy,
"we shall see, shall we not?"

"Yes," Sneezy said. "We're antiterrorists. Hell, yes!"

Getts slowly lowered his weapon. "And your assignment?"

"They haven't told us yet."

"You lie! Your mission is in Libya. You work for a white
pig called Wallis. He kisses the ass of your sick President."

Sneezy did not respond but merely waited.

"Well?" Getts demanded. "What is the mission? Exactly!"

"Shut up, Sneezy," Valentino warned from his position
on the floor.

Peach swung a booted foot into Valentino's midsection.
The trooper fell sideways, vomit spewing from his mouth.

"Easy for you to say," Getts said to Valentino. "In a few hours, you will be a woman. Carla has promised."

Carla removed her own balaclava, her face remaining unemotional, entirely unreadable.

Outside of the hut, a dirty, bleeding Huck Finn stalked the perimeter. There was a single guard with a rifle across his knees, who squatted near the doorway leading into the hut. Huck Finn searched around him for a weapon and chose a thin but strong vine from nearby lush shrubbery. He silently stripped the leaves from the vine, doubled it, then tied a knot in its center creating a garrote. He moved silently into position behind the guard. Just as he was about to strike, a runner arrived from out of the dark. The runner spoke Arabic as he addressed the guard.

"Yaral?"

"Inside," the sentry responded, also in Arabic.

Within the hut, Getts was beginning to make progress. "How many men form the task force?" he demanded of Sneezy.

"A brigade."

"A lie!"

"I'm not lyin'," the young man said with a trace of belligerence.

At a nod from Getts, Peach stepped forward and quickly threw a leather thong around Sneezy's head, then inserted a simple wooden stick and began to twist. Sneezy screamed aloud. At another nod from Getts, the pressure was eased slightly.

"How many men? Total," Getts repeated.

"They told us . . . told us when we volunteered . . . about one hundred," Sneezy admitted.

Getts and Peach exchanged glances. They smiled in satisfaction. "That is so," Peach agreed. "We know it."

"Good, Mr. Sneezy," Getts said, leaning closer to the trooper. "Your target; where in Libya? Be careful you do not lie."

"You were right. We're going after Khadafy," Sneezy said.

Again, Getts and Peach exchanged looks. At that moment, the runner entered the room, and stepped toward Getts.

"Yaral," the messenger began. "A message. High priority from the leader. It is for your eyes this moment."

The messenger held out a small piece of paper, which Getts immediately read. He jerked his head toward Peach, who, leaving the two guards and the messenger to watch the prisoners, moved to the door with Getts. "I must go," Getts said. "I will meet you in two days."

"What about these?" Peach indicated toward the prisoners.

Getts glanced over his shoulders, then shrugged. "Kill them."

Getts turned on his heel, and passed through the door of the hut.

Outside, Huck Finn waited for Getts to depart and leave the solitary guard alone. When he was certain he was unobserved, Huck Finn moved quickly. The guard sensed movement behind him but was too late to act. Huck Finn slipped the deadly green vine over the terrorist's neck and, with powerful hands and shoulder muscles straining, strangled the guard by crushing his larynx. The guard slumped quietly to the ground. Huck Finn retrieved the man's assault weapon, stuck an extra magazine into his pocket, and moved slowly toward the door of the hut.

Inside, Peach regarded his prisoners with relish. "So? How do you want to die? I can shoot you with cyanide bullets. I made them myself. Or nicotinic sulphate. Very painful," he smiled at the thought.

"I think we'll just drive a wooden stake through your heart."

The voice suddenly emanated from behind Peach and the others. The terrorists spun to behold Huck Finn, his face a portrait of livid anger. Peach, Carla, and Bartender all dropped their weapons without being told.

Peach spoke rapidly to save his own life. "Hey, man, that looks like a real gun with real bullets. You win. This is a training exercise."

Huck Finn's mouth twisted into a cruel grin. "Nice try, comrade," he said, lifting his weapon and pointing it directly at Peach.

Peach inhaled deeply. "I need help here, Lurch."

Lurch rose slowly from his prone and bloody position on the floor near a wall.

"Oh, oh," Lurch said, "the man means business."

The sight of "dead" Lurch coming back to life made Huck Finn hesitate, his finger on the trigger.

"Must have fallen asleep," Lurch said, forcing a smile. "It's okay, Huck, Peach here isn't bullshitting. War's over, man."

The truth slowly washed over Huck Finn and the other Blacklight volunteers. Huck Finn's gun muzzle slowly lowered.

"You . . . you're okay?" he asked of Lurch.

"I'm okay, trooper," he said, indicating his shirt. "Cattle blood an' blue ink. Realistic stuff."

Huck Finn looked slowly around at the group. "Oh, Jesus," he said. "I just killed a man."

Chapter Five

Conrad, using a disguise and the passport of one Señor Alfonso Beniquez, boarded an *Air Syria* Russian-made IL76 aircraft in Beirut. He flew four hundred air miles to Egypt. Once in Cairo, between concourses, Conrad stepped into a rest room, removed the mustache and glasses, dropped his passport into a trash can and withdrew a different passport from the lining of his attaché case. Now using the name of Johann Van Meter, age twenty-eight, an Amsterdam optometrist, Conrad bought a ticket to Rome by way of Athens. He made his way briskly to the American Express office. "My name is Johann Van Meter," he said to one of two men working behind the counter. "Do you have a letter for me?" The dark complexioned Egyptian turned away to shuffle through papers contained in a wire basket. He withdrew a manila envelope. The clerk hardly glanced at Van Meter's identification as he handed it to the blue-eyed man on the other side of the counter. Conrad left a two dollar tip as he walked out of the office and into a skyroom restaurant. He chose an outside table, ordered mineral water, then opened the manila envelope. The letter inside, written on a single sheet of paper in a rather shaky script, informed Johann that his mother was no better and that he should make plans to return to Den Helder at his earliest convenience. The letter was signed *Your loving aunt, Elizabeth.* Conrad considered burning the letter but at once rejected the idea. Less conspicuous to simply tear it in two and drop it into a trash receptacle. There was, after all, only a single word in the letter that meant anything at all.

Conrad immediately took a taxi the few short blocks to the Hilton Cairo Hotel and registered for a room. He informed the concierge that he would need the use of a computer in the room, one that was equipped with a high-speed modem. Within ten minutes after moving into the room, an American portable computer was delivered. Without so much as removing his coat, Conrad accessed the Internet then typed in the site letters for the interactive edition of the *International Wall Street Journal.* When the *WSJ* appeared on his screen, he scrolled through the electronic pages until he found mutual funds, then money markets. Most people would have had to use a calculator to get the numbers precisely, but Conrad was able to add the total value of assets contained in the first, second, and third money market funds. The resulting number was a six figure integer. He inserted a 3.5 MB disc, which contained an initialization vector determined from the system clock within the computer. The information also contained the system ID, user ID, date, time, and system interrupt registers.

There was a second file contained on the 3.5 floppy. It was the entire book of *Heart of Darkness* by Conrad. A letter to the Editor in the *Journal*—written under the name of Leon Gills—provided the key. The third letter in every second word of the article corresponded with a logarithm formula in letters of words from *Heart of Darkness* by Conrad.

Conrad, using the *Wall Street Journal* key, could then underline the words from the text that was being sent to him. *Special military unit composed to target Conrad. Commander is Robert Getts, United States Navy, real*

name not yet known. Organization code named Blacklight.
Details Getts and his unit forwarded to AAL, New York.
Fanus.

Conrad cleared the screen of the message, removed his 3.5 disk, dropped it into his coat pocket and exited the room. He would not need to sleep here. Descending in the hotel elevator, he considered the message. His plans for the warheads were too far along to worry about some clumsy military unit interfering with them. But Robert Getts was something else. He knew of Getts from when he was attached to the British SAS in Libya. In that same year, on a black ops mission, Getts had mutilated General Ernesto de Palmas. Cutting off his genitals and letting the general live was genius. The general would never lead again because no one would follow a man without balls. Conrad begrudgingly respected Getts's tactical brilliance and his emotionless devotion to completing his mission.

Conrad had not heard of Getts since, but it appeared that now he was back. If so, Getts would have to die. But since Getts had no idea Conrad was on to him the task would be easy.

There were nineteen days remaining of the original sixty allotted to Conrad on the Van Meter visa for Israel. Of course the real Van Meter lay buried in a shallow grave under the broiling sands of the Dara desert. Nevertheless, an exit stamp was affixed to the Van Meter passport before Conrad boarded Olympus Airways Flight 40 for Rome and Athens.

Carrying Van Meter's passport, Conrad disembarked in Athens but did not leave the international terminal building. He pretended to browse through the racks of a book kiosk but used his position to watch ticket lines and boarding gates at BOAC, Pan American, and Air France. He had two reservations at each, under identities including Van Meter. The nearest departure time, a BOAC flight, was still fifty-five minutes away.

The scene before him seemed normal. There were a number of passengers sitting in chairs, some reading, some sleeping, some tending children. He paid for a British automobile racing magazine, then began to walk across the terminal lobby when he noticed two men near the boarding gate. Conrad sensed something unnatural about them. He altered his direction slightly so that he would pass by their left side a dozen meters away. As they talked, he could see that though their lips moved, they did not look at each other. No eye contact at all. Despite their casual dress, one wore fashionable jeans and a sweatshirt, the other loose fitting corduroy trousers and a cheap jacket.

Conrad continued walking toward the Pan American ticket counter. He took a seat in a nearby waiting area and pretended to read his auto racing magazine. The two men at BOAC were, he was convinced, police. They were not necessarily looking for him or, for that matter, anyone in particular. They might be part of airport security apparatus. After several more minutes, he rose from his chair, approached the ticket counter, and paid for a first class fare using one of Van Meter's credit cards.

He waited until all of the other passengers had boarded and the gate doors were beginning to close before he hurried to the ramp and got on the plane.

In Rome Conrad took a taxi to Il Grande Vittorio hotel where a single room had been booked and paid for in advance. Inside the hotel room, Conrad stripped to the skin, removed contact lenses from his eyes, then showered and shaved. He used a bottled treatment that removed the dark coloring from his hair, leaving his natural color, if not its luster, exposed. He opened the room's only closet and found a suitcase, which he laid on the bed and opened. From the suitcase, he removed clothing made in Europe. He burned the Van Meter passport, then placed the clothes in which he arrived into a plastic bag along with the contact lenses. As he left his hotel room scarcely an hour later, he dropped the plastic bag along with his briefcase into a refuse chute, took the stairs to the lobby of the hotel, and stepped onto an airport bus.

One hour and thirty minutes later "Erich Friedrich von Eisler" stepped onto Lufthansa Flight 312 bound for Frankfurt. He carried a genuine passport, stamped to reflect his arrival from Buenos Aires, Argentina.

Kronberg, in the state of Hessen, was the seventh train stop from Frankfurt, about 67 kilometers away. The town boasted an ancient castle, its ruins meticulously preserved by the state. The mountains behind Kronberg provided first-rate skiing and attracted a large number of tourists each winter. During the spring and summer, tourists from all over arrived in Kronberg to drink its mineral waters and relax in its several spas. The nearby towns of Lozenstein and Konigstein each boasted castles of their own.

There would never be a skyscraper built in Kronberg. A number of its streets were still lined with their original cobblestone, several hundred years old. The town's houses had heavy walls, small windows, and beautifully landscaped and carefully tended gardens.

There were three high schools in town, all public. There was a private school in nearby Schonberg, over one hundred years in the same location. It was called the Winter School after the family who donated its land and buildings in trust, that it always be used to educate the children of "deserving families." These young trust fund heirs would begin attending Winter School at the age of ten and complete their studies by age seventeen. The school was run by Herr Professor Wilhelm Klostermann and his wife Frau Doktor Hildegard Klostermann, both regionally noted educators. The Winter School was widely known and respected for its liberal arts curriculum, and its science program was respected throughout Germany. Few Winter School alumni failed to matriculate at university.

Heinrich von Eisler and his wife had both attended Winter School. Their tragic death aboard Flight 280 had shocked the entire community. There had been an Eisler family in Kronberg for over a hundred years. As there were no children from that marriage, it seemed that the Eisler line was ended.

The quiet arrival of a new Eisler, a proclaimed cousin from South America, created whispering, in hopes that Erich von Eisler would like what he saw in the baronial estate and would settle in town.

Conrad was greeted effusively by Jakob, a nearly blind family retainer, whose spine bent forward as though constantly searching for a next footfall. The old servant took Conrad's bag and clutched with twisted arthritic fingers at a nearby bell cord. As though from the woodwork, two more scr-

vants materialized—Helga, the cook and housekeeper, and
a younger woman of about half of Helga's fifty years. Helga
was, Conrad noticed with distaste, severely overweight. Her
forehead supported heavy brows and drooping eyelids,
framed by dull gray hair pulled tightly behind a round face
and fastened in the back with a rubber band. Helga smiled
infrequently, as her attempts to seem pleasant were trans-
parently false and she was bright enough to know it. On
the occasion of meeting a potential new master of the
household, Helga forced the edges of her oversized lips and
mouth upward a discriminating millimeter.

Conrad mumbled insincere greetings to her, then turned
toward the smaller, less intimidating presence of Fraulein
Lena Milch, maid and First Assistant Housekeeper. It was
a Germanic tradition to assign titles to the most pedestrian
stations in life as though by doing so the designee could
avoid social ennui. Fraulein Milch was, Conrad thought, not
as beautiful as she believed she was. He assured them all
that their positions with the Eisler family would continue
into the foreseeable future and that he would show himself
around the house and grounds. He nodded dismissively as
he walked past them all through the massive foyer, down
the picture-laden hallway leading to the mansion's main
room. Conrad noted that the Persian carpets and lush tapestries were crafted with the special dyes of eighteenth-
century "Prussian Blue" and embroidered with the crest of
the German Weimar Republic in gold thread.

As he turned toward the library, he spoke to Jakob, who
followed a discreet few steps behind. "I'll take coffee in
the library, Jakob. And see if you can't find something to
eat with it."

"Of course, sir," the servant responded. "It's good that
you have come, Herr Eisler."

"Well, in that case you will be saddened to know that I
won't be here often," Conrad said. "I travel."

"I see," Jakob said, his face drooping at the news.
"Would you like cake, Herr Eisler?"

"Cheese."

Conrad passed under a vaulted archway into the library,
once his "cousin's" favorite room, he reminded himself.
The fool Heinrich had carried photographs of the house

and a personal diary in his luggage. Conrad's stock in trade, he believed, was good research.

He idly regarded a section of books by Schiller. *William Tell* sat beside "Ode to Joy" and *Don Carlos*. Idealism, Conrad inwardly snorted. How could audiences have read such pap? They were, he thought, intellectual fairy tales. Conrad took in walls of books in twelve-foot shelves, filled with the ridiculous notions that God would send a democratic angel to solve their problems, to forgive their lusts, their sins, their animalism.

He sat heavily into a wingback chair, picked up a nearby telephone and dialed. A woman's voice answered. "Lisa," he said simply, "I'm here."

"Conrad? My darling, where? In Kronberg?" she said excitedly.

"Ja. Das Gipfel Haus."

"But when? I didn't know you were coming. But then I never know. How are you?" Lisa asked, her voice breathless.

"Come over," he said. "And my name is Erich. Understand? Erich von Eisler."

"Yes, I understand. But the children . . ." she began.

"How far away is Belden?" he asked.

"An hour and one half, by autobahn. I can be there in two hours," she said.

"Bring a bag," he commanded. "And hurry. I need you."

Conrad sipped dark European coffee and nibbled at the cheese and crackers Jakob brought. He had been hungry, but the thought of Lisa's physical nearness replaced his appetite for food with lust. She completely dominated his sexual desires to the exclusion of all other women. It was late in the evening when Conrad finally heard the thunderous clap of the front door knocker.

He strode through the library door, through a room replicating a full-sized English pub, into the main foyer. To his irritation, he had not been the first to answer the door. It was Fraulein Milch who greeted Lisa into the mansion.

"Con . . . Erich!" Lisa virtually gasped, a huge smile on her face, arms wide open. Conrad was aware that Fraulein Milch was watching them carefully, judgmental of their transparent desire for each other. The corners of her mouth twitched at once. She made no excuse to take her leave as she should have.

"Lisa," Conrad sighed, choked with passion. His head swam. "Uh, Lisa, this is Lena Milch. She is new, I am told," he said, turning away from the maid, refusing to finish the introduction.

Lisa smiled warmly. "Hello, Lena. I am Lisa Hohelganz."

"Frau Hohelganz." The maid almost curtsied.

"Uh, darling," Conrad said quickly, "I've brought you something from Egypt. I can't wait for you to see it. Come." He almost pulled her across the entranceway of the mansion and toward the huge winding stairway that led to the second floor. "It's in my bag in my room," he said in a voice intended to carry back to anyone who was listening.

"Really," Lisa said *sotto voce,* a throaty chuckle of amusement escaping her lips, "is that where you keep it now?" Conrad forced himself to keep a discreet distance from her until the two had moved out of sight of Fraulein Milch's peering eyes. Once they were behind the heavy walls of the hallway, he fairly ran, pulling her along insistently until he reached the door to his room. He thrust it open and pushed her inside.

"Oh, I am so sorry!" Helga blanched, her eyebrows arching upward. "I was only making ready your room, Herr . . ."

"Get out," he commanded. The door had hardly clicked shut before Conrad encircled Lisa with his arms, pulling her fully into his own body, his mouth pressing upon her lips, his hands hungrily caressing her. Soon they were on top of the huge bed, tearing at their clothing.

While Lisa rested before dressing for dinner, Conrad rang for Jakob. The old man appeared at the door of the master bedchamber, breathing heavily from the climb upstairs. "Heinrich often spoke to me of his darkroom," Conrad said. "I am an amateur photographer myself." Conrad raised a small black bag he held in his hand. "Would you show it to me?"

"Of course, sir," Jakob said, turning toward the balcony and stairs beyond. They walked down the main staircase, down a long hallway past a library, a sitting room, a game room complete with billiard table, skirting an indoor swimming pool to the large kitchen. Jakob continued by the massive walk-in refrigerator and opened a large oak door.

He flicked a wall switch, which illuminated the stairs and rooms below.

"Thank you, I'll find my way from here," Conrad said.

"The door of the darkroom is locked, Herr Eisler," the servant said.

"Then give me your key."

The darkroom door opened easily. Conrad reached instinctively for a switch on a wall. There were two: one that operated a red light, the other white. He snapped on the white bulb. He opened another door and stepped into a well-ordered store room. Supplies of raw film stock, cassette covers, papers of various kinds, cotton rolls, a rubber apron, and bottles of chemicals for developing and printing sat neatly on shelves.

Conrad searched, moving around jars and tins but did not find what he was looking for. Dipping into the bag he carried, Conrad came up with a four-ounce bottle marked with a glaring red danger label that read SODIUM CYANIDE.

Conrad wandered around the basement until he found a screwdriver and a few other miscellaneous items. He retrieved a compressed-gas cigarette lighter from his pocket, which he placed on the darkroom workbench. Next to this he put a common laboratory glass tube, a roll of cotton, and a small opaque bottle.

He applied the edge of a screwdriver to the valve of the cigarette lighter. He waited until the hiss of escaping butane gas abated entirely, then used the screwdriver again to remove the screw-valve. He tore off small pieces of cotton from the roll, wetted them with water from a nearby sink, and wedged them into each nostril. Afterward, he very carefully began to remove the cap of the sodium cyanide bottle. Dipping the hollow glass tube into the bottle, he placed his thumb over one end to produce a seal, and transferred a good amount of the acid into the cigarette lighter.

Conrad then opened his small black bag and removed a bottle of astringent. He rinsed the glass tube in clear water, dried it, then dipped it into the second bottle. Despite the number of times Conrad had performed this very same operation, he was aware of sweat beading on his scalp. He held the glass tube filled with astringent above the open

chamber of the cigarette lighter allowing just two drops
to fall.

Very quickly, Conrad replaced the screw valve onto the
lighter. As he tightened the valve, he could not help but
turn his face away from the threat of what was now prussic
acid, instantly deadly if even a minute quantity were to
penetrate the cotton filters in his nose.

When the valve was tightened as far as it could be, Conrad felt like fleeing backward from his lethal canister. But
there was one more operation. He pulled out a CO_2 cartridge from within his small shaving bag. He pushed the
cartridge firmly against the valve until he heard compressed
gas flowing into the now deadly cigarette lighter.

Before rejoining Lisa, there was still another vital piece
of business for Conrad to attend to. He returned to the
library, picked up a telephone, and dialed a long distance
number he had memorized long ago. "Yes," he said when
a voice answered from across an ocean. "I am calling the
Arab American League. To whom am I speaking? Ah. This
is Conrad. That's correct." Conrad's voice slowed so that
he could speak very distinctly into the mouthpiece. "Please
notify Mr. Hixx that I have an important job for him. Tell
Mr. Hixx that he will need a special tool, which I will send
him by overnight freight. Details will be in the package."

Lisa was still drying from her shower as Conrad entered
the master suite. He again marveled at his sister's lush
body, perfectly curved, breasts hanging freely as she dabbed
at her foot perched on a step near the shower. He had
adored her all of his life, hated the man she married, re-
joiced at his death because now she could be his own. That
death, Conrad thought, visited upon people who opposed
him, was both useful and comforting.

Dinner was prepared by a live-in French cook. The menu
consisted of pork tenderloin, vegetables with a Bernaise
sauce and a robust claret. The French were born to be
cooks and waiters, Conrad mused as he bit into a fresh
strawberry. Hitler knew that when he began his attack
through the Low Countries in 1940. "On the other hand,"
he said, "there was not a dish worth fighting for in Russia.
Unless it was blintze. With lots of butter and sour cream."

Lisa was amused. "And the food the Arabs offer," she

said. "Is it any good? Do you suffer down there with the heat and the flies?"

Conrad guarded his real feelings about Arabs from Lisa lest she avoid traveling to those countries with him. "The food is quite good, in fact. The desert is maddeningly romantic. And one can live well."

"But can you drink wine with meals? Muslims are religious to a fault, eh?" she said. "How about America?"

"What about it? I haven't been there for some time," he said.

"I had the impression that you go there often on business."

"If I had to go there often for business, I would get out of business," he said, scowling.

"I was there two years ago, remember?" she said.

"More's the pity," he said.

"I loved it. America is fun," she said.

"Filthy people. They encourage the dregs of humanity to live there. Like the blacks. They are not even masters of their own destiny in Africa, and any collection of idiots could improve life there. And the Jews run the country while they lower their pants and allow their filthy politicians to kiss their fat asses. America is a pestilence to the entire world."

Lisa had stopped eating her food. She slowly lowered her knife and fork. "Good heavens, Conrad. I had no idea that you felt that way about the Americans. How could I have not known?"

"But you have known, my darling," Conrad said. "I've told you that they buy everything and everyone. They seek to make the rest of us like them."

"And your Arab colleagues?" she said.

He shrugged. "The enemy of my enemies . . ."

"Conrad—" Lisa began.

"Yes, yes, well, let's talk about something else. How do you like this house?" he asked.

She looked around as she lowered her voice. "I am very frightened for you, Conrad."

He was pleased that she cared so deeply for him. "But I am doing what we had always said we would do. Remember? And you are not to be frightened. I know what I am doing. Believe me."

Chapter Six

One week later in Los Angeles, Conrad rented yet another car at the airport, this time from a different rental company. From LAX, Conrad turned left onto Century Boulevard and picked up the 405 freeway to Beverly Hills.

When Conrad arrived at St. James's Place on Sunset Boulevard, gone were his eyeglasses, elevated shoes, and mustache. Also discarded were the passport and driver's license belonging to Jacob Bartholoma. He registered at St. James's Place under the name of Udo Christhanson of Stockholm. When he later left his room, he decided to drive his rental car despite the heavy Los Angeles traffic. He drove along Wilshire Boulevard and left the car in a valet lot near Camden.

Conrad walked two blocks along Wilshire carrying his fabric luggage case, and entered the lobby of Banque de Suisse. He approached the young woman at a reception desk, handing her a business card with a Stockholm address.

"My name is Christhanson," he said. "I want to speak with Herr Otto Jodel."

"Do you have an appointment?" she said.

"No, but he is expecting me," Conrad said.

"I'll see if he is in, sir," the receptionist said as she reached for a telephone and touched four keys. "Mr. Christhanson is here to see you, Mr. Jodel. He doesn't have an appointment but . . ." The girl listened for a moment, glanced at the business card, and said "Yes. From Stockholm."

She hung up the telephone and widened her smile as she turned back to Conrad. "Mr. Jodel is on his way out, Mr. Christhanson. May I get you something to drink? Coffee? Tea?"

"No, thank you," Conrad said. Within moments, he could see a man he had never met but assumed was Jodel coming across the lobby of the bank. Conrad could see a look of curiosity behind the foreign-born banker's rimless glasses as he offered his hand. "Herr Christhanson?" the banker said in a statement rather than question. "Otto Jodel. Come in, please."

The banker led Conrad through the lobby, past several desks and into a private office. "I am sorry," he said, motioning Conrad to a chair as he closed the door, "that all I can offer a thirsty traveler is cognac, but if you like the year, I can guarantee the quality."

"Would that be 1966?" Conrad replied, blandly.

"Yes," the banker said, tense but trying not to appear so. "That is the year."

"An outstanding vintage, I understand," Conrad said. "Unfortunately, it would be wasted on me. I don't drink."

"Quickly to business, then?" Jodel said.

"I'm afraid so. We have so little time to enjoy life. Smelling the flowers, as it were," Conrad said as he produced a piece of paper from his pocket. He handed it to the banker. "I require that amount of money in American currency. No bills larger than one hundred dollars. The balance is to be Crédit Suisse Nationale bearer bonds in denominations of ten thousand francs."

"Yes, ah, I shall need your account number, Herr Christhanson," the banker said.

"The account should be listed on the sheet," Conrad said.

"Yes, yes, naturally," the banker agreed.

Conrad was certain the banker had recognized the account number at first glance. Herr Jodel turned to a small computer terminal behind his chair and began typing on his keyboard. The screen was discreetly laid into the back cabinet so that its face was visible only from Herr Jodel's side of the desk.

Within moments, he turned back around toward his guest. "Please make yourself comfortable, Herr Christhanson. I will be only a short while." Jodel closed the office door behind him before walking down a flight of nearby stairs to the bank's vault.

He returned within minutes. In his hand he carried a

single leather case, which he placed on a table near Conrad. "The cash is here, Herr Christhanson but I am instructed to inform you that the bonds are to be issued at *Crédit Mimmier* in Bordeaux, France. Also, the amount authorized by the principal is 2.5 million francs." Jodel passed a letter from which he had read across his desk to Conrad. The terrorist scanned it quickly.

"This is not convenient," Conrad said.

"With apologies, Herr Christhanson, the bank is acting under direction from the principal. Naturally, your expense reimbursement reflects this diversion," Jodel said. "Also," he added to assuage nervousness, "they assumed you would prefer to make your own travel plans."

Conrad grunted. *Ridiculous,* he thought. *Do they not understand the logistics involved in my projects?*

"I am sorry?" the banker said.

"Nothing," Conrad said. He was receiving funds from certain nations in the Middle East, and, in the end, he could hardly complain that there was never enough. In fact, they had been quite willing to pay well for the Western blood that he had caused to flow in their behalf.

In Baltimore, Getts stood under a weathered street sign that read *Nimbus.* He turned up his collar against the chill of a foggy night and walked along a sidewalk in this ill-kept part of the city. His eyes swept from one side of the street to the other, watching between old clapboard houses built only a few scant feet apart. Few lights were on. He arrived at number Twenty-One. A bright porch light illuminated the front door. As Getts rang the bell, he noticed that the windows of the house had been replaced with extra thick glass. Probably bulletproof. He also had the feeling he was being scrutinized through the one-way peephole in the door.

The door was eventually opened by a small, elderly woman, with gray hair piled atop her head. Her feet, Getts noted with amusement, were quite long, and her nose had probably doubled in size since her early years.

"Yes?" she said, looking up at Getts.

"Excuse me, madam. I'm looking for the Priestly family," he said. "Are they at home?"

"No," the old lady responded. "They moved. I don't know where they live now."

"I have a number for them," he said. "May I use your telephone?"

The woman said nothing. Then she looked questioningly to one side. After a moment, the door opened wider. A man in his early thirties with dark hair and mustache appeared from behind it. Getts glanced at the short-barreled shotgun the man carried easily in one hand as he nodded for Getts to enter.

"My name is Ebber," he said with a pronounced European accent. "This way, please, Commander."

Getts followed him through a short hallway and into a living room that fronted the street. Ebber then led Getts through a set of sliding wooden doors into a dining room. Several maps littered a table next to an overstuffed couch and several straight-back chairs. The room was otherwise shorn of accoutrements that would make long-term habitation comfortable.

Seated at one end of the large dinner table was Rabbi, a face Getts had never seen and knew only by description. "Ah, Commander Getts," Rabbi said, rising to his feet. "A pleasure, sir."

Getts shook the Mossad agent's hand. Accompanying Rabbi was a subordinate, a dark-haired muscular man in his late thirties, who sat rigidly, eyeing Getts. "This is Maas," Rabbi said, simply. Getts was at once impressed with the intelligence in Maas's eyes.

"Have we met before, Maas?" Getts asked.

"No. I would have remembered," Maas responded.

"Could it have been Italy? I skied there years ago," Getts pressed.

Maas smiled patiently. "Jews are not permitted near snow."

Appreciative laughter circled the table.

"And this," Rabbi said continuing his introductions, "is Tomaz, our guest of honor."

Getts turned to study the man, who was in his late twenties, light complexioned but with clear Semitic features. His dental work was extensive—Getts noticed as the man's lips pulled back in a slight smile—done in gold rather than the more expensive porcelain capping favored by Westerners.

He sat on the edge of the sofa, his hands moving continually as though his fingers were playing an endless concerto. Getts extended his hand. "Tomaz," he said.

Tomaz shook Getts's hand nervously. "Yes," he said.

"How do you wish to speak?" Getts asked in passable Arabic.

"I am fine in English," Tomaz responded.

A swinging door opened to Getts's left. Through it emerged the old woman who carried a large tray of hot Oriental tea and pastries. Wordlessly, she deposited the fare near Getts, then took her leave. As she passed through the door into the kitchen, Getts caught a glimpse of other men seated around a small table, eating.

Getts's eyes turned back to Tomaz. "Are you Libyan?" he asked.

"I was born in El Gatrun," the defector confirmed.

Getts noticed that Tomaz's hands were still working. "Did you attend school there?"

"Yes. And two years university. Madrid."

"Ah. Your soul has been softened in one of our decadent democracies," Getts jibed.

Tomaz smiled, his teeth glittering. "My mother was European. I lived with her there."

"Did you travel in Europe?" Getts asked as he sipped his tea.

"Yes. Sometimes. Vacations, you know."

"When did you return to Libya?"

"In 1982," the defector responded. "I was in the army that year."

"Combat?"

"No. Training only. I was chosen for security duty."

Getts noticed that Tomaz's hands ceased to move. "Where were you trained?"

"Kazan," Tomaz said. "A small village near Hammud Tinghert."

"In the Idehan?" Getts asked.

"Yes."

"East or west?"

"West."

"Would you point to it on a map?" Getts asked.

For a long moment, Tomaz said nothing, his eyes drifting slightly, focusing above Getts's head. "Yes," he said.

Getts leaned forward in his chair to retrieve a cookie from the table. As he did, he made sure his arm shielded his surreptitious glance over at Rabbi. The old spy's eyes flashed back.

"How long?" Getts wanted to know.

"Six months."

"And after your training?" Getts gently urged.

"I was assigned to the Colonel."

Getts as well as the others in the room understood that Tomaz was referring to Moammar Khadafy. "To do what job? Protect him?" Getts asked.

"Yes," Tomaz responded.

"Who made the staff assignments? Was it a function of the army?" Getts asked.

Tomaz shrugged. "It could be so. We wore no uniforms, but I think General Khurom made the decisions."

Getts knit his brow. Strange that with all his experience regarding Libya Getts had not heard the name before. "Khurom?"

"Head of security detail," Tomaz responded.

Getts made a mental note to return to Khurom at another time. "How long did you protect the Colonel?"

"One year."

"Did you go on any military operations?" Getts received a questioning look from the Arab.

"Ah. No, no. Only protection. That is all."

"Tell me about the man called Conrad. What is his real name?" Getts asked.

"His real name I don't know." Tomaz's hands were fidgeting again.

"What does he look like?" Getts asked.

"European, this tall . . ." Tomaz stood up and raised his hand in the air near his forehead. "Brown eyes."

Getts considered the color. Conrad would most likely use color contact lenses if he could. But desert sand, Getts knew from experience, made contact lenses painful.

"How did he speak?" Getts said.

"Like an Arab," Tomaz replied in a slightly sour tone.

"Like a European Arab? Or one who was born in the desert?" Getts urged.

"No question, he is European."

"Where? Italy? France? Germany? Farther north?" Getts suggested.

"I don't know," Tomaz responded, his hands halting their fidgeting. "I am not, what you say, a good ear."

"All right. Tell me more about him. Anything that comes to your mind." Getts could feel the intense interest of the Israelis. They were professional, trained to remain emotionless, to hide their feelings behind bland masks. But Getts sensed that these men, like him, were beginning to believe Tomaz was genuine.

"He is not like this . . ." Tomaz's hands indicated a stout man, "but he has power. Sometimes when he came to see the Colonel, he would join us in our exercise. Karate. He was good." Tomaz thought for a moment. "He reads books, but I don't think he likes them."

Tomaz paused as though waiting for more questions, but Getts merely sipped his cooling tea.

"He can change his face," Tomaz continued, finally breaking the silence. "He could sometimes get by one of us, and we did not know it was him."

"He have any women?" Getts asked.

Tomaz responded with a vigorous shake of the head. "No, but it was not men instead. He is not that way."

"Not that you know about," Getts insinuated.

"I would have known," Tomaz said, confidently.

"Did you like him?" Getts asked.

Tomaz eyes darted about the room at the others. His demeanor suggested embarrassment, as though an inner, personal, boundary had been penetrated. "At a time, yes. But . . . he is a monster. A sick one."

"Like Khadafy?"

"The Colonel is not sick. Khadafy works for Arabs. Conrad works for death. He reaches out for it. He is evil."

"So," Getts continued, "you were reassigned to Conrad?"

"Yes. But not operations. Only security."

"Security where? Did you travel with him?" Getts asked.

"We were with him only in our country. Outside, he goes alone," the defector said.

"Were you with him at Kismere Road? At the American tour bus," Getts prodded.

Tomaz did not answer at once. He glanced sideways, first

at Rabbi, then Maas. "No," he said. "I would have nothing to do with killing children. Or women. No, I was not there."

Getts nodded his head as though sympathizing, believing.

"Why did he do it?" Rabbi's voice thundered abruptly.

Getts felt a stab of annoyance. He was making progress with Tomaz, leading him in a specific direction.

"It is obvious, is it not?" the Arab said. "A freedom fighter creates terror. It was Conrad's plan."

"Freedom?" Rabbi's voice began to rise.

Getts caught his eye, silencing Rabbi's indignation with a pointed look.

"How did you travel from Libya?" Getts asked.

"Four of us were to escort Ambassador Fiez to Lebanon. In Beirut I know a man with a boat. We sail to Haifa. Very easy. Nobody was looking for us."

"What would happen if you went back?" Getts asked Tomaz.

"They would kill me," the witness said, simply.

"Where is Conrad now?"

Tomaz shrugged. "Syria, maybe. It is where he lives, I think."

"Where, in Syria?" Getts pressed.

The Arab shrugged again. "One does not know. He has protection of the state, you see, because he does their work."

"Weapons? Supplies? Personnel?" Getts asked.

"Yes. All support."

Rabbi, Getts saw, leaned slowly back into his chair. Maas continued to scrutinize Tomaz.

Getts thought Tomaz knew Conrad's whereabouts but would not tell. Not yet, anyway. "Thank you, Tomaz," Getts said. "We would like to talk more tomorrow, if you will," Getts said, rising to signal the end of the interview.

Tomaz nodded his head eagerly.

"I have to be honest with you, Tomaz. You have told us very little that we did not know. We are people of our word. You will receive a reward but . . ." Getts looked down at his own hands, now turned palm upward.

"I have more to tell," the Arab blurted.

"And that is?" Getts asked.

Tomaz's eyes flashed, excitedly looking around the room, from one man to another. "Among you is a traitor."

Rabbi leaned forward as did Maas and Ebber. "Who?" Rabbi croaked.

"I do not know," the former bodyguard said. "Only that he is our best agent. He works against the Jews."

"You know the man personally?" Getts asked.

Tomaz shook his head. Rabbi's eyes shone. "Is he a Jew? An American?"

Tomaz shrugged. "He is not a Jew. His code name is *Fanus*."

Ebber constrained himself to speak civilly. "You are making this up. It is clear that all you want is a larger reward."

"No," Tomaz protested. "I know I am speaking truth."

"How do you know of him?" Rabbi asked, fascinated.

"He uses radio, and satellites of course, and other ways, but he speaks only to one man."

All in the room were aware that satellite transmissions were not so easily intercepted given the sheer quantity of radio traffic on Earth. And decoding took time.

"And how did you know," Getts asked, "when Fanus transmitted? And how did you know what business the message discussed? It might have been anything."

"The men on the detail take turns carrying a UHF burst receiver. Ours printed a tape, but it also had a memory in case the tape was destroyed. We would at once give the tape to Conrad or General Khurom."

"And of course you had no key to read the tape," Rabbi said, skeptically.

"Yes, sir," Tomaz said almost obsequiously.

"And then," Maas said to Tomaz, "Conrad would move."

"Not always," Tomaz said.

"No," Maas corrected himself. "If he was preparing to move, he sometimes changed his plans."

"Yes, sir. It seemed to be so."

"Where did the messages arrive from? Always the same place?" Getts pressed.

Tomaz shook his head. "Sometimes the U.S.A., sometimes Europe, sometimes . . ."

"Anywhere," Rabbi interrupted.

"Yes," Tomaz agreed. "Anywhere."

"And that's all you know about a mole, here? Nothing else? Not his age? What he looks like?" Getts urged.

"No. That is all I know, but it is much, I think."

Getts considered a moment. "Thank you, Tomaz. I'd like to talk more tomorrow. Okay with you?"

"Okay," Tomaz said, rising.

When the Arab had been led out of the room, Getts spoke with Rabbi, Maas, and Ebber. "How long has he been here?"

"Ten days," Ebber replied.

"Well? What do you think?" He directed the question to everyone.

Ebber spoke first. "He is lying," he said with finality.

"Why?" Getts wanted to know.

"His hands. You saw them. We all did. He is a poor liar," Ebber said, dismissively.

Maas was equally certain. "There can't be a mole. No men have been so sanitized as we. Not a minute of a day of our lives has been missed in background checks. We have all made sacrifices . . ." His anger halted his speech. "And many of my friends have given their lives hunting terrorists. Who here would betray them?"

"Maybe he is not lying," Rabbi offered, "and who says the traitor has to be inside this room? He might only be connected with our mission. Fanus is a code name we can check on. We plan an operation. Wait for Fanus to transmit. Even if we can't break his code, we will know the circle it came from."

"I'm not so sure he is even real," Maas said. "We have checked out much of his story. We know people who went to school with him in Madrid. The boat man from Lebanon is still with us in Israel. He has no black background. We spoke with two of his childhood sweethearts. It was all too easy."

"Ahhh," Rabbi scoffed. "Of course he went to school in Madrid. Do you think they would fabricate his entire background? No, they would stay close to truth. And the fisherman with the boat; what does it show us? Nothing. I believe Tomaz is who he says he is."

"Then who is he?" Getts asked.

Ebber shrugged. "Just someone who wants to fuck

blonde girls in the West. We are going to give him reloca-
tion money. Sounds good. Maybe I'll do it myself." Getts
caught a twinkle in the Mossad agent's eye that amused
him.

"What about the school bus?" Getts threw out. "Is he
lying about that?"

"That's the point, isn't it?" Rabbi argued. "How can
you tell?"

"I think he knows more about the school bus than he
has said," Maas put in.

"Why would he hold back?" Getts asked.

Maas considered. "Because he is afraid of us. He might
think we'd kill him in anger."

"He is a hard man," Ebber observed, softly. "I don't
think he is afraid to die."

Getts hoped that was not the case. He also sensed that
his Israeli colleagues were holding something back. "Let's
talk about motive, again," he said to them all. "Tomaz is
trying to do what? For who?"

Rabbi glanced quickly at Maas, then turned his attention
back to Getts. "To move your Blacklight. Disrupt us. Con-
fuse you. Maybe to kill you."

"Why?" he asked.

"Because you are in their way," Rabbi suggested. "Do
you have something planned?"

"They are still training," Ebber said.

Not a bad guess, Getts thought, but still it was a guess.
It was a question that Rabbi could not expect Getts would
answer. So he ignored it. "Or they may have something
planned," he said.

"Another Flight Two-Eight-Zero," Maas suggested almost casually.

Getts did not answer.

"Remember, he promised more," Maas added.

"Yes," Rabbi nodded emphatically. "I say we take
Tomaz at his word."

"He lies." Ebber.

"We all lie," Getts said. "The trick is to know which is
the lie that can kill you. I want him to be debriefed by our
people at Fort Meade. Communications are their business."
He thought further. "Rabbi, I can tell you that the United
States is going to operate in the Mediterranean and Middle

East. The French, British, and Germans will concentrate in Europe. If I have to go into, say, Iran or Iraq, can you provide air extraction?"

"No, no," Rabbi shook his head emphatically. "We will not supply air units. Intelligence, yes, but not Israeli soldiers for U.S. operations."

"We may need your expert extraction units. They are the best in the desert. We all know that," Getts exaggerated only slightly. But if his SpecWar superiors were being perfectly honest, they would agree that Israeli helicopters are without equal in their own backyard.

Rabbi considered for a moment. "We can do nothing from here. I can only ask Tel Aviv. I need authority from the prime minister himself."

"How long will that take?" Getts asked.

"A little time, but not long," the aging agent said.

Getts considered for several moments, then said, "Before I go, I want you each to play a game with me." Getts glanced around the room for assent.

"Wonderful. I like games," Rabbi said.

"Ebber? Maas?" The two other Israelis nodded in agreement.

"The last time you and your men had dinner together in an American restaurant," Getts said to Rabbi, "where was it?"

Rabbi did not need to think hard. "Last night," he said. "A French place called Marceau's. Does that count?"

"Sure," Getts said. "Who was at your table?"

"Ebber, Benjamine, Ellul, Maas, and myself," the senior spy recalled.

"Five of you. Now, who got the check?" Getts asked.

Ebber said, "Rabbi. He paid the check."

"All right, here's the game," Getts said. "I have only one guess. The point of the game is to guess not who paid for the meal, but by whose plate the waiter placed the check when he delivered it to your table."

"A good game," Ebber said enthusiastically.

"Yes," Rabbi agreed. "Go ahead."

"Maas," Getts stated immediately.

The Israelis looked at each other in amazement, grins spreading across their faces.

"That is very good. How did you do it?" Rabbi said approvingly.

"A lucky guess," Ebber said.

"It seldom fails. A waiter hovers about a table during a meal." Getts said. "The people at the table are careful not to be overheard so the waiter hears nothing of value. But subconsciously messages are sent to him. He senses the most powerful man in the group, no matter what is said. Or what is not said. The others silently defer to him. So when the waiter presents his bill, he places it before the most powerful man present." Getts slowly leaned back in his chair to watch the reaction of Maas. Getts was certain that Maas was far more powerful than the mere field agent he seemed to be.

Maas and Rabbi exchanged looks. Then Maas spoke, a slight, reluctant, smile flitting across his face. "You are, Commander Getts, as they say in this country, a piece of work. Your game is amusing. I'm going to use it myself."

"But it's not just a game," Getts said to Maas, in a level tone. "You're not Rabbi's assistant. You're nobody's yes man, are you?"

Maas considered for a moment, then nodded his head slowly. "Very well, I am the Director of Action Group I of the Mossad."

"General Maas, I assume," Getts said.

Maas nodded his head toward Getts. "Thank you. I want your word that you'll provide helicopter extraction for my Blacklight force wherever we have to go to get Conrad."

"It's possible I can arrange that," Maas said.

"Alive," Getts added.

"Ah, that's much harder," Maas said, his brow knit.

Everyone at the table laughed at the general's black humor.

Getts rose to leave. "By the way, Kazan, that location Tomaz talked about in the Idehan. It's not a security training school—it's a terrorist camp."

Maas nodded his head. "Yes. We know that. Good night, Commander."

The restaurant was called "Old Havana," but the clientele were in fact Castroites, not expatriate Cubans who wanted to regain their land from Communist rule. Their particular cafe was three miles away. Old Havana was a block from Venice Boulevard on the beach by the same name. Its bill of fare offered lime-cooked pork and chicken, fried bananas, rice, and black beans. On the walls were photographs and paintings of pre-Castro Cuba—automobiles, cafes, crowded streets, happy faces. The sun had hardly set, and Conrad was surprised that restaurants in America were always crowded so early in the evening. He had to wait fifteen minutes before being seated at a small table. He barely glanced at the menu, ordering Malta Tuey when a waiter arrived at his table. He asked for chicken, number four on the menu.

"Is Carlos Ochoa around?" he casually asked the waiter. Conrad added a Castilian accent to his words

"He don' work here no more," the waiter said.

"Oh, well," he said, "too bad if I miss him."

"He comes in time to time, you know. You want to leave a message?" the waiter asked, one eyebrow raised.

"Sure." Conrad took the check out of the waiter's hand knowing that it would not be lost or misplaced, and wrote on the back. "I am staying here," he said, returning the check to the waiter along with a ten dollar bill.

He took a few bites from the chicken, tasted the black beans, then left.

He had written his extension number on the waiter's check so that a call, no matter what hour, would go directly through to his room. He waited more than three hours before the telephone rang. "Yes?" he answered.

"Carlos Ochoa," said a distinctly Latino voice on the other end.

"Ah. My name is Udo Christhanson," Conrad said. "I'd like to meet you to discuss business."

"What kind business, meng? I don't know no Christhanson," Carlos said cautiously and with a cockiness that Conrad thought unprofessional.

"No, we have never met, but we have a mutual friend. His name is Fanus," he said.

At the other end of the line, there was a long moment of silence. Then Carlos finally replied, "I meet you at the Versailles. Know where that is?"

Conrad did indeed. It was located near a famous movie studio in western Los Angeles, and it was a strong anti-

Castro institution. Very clever of Carlos. "I'm sorry," Conrad lied. "I don't have access to a car. Will you come by my hotel? I am at the Belage, off Sunset Boulevard."

"Fuck, meng . . ."

"I'll meet you in the hotel bar in one hour. What are you wearing?" Conrad wanted to know.

"I wear a black shirt, meng, white tie I leave open."

"Good," Conrad approved. "And Carlos, I don't like company. Come alone."

"Hey, meng, I don't need nobody to wipe my ass for me."

"Give me a number to call if I need you," Conrad said.

"You don't need no number . . ."

"Please don't waste my time. You carry a pager. What is the number?" Conrad said.

After a pause, Carlos reluctantly provided Conrad with a telephone number. Conrad hung up.

He took a taxi to the Belage immediately, some forty-five minutes before the scheduled meeting. He entered the bar and sat in a dark corner of the room at a table. He ordered a concoction of blended juices. This was not an unusual drink order in Los Angeles, and it was delicious, Conrad thought.

Business was moderate at the Belage, as usual, and Conrad watched people enter and leave. Twenty minutes before the meeting was to take place, a Latino man entered the room, took a seat at the far end of the bar and ordered bottled beer. The man looked around the room with studied casualness, noticing Conrad but not paying him any particular attention. He then sipped his beer disinterestedly.

At the appointed time, Carlos entered the room, took a seat at the bar and ordered beer. He was, true to his description, wearing a black shirt and ivory tie left untied. Conrad pretended to read a book while he watched Carlos.

The Cuban began to check his watch with increasing frequency, glancing more often around the room. Twice, he looked directly at Conrad. Carlos drank three beers until, thirty minutes after the appointed time, he paid for his drinks and strode out of the bar.

Conrad remained seated. After a couple of minutes, the Latino man who had been sitting at the far end of the bar also rose, and walked out of the lounge and into the lobby.

Conrad followed. From within the lobby, he could see Carlos and the second Latino speaking animatedly together in the valet parking driveway. Conrad remained inside the lobby of the hotel until they both had gone.

Conrad placed his second telephone call to Carlos at three o'clock A.M.

"I said I did not want to see you with company," he said to Carlos.

"Hey, meng, I don' know the hell you mean. I waited for you—where the fuck were you?"

"You brought somebody along. This is your last chance. Do you want to do business or not?" Conrad demanded.

"Sure, sure," Carlos's tone had softened considerably. "Where you gonna be tomorrow, meng?"

Conrad ignored the Cuban's suggestion. "Drive your car to the end of Washington Boulevard by the beach. Leave it on the street, and walk into the public parking lot. Thirty minutes."

"Now? Shit, meng . . ."

The protest was weak, and Carlos relented to the rendezvous. It was, for Conrad, an elementary guess that Carlos would live within an easy drive of Marina del Rey from west Los Angeles' Latino community. "This time make sure you're alone." He hung up the telephone.

He was waiting in his own parked car on Washington Boulevard's cul-de-sac when Carlos Ochoa drove slowly toward the beach and parked on the opposite side of the street. Carlos got out of his car, pausing as though considering whether to lock it and, evidently deciding against it, turned toward the public lot as Conrad had requested.

"Over here," Conrad said in a voice just loud enough to carry over the sound of surf.

Carlos turned and saw Conrad, then walked with unhurried steps toward him. The Cuban made a circuitous approach, arriving slightly behind Conrad who sat behind the wheel. Conrad was amused at Carlos's caution, but he let the Cuban have his fun.

"Christhanson?" Carlos asked as he neared the car.

"Get in," Conrad said.

The Latino made one more sweep around the street before slowly circling the rental car to the passenger side.

"Hope you gotta big fuckin' deal to do, meng," Carlos said as he got into the car and shut the door.

"I need a Redeye. Or a Stinger. Doesn't matter which."

"Huh? You don' wan' much, meng. A Steenger," he groaned. "Very hard to get. Very, very hard, meng. Redeye, too."

"How much?" Conrad asked.

"Hey, pro'lem is, how to get it, eh? Lot of risk. Anything else you need, meng? M-16s? Make you a hell of a deal. Grenades? Ammunition?" Carlos asked, smiling.

He was showing off, Conrad knew. "How much for a Redeye?" he persisted.

" 'Pends how hard to get it, you know," the Cuban responded.

"You already have a Redeye, Carlos. I won't haggle about the price. Whatever you say it is, I'll pay it," Conrad said calmly.

"Hmmmm," Carlos said, beginning to smile broadly. "Good chance I can find one tomorrow."

"Tonight," Conrad insisted easily. "Right now."

"Hey, meng, how d'you know I got a Redeye? Huh?" Carlos casually produced a gun and pointed it at Conrad. "You keep both you' hands on the wheel, Señor Christhanson." He carefully leaned near Conrad and patted locations on his body that might conceal a gun. Satisfied in finding none, Carlos eased his own pistol back into his belt, allowing Conrad to know it was still quickly accessible.

"Because I'm in the business of knowing these things." Conrad started the engine of the rental car. "Tell me where to drive." Conrad's network, which included top intelligence officials of an Arab government, tracked weapons shipments all over the world.

He knew that ten Redeye and five Stinger ground-to-air, shoulder-launched missiles had been stolen from a marine armory in the California desert six weeks prior. Other military hardware missing in the armory "break-in"—which was not a break-in at all but an inside job made to look like a burglary—included a dozen cases of hand grenades, several sets of valuable night vision glasses, and two Armbrust 300 antitank rockets on loan from Germany's Messerschmitt Bolkow-Blohm GmbH for field testing. If one were contemplating opening a safe or an armored car, the Armbrust would be the perfect weapon.

"You got money, meng?" Carlos asked, now in a better humor.

Conrad tapped his jacket pocket in response. "Which way?"

Carlos directed Conrad back up Washington Boulevard. They turned onto a freeway ramp and drove north toward what Angelinos call the Valley. At the bottom of a long hill, they exited the 405 freeway, then turned south on Ventura. Carlos insisted on using a number of turns and cutbacks, obviously designed to elude a tail should one be there. Once he had Conrad park on top of an overpass and wait several minutes before making a U-turn and retracing their original route. Conrad protested none of the evasive strategies. At last, Carlos allowed them to park in the driveway of a house not more than two hundred meters from a Highway 101 entrance ramp. The neighborhood was lower middle class, the houses on the block kept in decent condition, including number 1344.

A four-foot-high chain-link fence, designed to keep out pets, ran across the driveway and around the back yard. Carlos used two keys from a ring on the end of a chain to unlock the front door. He stepped inside, followed closely behind by Conrad.

The house had been built during the 1950s; it had hardwood floors, and lath and plaster walls. There were a few pieces of cheap, fifties-style furniture in the living room, and a card table was placed in what would have been called the dining room if anybody lived in the house, which Conrad doubted was the case. He followed Carlos past of den that was littered with old papers, magazines, and books of all descriptions. A new telephone sat on a small table. Attached to it, Conrad could see, was an answering machine. Down a short hallway, were three more doors.

They passed through this part of the house into a kitchen that seemed to have been unused for some time. Off the kitchen was another door, which Carlos opened with another key from the ring he carried in his pocket. Steps led down into a basement. Snapping on a light, Carlos looked at Conrad long enough to let a smile broaden his face. This was, Conrad thought, the superior smile that little boys beam at each other when showing off their secret fort. Carlos offered to let Conrad go first, but Conrad politely declined the honor and waited for Carlos to descend.

The basement was pleasantly cool compared with the shimmering heat of the entire valley above. A certain similarity of careless housekeeping was evident down here as well. Crates, some opened, some still sealed, were stacked precariously one upon another. Boxes were shoved into whatever space would hold them. Conrad could see that there was an assortment of armaments sufficient to fit out a full rifle company. Such a group would also have the capacity of killing tanks, judging from the abbreviated identifications stenciled upon the sides of wooden crates and laminated plastic boxes.

Carlos stood, hands on hips, looking proudly about, expecting Conrad to be suitably impressed. Though he did not feel like doing so, Conrad obligingly smiled his approval. "Excellent," he said. "I knew I was coming to the right man."

Carlos's chest expanded noticeably as he walked about, showcasing a hand grenade or an assault rifle, working a mechanism on a handgun. "The best, meng," he said. "I got a organization, eh? People"—he pronounced them pipple—"work for me, the best. Goo' ma'gement," he laughed. "Hey, you wanna buy it all?" He laughed expansively. "Make an offer."

Conrad moved about the room, immediately seeing the equipment he was interested in. A crate was stenciled "XM-41EZ antiaircraft missile," another mark revealed its manufacturer, "General Dynamics Corporation, Pomona Division, U.S.A."

Conrad turned toward a still beaming Carlos, pointing to the already opened crate. "I'll take one of these."

Carlos made an inviting gesture toward the container, and Conrad helped himself. There were three missiles to each crate. Carlos carefully inspected each of them to detect if there had been any tampering of the sealed shoulder-held system. He was quite familiar with its operation and knew that its infrared sensing and booster motor firing mechanism must be entirely closed and complete to guarantee the missile would fire and hit its target.

"I will take this," Conrad said, holding the Redeye of his choice. "How much?"

The Cuban pursed his lips a split second long enough for Conrad to know that the "going" price was about to escalate. "Ten thousan' dollars," Carlos said, his eyes half closing in pretended firmness. "Tha's special price to a frien' of a frien'."

Conrad pretended to be concerned. "A lot of money," he said, "but I know that there is danger in acquiring these things." He reached inside his shirt and withdrew an envelope from which he counted, then extracted, the required tariff for the weapon. He handed over the money, smiled, and said, "My pleasure."

Conrad could see, and hear, the Cuban licking his chops as they retraced their steps into the house above. "Let me remind you, Señor Carlos Ochoa, that my friends know who I met tonight."

"What? Oh, sure, sure. We are professionals, you an' me," he reassured his customer.

"Good. Then in celebration of this deal and many more deals to come, I offer you a genuine Cuban cigar." Conrad opened a cigar case and extracted two cigars, one for himself, one for Carlos. He smiled, and made a slight bow with his head.

"Ah," the Cuban said, "I save it for later." He stuck the cigar into his pocket and turned toward the door.

Conrad touched him lightly on the arm, gently withdrew the cigar from the Cuban's shirt and placed it into his mouth, put his own cigar into his own mouth. "In my country, it is a custom after business to smoke either a pipe or a cigar. A cigar seems fitting in these conditions," Conrad smiled widely.

Carlos shrugged as he bit the tip off the cigar. Conrad was the first to produce a compressed gas lighter. He held it near Carlos's face. Carlos leaned forward to take advantage of the gesture. As he did so, Conrad actuated the lighter's mechanism, spewing a mist of prussic acid in Carlos's face. The Cuban's head immediately snapped backward, his hands grasping futilely at his throat. Within seconds, he had fallen to his knees, then fully onto his face.

Conrad touched Carlos's carotid artery to make sure he was dead. He then reached inside Carlos's trouser pocket

and withdrew his recently spent cash. He also relieved the
corpse of its pistol, a 9mm PPK automatic. Sensible, Conrad thought. Capable of doing close range work but small
enough to conceal easily. There was no need to dispose of
the body, Conrad knew. His colleagues would come here
to look for him. Naturally, the police would not be notified.

Conrad was glad that a freeway entrance ramp was near
the house. He would not like to drive around Los Angeles
traffic for very long with a Redeye missile in his trunk.

All of the Blacklights were parachute qualified before they
arrived at Camp McReynolds. Most had advanced infantry,
recon, weapons, and ranger qualifications. Toni was the exception, lacking recon and ranger work, as she had arrived
not long after her academy graduation. It was 2200 hours
on a moonless night as Getts surveyed his platoon. They
were all wearing jump suits, including Getts. They carried
neither weapons nor field packs. They had made thirty
jumps in less than six weeks, and Getts thought each
trooper had done very well.

Tonight would be different. On one arm, they had
strapped a barometric pressure indicator, the face of which
was similar in size to a large wrist watch. On the other arm,
they wore timing devices. Tonight would be a high altitude
jump, low opening, an insertion method that was commonly
used by elite airborne units. They would jump from 20,000
feet, free fall through the black of night until they were a
bare 1,000 above the ground at which time they would pull
their ripcords. There would be no use of automatic pressure
opening devices. No one wore an emergency chute, because
there would be no time for a second parachute to open if
the first failed. Traveling at about 130 mph, a falling body
had less than eight seconds before it hit the ground, unless
the chute fully deployed at 1,000 feet altitude.

"Okay, troopers, listen up," Getts said. "Remember not
to look for the ground as a reference. You won't be able
to see it. Don't ever panic. If you believe you have a horizon, get your eyes off it and get 'em back on your altimeter.
You've got a choice to open on that or on the clock. Everybody do the arithmetic on the clock? Your body attitude
is going to affect your velocity so you have to make your
own calculations. It better be close to 1.8 minutes to fall

20,000 feet. Anybody want to use an automatic opening rig? No? Okay?"

"I don't see any stars, Bobby," Valentino said, nervously.

"The fuck you need a star for, man?" Redskin said. "That's why you got the altimeter."

He was right, of course. "That's one of the reasons you don't look for the ground. You might be looking at a cloud instead. So pull on the clock or the altimeter. If you panic or lose your reference, pull immediately. Guide on the light on the back of the man in front of you. Questions?"

Each man would snap a plastic chemical capsule on the back of the man in front of him. It would glow green in the dark. Each jumper would keep himself aligned with the others in the dark, preventing separations as they descended through the night.

The C-130 lifted off the ground and began a shallow left turn at Vy—most efficient angle of climb—at twelve hundred feet per minute. The aircraft would level off at 21,000 feet and fly about five minutes to a practice jump area near the airfield. Peach, acting as A team leader would then lead his team out one side of the rear door while Getts, the B team leader, would jump from the opposite side of the yawning open ramp.

Each member of the team, no matter how many times he or she had done a HALO jump, was nervous. Timing had to be correct, or the result would be instant, shattering death. Each jumper checked his own equipment, then helped another check theirs. The checking, calculating, and rechecking, went on until it was time to go out the door.

As the heavy aircraft passed through eleven thousand feet Getts gave the order for oxygen masks. The troopers went dutifully to oxygen, now feeling the rapid change in temperature, cooling at the rate of 4.5°F per thousand feet.

Sneezy occupied the seat next to Busboy. "You scared?" he said.

"Hell, no," Busboy lied.

"I am," Sneezy said. Busboy did not respond but swallowed hard.

"How old are you?"

"The hell difference does that make?" Busboy said. Then, "Twenty."

"Me, too. I mean I'll be twenty in March." A beat. "You like this kind of work?"

"Hell, yeah. Most times. You?" Busboy said.

"Not now, man. Truth is, I never liked HALO jumps. Especially at night."

HALO jumps were seldom done at any other time.

"Hey, Redskin," Lurch said, "bet you pull before me."

"How about three months pay, big mouth," the Native American said.

"Braves are brave, huh?" Lurch said, grinning.

"You got that right, Lurch. You pull after I pull, and you might die, man, 'cause I'm going to the deck." Redskin punctuated his bravado with an inadvertent swallow that escaped no one. But everyone else was too concerned with their own safety to laugh.

"You got a bet, Wahoo," Lurch laughed. Lurch had made HALO jumps before in Special Forces, and regarded himself as a crack paratrooper.

"Shit," Sneezy whispered to himself as he looked out of a window, then quickly back into the plane.

"What's the matter?" Toni said.

"Nothin'." Sneezy said, his eyes now fixed on his hands.

"Then what's wrong with you?" Toni persisted.

"It's dark out there, that's what. Why don't we jump when the moon's out? Wouldn't hurt a fucking thing," he said.

Toni had wondered precisely the same thing.

"Stand up!" Peach yelled when the red light signal was turned on from the cockpit to indicate they were approaching the LZ. Thirteen people stood up and took their places on each side of the Hercules aircraft. Suddenly, the sound of high pressure hydraulics, then the wind screaming around the jump door caused more than one team member to jerk alert. "Stand by!" Peach shouted while, at the same time, giving hand signals to the jumpers. As he watched for the green jump light, he placed his oxygen mask securely over his face. Their bail-out bottles contained a five-minute air supply for this operation, which would enter their lungs under pressure. They would not have to breathe, only receive the forced air. From this point on, jump signals would be made by hand only. At Getts's command, each trooper broke the seal on the chemical light of the man in front of him.

Green light.

Peach made another explicit hand signal then turned, ran several steps to the outer limit of the cargo door, and allowed himself to fall into the blackness. His team followed. On the opposite side of the ramp, Getts stepped into the ether.

Getts felt his skin flutter as his body began to approach terminal falling velocity. He could see the glowing light on Peach's back but because of his angle, could not see the other Blacklight behind him. Nor, at this minute, were they his responsibility. Each man and woman had to be watching the trooper in front, configuring his body to avoid tumbling, and monitoring instruments as precious seconds ticked away.

The horizon that could be seen at the moment of bailout was gone. Clouds obscured the faint green homing lights of the troopers. Then the clouds were suddenly gone again, and the ground took on various shades of darkness.

Toni felt a mixture of extreme exhilaration and fear as she straightened her spine in an effort to keep pace with the jumper directly below her. The air temperature, freezing at 20,000 feet, now warmed at the rate of 2.4° Celsius per thousand feet of fall. Because of their protective thermal clothing, by the time they reached the ground, they would feel excessively warm.

The fear each carried down with them was like that of an experienced fighter during a match, or a firefighter when dealing with an explosion of flame. Fascination, caution, a feeling of triumph not yet realized but certain to come.

Toni's altimeter indicated 1,600 feet, unwinding fast. 1,300, 1,100 . . . She pulled her ripcord and saw, in relief, that her chute had deployed when her altimeter was reading only 500 feet.

Then she was jarred sharply upward, straps cutting into her crotch and shoulders. She had hardly a fleeting moment to appreciate that she would not hit the ground at more than one hundred miles per hour when indeed her feet touched the ground. "Lighter," she would say later, "than a butterfly with sore feet."

Lurch had no fear. Eyes riveted to the face of his altime-

ter, he arched his body, deflected his arms and legs to slow
his descent, planing himself well below the speed of terminal velocity. For good measure he waited a full second beyond minimum chute deployment altitude (MCA) before
pulling his D-ring. His grip on the ring should have been
established several seconds earlier. He fumbled a split second for a firmer hold before tearing the holding pins. By
then it was too late. He struck the soft earth at more than
one hundred miles per hour, his parachute not fully open,
streaming down atop his mangled body.

There was no official burial, no ceremony. His death was
referred to as "Gone to the gold." Lurch's real name—
Enos Burch, age 23, from Yakima, Washington—and army
serial number were reverentially placed on gold leaf parch-
ment paper that was kept in a vault, unavailable to the eyes
of anyone without expressed permission from the President
of the United States or the commander of Blacklight.

Chapter Seven

Getts was in his quarters packing a bag while Peach
sprawled carelessly on his CO's comfortable bed. At his
elbow was a bottle of vodka that he used to reinforce his
already potent drink. He still wore a fatigue uniform from
the day's training while Getts, showered and shaved, had
donned a pair of jeans, a dress shirt without tie, and a plaid
wool blazer. "So, how's Buzzy?" Peach asked referring to
Getts's mother.

"She's okay," Getts said, tossing extra socks into his bag.

"I thought you were home three months ago," Peach
said, his curiosity piqued by Getts's sudden urge to travel.

"I was. Okay with you if I go again?" Getts said.

"Goodness gracious, aren't we sensitive? Have you been
taking your medication like you should?" Peach said.

Getts turned and looked hard into Peach's eyes, temper

suddenly flaring. His sudden flash of anger disappeared as quickly as it had begun. Hell, they were about to hang their collective asses out to dry. Peach had a perfect right to know what kind of shape his CO was in before it got too late to matter. "Yeah, I'm okay, Peachy. I'm not suicidal."

"Never thought you were. I just want to know how you feel. Want to know how I feel?" he said.

"Sure. How do you feel?" Getts said.

"Horny. I got to get laid."

"Sorry," Getts laughed, "like to help you out."

"I don't think you really mean that, Bobby. You keep telling me that you love me but you never kiss me," Peach said.

"Yes, but we do lots of things together," Getts said.

"Oh, sure, we jump out of airplanes, and we shoot off our guns, but sometimes I think you don't even know I'm there."

"There's someone else," Getts said.

"There. You see? I knew it. Who?" Peach said.

"Anybody."

"Oh, how can you talk to me that way? Don't you know I can't stand the thought of you seeing somebody else?" Peach said.

"Now that I think about it, I think Carla loves you," Getts said to Peach.

"Well, certainly. All women do."

"So?" Getts said.

"So? What? I'm not going to mess around with the employees," the gunner's mate said.

"Well, she's a short timer, remember. If she goes with us on this operation, it'll be her last," Getts said, hoisting his bag from a chair to the floor and zipping it up.

"Women love me because I use 'em. Women *want* to be used. It's in their genes, or something," Peach said.

Getts placed his hand affectionately on his friend's shoulder. "Actually, Peach, you're not nearly as good looking as you think you are, and if you ever had a mother she would have told you that."

Chapter Eight

It took only a few telephone calls to a travel agency for Conrad to obtain the flight schedule information he was looking for. Among important criteria was that it be an airline other than United so that the public would not think only one airline was being picked on or that others were safe; that take-off time for the flight would be as close to sunset as possible, preferably a few minutes after; that the aircraft be on an international route and that it have a destination in Europe. There were several flights that fit the bill. He chose American Airlines Flight 1421. The flight was scheduled to leave LAX and fly to Charles De Gaulle Airport in Paris, France. According to a newspaper official, sunset would occur at 7:36 P.M. the next evening. Flight 1421's scheduled departure was 7:45 P.M. Conrad's experience told him that the flight would likely be ten to twenty minutes late on its roll down runway 24-R. Still, he would be there early.

On his way back from a morning drive past LAX, Conrad stopped at a large department store and visited the camera/electronics section. He picked out an expensive and relatively powerful telescope and tripod. Radios were sold in the same department, and he chose a top of the line Halicrafter that received short wave transmissions. He also stopped in the hardware section and picked out several tools including a hammer, screwdriver set, and crescent wrenches. He paid for everything in cash. He placed his purchases next to the Redeye missile launcher in the trunk of his rented car and covered them with a blanket.

After referring once again to his Los Angeles County map book, he drove north along Pacific Coast Highway. As he passed through Malibu, he began to see a part of the south coast that he had never before seen. He thought it was quite pleasant. Traffic began to thin out as he drove beyond Pepperdine University. After five more miles, he arrived at a canyon road that traversed the Malibu mountains heading east. He drove slowly, seldom seeing other traffic, until he found an unpaved utility road. Checking his area map, he saw that the road was not marked. He left the surfaced road and turned onto the rural utility path. He followed it for less than a mile before it became little more than a trail. It finally dead ended in a cul-de-sac surrounded by dry brush and wild flowers. On the ground, the dross from years of broken liquor bottles and bits of litter strewn about by teenage partiers or trysting lovers.

He turned the car so that it pointed downhill, shut off its engine, and set the brake. He then opened the trunk of his car and took out everything but the spare tire. A reasonable person would have stood slack-jawed at the sight of what the terrorist calmly did next. He took a hammer in one hand, balanced the telescope in the other, then began to smash out the lenses of the telescope, including the mirrors inside its housing. The glass was necessarily thick, and Conrad was surprised at how hard he had to deliver each blow. He found the car's lug wrench, ideal for poking into the cavity of the now-blinded instrument.

Once the tube had been sufficiently cleaned of glass fragments, Conrad inserted the Redeye missile launcher packet into the larger casing, once useful for gazing into the heavens. There were several inches of room on all sides. An exact fit was not essential. He used a ten penny nail to punch four holes along the bottom of the telescope tube, then used pieces of styrofoam from the telescope packing box to wedge between the Redeye and the telescope tube until the missile launcher was held as firmly as possible. Using four self-tapping metal screws, Conrad carefully twisted each into the holes he had made along its barrel until their tips pressed against the launcher inside. He tested the launcher's position within the telescope barrel and found it to be entirely secure.

In the interest of the thoroughness Conrad prided himself on, he attached the tripod to a fixture on the telescope. It easily supported the added weight of the launcher.

Conrad carefully placed the modified Redeye back into the trunk of the car and once again covered it with a blanket. He tossed each tool far enough into the brush so that it would not soon be found. Then he drove back to Los Angeles via Sunset Boulevard. He felt good for the first time in several days, excited with what the next thirty-six hours would bring upon the United States of America and its allies.

Major General Cornelius R. Lathrop was in the blackest of moods today. He felt the same combination of frustration toward the Chief of Staff as he had at Schwarzkopf when that button-popping pachyderm ordered him to remain in Washington when the rest of the army deployed to where the action was. He surveyed his own staff. They occupied plush leather chairs in his conference room staring straight into a void, or rereading papers, or writing memos while they waited for a man who would not come.

General Lathrop was 52, too old by several years to head up a special warfare command. He knew that if he did not make another star he would be retired. He was the third most decorated active duty U.S. soldier and did not deserve retirement when he clearly had so much to offer his country. But no commander could expect advancement when he was left out of the "need to know" loop. A soldier always had to identify the enemy that stood behind him as well as those who faced him. Lathrop had the distinct feeling that a saber was being aimed straight at his back.

"Nash!" General Lathrop barked at his aide-de-camp, Major Jessie Nash. Other field grade officers around the table flinched at the general's booming voice.

"Sir?" the major said.

"What time did you tell that son of a bitch to be here?" the general demanded.

"Fourteen hundred hours, sir," the major said. Then added, "Sharp."

"Then get Wallis on the blower. Now."

"Yes, sir."

The general shoved a coffee cup toward the middle of his mahogany conference table, then resumed pacing. He stuck a cigar in his mouth, patting his pockets for matches. When obedient hands held out lighters, the general just threw the unlit cigar into a trash can.

"I have Mr. Wallis on the telephone, sir," Major Nash announced.

General Lathrop jerked a handset from its cradle and stabbed a button on his communications console. "Wallis, my entire operations staff including G-2 through G-7 are sitting in my goddamn conference room with their thumbs up their asses. Now where is Commander Getts?"

Wallis sat comfortably in a dark oak paneled office among functional antiques. He favored his overstuffed sofa when there was much reading to do or when speaking for a long time on a telephone. He was on the sofa now, a silver tea service nearby, when Lathrop's priority call was put through. "He's here, General," Wallis said. "He doesn't think it's advisable for him to be seen unnecessarily in public."

Lathrop allowed the handset to fall from his ear momentarily. He regarded it for a long moment as though it were a piece of rotting fruit. "Advisable? Unnecessary?" he screamed into the mouthpiece. "Who the hell does he think he is? Doesn't he understand an order when he hears one?"

"I'm sure he doesn't mean to . . ." Wallis began soothingly before being interrupted.

"Listen, Wallis, you're a civilian, so there's not much I can do about your insubordination, but there's damn well is something I can do about Commander Getts. When I tell him I'd like to see him in my office, I'm not asking the bastard, I'm telling him!"

Back in his own office, Wallis caught Getts's eye while struggling to temporize with General Lathrop. Today, Getts was wearing charcoal wool slacks, a blue and white striped cotton shirt, and a herringbone jacket with a navy blue and red striped tie. His hair was neatly combed, and his face shaved clean.

"I understand your feelings, General," Wallis said into the telephone, "but Commander Getts suggested that you might be able to handle your business with him either over the telephone or in a less conspicuous place . . . Hello?"

Wallis hung up the telephone. "He's upset, Bobby. He said that he would be here in twenty minutes. Maybe you'd better wait for him."

"Sure. I know I'm paranoid. And I don't blame the man

for being upset," Getts admitted. "By the way, your clock is six minutes slow."

Wallis regarded the huge grandfather clock standing against a wall of his office. "If it is, so be it. I run my business by it, not one of these shoddy little battery watches." As if to underscore his point, Wallis crossed the room and wound the clock with a large key kept on top of his desk.

Getts leaned back from paperwork in front of him. "This everything we have?" Getts was referring to a stack of carefully transcribed reports from a number of locations in the Middle East.

"Yes. All I have, anyway. It's difficult to get DIA to come up with everything that all their shops have. They each want to hang on to their own sources, you know."

"This brings us back to your friend Rabbi. Is he a possibility?" Getts asked. "And, if it's our reward money, how come the Israelis have Tomaz?" Getts wanted to know.

"The defector feels more secure in the hands of the Mossad. Can you blame him?" Wallis challenged.

"What about Rabbi?" Getts asked.

"What about him?"

"Reliable?"

"I met him through his brother in Israel, 1947. His brother was Rudyeh Gurin, a barber by day, but at night he smuggled guns into Israel. In those days my job was to see to it that Israel found arms on the so-called open market. You see, the British had been there, and the Arabs were there, but nobody wanted the Jews. Except America. In Britain, we just wanted them someplace else. We've never admitted that, of course. Rudyeh was my contact man.

"One day Rabbi went to the Mossad and informed them that his own brother was a double agent for the Arabs. That night Rudyeh was arrested by an Irgun tribunal. In the morning, he was hanged. Rabbi was cold as ice when he sent his brother to his death."

Wallis had Getts's full attention. "Ever had a reason not to trust him?" Getts wanted to know.

"Why should I? I've never known him to deceive an ally," the elder spy responded.

"Seems to me he'll say whatever he thinks is good for Israel," Getts observed.

"Yes, and you'll say whatever is good for America. Fortunately, we're all on the same side in this one."

"Against a terrorist. Not against other Arabs, necessarily," Getts submitted.

"If you think he is using us, then cut him out of the loop," Wallis countered.

Getts thought for a long minute. "If his intelligence is good I don't care about his motives."

A Buick army staff car pulled up sharply in front of the gates of Carlisle Foundation. A U.S. Army sergeant sat behind the wheel. In the backseat was General Cornelius Lathrop. The gardener, Mr. Bucks, put aside his rake and, stepped over to the car, smiling.

"Afternoon," he said, touching the brim of his hat. "Beautiful day."

"Open the gate," General Lathrop said.

"Sorry," Mr. Bucks said, pleasantly. "Don't believe I've had the privilege."

"Well, it's a damn shame we haven't been formally introduced. Now open that goddamn gate, or I'll have my driver open it for you."

The gardener revealed a wisp of a smile. "That gate is tool steel, General. It hasn't been tested against a Buick, but we tried running an armored personnel carrier through it before we installed it here. The APC didn't bust it open. May I see your identification, General?"

Lathrop felt his anger turn to blue rage, but he nevertheless produced a plastic identification card and handed it to the "gardener."

"Much obliged," the New Englander said, his flinty eyes not matching his outwardly pleasant demeanor.

Mr. Bucks nodded toward his "assistants," one of whom actuated the electrically controlled gate from the inside the grounds.

General Lathrop's sergeant gunned the engine of the staff car as they sped toward the main house. "Goddamn civilian knew who I was all the time," the General growled.

"World's full of 'em, sir," the driver agreed.

Inside, Cletis interrupted his employer and Getts in the

midst of their conversation. "Begging your pardon, Mr. Wallis. General Lathrop is here."

"Ah, wonderful," Wallis responded. "Show him in, Cletis."

But General Lathrop had already pushed the butler aside and walked into the spy's sanctum.

"Come in, General," Wallis invited. "Good of you to find the time to stop by, sir."

"Stow the bullshit," Lathrop said.

Getts rose to his feet in the presence of a superior officer.

"Commander Getts," Wallis beamed with effort, "I have the honor to present General Cornelius Lathrop, Director of U.S. Army Special Operations."

"My pleasure, sir," Getts responded. He did not salute because he was not in uniform. He did not offer his hand because protocol required that the gesture, if made, would come from the man of superior rank. There was no such offer.

"It is, huh?" Lathrop grunted.

"Yes, sir. When you were a deputy brigade commander in Vietnam you mounted an airborne assault to rescue an 'I' Corps recon platoon. My uncle was one of them you brought in," Getts said with open respect.

"That so?" Lathrop visibly brightened. "What's his name?"

"Sergeant First Class Marion Clark, sir," Getts responded.

"Clark," the general mused, "Clark. Hmmm. Well, that's great. Ever see him?"

"No, sir. He died of a drug overdose. Someone sold him some high grade smack, and he didn't cut it."

General Lathrop stared at Getts for a long moment, his eyes narrowed into slits. "You kept me waiting today, Getts. I don't like that, but I'm going to put it out of my mind. I've got a big ego, but I know how to control it. I haven't seen your service record yet, and until I do, you haven't got a job."

"General Lathrop . . . " Wallis began.

General Lathrop continued to speak directly to Getts, ignoring Wallis's interruption. "Wallis here is a civilian. I don't care who he answers to or who he gives orders to. But if you do SpecOps, you answer to me. Chain of command. What you do is a reflection on the entire U.S. military. It's nothing personal, Getts. An army without control isn't an army. It's an armed mob. Understand?"

"Yes, sir." Getts responded.

"Good. Then maybe this won't be so hard after all. Commander, I'm going to give you two simple orders. First, I want you to present yourself at my office at 0900 hours tomorrow in uniform. Second, be prepared to brief me and my staff on the exact table of organization of your unit, name, rank, and serial number of each man assigned to your TO, and a complete description of your current mission. Are you clear on all that?"

"Yes, sir. Very clear," Getts said.

General Lathrop smiled, obviously relieved with the course of events. He turned gracefully for a big man and walked toward the door in preparation to leave. "Very well," he said. "Brad, I'll leave you to your work. Commander Getts, see you in the morning. And take that goddamn ring out of your ear."

"Tomorrow morning will be a problem, sir," Getts said, easily.

"Why should it be a problem?" the General asked.

"My work is secret, General. Secret means secret. The identity of my men can't be disclosed to anyone. That's the deal I made with them, sir."

General Lathrop nodded his head as though this was the reaction he had expected all along. "Okay. I should have known. Should have figured you'd come up with something like that. Well, you just buried your military career, smart-ass."

Lathrop rocked from heel to toe while he struggled to control his anger. "Your rich old man put you through Harvard or Princeton or Yale so you thought you'd have some interesting experiences in the army or navy before you settle down to spending the family money, huh? And if someone along the way gives you static, your family will lay on some political muscle and that'll take care of that. Why, I'll bet you even know the President personally. Let me tell you something: I've got a few political friends of my own, and by the time I get through with Commander Robert V. Getts he'll think resigning his commission was an act of mercy. And something else. At 0901 hours tomorrow morning orders will be issued to military security forces to arrest your ass, put you in handcuffs, and deliver you to my office at the Pentagon. In other words, Getts, either way, you'll be there in the morning."

"Gentlemen," Wallis said, "I think I'll let you discuss military matters in private. Excuse me." Wallis crossed the room and shut the door behind him.

Getts made sure the door was closed securely before turning toward the general. "General, my file has been removed from the adjutant general's custody. It is unobtainable until I choose to produce it." General Lathrop's face reflected momentarily disbelief as Getts went on. "My name isn't Getts. It isn't even Robert."

"Then who the hell are you?" Lathrop demanded.

"I volunteered for counterterrorist work, sir. The people we're up against will try to find out who I am. When and if they do they'll kill me, my family, my friends, and my cat. And they'll do it as painfully as possible. They will regard their search for me and my loved ones as a form of spiritual fulfillment."

"I'm not just anybody, Getts, or whatever the hell your name is. I am your commanding officer. I run Special Operations for the armed forces of the United States. Not you. You give me the information I ordered, and I will decide whether or not to approve your missions. We are either an army or a mob, just like I said. Be in my office at 0900, or I'll have your butt dragged in," Lathrop said.

At 0930 hours the next morning, military police, acting under orders of Major General Lathrop, arrived at Carlisle Foundation demanding the person of Commander Robert Getts. The police were informed that they were trespassing on civilian property. Nor was Getts on the grounds. When they refused to open the gates, the army police returned to their cars and drove away.

The Blacklight team flew cross country, arriving over Vandenberg Air Force Base at 0400 hours, 12,000 feet. The briefing by Peach had been clear and straightforward. "The package delivery system is a highly automated method of moving an important item from point A to point B. It will determine in a unique scientific way who is an outstanding trooper and who isn't worth a shit. Winners of the package delivery game will be superior troopers worthy of our deepest respect and admiration. Losers will shine their shoes for one week, bring their food from the chow hall, and kiss their asses. Winners have pride, losers have none.

"It is the business of Blacklight to kick total ass and not to be kicked in return. The enemy dies, we continue to live. A happy trooper is a successful trooper, and success is within our hearts, within our brains, and within our capabilities. Make me happy. Troopers who fail in the package delivery program will be sent home with a stern note written to their mothers. Do not, I repeat *do not*, disgrace your mommies. That is all."

They would "insert" at 34.399 n. lat/120.278 longitude using global positioning satellite (GPS) hand-held receivers to guide by. Those coordinates would put them at the south end of Vandenberg AFB, the second largest military installation in the United States. Each team, A and B, was to secure and transport what was only known as Item Alpha and Item Bravo a distance of 32 statute miles to another coordinate on a map, which would place them near Point Sal to the north within a period of 36 hours. In moving their items, they were instructed, the use of civilian railroad tracks or vehicles was not authorized.

This time, the night jump sky provided the faint light of a quarter moon. Each trooper was able to steer his chute to the LZ, a location known on the map as Espada Creek. The effervescent reflection of moon and surf acted like a beacon to guide them to the beach. They buried their chutes in the sand, then spread out to locate their transport items. Carla was the first to spot them. "Holy shit." She pointed at the surf.

There were two floating buoys, each marking the shallow but watery graves where the items were buried. Each team had to wade through water over their heads into cold Pacific Ocean waters to dig the burdens from the sand. Their equipment was practically nil. They carried nothing but what their fatigue pockets could support—concentrated packages of food, small knives, and water.

Both teams dove into the frigid water at once, digging away at the sand, pulling and pushing, knocked flat by relentless incoming breakers. Team Alpha, consisting of Bartender, Sneezy, Valentino, Razorback, and Carla were first to free their item—a twenty-foot log. The effort took forty minutes as hands were cut and bruised, their body temperatures dropping to near hypothermia levels in the 10°C environment.

There was no time to rest. Team Alpha hoisted their log to their shoulders and set off along the coastline attempting to find a pace that they could sustain. Sheer rock cliffs rose to their right, obviating the possibility of finding a road on which to travel. So they stayed with the sand. "Fucking asshole Peach thought this one up," Valentino grumbled.

"Save your breath," Bartender said. Peach was jogging with Alpha and could easily hear the team's dialogue. He didn't care. Nobody else did, either. They all knew it would be a bitch.

Getts jogged behind team Bravo.

"Let's pick up the pace," Razorback said. They were in a slow trot.

"This is good," Sneezy said. He already had experience with the log.

"No, let's move—I can keep up with you guys," Carla said. She sneaked a look over her shoulder and noted that Bravo team was out of the water and starting to book it. The effort of turning her head with a 100-pound load on her shoulder, however, was painful. Her shoulder already hurt, and she shifted her hands more directly under the log.

The first two miles were relatively easy for the troopers, except for chafing between the legs caused by sand, salt water, and friction. Forewarned of a pending long march, each trooper carried a pair of hiking shorts into which he/she could change when necessary. After three miles, every trooper had changed. Shoulders were rubbed raw, and the load felt increasingly heavier as they moved at their best pace.

After five miles, the pace had slowed, partly from fatigue but mostly because the tide had risen. Footfalls were now made more difficult because of the soft sand as well as the sharp rocks from the cliffs that spread right down onto the beach. It was impossible to keep out beach sand and sea water. The result from their specially made hiking boots was like sand paper rubbing against flesh. Because of her short stature, Toni struggled to maintain her share of the load, but it was taken up by the others, who did not complain.

After eight miles, Team Alpha broke for a ten-minute rest. Team Bravo opted to continue as long as they were able, but their fatigue and injuries stopped them after only an additional mile.

Bravo took stock of their condition. All were rubbed raw by the salt water and sand. T-shirts had been removed to add padding to their shoulders, but their black shirts could not be kept in place for long, causing them to be a nuisance.

At mile twelve, Busboy slipped on a rock and fell. "Goddamn it," Redskin snarled as he went down as well. The log would have fallen but for Crush, Toni, and Huck Finn. As it was, the three placed it down in order to tend to a gash on Busboy's knee. "Fuck this," Crush said, his body beaten. All members of the team had open sores on their shoulders and hands and burning rashes between their legs.

"Fuck what?" Redskin said as he placed medical tape on Busboy's leg.

"I mean fuck this log shit," Crush said. "Let's sit on this thing instead of packing it twenty more miles. What are they going to do? Fire us?"

"No guts, that's you, Crush," Redskin said. "Big, strong, tough guy with jelly where your heart ought to be."

"Hey, I still got enough in me to rip your heart out, Wahoo," Crush said. Exhausted, he made no move to stand.

"Knock it off, morons. Makes it harder," Toni gasped. "Come on," she said, "I'm going to push." As Crush, Redskin, Busboy, and Huck Finn once again shouldered the hated log, Toni made no pretense about carrying her load. She couldn't. But she could do something else. She got behind Busboy, the last man in line, and put her hands on his hips and pushed. It helped Busboy enormously. A half mile later, she had Busboy move up in the line, and she did the same with Crush, then Huck Finn. Team Bravo passed Alpha that evening just after twilight at 1842 hours.

Peach grinned.

Twenty-eight miles and 29 hours into the punishing march Huck Finn's legs were so badly injured that blood flowed freely from wounds. "That's all for you, Huck. Sit down," Getts said. He began administering first aid to Huck Finn's wounds.

"Just a bandage, Bobby, then I can go," he said, his head lolling backward as blood oozed from both shoulders.

"Sorry, man, you're government property. If it were up to me, I'd let you cripple yourself," Getts said as he worked on his battered legs. Getts then removed a folded tinfoil-thin survival blanket from his pack, and snapped it open around Huck Finn. He dropped two extra food supplement bars into his lap. "Wait here till we come for you," then jogged off after the Bravo team.

With the loss of Huck Finn, Team Bravo had fallen to a grinding, slogging pace, fighting their way through sand, and chaparral that ripped clothes and tore skin. The entire team was a mass of blisters, cuts, and abrasions. Their minds were numb, their actions automatic and unthinking. They could not concentrate on anything beyond the next step. Carla had placed a piece of her torn uniform in her mouth to protect the enamel on her teeth as she gritted them together.

"Half mile, troopers," Peach said. There was admiration in his voice for all of them, as they had done no less well than many navy teams that had struggled through this important phase of their training. His own shoulder ached with sympathetic pain as he recalled his own grinding agony under the log. But the exercise was the most effective means ever devised of teaching team unity. And grinding pain and exhaustion were facts of life in combat; troopers had to learn to think even while they suffered.

Life was momentarily improved when they heard that they were only 2500 feet from the end of their ordeal. They tried to look up from the ground, but they were punished for trying. But they could feel what was coming.

"Oh, God, no . . ." Carla groaned. The terrain was beginning to steepen.

Valentino fell. Bartender collapsed under the extra weight, and Carla went down as well. Razorback, the work-horse from the gridiron of Arkansas, broke his collarbone when the full weight of the log rammed him to the ground. He grunted, his good arm going to the injury. "You okay, man?" Valentino asked Razorback.

"Yeah," Razorback said, unable to utter more. The team, with determination and great difficulty, shouldered the log again and willed their feet to move. With each step of the way, the terrain gained a sharper angle, slowing their walk to half steps, then to a crawl. They ploughed through ice plant that snatched at their ankles, which would then give way to soft sand causing them to slip back.

"Hold it," Carla said. The group fell to the ground, gasping. The last of their water ration was gone. "I got an idea," she said. "Let's quit carrying this thing and slide it. We stay in one place, push it up the hill, move ourselves up, repeat."

Without comment or argument, the team took new positions and tried pulling, sliding, and repositioning. It was slow, but easier than the impossible method of trying to walk up a 40° hill.

Team Bravo was only fifty feet to their right.

The last fifty yards, marked with a finish line drawn between two pine trees, was flat. Both teams ran, or tried to. Twenty yards from the finish line Team Alpha had clearly won the race. They had only to shuffle a few more steps and they would beat Team Bravo who, equally exhausted, could not increase their pace for a dash to the finish.

Then without signal, without plan or discussion, Team Alpha stopped. They waited with the log on their painful shoulders several long minutes for Team Bravo. Words of encouragement escaped their dried and swollen lips. "C'mon, you guys . . ." they called out. "Go, Redskin." "C'mon, Crush. C'mon." "Go, Toni . . ."

Carla's eyes were fluttering from fatigue, and she was on the verge of passing out, but when the finish line was crossed, they all did it together. They dropped the logs and dropped into each other's arms. Some cried with relief, patting each other's backs.

Instead of waiting to be picked up, Huck Finn had walked painfully behind. But he had finished.

Razorback sank to his knees in pain. Everyone could now see the swollen, bruised injury to his collarbone. Other soldiers came their way from an area where transportation had been assembled; an ambulance, a personnel van, and a truck. Medical staff quickly moved among the Blacklight, with Razorback getting particular attention for his broken bone.

"They nuts?" one airman, a driver, said to a colleague.

"Guess that's how they make killers," the other said.

"Good job, troopers," Getts said. "Thirty-one hours and eleven minutes. Fifty-one minutes off the record set by the SAS team that did it three years ago. But we have a problem. We only borrowed the logs. They have to go back. Right now."

"That a fucking joke?" Razorback said.

"You heard the order," Getts said. "On your feet! Move out!"

One by one they struggled upright. With supreme effort, each team hefted their hated log to their shoulders. They had not yet begun to retrace their steps when Toni spoke in a tone heard only among the teams. "Let's take the truck." For a long moment, there was no discussion and no movement among the Blacklight. Then, without a verbal signal, they advanced toward the 2.5 ton truck and its drivers. Redskin pulled open the driver's door, reached inside the cab and pulled him out, dropping him unceremoniously to the ground.

Getts, Peach, the medics, and all the others stood watching in disbelief as Blacklight troopers heaved the logs into the back of the truck and climbed in. Redskin punched the engine into life as Peach, hands on his hips, yelled at his troops. "Hey, goddamn it, you do not have permission to . . ."

But the truck pulled out, its big wheels spinning on soft sand. Peach turned to look at Getts, who was now grinning ear to ear.

The speed limit on Vandenberg Air Force Base was, in most places, 25 mph. Redskin took the corner of a secondary base road at 65 onto California Boulevard, the main street running through the base complex. Despite the large geographical size of Vandenberg AFB, like most bases, it has a relatively concentrated center of barracks, officers' quarters, a theater, BX, NCO, and officers' clubs, and administrative buildings. When a large truck rumbles through this small grouping like an avalanche over a ski chalet, the effect is startling. Redskin floored the gas pedal to kick the truck up to 70 mph and was headed for the main gate.

"Do you know where the fuck you are going?" Valentino yelled at him.

"Hell, no. Never been here before."

"Ah, shit." Valentino looked at his hand-held GPS navigation system. "Southeast, man. Pick any fucking road you see 'cause that's where we gotta go."

As Redskin fired through the main gate, Air Force Security Police personnel frantically waved their hands before leaping out of the way of the careering truck. Blacklight troopers in the back of the truck yelled back and waved their arms before sprawling sideways as the truck bounded onto Santa Lucia Canyon Road.

Security Police cars and trucks took up the chase, their sirens blaring. "Step on it, Redskin!" Sneezy yelled from the rear, his elated face reflecting the adrenaline that was pumping through them all. The truck sped by the Lompoc maximum security prison, shooting past triple fencing, guard towers and quadruple rows of razor wire. Redskin narrowly missed an automobile coming from the prison personnel housing on their left.

Inside one of the pursuing cars, Captain Walls spoke again into his mobile radio. "Base Ops, this is Captain Walls, Security Police. Locate Major Diehl and tell him that we're in pursuit of a stolen truck in area twenty-one. Subjects are heading south toward highway two-forty-six. We need helos."

Meanwhile, a personnel van had arrived at Point Sal. An air force lieutenant and several armed security personnel confronted Getts and Peach. "Commander Getts, General Schroeder requests that you come to his headquarters. That's immediately, sir. You too, Peach."

"Thought I might stop at the BOQ and clean up first," Getts said to the lieutenant.

"Sorry, Commander, the general was real specific. We're to use force if you resist." The junior officer was embarrassed as he searched for softer words. "That's what he said, sir, begging your pardon."

Getts smiled, straightened his filthy camo uniform, then nodded to Peach. The two men stepped into the waiting van.

When Redskin and the rest of the Blacklight team came to California 246, a state highway near Vandenberg Air

Force Base, they hung a right. With the pedal to the metal the truck sped on at its maximum speed of 79 mph. Six miles later, the truck slowed to a stop at a map coordinate marked only as "surf." There was a line of police security vehicles a quarter mile long and a helicopter circling on station overhead.

"Get going, Redskin," Razorback yelled from the rear of the truck.

"Which fucking way? There's no road, man." Redskin said.

Unless one counted a railroad track. When the Blacklight team took the stolen truck down the old SP&S line, the pursuers ruined suspension systems on three vehicles before giving up the chase.

General Andrew Schroeder paced back and forth behind his massive desk until his office door opened. The escorting lieutenant stepped into the office and announced Commander Getts before standing to one side. Getts entered, came smartly to attention and saluted the general. "Commander Getts reporting as ordered, sir."

"Getts? Getts? What's your full name and DD number, Getts?" the general said.

"Robert V., sir. DD-2 3990430."

"Your unit?"

"344 Theater Group, sir," Getts said.

"Theater, my ass. You're the leader of a gang of thieves. Your men assaulted air force personnel, stole an air force truck, wrecked at least one of our cars, and at this very minute are being pursued by an air unit. Somebody's going to jail, Commander, and that someone just might be you."

"I understand the general's position, and I take full responsibility for the conduct of my men and women."

The general continued to pace. "Stand at ease. You look like a sorry sack of shit. How did you get to this base? You damn sure didn't come through the gate."

Getts considered quickly. In his moment of desperation, he decided to try the truth. "Parachute, General."

The general nodded knowingly. "Good thing you didn't try to bullshit me. This is a ballistic missile test range. Our security is pretty goddamn good. We had a fix on an un-identified black plane two days ago. We found your parachutes this morning. Quite a play your theater group is putting on for our people."

"Yes, sir," Getts said.

"Are you sticking to that stupid line, Getts?" the general said.

"It's the only line I have, General."

The general stopped pacing, placed his hands behind his back. "Okay, that's your privilege. You're some kind of commando unit, I think that's pretty obvious. Carrying logs around, well, I've heard of that, too. Tough training, but I know what it's for." The general waited for any kind of confirmation from Getts that his surmise was correct. There was none. "But I'll tell you this, if any one of my people are hurt, you and yours are going to pay for it big time. You can kill your own goddamn selves but, when you involve my people then you're over the line. Do I make myself clear?"

"Exactly, sir," Getts said.

"And the wrecked equipment. We have this thing you've probably never heard of. It's called a budget and I'll be damned if . . ." The general's words were cut short by his desk telephone. The general snatched it from its cradle. "Yes?" He listened for a long moment then said, "How is that possible? What? No. He's here. Standby until you hear from me." The general replaced the telephone and turned a wary eye on Getts. "Helicopter reports that your loonies dropped two logs near the water at the south end of the base. They left the truck at Jalama State Beach. We don't know where they are. But we'll damn sure round them up."

"I doubt that, sir," Getts said.

"What's that supposed to mean?"

"You won't find them if they don't want you to find them, General. Part of their training. As actors, that is."

The general considered this for a moment, then his shoulders slumped in resignation. "Okay, Getts. You do it. Blow the whistle or whatever you do but get them out of my hair and off my base."

Getts gathered himself into attention and saluted the general again. "Yes, sir, thank you, sir." He did an about-face and strode to the door. Before he could exit, however, General Schroeder spoke again. "Getts, your people are pretty tough. For actors. You must be proud of them."

"Yes, sir, I am." Getts closed the door behind him.

                              *   *   *

Conrad parked his car on the opposite side of Vista del
Mar. From the trunk of his rental, he removed an item
that appeared to be an amateur's telescope. He placed the
instrument over one shoulder and slung a canvas bag over
the other. He had to wait for an opening in traffic before
hurrying across four lanes of roadway.

It was only seven o'clock when he set foot on the grass
of Vista del Mar Park and, as he expected, he was alone
at this hour. It was still early spring and the evening air
was turning chilly. He zipped up his jacket to his chin.
Motorists speeding by hardly noticed the man who peered
through the telescope pointed toward the evening stars.
Conrad munched on a barbecued ham sandwich as he
aligned his deadly tube along the flight path of outgoing
aircraft almost directly under runway 24-R. He estimated
that the widebodied jets were not more than eight hundred
feet above him as they climbed slowly, laden with fuel for
nonstop trips to distant lands. It would not matter, of
course, if they were much higher since the Redye had a
range of three thousand meters. A blind man could make
this shot, he knew.

At seven-thirty he turned on his Halicrafter radio, raised
the antenna, and tuned the instrument to LAX tower frequency. There was no interference of any kind. Conrad
could hear ground control instructions and air traffic directions to and from aircraft as though he were sitting in the
cockpit with the flight crew. The "telescope" with its de-
structive Redye was now in position, its systems checked
and fully operational.

"Ramp control," a voice crackled over the radio, "American 1421, Gate 32, ready to push."

Conrad bent closer to the radio. This was the transmission he was waiting for. He knew that American Airlines
Flight 1421 was now ready to leave the gate. In his mind's
eye, he could see the small tug in front of the aircraft, its
metal spar hooked to the airplane's nose wheel.

"American 14," the return voice abbreviated the flight
number, "standby one; there's a Delta 737 behind you . . ."

After several moments, as Conrad listened intently, ramp
control again directed its transmission to his target. "American 14, you're clear to push."

Conrad controlled his heightened excitement as he imagined the huge jet rolling slowly backward until its nose was pointed outward from the safety of airport terminals. Passengers would be making last minute adjustments of the luggage under their seats, choosing reading material, and checking seat belts. Air crew members would patrol the aisles, pleasantly reminding people to put their seats in an upright position.

Conrad glanced at automobile traffic. It was almost dark now. He seldom got so much as a glance from drivers heading north, none at all for those heading south on the opposite side of the highway. It was prime time for late afternoon air traffic, and jets were taking off overhead at intervals of about three minutes. The noise from their engines, thrusting at maximum power, was shattering from where Conrad waited in ambush.

"Ramp control, American 1421, ready to taxi," the co-pilot's voice said over the radio.

"Okay, American 14, taxi to spot nine," ramp control responded at once.

Conrad could feel his heart beating faster. He had hardly straightened up when a police cruiser drove past him in the nearest lane. It did not slow, he noticed, and the policeman sitting on the passenger side of the car looked away, with no indication that he suspected anything.

The terrorist then reached down and placed his finger on the actuator of the supersonic missile system. A green light immediately winked on, indicating that the arming mechanism was on line.

"Tower, this is American 1421, we're ready to go."

"American 1421," the tower controller said, "take position and hold."

"Roger, position and hold," the pilot confirmed.

Conrad again checked the system of his Redeye, then placed a set of earphones that resembled medical stethoscope earpieces around his neck, ready to insert when the moment arrived.

He referred to the sweep hand on his wristwatch. Without taking his eyes from his timepiece, Conrad placed the listening device into his ears. Conrad watched with intense concentration as Delta 1210 flew directly into the path of his "telescope." Conrad was using an optical sighting device as the aircraft flew into its range, maintaining a departure speed of approximately one hundred eighty knots. He could have fired on the optical indicator, but he waited until he heard the missile's audio system inform him that the missile had locked onto the jet engine's exhaust with its infrared homing. Conrad watched as the jet continued seaward, his finger on the trigger, the missile fully armed, the audio targeting adviser now screaming into his ears.

But this was not his target.

Conrad knew that American 1421 had moved from its right-angle waiting position to square itself with runway 24-R. His mental image was confirmed by the voice of a tower operator.

"American 14, cleared for takeoff. Nice day."

"Roger, Tower, we're rolling," the copilot said.

Conrad knew that passengers would soon feel four giant Pratt & Whitney fan-jet engines lifting the massive eight hundred thousand pounds of aircraft off the ground. They would feel a slight pressure as fractional G-forces carried them along a ten-thousand-foot runway. Many a passenger's palms would be sweaty. And, Conrad thought, this time for good reason.

Twenty-two seconds passed.

The jet would have rotated by now, its incredible bulk lifted through ethereal matter by combinations of titanic force and delicate balance.

He could hear its engines now, could feel first the vibrations of the earth under his feet as the aircraft suddenly broke into view over the top of his head. Conrad placed earphones to his head. He looked down at the indicator lights of the Redeye system. The fire control switched from irresolute blinks to a sudden steady red as American 1421 flew into both visual and infrared tracking fields.

Conrad pulled the trigger.

A screaming missile, seventy-six millimeters in diameter and one hundred twenty centimeters in length, exploded out of its carefully compacted tube by means of a booster motor. Almost immediately, its main engine ignited and, flashing quickly through supersonic speeds, streaked after the right inboard engine of American 1421.

In less than three seconds, Conrad could see the first

explosion. That would have been the HE warhead. Then instantly, almost indistinguishable from the first, there was a second explosion as the aircraft's fuel tanks erupted.

The 747's wing snapped and it did a slow roll, like a rhinoceros in a wading pool seeking relief at the bottom from an unbearable sun. No longer flying, it began to fall backward and sideways.

As he removed earphones from his head and watched in momentary fascination as pieces of the giant machine began striking the water, Conrad felt a surge of exhilaration, a sense of fullness. Accomplishment.

Conrad withdrew a plain white envelope from his pocket and, bending it slightly, placed it into the end of the still smoking rocket launcher tube. Inside the envelope was a reminder of Conrad's prophetic words he had uttered on the desert of Palestine that the Jews had stolen. The war America had so foolishly begun in the Middle East was far from over and would ultimately extract a penalty that the West would not be willing to pay.

He was already walking deliberately down a short grass slope of the park toward Vista del Mar Boulevard when a passing motorist slammed on his brakes and swerved to a stop nearby. The driver stepped out of his car with a concentrated look at Conrad, a glance back toward the abandoned "telescope" and radio. Conrad's attention was focused upon his own car on the opposite side of the road. Other automobiles were now slowing to complete stops while motorists stared with wonder several hundred yards off shore. Flames and smoke were quickly dissipating on the surface of the water.

"Hey!" the driver called to Conrad as he approached. "Hey, you. Hold it, fella." The man broke into a trot until he was close enough to reach out and touch Conrad.

Conrad calmly turned toward the approaching stranger and placed the barrel of the PPK inches from his eye. He pulled the trigger rapidly three times. The rounds tore through the man's eye socket and exited the back of the head.

The shots did not attract immediate attention among the people shouting, car tires screaming, and another jet taking off on 24-L.

Conrad calmly stepped into his rented car, started the

engine, made a U-turn through congestion of Vista del Mar, and drove off. He continued on Vista del Mar to the first stoplight, which was Manchester Boulevard. He turned right, up a hill, until he reached Lincoln Boulevard. As he turned right again, he could hear the wail of distant emergency vehicles and could see helicopters lifting into the air.

In less than a minute, his rental car was traveling immediately adjacent to the fence separating Lincoln from runway 24-R. He continued in a sweeping turn that carried him, within a few blocks, into an entrance of LAX. He stayed in the inside lane, taking an elevated ramp to the top airport roadway that circled the huge terminal complex. He continued halfway around the oval until he arrived at the international terminal, where he took an exit into a public parking garage. He picked up his metered ticket and, leaving it on the seat, wiped his fingerprints from the car and locked its doors.

Inside the terminal, he could hear passengers anxiously speaking with each other, still others watching television, which had begun to cover the disaster of a jumbo jet exploding, falling into the ocean near LAX.

"What's happening, here?" Conrad asked the clerk at the SAS ticket counter.

"Seems that a plane went down," the tight-lipped clerk said, his eyes scanning his reservation computer terminal for the name Udo Christhanson.

"Mein Gott," Conrad uttered in what he knew was proper shock. "But why?"

"I don't know, sir. The news just came in. It only just happened, you see. Would you like to pay for this with a credit card, Mr. Christhanson?" the clerk asked, anxious to change the subject.

"Ah, no. I think I would like to get rid of this American currency. All right for you?"

"Of course," the clerk said, accepting the cash. "Your flight may be delayed, sir, and there's no telling how long. Watch the monitors for boarding instructions."

"Ach," Conrad smiled, "I am a patient man."

Not in decades had any single event received such media attention, such analysis, such speculation, as the downing of a second American international jet by means of terrorism. Three hundred fifty-seven souls went down on Flight 280; 312 passengers and crew perished on American Flight 1421.

The nation, indeed the world, was horrified. Everyone and anyone who knew anything of the habits of terrorists or guerilla fighting was interviewed, cross-examined, asked to predict.

Government officials made statements, some averring that America had brought it all on itself by its reckless commitment to violence. All bemoaned the tragic loss of life, but, out of the ashes, they said, maybe we could now learn a deeper, more cautionary lesson of how to live with our neighbors.

Others felt that we had tolerated our "friends" to the point of grace and beyond. Our mistake in the Middle East, they said, was in stopping our forces short of Baghdad. We should have dragged Hussein out of his desert rat hole, held a brief tribunal and hanged him for the war criminal that he so clearly was. Then we should have moved against Syria and Hafez al-Assad's regime, officially named just months ago by the State Department's report to Congress, as the world's most ardent sponsor of terrorist groups.

International intelligence agencies friendly to America were pushed for any scrap of information on the man who called himself Conrad. Indeed, it was not just America that required to know this information but the entire West because, as Conrad had so accurately forecast, the effect on trade and international relations was almost immediate.

No sea vessels were kept in port. Cargo aircraft maintained cut-back schedules. The tourist trade stopped so quickly that airlines were forced overnight to furlough flight crews. Airports began to look like athletic stadiums in off season. Travel agencies went out of business by the hundreds. Equally bad for world economics, foreign carriers canceled normal scheduled flights from their countries to North America.

Airport security was intensified. No one could remember such precautionary measures since the 1940s. Armed patrols watched approaches and exits to airports. Every package, every bag, regardless if checked through or carried aboard, was sanitized. Still, experts agreed among themselves, publicly, that there existed myriad ways to bring down any of the fragile giants, so that in the end there was no way to stop a determined plane killer.

The President of the United States had laid on every available intelligence and military resource available to him, but it was Wallis who believed Bob Getts had the best chance of paying off the President's promise.

Peach had parked his car at Dulles Airport in Washington, boarded a morning commuter flight to Kennedy International, then caught a bus to Manhattan. He had never liked New York. He was not intimidated by street toughs, crowds, or noise. But it seemed to him that everybody had a hand out in New York, and Peach did not feel it was his purpose in life to fill other people's extended palms. Unlike some other career army types, Peach stepped easily out of and back into civilian clothing. As well as attitude. He wore plaited cotton trousers, loafers, and an expensive cotton sweater that hung attractively on his muscular frame.

He used a subway, got off near 118th Street, and began looking for an address. He found it within a block. He pushed an entrance button near a door upon which was affixed a sign, written in both English and Arabic: *Arab-American League*. The door, made of exterior wood veneer and augmented, Peach guessed, with inner layers of tool steel, was equipped with a "see first" glass several inches thick. There was a two-way communications speaker nearby. A heavily Middle Eastern accented voice sounded from the speaker.

"Yes? You have an appointment?"

"Naw. No appointment, but I want to see somebody inside," Peach answered.

"What is your name, please?" the voice queried. "And who do you wish to see?"

"My name is Jones. Wes Jones. And I want to talk to your president or whoever runs your league."

There was an extended period of silence, which Peach bore with the knowledge that video cameras were recording his demeanor. He waited with patience.

The voice returned. "We are sorry, Mr. Jones, but there is no one here who can help you. Is it possible for you to return tomorrow?"

"Hey, I'm from out of town. I'm here to help you, not

the other way around. Gimme a break," Peach said to the speaker.

Another prolonged silence ensued. Then Peach heard the decisive clack of a heavy metallic bolt being slid back on the other side of the door. "Come in, please," the voice said through the speaker.

Peach stepped inside the foyer, which was nothing more than a security chamber. The doorway itself was framing for a metal detector. Directly in front of him was a "reception" desk fronted by ten-inch hardened glass. There were no chairs, or tables, only a second door, which Peach assumed led into the offices of the League itself. He stood in the foyer and waited until the "receptionist" scrutinized him. "Mr. Jones? Someone will be with you directly."

Within a few moments, the second door, also mounted on heavy reinforced hinges, opened to reveal a Semitic man ten inches shorter than Peach but broad in the shoulders. The man had eyes that reflected intelligence as he spoke.

"I am Fadwa," the Arab said, extending his hand.

Peach took it. "Wes Jones."

"Mr. Jones," said the smiling Fadwa, "if you tell me the nature of your business, maybe I can bring you to the person you should see."

Peach, with an ear for voices, guessed that this man who called himself Fadwa—undoubtedly not his real name—had been born and raised in the Middle East, probably near Jordan, then educated in America and had lived here for several years. He was even likely a citizen, Peach would have bet.

"I got some information that your people would like to know about, Fadwa. Security stuff, you know," Peach said.

Fadwa chuckled softly, "I don't think you know what our organization is about, Mr. Jones. We're American Arabs. We try to promote peaceful understanding between this country and the Arab countries we come from. Don't let all of this . . ." Fadwa gestured toward the bulletproof glass and heavy doors, "give you the wrong idea. Violence can come from anywhere."

"Yeah, well, it's violence I'm here to talk about, Fadwa, old boy. For example, I know a guy in your organization named Habash who's about as violent a motherfucker as Allah ever sent down the street. He ain't passing out pamphlets for you folks, is he?" Peach asked, his voice soft, easy in modulation.

Fadwa hardly blinked. "Habash? No, nobody by that name is here, Mr. Jones. I'm really sorry . . ."

"Just in case you suddenly remember the name, tell him or somebody like him that I was here. Mention the name 'Blacklight.' I guaran-fucking-tee that'll get their attention. I'm staying in town one night," Peach said, handing Fadwa a slip of paper with an address written upon it. "I'm gone in the morning, Fadwa. Early."

Peach turned his back on the Arab and retraced his steps to the sidewalk outside.

The address Peach had left was a comparatively low-rent hotel in Jackson Heights. Peach was watching baseball on television without sound, while on the floor of his small room stretching lower back muscles, when there was a knock on his door.

He rose, stepped lightly to one side of the door and said "Yeah?"

"Mr. Jones? I am from the Arab-American League."

Peach unlatched the door and turned the knob, but kept to one side of it as he swung it open far enough to see the man on the other side. Peach's visitor was the opposite in stature from Fadwa. This man was so slender as to appear emaciated, not quite as tall as Peach, although he appeared so because of his narrow frame. Peach opened the door fully and, by motioning with his hand, beckoned the Arab to enter. Peach looked up and down the hotel hallway before closing and locking the door.

As Peach turned to regard the Arab, he knew the man would not be carrying a gun nor, likely, any other weapon, so he nodded toward the only chair in the room. Peach sat on the edge of his bed.

"My name is Magetz, Mr. Jones," the Arab said, the hint of a knowing smile tugging at the corners of his mouth as he uttered Peach's alias.

"Pleased to know you," Peach said. "Want to talk business?"

Magetz's nose wrinkled slightly in subdued disapproval of the American brusque, even discourteous, approach. Peach enjoyed the knowledge that he could make his visitor feel culturally uncomfortable. This one, he could tell, had been in this country far less time than his colleague, Fadwa. It was likely, Peach felt, that Magetz still spent more time in the Middle East than in America.

"Of course, if that is your pleasure, but I cannot imagine what business we have in common," Magetz said.

"Okay, here it is straight ahead, Magetz, and don't jerk me off. I happen to know who supplies you people with your money to operate your club, your organization, or whatever the fuck you want to call it. I also know some of the people that you front for. I gave one of his names today to your buddy Fadwa. Want some more?"

Peach waited for a response, but the Arab said nothing, not moving not blinking his eyes.

Peach continued. "I also happen to know you people know what Blacklight is. Nothin' against the Delta people but let's just say Blacklight will work in places where Delta doesn't. Put it on a level with SAS. Plus a lot of hardware the SAS would give their collective balls to have. Here's my deal. I got access to everything Blacklight is capable of doing. Lot of times, I know when it's going to do it, who's going to carry it out. Bullshit aside, my information is the best, and it's for sale. Like I say, if you're not interested, don't jerk me off, just walk out the door, and we're done."

Magetz sat for several long moments. He moved not a muscle in his body save for a vein at his temple, which, Peach could see, pulsated slightly.

"I am interested, Mr. Jones. But talk, as they say, is cheap. I do not pay for rumors," he said.

"Rumors, huh? Okay, here's a sample. A Libyan defected from one of your boss's bodyguard detail. He's in a safe house in this country being watched over by the Mossad. The defector's name is Tomaz. How's that for quality information?"

Peach was satisfied to see the excitement glow behind the eyes of the Levanter. "Where is this man being kept?" Magetz said.

"I don't know right now, but then you haven't come up with anything that looks like money, either. Huh?" Peach scribbled on a small note pad near his nightstand and passed the paper to Magetz. "Post office box. Mail cash, Mr. Magetz. You put me on retainer at, say, ten thousand dollars a month, paid every two weeks. Along with the first payment, you tell me where to mail you the information. Easy."

"The money is too much, Mr. Jones, considering . . ."

"Hey," Peach's voice rose, his eyes narrowed as he interrupted the Arab. "Then just don't send the cash. I ain't gonna fuck around with you. I'm not in fucking love with you rag heads anyway so if you think you can't afford a few barrels of oil to find out what I know, then fuck you. Got that, *effendi*?"

Peach stepped to the door, and opened it. The man called Magetz rose gracefully from his chair, paused in front of Peach and smiled. "Truly a pleasure meeting you, Mr. Jones."

Chapter Nine

Bob Getts had put in a long day in the field with his men. Their training consisted of a predusk trot of twenty miles, then a ninety-meter rope ascent on a cloudless night. Driven to the point of exhaustion and beyond, the team would then be required to perform a different exercise altogether—psychological evaluations on scores of filmed "travelers" interrogated as they prepared to board airlines, railroad stations and simply walked along streets.

Getts would look in retrospective irony at the call he received in his office minutes before he was to rejoin his Blacklights.

Peach, equally tired and dirty, held a telephone for Getts as he entered the headquarters office.

"Are you in a place to talk?" Getts immediately recognized Rabbi's voice.

"Yes," Getts replied with confidence. Camp McReynolds's telephone lines were gas-shrouded and buried in concrete.

"I thought you should know that Tomaz is going to move," Rabbi said.

"Tonight?"

"Yes."

"His idea?" Getts asked.

"Yes," Rabbi responded in a voice of forced calm. "He is your guest, but I am responsible for his safety. He says he worries about fire in these old neighborhoods," the master spy said.

"Think you really ought to move, or do you just want to show Tomaz some other parts of the city?" Getts said impatiently.

Rabbi's response was unruffled, as though he could understand the strain Getts was under. "A man from the electric company came to the house today and read our meter."

"So?" Getts responded.

"The man from the electric company did not appear to read the meter of any neighboring houses so I called the power company. I was told that they had no scheduled readings for this area," Rabbi declared.

"Okay, I understand," Getts said. "Why don't you wait until I can help? Peach is with me."

"We have enough, thank you. Sometimes the fewer the better, you know."

The remark stung Getts slightly especially after Tomaz's revelations about a mole. "Can I still see him tomorrow?"

"Of course. He won't be going far," the Israeli spy said.

Getts hung up the telephone, grabbed a half-eaten green apple, and finished it as he regarded Peach. "Hear you lost some money shooting craps."

"I don't know why I play that game," Peach said. "I always lose."

"Need money?" Getts asked.

"Nope," Peach said.

"Listen, Crosley, I'm your best friend. And you're mine. What I have is yours. I don't care if you're short the price of a car or a candy bar. You want it, it's yours."

"Thanks, Bobby. Figured you'd say something stupid like that."

"Well, you got to talk down to simple people, Peach, and they don't get much simpler than you."

"Tell me something, Bobby, why don't you get out of this military bullshit and do something in civilian life?"

* * *

Beyond the old parade grounds among white pine and Juniper trees was a concrete-block building identified only as T-1044. It was surrounded by two chain-link fences and topped with razor wire. There were signs along the road informing all personnel that the area was off limits without written authorization. Peach and Getts had visited building T-1044 approximately one hour before with the Blacklight team rolled up in a troop carrier near the outer gate. Getts was standing at the outer perimeter.

"Gather round," he said, and waited for the troops to form a semicircle around their commander. "Within forty feet of us is a man armed with hand grenades and a HRF weapon. He is considering whether to kill us one at a time or all at once." Getts paused for effect. "See him?"

The Blacklight turned almost as a single person and scanned their immediate surroundings. "He's dug in," Valentino said.

"In ghilley suit," Sneezy added, moving several steps in different directions as he scanned the tree line.

"What do you think, Huck Finn?" Getts asked.

"Why would he want to kill a bunch of nice people like us?"

"That's good, Huck, but the fact is if you can't see him, you can't kill him." Getts waited while the troopers began to look around in earnest.

"Okay, this is what you're going to be wearing someday," Getts said. "Come on out, Peach."

Even in off-the-shelf camos, a guy could disappear inside the pine. None, however, were prepared for the figure that loomed out of the very concrete walls of building T-1044. There was a collective gasp as the form of Peach, unrecognizable except by his size, morphed from cement blocks. Slowly, a shimmering arm reached upward to his head, padded fingers begining to manipulate a ninety-million-dollar camouflage suit. Turning slowly like a stripper showing her wares, Peach wriggled out of one of the U.S. Army's latest top secrets.

"It's ionically charged PPE—photo pixel electrical particles—responding to external stimuli in the near-infrared wavelength. The material needs no power source. It absorbs whatever environment it is exposed to and takes on the precise coloration of that environment. Just like a lizard," Getts explained.

Blacklight quickly crowded around Peach to look at the camouflage suit closely.

"Jesus Christ . . ."

"Hey, Crush, you could snare yourself a date with this . . ."

There were other goodies that Peach and Getts would carefully point out to the team. "We're going to practice with this equipment, and we're going to get very good."

"You can see him when he moves," Valentino said.

"Right," Getts said. "Everybody keep that in mind. Let's see what else we have."

Also demonstrated were "mini-agents," golf-ball-sized units that could be made to look like anything that lay on the ground—pine cones, rocks, walnuts—that when activated, blossomed, opening up like flower petals. Tiny silicone sensors would send moving images to a satellite up-link or to a receiver on the ground within a thousand meters. The units were capable of audio input and transmission, and were both IFR and motion sensing. The data would be transmitted back to a specially designed Blacklight helmet constructed with heads-up displays inside the visors, hopping between optical, IR, near-IR and vibration-detection modes.

Each helmet would contain auditory enunciators giving each trooper extraordinary powers of hearing. High resolution GPS receivers attached to the wrist of each trooper would receive position reports from orbiting satellites to a half meter on the ground. Another receiver attached to the inside of the trooper's helmet would display a small green dot, indicating where all other troopers were at all times. Each Blacklight had an auto-talk lip mike built into his headband for instant verbal communication with other members of the team. "At night," Peach said, "we are warriors from the Other Side."

"And this little hummer," Peach said, holding a strange-looking rifle aloft for all to see, "is a smart shooter. An OICW. Stands for Objective Individual Combat Weapon. This weapon will kick serious ass. It's scheduled to go to our troops next year, but we got it now, and we're going to use it. Bobby?"

Getts took the gun from Peach's hands, and held it up. "Over and under barrels. The bottom fires a 5.56mm standard NATO round. Clip holds either 20 or 30 rounds. We'll use 30 on our missions and we'll tape 'em up in packages of three. The barrel up on top, shoots a 20mm high-explosive round from a six-round magazine . . ." Getts paused to listen to the incredulous murmurs from the troops. "And it's a killer. What really sets it apart from everything else on the face of the earth is the fire control and sighting system. Here, it has an optics selector for firing during the day or night, and a 6X zoom lens laser ranging system, dead certain to be on target at one thousand meters." After collective gasps, Getts continued. "That's right. We won't carry traditional sniping equipment anymore. This baby will do it all. The 20mm HE round contains a proximity fuse. You don't have to make contact with the target. The laser sighting system will automatically set your fuses to explode either on impact, with a delay if you choose, or in an area. The laser range finder measures the distance to the target and communicates that data to a computer chip built into the fuse of the HE round, which calculates the detonation time. This is a real force multiplier, people. Ten of us can take on a company of infantry. Don't take it home to hunt deer."

Peach spoke again. "All right. We're going to have chow, then we're going to fall out on the firing range and learn how to become instant killers."

That night Rabbi, his khaki-colored raincoat draped carelessly over his shoulders, stepped through the front door of 19 Nimbus Street and onto its porch. He looked up and down the entire street. Rabbi noted that two cars, both dark in color, were parked on opposite sides of the street. Nothing untoward seemed present. Two women pushed a baby carriage slowly down a sidewalk.

Most house lights were out at this hour, and street lamps emitted a kind of golden halo, diffusing an eerie glow in the misty evening. Rabbi, a man of long experience in darkness, preferred less illumination. Still, he satisfied himself with the layout of the street and made a movement with his hand. At once, the two car engines fired into life and pulled rapidly into position in front of Number 21. The car on the opposite side of the street made a U-turn, positioning itself behind the larger sedan. Car doors opened. Men stepped out and waited. Their coats were open, and anyone standing in Rabbi's position could see that under them were slings containing automatic weapons.

With another flick of his head, Rabbi exited the house with a group of bodyguards, including Ebber and Benjamine. Benjamine and Ebber scanned the length of the street. They knew from their advance recon that they would have an easy ride to the outskirts of the city. Each car was heavily armored, with four-inch hardened glass on each of the windows. Rabbi, armed with an automatic weapon, entered the second car.

Maas stood alone with the housekeeper, who had her own two small bags packed.

"Where will he go?" the old woman asked.

"Boston, Massachusetts," Maas said. "Rich in American history."

"Ah, well, then," she said. "I hope he enjoys seeing it all."

"Each life has a different value, Missus. His might increase."

The two automobiles pulled away from the house, the security car accelerating past the limousine into the lead. Both cars ignored the stop sign at the intersection. As the cars slowed to make the next turn, a manhole cover placed precisely in the middle of the road moved to one side. A black-shrouded head emerged from the sewer cover and pointed an RPG at the approaching cars, firing a rocket at the limousine.

The limousine was ripped apart by the extraordinary impact, the charge designed to penetrate tank amour. The limousine was disemboweled, its occupants killed outright. It free-wheeled out of control, burning, careening across the street, jumping a curb, and coming to rest upon a well-manicured lawn.

From the same manhole, a second RPG appeared in the hands of a shooter who fired again, this time launching a missile at the lead car. Attempting to reverse directions in midstreet, the sedan was struck directly in the front of the engine. The two guards in the front seat were wounded severely, the three in the rear seat, including Rabbi, managed to escape the fire that followed, hurling themselves out the door.

Seeing the carnage from the house, Maas sprang into action. He raced for the front door, retrieving an automatic shotgun, then ran as fast as his legs would carry him toward the manhole. When he arrived, the heavy cover was being replaced. Fingers protruded through two of the four ventilation holes while the person below attempted to wrestle the cover back into position. Before they disappeared, Maas jammed a heavy heel onto them, breaking them but, more important, holding them in place.

Rabbi arrived, his face burned, traumatized from a concussion. Without wasting time on words, he placed his automatic weapon into one of the unoccupied ventilation holes and fired blindly. He and Maas heard grunting sounds that indicated they had scored some kind of hit.

Below, Conrad, still wearing a black hood, as did his three other colleagues, moved to activate the locking mechanism. The manhole cover was secure.

"Conrad!" yelled one wounded terrorist at his leader, who was dashing ahead of the others, leading the way out of the city's underground maze. Conrad hesitated. He saw the extent of his wounded mate, kissed him fully on the forehead, and left him with an extra magazine of ammunition and a grenade. "We need time. Remember, Wallid, you fight for the glory of Allah." Conrad then turned away to join three surviving terrorists making their escape.

"The next manhole," Rabbi snapped at one of his security men, Benjamine. "Try it. Then the next."

As Benjamine trotted down the length of the street, indiscriminate gunfire emerged from the sewer below Maas and Rabbi. They ran to keep their heads back out of range. After several moments, the firing stopped. Looking down the street, Maas saw that Benjamine had tried without success to raise a manhole cover, no doubt previously locked by the terrorists, and began moving off toward yet a third intersection.

As he stopped at the next cover, there was a loud explosion as the man below pulled the pin on a hand grenade, placed it onto his chest, and exited this transitory world.

Chapter Ten

The rural setting fifty miles northeast of Washington, D.C., was ideal horse country. Expanses of rolling green hills, oak trees, and white fencing were favored by those who had the time, interest, and, of course, the money, to breed horses.

One large house, set back among evergreen trees, expanses of manicured lawn, and a curving drive, dominated an elevation that overlooked a valley below. Built in the plantation style of 160 years ago, the house was surrounded by a variety of parked automobiles, all of them testifying to their owners' wealth. Among the flock of iron horses tended by gray-suited men who took turns speaking into small, hand-held radios, was a Buick belonging to the United States Army, and bearing the two stars of a Major General. From outside, strands of Dave Brubeck jazz played by a capable group provided afternoon entertainment that could be heard above genteel laughter and the burble of conversation.

A cocktail party was in progress with smart, fashionably dressed people milling about, talking in groups, taking small bites of food from one of several tables covered with white linen and piled with sumptuous dishes. French doors were opened from the living room into a patio area and the pool beyond.

General Lathrop appeared uncomfortable out of his uniform. It seemed to the more stylish Washington guests that career military types buy civilian clothes with the idea of wearing them only a few times each year, therefore spending as little as possible on fabric and fit. They also tended to wear military stockings and service shoes. Black is black, brown is brown, after all. Lathrop clutched a tumbler of straight bourbon in fingers large enough to obscure most of the glass while speaking animatedly to an old man who wore an ill-fitting toupee. He was Senator Toby Johns, member of the Budget Committee as well as chairman of the Armed Services Committee, and while second most senior senator in the capitol, he was clearly, in his eighth decade of life, its most powerful.

Standing next to him was his third wife, Virginia, a physically attractive young lady in her late twenties. Others, paying homage, were standing as near as possible to the senator, hoping to catch a cosmic particle of the influence he emitted. Senator Johns seldom glowed more radiantly than when in the proximity of Cornelius Lathrop, a man he regarded as his moral and personally courageous equal. Senator Johns, having been deprived of the experience of actual combat by serving as a Washington liaison, with the rank of lieutenant, to the Seattle shipyards during World War II, had nevertheless managed to attain the rank of rear admiral in the Navy Reserve before his "retirement" twenty years past.

"You're not eating, General Lathrop," Senator Toby Johns said to his favored guest. "Virginia," he said turning to his wife, "see if you can't put together a plate of food for this hungry young man." Senator Johns affectionately patted the large-boned general upon his ample chest.

"I've already eaten from your fine table, Senator, thank you," the general responded.

Reacting to a gentle nudge from his young bride, Johns said, "You know my wife, Virginia, of course."

"Don't be silly, Toby," Virginia demurred from recognition. "I was just a secretary in your office when I was introduced to the general. He wouldn't remember me."

"You were always far more than just a secretary, Mrs. Johns. Everybody in Washington knows that," the general said graciously.

Mrs. Johns's smile increased in intensity until she was struck by the notion that Lathrop's response might have meant something else.

"Yes, I have leaned heavily on Virginia's help and guidance both at the office, and here at home, too," he said as he warmly patted the back of his wife's hand.

"I hate to impose on you in your own home, Senator

Johns, but I believe we have a problem. I'm going out of my chain of command, but . . ." the general began.

"You are doing no such thing, now, General," Johns interrupted, putting his arm up uncomfortably in order to get it around the larger man's broad shoulders. "We're friends. An' you call me Toby. Come on, let's talk."

The two men gravitated toward a small room off the study. It was unoccupied, so Senator Johns closed the door, leaving them alone. On a table was a cut glass decanter surrounded by small crystal tumblers.

"Brandy?" the senator asked.

"I'll stick with this, thank you," the general said.

The senator poured a drink for himself. "Well, Lath, nothing serious, I hope."

"In my judgment, we have a situation that could get out of hand. Far as I know, it might already be."

The senator's eyebrows arched at his unspoken concern.

Lathrop continued. "We've got a group of renegade soldiers playing cowboys and Indians. Unless we can get a handle on 'em, they could get this country into a lot of trouble."

"Renegades? Who are they?" the senator asked.

"That's part of the problem. I don't know who their commanding officer is . . . That is, I know what he calls himself, Senator, Commander Robert V. Getts. Navy. But that isn't his real name. I can't trace his service record. Nothing. And by God I've tried," the general said with energy.

"Well," the senator said, "what the hell are they supposed to be doing? Why hasn't my committee been briefed about these people?"

"I don't know for sure, sir, but my staff and I believe they're working in the counterterrorist business. As you know, Senator, I have first-rate commandos under me that can do the same damn job. We think this Getts character is going to roam all over the world including the Middle East. We also have reason to believe their whole operation is supported on the authority of the President."

"That asshole," Senator Johns said.

"I can't comment on that, sir."

"I can. If Elling is behind this, it must be a bad idea. He's never had a good one in his life. He knows if he tried to run it through my committee I'd shoot him down like a dog. That's why it's secret, you see," the senator said, certain of his deduction.

"What concerns me, uh, Toby, is that without our best military staff involved in planning and support of hot missions, they've got a chance to make us look stupid. Know what I mean, sir? Like that Delta fuckup in Iran."

"No question about it," Senator Johns replied. "All right, what do you need to get these squirrels back into their cages?"

"No matter what they have planned, they have to use communications. The National Security Agency monitors everything we put out. If I had access to NSA intercepts, I'd know their game plan," the general said.

"Okay, get in touch with Admiral Wrench. He runs the show over there."

General Lathrop frowned. "Admiral Wrench doesn't respond to our requests."

Senator Johns's sardonic grin reminded Lathrop of a piranha. "Then I'll get hold of Wrench myself. He can play ball on our team or apply for a job with AT&T as a switchboard operator." Senator Johns nodded his head emphatically.

Chapter Eleven

Colonel Barnes was briefing his boss, Bradley Wallis, and Commander Getts, who, as per his usual visits to the Carlisle Foundation, wore civilian clothes.

"They used an RPG on both cars," he said. "Standard PZF44 rocket. Made in Germany, but you can buy the same model from the Czech Republic or go for the Russian RPG7. They had four down there in the sewers, in case they missed with the first two."

"Were either of the Mossad cars armor plated?" Wallis asked Barnes.

"Wouldn't matter," Getts said.

"That's right," Colonel Barnes agreed. "That ordnance would penetrate tank armor. There wasn't much left of the man who blew himself up, but we took prints. No matches on anything we can get from DDI or the Agency."

"Was the poor fellow Arab?" Wallis asked.

"Probably. Hair samples suggest that," Barnes said.

"How many sewer gratings were locked from the inside?" Getts wanted to know.

"Six," Barnes said.

"In a straight line?" Getts said.

"Pardon?" Barnes said.

"Were they locked down in a row, like straight down Nimbus Street, or were they locked down in a circle around the neighborhood?"

"Ah," Barnes referred to his notes that included several sketches. "Looks like they went south three blocks, then the next lock-downs were to the west."

"Was there a lock-down on each side of the house on Nimbus Street, or just one?"

Barnes again glanced at his notes. "One."

"Anybody get out of the lead car?" Getts asked.

"Yes," Barnes responded without needing to refer to notes. "The missile struck the front left wheel area and exploded inside the engine block. All five men got out alive, but the two in the front seat, nearest the blast, were wounded. One serious, one critical. The driver . . ." Barnes paused. "Do you want his name?"

Getts shook his head.

"Driver died this morning. The others are stable."

"Good god," Wallis said, turning his back on Barnes. "Six men."

"How far away was the lead car from the manhole cover when it got hit?" Getts wanted to know.

"About 20 meters, give or take," Barnes responded.

"Lucky that PG round didn't hit the car a few more feet back. It would have taken out everybody," Getts responded.

"Yes, I suppose we're lucky about that," Wallis agreed.

"Possibly," said Getts. "But something still bothers me. Why didn't they nail down sewer covers all around the house at Nineteen Nimbus? Why didn't they nail down the one at the far end of the street?"

Barnes was already nodding his head as he said the words. "Because they already knew where Tomaz was going."

"Right on," Getts agreed.

Each man in the room kept his thoughts to himself for several minutes. Finally, Wallis spoke. "Frankly, when you told us what the defector said about a mole, I didn't believe it. I still don't."

"Believe it," Getts said with finality. "And we know where to look."

"And where is that?" Wallis demanded.

"Somebody sitting in the backseat of the first car who knew that a well-aimed shot with an RPG would only cripple the car, not destroy it completely. Or maybe somebody not in the car at all," Getts ventured.

"Like Maas," Colonel Barnes thought aloud. "He did the planning. Gave the orders."

"You're talking about the Mossad. There has never, and I repeat never, been anything close to a traitor in that group of people. The very essence of background investigation is defined by them. Why, we adopted most of their methods when I was with MI6," Wallis fumed.

"You think it was one of us, Bradley?" Getts asked, softly. "Me? Or Barnes, here? Or you? Hell, you Brits are famous for selling out."

"Damn you, Getts!" Wallis roared, "I resent that. Do you hear? I want your apology at once!"

Getts smiled wanly. "If you want an apology Brad, you can have it. But you're just pissed off because good men were killed by a rat."

Wallis rose stiffly from his chair and walked slowly toward the door. His voice was almost a whisper. "Of course you're right, Robert. No one is above suspicion. All right, Fanus is real. And if he's real, then they know who you are. Be careful, Robert." He opened the door and closed it behind him.

Rabbi was using a cane to walk as he paced. Getts leaned backward against an iron railing built above a cement retaining wall along the Potomac River. His face was flushed red, and not from the chill of the day.

"Well," the ancient spy spat at Getts, "Tomaz was

wrong. He was wrong in thinking that we could protect him."

"I can vouch for my people," Getts said.

"You will excuse me if I don't have my people executed on the strength of your reassuring words, Commander," Rabbi said.

"Someone in our organization thinks Maas is your mole, Rabbi," Getts said casually. "Some think it's you."

Rabbi stopped pacing and leaned heavily on his cane as he put his face close to Getts's. "That should cover just about everyone, eh? All of us Jews, anyway. And as for you, Getts, even repeating those kinds of words makes it hard to work with you again."

Rabbi turned to go, but quickly stopped, and faced Getts. "If you had been doing the work your country has paid you to do, you would know that your NSA has intercepted two signals from Fanus."

Getts did not know this, and his eyes betrayed him.

Rabbi's face lit up with unhidden pleasure at Getts's reaction. The spy went on. "They were sourced from New York the day before Tomaz was ambushed and my men were murdered. It may also amaze you to learn that I have not been out of this city in more than ten days, a fact to which Maas and others will swear. Unless you think, Getts, that we're all in this together."

Getts watched the older man hobble down the riverside walk. He did not bother wondering how Rabbi had been privy to signal reports out of NSA. He was, after all, a man of incredible resources and held in great respect within the Western world of espionage. No, Getts knew that to probe Rabbi's already well-known service record would only further strain relations with a badly needed ally. And Getts had further need of the aging spy.

Chapter Twelve

Conrad rented a conservative BMW in Frankfurt, then drove leisurely south to Stuttgart, turning southeast toward Augsburg.

From an Augsburg parking lot, he caught a train to Munich and then a cab to the airport. He carried a garment bag over his shoulder along with a smaller fabric utility piece. He entered the international terminal, found a rest room, and stepped inside. He took his time washing his face, combing his hair while other passengers came and went, paying him no special attention. When he had finished grooming, his upper lip was covered with a neat mustache, he was wearing dark-rimmed correction glasses and shoes that elevated his height almost two inches. He carried a passport with a photograph of suitable likeness that bore the name of Jacob Bartholoma, age thirty-four. He passed easily through security toward the flight concourses.

His carry-on bag moved smoothly through the X-ray machine, revealing none of the false passports contained in the linings of the case. He checked his garment bag through to New York via British Overseas Airlines.

He had, as usual, made not less than three reservations, including one on Lufthansa. He retired to an open-sided café and ordered coffee and a croissant. When boarding time neared for the BOAC departure, he decided to wait for the Lufthansa flight instead, knowing that he could claim his garment bag at the same airport in New York.

Conrad flew first class, as was his custom. It fitted the image of a successful business man he intended to project, and it was more comfortable than coach. As the hours passed, he covered himself with a wool blanket, politely declining both alcohol and dinner. In fact, he had found himself with a pleasant loss of appetite since the fortuitous passing of Lisa's lightly lamented husband, Alexander, only a few months ago.

The latter's estate was quite substantial and complex. Family and corporate attorneys were only beginning to assess the value of Hohelganz's holdings. Meantime, however vexing it was to appear properly mournful of Alexander's loss for Lisa's sake, there had been weeks of excitement in his life that had been unmatched for more than a decade.

Lisa was not unemotional about the abrupt passing of her husband, but her sexual relationship and deep love for Conrad was in a place entirely apart from her memory of Alexander. Or from any other man, for that matter.

Their intimacy went beyond sex. There was nothing they could not discuss. They were more than symbiotic, they were one. There was a single secret that Conrad kept from Lisa but one that he would share with her when they had settled safely in Syria. She would not only understand, he thought; she would want to participate in his work. He had resolved long ago, however, never to expose Lisa to danger of any kind. She would have to be content to share the life of a freedom fighter vicariously.

He was not yet sure about her children.

Conrad, alias Jacob Bartholoma, was given only cursory examination as he entered the United States and passed through customs at Kennedy International Airport. He took a shuttle to the BOAC terminal, claimed his garment bag, and rented a car at Avis. He placed his luggage in the trunk of the car and took the Van Wyck Expressway to Highway 25. He crossed the Queensboro Bridge then followed East River Drive as he had so often in the past, to an address on 120th Street in Manhattan.

He planned to spend only a few minutes in the offices of the Arab-American League, long enough to drop off a package for Mr. Hixx, so he parked his rental car at the curb rather than in a subterranean garage provided for guests and tenants at exorbitant rates.

Less than an hour later, he returned to his car to find it vandalized, its radio and tape deck stolen. The trunk, however, was not touched, and his luggage was safe. Conrad cursed crime in general, his stupidity in particular. He drove in a light drizzle to La Guardia Airport, left his car not with Avis but in the general terminal area. He could not afford to deal with people at the car rental counter over the stolen radio. He entered a public lot and parked the car in the first open spot. He left the keys in the ignition, the doors unlocked, then caught a shuttle bus to the terminals. He had multiple reservations as usual, and was able to travel business class on American Airlines to LAX. Twenty minutes later, he stepped aboard. As he settled into the relative luxury of the aircraft, he smiled. He was contemplating the removal of the single most important threat against his life, Commander Bobby Getts.

Back in New York City, Avis Car Rentals had reported one of their automobiles thirty-six hours overdue. A trace was begun to locate Herr Jacob Bartholoma of the *Kalte Roll Stahl Mühlen, Stuttgart.* The assistant director of personnel at Cold Roll Steel Mills of Stuttgart informed the Avis caller that Herr Jacob Batholoma was no longer employed there because of his death four years prior. After a delay of several hours, the personnel officer obligingly supplied the Avis representative with Herr Bartholoma's last known address.

The Avis insurance coordinator, by now certain that fraud had been involved in the rental and probable theft of one of their automobiles, routinely filled out a police report and filed it with New York City Police, Interpol in Germany, and eventually the FBI, for information purposes.

Chapter Thirteen

The USSR had manufactured 36,000 rounds of weapons-quality anthrax artillery rounds, each with 10 kg yields for their massive but mobile 180mm S-23 gun. The heavy cannon and its projectiles were an integral part of the Warsaw Pact forces that faced the Western NATO armies until the end of the Cold War in 1991. Among the many bio-weapon storage facilities were the "crystal" bunkers at Neustrelitz, East Germany. With the disintegration of the USSR and gradual withdrawal of the Red Army back to the confines of Russia, chemical and biological warheads were also moved.

As the fortunes of the Russian economy foundered on the shoals of the nation's economic low tide, its military forces, once the pride of that preeminent world power the USSR, were among the hardest hit. In the social chaos that ensued, Russian foot soldiers went unpaid, reduced to begging in the streets for food. Field grade officers drove taxis to make up for their absent income, and Russian military pilots gave rides to tourists in complex combat aircraft for enough money to buy fuel for their planes.

Along with military ennui came indifference about maintaining inventory records. The Russian government became a huge rummage sale of military weaponry for international shoppers. They were bargainers for every Third World nation or well-financed revolutionary forces who needed aircraft, tanks, field artillery, trucks, machine guns, ammunition, night vision equipment, and all the other vital ingredients that go into making modern warfare.

Keeping track of its vast materiel was more than the disordered Red quartermaster corps could manage, even had had it the will to do so. Soldiers, now working for themselves, sold everything they could get their hands upon. The biological artillery shells of Neustrelitz were moved in 1993 first to Yekaterinburg, Russia, where they were originally developed, then, in that same year, to antiquated bunkers located in Belgorod, Russia.

Belgorod was 120 km from Kursk, site of the largest tank battle ever fought in history. Belgorod was conveniently located near rail centers and excellent highways. When the senior officer in charge of the KZ-12 weapons storage facility there was approached by Conrad several months earlier, the devious terrorist offered him a way to secure his future—and that of his extended family. Major Vladimir Valitnikov realized that he would have to take more than a dozen others into his confidence, but there would be enough money to make shared risk worthwhile. His offer of 50,000 Swiss francs plus the cost of fuel for a flight to Prague was snapped up by the pilots and their crew of an

An-26. The twin-engine cargo plane had a 1,400 mile range with a payload of 120,000 pounds, more than enough to transport the 4,600 pound biological shells and their shock-proof inconel canisters. Each container was plainly marked *ORE SAMPLES.*

After Major Valitnikov paid his colleagues generously for "adjusting" storage records for the stolen rounds and transporting them to the airfield, he was still left with more than $1 million American in the form of Swiss bonds. As he stood watching the Antonov lifting easily into an overcast sky, he could not help but grin.

The apartment building on *Northsea-Weg* in Bremerhaven was part of a modern complex of urban condominiums and hotels designed near the waterfront area of the German port city. It was a successful venture, invigorating an otherwise decaying part of the industrial area. Conrad took an elevator to the twenty-third floor of the building and knocked on the door of apartment 2206. It was answered by a waiter in a white serving jacket. "I am Ernst Jung. Colonel Schneller is expecting me."

The waiter nodded and stepped back for Conrad to enter. In the center of the large suite was a well-laid table of lobster and other dishes. A champagne bucket sat at the elbow of Colonel Sig Schneller. Conrad judged his age at about forty-five. A linen bib was tied about his neck as he stood to greet his guest. He was not tall, a bit shorter than Conrad, barrel-chested, with large forearms and thick neck. What remained of his thinning hair was cropped well above the ears. "Ah, Herr Jung," he said, hand extended. "I am dining late this evening. Please join me."

"I have had dinner, thank you," Conrad said, seating himself in a chair.

"Champagne, then?" Schneller offered.

"Coffee, if you have it."

Schneller motioned to the waiter, who poured coffee into a porcelain cup. Schneller spoke a few words in crude French to the waiter who immediately withdrew. "They still hate us. They make good cooks but poor soldiers." Schneller laughed at his own humor, then eyed Conrad with interest. "Now, then, Herr Jung, down to business, eh? What may I do for you?"

"To the point—I need well-trained men who can handle guns. I am told you are in the business," Conrad said.

Schneller continued to eat. "What do you need them for?"

"I am expecting a valuable cargo to arrive in Prague within three days. It will travel by train to Marseilles. I want it protected," Conrad said.

"And the cargo?" Schneller said.

"That is not your business."

"But the kind of personnel required to guard a shipment will depend upon what it is they are being asked to guard," Schneller said.

"I will tell you how many men I will need, and I will tell you the kind of equipment they will carry," Conrad said.

Colonel Schneller's jaws stopped chewing as his he wiped drawn butter from the edges of his mouth with a white linen napkin. "I am the military expert here, Herr Jung. Not you."

"I am the buyer, Colonel Schneller. As it is my money, I give the orders," Conrad said.

Schneller regarded Conrad for several moments. "I provide outstanding personnel. And support equipment. They do not work cheaply. Do you have $1 million, Herr Jung?"

"Is that your price?" Conrad asked.

"Not necessarily, but military operations are luxuries only for the rich, make no mistake."

Conrad rose. "Of course. Here is a list of men and equipment I believe we shall need. I'll be back here tomorrow at 10:00 P.M. By the way, I understand that you have an employee by the name of Southwith?"

Schneller's eyes widened with surprise. "Ja. He is a lieutenant of mine. Why do you ask?"

"I would like to meet him. Can it be arranged?"

"Anything can be arranged," the colonel said turning back to his meal, "for a price."

Getts was pleased with the progress of Blacklight in their efforts to achieve precision teamwork. They had flown to Panama to exercise in the Army's Special Warfare jungle Ranger school, ten weeks of rugged warfare that tested the endurance, navigation, and survival skills of each member. But Getts had expected them all to do well in the course since most of the Blacklight team had similar training in the past. What was key to their relentless training program was the durability of their psyches to operate efficiently under extreme pressure.

Taking more than a page from the navy's Seal 6 team, Getts, and Peach put Blacklight troopers into civilian clothes and provided them with urban warfare weapons and ammunition. In cities along the eastern seaboard, they practiced infiltrating airports, placing "bombs" aboard aircraft, penetrating "secure" buildings, and setting up selected targets to be removed by a variety of deadly means. At port locations, they surreptitiously boarded ships, "took over" command, and simulated sabotage to machinery and communications.

Getts sometimes materialized before, during, or after a training operation as his schedule permitted, but Peach was a constant in their honing of a cohesive unit. If Getts was unable to see Peach personally, he talked to him every day via secure land lines.

They now met in a Manhattan cafe on West 54th Street. Peach ordered chicken-fried steak, Getts went for roast turkey with rice. Each drank local beer. "How are the women doing?" Getts asked.

"Carla can sure shoot a fuckin' gun. Did you know that she made the U.S. Olympic team in riflery?" Peach said.

"It's on her record. Maybe we should send her to the marine sniper course," Getts said.

Peach shrugged. "Suits me. We loaded her down with seventy pounds of ammunition and some food, and she ran all over the goddamn mountains in Panama. Never slowed us up, never asked for a break."

"How about Toni?"

"She's got guts. She's not as strong as she should be, but she's a quick study and doesn't mind pulling the trigger, either," Peach said.

"Feed her bananas and put her ass to work in the weight room four hours a week. How about the force multipliers?"

"They love 'em. If it wasn't such hard work, I think they'd wear their helmets to bed," Peach said.

"I hope so, because we're going into action soon. Get 'em back to McReynolds. Check out all our gear, then let them have some time off—except for Carla and Razorback." Getts thought a moment. "Anybody else speak German?"

"Sneezy. He's pretty good," Peach said.

"Okay, send those three over to Germany. I'll provide you with the address when I know what it is. Make sure you can get the others back within eight hours."

"Where in Germany are you going to be while I'm doing the hard work?" Peach asked.

"Bonn. Conrad's a kraut, not much doubt about that."

"Going alone?"

"I'm meeting Rabbi there," Getts said.

"What about commo?" Peach asked.

"Sat phones will do. I don't think Conrad's people are running radio intercepts," Getts said. He was referring to PR-2000 telephones that could be carried in a briefcase or even in a pocket. The PR-2000 uplinked to a defense satellite anywhere in the world, which would then downlink the signal to a designated ground receiver. That, and the handheld GPS that could navigate the user to any spot on the surface of the earth to within a single meter, were the most valuable tools in the bag of insurgency forces. The PR-2000 was not 100 percent security proof, but it was close. "Just be careful."

"I'm glad it's you going and not me," Peach said.

Getts boarded an administrative military flight from Andrews Air Force Base that took him directly to Bonn, Germany. An envelope with his name on it was left with the Officer of the Day. There, he politely declined the use of a military car in favor of using public transportation to the address listed inside the envelope.

Bad Honnef am Rhein was a small, nonindustrialized community on the Rhine River a scant twelve kilometers south of Bonn. The hotel to which Getts had directions on 137 Freiheit-Weg was a rather old but recently remodeled twelve-story building. Getts paid the cab driver, then carried his own bag to the desk and checked in. Before Getts could unpack, there was a knock on his door. Rabbi was wearing suspenders to hold up his trousers because, Getts suspected, he was visibly losing weight. He wondered if Rabbi was ill.

"Come in. Have a good trip?" Getts said.

"Yes. I know the city well," Rabbi said as he followed Getts into his room. "I enjoyed seeing it again." Rabbi walked around the fourth-floor suite, admiring the decor, a mix of baroque and modern tastefully interwoven to conserve the rich textural history of a building that was likely more than one hundred years old.

"How is Bradley?" Rabbi said.

"He's tired of the business, he says. I think he means it this time."

"Aren't we all," Rabbi said. The aging spy looked out of a window at the city below. "I was born ten kilometers from here. Did you know that?"

"No. I thought you were a desert rat."

"Yes, well, that came later. My father was born in the same house and never lived anywhere else until he died," Rabbi said.

"Like Kant," Getts suggested a comparison with the German philosopher who, in his lifetime, ventured no farther than sixty miles from his town of Königsberg. "We need telephones," Getts said, changing the subject.

"I've arranged to use a room at the state security police headquarters. They have made space for us in their basement near Cologne. I told them we would be in tomorrow," Rabbi said. "Tonight, I attend synagogue. You might want to rest."

"I'm impressed with your faith," Getts said, and meant it.

"You shouldn't be, Commander Getts. I haven't been inside a synagogue in years. I am a very bad Jew."

"How about this room?" Getts asked. "Is it clean?"

"We already sanitized it. The state security police use it for guests and meetings. If there are bugs in here, they are probably ours," he said. He then lowered his voice as he spoke again. "We confirmed a bit of information omitted by Tomaz," Rabbi said. "He was a graduate of the Bekka Valley academies. Ras Kilal, Tomaz's colleague in Libya, was caught three days ago in Toulouse with a briefcase full of plastique. He was an aide to al-Omar." Getts knew of an al-Omar, who ranked high in the Hizbollah. He would verify this later.

"I don't understand why he told us about Fanus. I don't think he was playing both sides," Getts said.

"You are naive."

"Nope. Conrad knows about Blacklight. And most likely he knows who I am.

"Who caught Kilal?" Getts said.

"Deuxième Bureau," Rabbi said. "Kilal was delighted to trade the names of his comrades in training school for the use of his hands. Your DDI can match the fingerprints taken with those of Ahmad Hassou. He was one who got away with Conrad."

"You people do good work," Getts said.

Rabbi shrugged, a smile tugging at his mouth. "We try. Well, he was bound to find out sooner or later."

"He?"

"Conrad," the Israeli said.

Getts watched as Rabbi poured himself a glass of water. "Yes. A man who matches the general description of Conrad rented a car in New York," Getts said as he watched Rabbi. "He was in disguise, of course. He scribbled directions on a piece of paper, which was later found in the car. The writer was lefthanded. The note was written with an expensive pen. Not a ballpoint. The people at the rental agency thought his voice sounded cultured. I think it's even money that Conrad lives well and has always lived well."

"What will your security people do with that intelligence?" Rabbi said.

"Wallis has people checking hotel reservations in New York and Los Angeles," Getts said.

"And?"

"Nothing's come up yet. It's a big job," Getts said.

Rabbi rubbed his eyes and pushed his bifocals over his nose. He allowed the glasses to fall into place again as he gazed languidly out of a window.

"I want us to come up with a list of every possible male terrorist who is between the age of twenty-two and forty-five," Getts said. "I think that Conrad might have a medical history. So I want to look first at any German who has ever been arrested for criminal behavior that would fall into the category of social protest; neo-left rosters; PLO and IRA publication subscription lists, student movements, campus extremists, anybody on police quarterly lists . . ."

"Those are not public information, Getts," Rabbi interrupted, softly.

"But you can get the cooperation of national police.

They'll give the Mossad anything you ask because they have a guilty conscience. True?"

"Broad parameters, Commander."

"If you have better ideas lay 'em on me," Getts said. "I've got three of my people arriving tomorrow to help. They all speak German."

Chapter Fourteen

Conrad could hear faint, distant crowd noises as he knocked on Colonel Schneller's door. It was opened shortly by a man in his late twenties. He was perhaps an inch over six feet and had a body, poorly hidden under loose fitting clothing, that had been assiduously fashioned by hard work. The man had a round, angry, burn scar on his neck near his windpipe. His nose was patrician, aiding to create the impression that he was looking down at others, perhaps in disfavor. "Herr Jung?" he said. "I'm Perkins Southwith." Southwith was obviously English and spoke in the accent of the upper class. He stepped back to allow Conrad to enter the suite.

Colonel Schneller's broad back was to Conrad while the mercenary looked through high-powered binoculars, mounted on a tripod, at something below. Conrad moved closer out of curiosity and looked over the side of the balcony. The view was of a racetrack, with a horse race in progress. Bright lights and the muted sound of roaring crowds provided a show that evidently interested the German soldier for hire, but held no fascination for Conrad.

"Ah, Herr Jung . . ." he said. "Something to drink? No? Let us sit where we can see a map." Schneller motioned Conrad to an overstuffed sofa that had been moved to face a large map mounted on a wall. The map was a projection of western Europe including territories from the Ural mountains in Russia to Spain and west Africa.

"Before we begin, Herr Jung, did you bring the money?" Schneller said.

"I did," Conrad said.

Southwith sat near Conrad while Schneller took up a pointer with which he touched locations on the map. "Good. We have made preliminary studies of various rail routes from the 'black earth' regions of Russia toward the west. We will provide you with specific routes to travel from . . . I believe you said Prague . . . to Marseille when we have completed our agreement. I can guarantee delivery of your cargo, of course."

"I have three million Swiss francs invested in this enterprise. Are you able to indemnify me against loss?" Conrad said.

"Absolutely," Schneller responded.

Conrad looked at Perkins Southwith. The Englishman looked impassively straight ahead.

"How much will it cost me?" Conrad said.

"Seven hundred fifty thousand U.S. dollars," Schneller said.

Conrad was silent for a moment. Then, "Does that include your personal fee, Colonel?"

"It does."

Conrad mused for a long minute before speaking. "Your guarantee is ludicrous. Your personal fee is exorbitant, and you don't have the assets to assure even the lease payments on this gaudy apartment."

The German exhaled, sitting slowly back into his overstuffed chair. He waved his hand in a defeated gesture. "Let us not argue. Suppose you tell me what you have in mind."

"I have something like this in mind," Conrad said. He casually rose to his feet, produced a Lambretta 9mm pistol from his pocket and shot the German through the heart.

Perkins Southwith reached slowly inside his lightweight jacket and retrieved a package of American cigarettes. He placed a filter tip in his mouth and lit it. He let the smoke curl slowly into the air, then turned his gaze toward Conrad.

"Your reputation," Conrad said to Southwith, "is considerably better than that of your late employer."

"Thank you."

"I have a special assignment for you," Conrad said as he removed a photograph from his pocket. "This is Robert Getts. He leads a group called Blacklight. Getts is well-trained in special warfare, and he is very smart. He is also an extreme threat to me. I want you to kill him."

Southwith studied the photo with interest. "I don't know the face. If he is in our business . . ."

"You don't know him because he has been protected. Getts is not his real name, of course. Not even the U.S. Army knows who he really is. But I know," Conrad said, allowing himself an assured smile.

"Then I'll need to know it as well," Southwith said.

"Of course. Can you do it?"

"If I can't perform the work, it can't be done," Southwith said with confidence that equaled Conrad's own. "How about the train? Do you still want the men?"

"Fifteen men is enough for the task. Eight on the train, seven in support. They should be lightly armed but with enough ammunition to feed the appetite of a weapon such as the Sweden M45. It's excellent for close work, but does well at 150 meters. Do you agree?" Conrad asked.

"Yes, a good choice," Southwith said. "We should also have night scopes."

"Of course. Your fee will be $400,000 from which you will pay all costs. Agreed?" Conrad said.

"Not if you include the work to be done on Getts," the Englishman asked.

"Six hundred thousand, and I won't haggle," Conrad said.

"Then I agree. Your cargo is valuable, I assume. Would you like to tell me what it is?"

"No. You don't need to know," Conrad said.

"We have frontiers to cross, inspectors to bribe," the Englishman said.

"They are my responsibility. But if you find yourself in an unforeseen emergency from which money will get you out, count on me to reimburse you. The train will leave Prague in thirteen days." Conrad removed a thick envelope containing cash from his pocket and handed it to Southwith.

"Here is my telephone number," Southwith said, writing it on a card. "I will be there for the next forty-eight hours. After that I'll be at the Chancellor Hotel in Prague."

          *   *   *

Captain Rudi Kubichenko had known about the money being spent lavishly by certain personnel at the KZ-12 facility at Belgorod. It took little effort to follow the trail of money from an enlisted corporal directly to station commander Major Valitnikov. Valitnikov, however, was a much tougher nut to crack than the corporal, and Captain Kubichenko worked around the clock for 36 hours before Valitnikov finally confessed. He dutifully reported his information up the line to Moscow.

Times at Dzerzhinsky Square had changed mightily in the past few years, and when General Nikolai Glavnoyi in the reorganized First Department digested the import of Valitnikov's confession, he perceived that sharing intelligence with the West would be wise both politically and practically.

Every national police agency has a quarterly file, consisting of men and women who pose a particular threat to someone high in the government, such as a president or a cabinet officer, even a visiting dignitary. They may have written a threatening letter or placed a call to a public figure, or they may have acted out their antipathy and failed. They may have been mental patients or still may be. They may have belonged to an organization that advocated the use of violence or the unlawful overthrow of government. Their names are kept on permanent record, pictures and fingerprints attached, and as lengthy a biography as possible.

Getts was hoping Conrad was on a quarterlies list.

The *Bundeshaus*, or parliament building, along with most of Germany's federal buildings, was located in the south part of Bonn near the banks of the Rhine. The buildings that housed the *Deutsche Staatsicherheit*, or German State Security Police, were several miles north of the city toward Cologne. Few people knew of their existence, since their physical location was not made public. The buildings were unobtrusively guarded, grounds well landscaped with heavy green hedges concealing cyclone fencing and barbed wire. The complex might be taken for a public utility or warehouse area.

In yet another section of the main campus, set in a basement on a south wing, was a division apart from the daily administration of routine state security called *Besonderer Fall Planen,* or Special Case Planning.

In eight days, with no time out for rest, Getts, Carla, Razorback, Sneezy, and Rabbi had gone through almost all of the German quarterly files, verifying through local authorities, the whereabouts and activities of those in the computer system.

"Why do I get the feeling," Getts said to no one in particular, "that Conrad died, moved out of the country or went underground?"

"I have the same notion, Bobby," Carla said, her nose still buried in a police printout of a left-wing student list. The list was seven years old.

"Fucks up my sleep," Sneezy said, yawning.

"You mean you've been getting sleep?" Razorback said.

"That isn't what I said, now is it? Didn't I just say it fucked up my sleep? If it's fucking up my sleep, how can I be sleeping?" Sneezy snapped.

Getts and Carla had been physically working out for 45 minutes each day at the extensive facilities on the *Deutsch Staatsicherheit* campus, but still found themselves struggling to stay awake. Razorback and Sneezy catnapped in their chairs for a few minutes at a time, a regimen that seemed to work for them. Rabbi alone seemed indefatigable, focused, resolute. They tried to eat regular meals, but salads wilted and bread turned stale before they remembered to consume them. They found that keeping fresh fruit nearby helped. Their work area soon turned into apple and banana groves of half-eaten fruits, with discolored peels scattered about.

A telephone connected into a hotline number rang on Getts's desk. He picked it up. "Yes," he said. "Getts here."

"Hello, Bobby," Bradley Wallis's voice sounded unmistakable and clear over the Atlantic ocean. "How are you getting along with my friend Rabbi?"

"I'm getting tired of looking at his face," Getts said, looking at Rabbi.

"Give him my best wishes," Wallis said.

"What's up?" Getts said.

"Any leads?" Wallis ignored the direct question.

"I didn't realize there were so many mental cases outside of America. Not yet, though," Getts said, exhaling. "We don't have anything worth going after with a team."

Getts waited for Wallis to continue.

"This could be nothing, of course, but a gentleman who runs United Airlines in Europe called his home office in Chicago. He told them that a German business traveler had his suitcase delivered to his home in Kronberg after it got temporarily lost by baggage handlers. His name was listed on the passenger manifest as Jacob Bartholoma, but the man they delivered the bag to was named Eisler. Erich von Eisler," Wallis said.

"That's it?" Getts said.

"Not all. It seems that Avis car rentals in New York rented a car to a man by the name of Jacob Bartholoma. The car was damaged and left in the general parking area of the airport."

"Did they run a trace on him?" Getts said.

"They tried, but apparently Jacob Bartholoma has been dead for four years," Wallis said.

"Hmm. Give me Eisler's address in Kronberg." Getts scribbled on a pad. "Thanks, Bradley. We'll have a talk with Herr Eisler." Getts hung up the telephone and walked into an adjoining room where Carla, Razorback, and Sneezy were working the phones.

"Hey Razorback, tired of dialing for dollars? I want a man interviewed. His name is Eisler, and he lives in Kronberg." Getts said.

"No problemo," Razorback answered, rising from his chair.

"Did you say Kronberg?" Rabbi piped up. "I know the town. I might even know Eisler," he said.

"I could use the help. Come on along," Razorback said.

The odds against striking gold with this next swing of the pick were remote, all agreed, but certainly worth a two hundred kilometer trip. Getts was grateful that the elder spy could go, since his experience with multifaceted interrogation techniques could be invaluable.

The town of Kronberg might have been copied from a postcard advertising the beauty of Europe. Razorback had almost forgotten the mission that brought them to this special city and the extraordinary mansions that marked their route.

It was already dark when the two men arrived at an old, well-tended estate belonging to the Eisler family. Razorback was groggy and hungry. The two men stood in front of the massive main door while Rabbi rang a bell.

The door opened slightly to reveal the figure of a short, hunched, elderly man.

"Ja?" the butler inquired of the strangers before him.

"Polizei Sache," Rabbi stated. *"Ist Herr Eisler zu Hause?"*

"Ja, aber . . ."

"Sagen Sie Herr Eisler daß Hauptmann Klaus und Herr Accardo hier sind," Rabbi ordered.

The butler inclined his head and stepped back to allow Rabbi and Razorback to wait inside the foyer. He then shuffled away, to inform Herr Eisler of their arrival. The butler soon returned, asking them to follow him.

Erich von Eisler, Razorback felt when first he laid eyes on him, was not Conrad. He was, among other things, not the right height. Clerks at both Lufthansa ticket counter in Munich and Avis car rental in New York could not remember details about Jacob Bartholoma except that he was well over six feet tall. While Eisler would not be regarded as short, he clearly was not tall. Nor, as he greeted Rabbi and Razorback, did he emanate the kind of animosity all terrorists show toward authority, the establishment, in spite of their best efforts to conceal it. Finally, few German social dissidents have sprung from such a lofty social status, at least since the 1960s to the mid-1970s, when to be against established societal strictures was *de rigueur.*

"Guten Abend, Herr Eisler," Rabbi said.

"Guten Abend," Conrad said, pleasantly.

"Es tüt mir leid, Sie zu belästigen," Rabbi apologized. *"Sprechen Sie englisch, Herr Eisler?"* he asked with great courtesy.

"Yes, of course I speak English," Conrad said easily. "Doesn't everyone, now?"

"My associate from America, Herr Eisler, Charles Accardo," Rabbi said, introducing Razorback.

Conrad extended his hand. "Delighted. Are you also a policeman, Herr Accardo?"

Razorback noticed that Eisler had not asked Rabbi for an identification card. Rabbi could have produced one had he been asked, but Eisler showed that he was not fearful of answering official questions. "Not exactly, Herr Eisler.

I'm kind of an interested party," Razorback responded. Over Conrad's shoulder he saw a beautiful woman with two children, a boy and a girl. The boy looked to be about seven years old, the girl a couple of years younger. They were meticulously dressed and their manners seemed impeccable.

Razorback nodded toward her as Rabbi spoke politely to the woman. "Frau Eisler, a pleasure," he said.

"Gentlemen, this is my friend, Frau Hohelganz," Conrad said.

"Oh," Razorback said, "pardon me. I thought . . ." The name meant nothing to Razorback, though the American commando saw Rabbi noticeably react.

"Ah, Frau Hohelganz. How do you do? Forgive us. We are sorry to intrude," Rabbi said.

Conrad had led the two men into a living area that was in fact a large den used by the family as a cozy evening room. A fire burned in the hearth. The children had recently played with toys on the floor while the adults, it seemed, had been reading.

"So. What is it?" Conrad inquired of Rabbi.

"Your name, Herr Eisler, is among many businessmen who travel on international flights. We are interested in learning from men, such as yourself about whether or not you have been approached by smugglers. What countries, airports, and the like," Rabbi lied.

"Well, it is true that I travel from time to time," Conrad said with an air of forbearance. "But I don't pay much attention to smugglers. I don't recall being approached, Inspector."

"Uh, *Hauptmann*," Rabbi corrected.

"Yes."

Conrad motioned with his hand for his visitors to sit while he took a place near Lisa. Razorback noticed that the boy, who was between his mother and Conrad when they sat down, moved to his mother's other side. Razorback dismissed the small signal as having no meaning. "You are in the oil business, Herr Eisler?" Rabbi ventured.

"Yes."

"A petroleum engineer, I believe."

"That is correct."

"And your work takes you to the Middle East, I suppose," Rabbi said.

"Not for some time. I have been in South America for the past several years."

Razorback noticed that Frau Hohelganz looked quickly at Eisler as though confused. But she said nothing. Razorback imagined that Erich von Eisler's line of work might cause long separations in their relationship. She was truly a beautiful woman, he mused. He found himself distracted by her composure and grace, by her eyes that seemed insightful yet innocent, like a doe's.

"May I offer you something to drink, gentlemen?" Conrad graciously offered.

Rabbi shook his head. "Thank you, no, Herr Eisler."

"Please," Conrad urged Razorback smoothly. "I have American bourbon."

"Okay. A little ice, if you have it," Razorback agreed.

Conrad fashioned the drink and poured himself a small amount of brandy into a snifter.

He handed the tumbler of liquor to Razorback, then raised his glass in salute to his guest. "To America," he toasted.

As Razorback sipped from his glass, he noticed that Eisler had hardly moistened his own lips with brandy.

"Tell me, Herr Accardo, just what do you have to do with finding smugglers who approach airline passengers?" Conrad asked blandly.

"We have the same problems in America, Herr Eisler. I'm here to watch and try to learn something," Razorback did not avert his eyes from Eisler's. When the German turned away, Razorback glanced at Lisa. Before he could speak to her, Conrad pursued his inquiry.

"Ah. But you say that you are not a policeman? You work for the American government, obviously. Are you an army man, Herr Accardo?"

Razorback regarded Conrad for a long moment. "Do I look like one?"

Conrad feigned embarrassment, "Oh, I am so sorry if I am, what do you say, pointing my face into your business."

Lisa laughed, tickled. "Nosey. That's what you are, Erich." Then, to Razorback, "He thinks he is so smart."

"I only mean it as a compliment, I assure you," the suave

terrorist said. "One pictures army men just as you are, Herr Accardo; sun bronzed, hard of muscle. I could feel your strength as we shook hands. And, if I were completing my imaginary portrait, I would guess that you know something of the martial arts. Professional soldiers do, don't they?"

Razorback realized that he had telegraphed his own message to Eisler. In not substituting a plausible reason for being with Rabbi on what was ostensibly a police matter, he might have carried a banner advertising his interest in . . . if not smugglers, then what?

"Are you a devotee of martial arts, Herr Eisler?" he asked.

"Ach, no, I am too much a house lizard. Lisa is disgusted with me," Eisler chuckled.

Razorback saw another quick shift of Lisa's eyes toward Eisler. She would not contradict him, but she could not hide her reaction of surprise. "United Airlines delivered a lost suitcase to this address. According to the airlines, the passenger's name was Bartholoma. Jacob Bartholoma," Razorback said. "Is that someone you know?"

"I hate to dispute the records of an efficient, powerful American airline, but in this case they are mistaken. My pun was intended," he chuckled. "My lost baggage was found on another airplane, but it had my own name on it. I use permanent name tags and my initials on my bags. Do you want to look at them?"

"Thank you, no, Herr Eisler. Frau Hohelganz," Rabbi said as he heaved himself to his feet. The Israeli spy apologized once more for invading Eisler's privacy. Eisler asked Lena the maid to show the two gentlemen to the door.

Razorback and Rabbi drove several kilometers in silence toward Saarbrücken. It was beginning to rain. Rabbi automatically reduced his speed, uncomfortable behind the wheel of any car, especially on a slick road.

"Smart man," Razorback said.

"Who? Eisler? Yes," Rabbi said. The tone of his voice seemed to suggest that he might have added "of course."

"Army. That was spooky."

"Spooky?"

"Strange. I mean, he could have guessed a lot of jobs

connected with the government. Even the embassy. But he said army," Razorback wondered almost to himself.

"Yes, well, he is an educated man," Rabbi said. "The guess was not so wild, I suppose."

"Know something?" Razorback said, a smile tugging at his mouth. "I don't think it was a lucky guess. I think Eisler could be our man."

"Conrad?" Rabbi asked. "Are you serious?"

"I think he's worth another look. Bobby can do it next time," Razorback said.

The gas gauge was moving slowly toward the empty mark and though he believed they could easily make it to Saarbrucken, Rabbi eased to a stop alongside the autobahn.

"Rest stop," Rabbi said, opening his door. By the woods and bushes near the highway.

"Again?" Razorback said.

"When I was your age I could hold on for many hours, but when old age attacks . . ." Rabbi shrugged.

"Prostate, huh? Guess I've got a few years to wait for that," the commando said.

Rabbi exited the automobile, and walked around to the passenger side of the car to shield himself from passing motorists. Razorback turned his head slightly away from the old man. Rabbi reached inside his overcoat and came up with a .22 pistol. Through the half-opened passenger window, he placed its barrel inches from Razorback's skull and pulled the trigger.

Razorback's body briefly convulsed, after which Rabbi opened the door with his free hand, closed his fingers around the dead American's collar, and dragged the body from the seat. Rabbi noted with satisfaction that the low-velocity bullet had caused no blood spatter on the interior of the car. He pulled the body near the shoulder of the road and rolled it into the thick vegetation. Then he stepped around the car, slid under the wheel, and drove off into the gloomy afternoon.

When Rabbi returned to the basement of German State Security Police Getts, Carla and Sneezy were still looking for promising names among the left-wing groups in the quarterly files. Getts asked where Razorback was. Rabbi, calmly making himself a cup of tea, said the interview with

Eisler was fruitless and that Razorback had stopped at the hotel to sleep. He would be in later at night.

Getts nodded and went about his business.

At 0100 hours that morning, Getts was brought a coded message from the Carlisle Foundation. Deciphered, it read: *Leave at once for Mozaisk, Russia. Meet with Captain Kubichenko. Aircraft waiting at Wiesbaden. Confirm. Wallis.*

Getts was waved through the gates of Wiesbaden Air Force Base and drove directly to BaseOps where, as Wallis had advised, a twin-engine courier jet was waiting for him on the ramp. It was wheels up at 0213 hours, and the aircraft covered the 1410 air miles to *Mozaisk* in less than three hours.

As the U.S. Air Force plane continued its descent into Mozaisk with Moscow in clear view on the horizon, Getts plumbed his memory for military information about the city. It had always been an important part of Moscow's air defense system, with large numbers of surface-to-air missile emplacements and corresponding radar installations girding its environs. In addition, he recalled that most of the important departments of Russia's Foreign Intelligence Service, the SVR, including all foreign departments, had moved from the old, intimidating concrete walls of Dzerzhinsky Square to new buildings outside Moscow. The new structure embraced western architecture and, like America's CIA headquarters in Virginia, was shaped in the form of a crescent. However, the impression of a newfound political freedom for its citizens was still incompatible with certain functions, like interrogations, that the state continued to carry out.

Getts was escorted from his aircraft to a concrete block building three stories high with steel shutters covering bars on all the windows. It clearly was a jail and, Getts assumed, most likely contained prisoners in whom the SVR had an abiding interest.

Inside the building, Getts was escorted to the desk of a reception area. Walls were painted institutional green and beige, and were deteriorating from neglect. The concrete floors in the reception area felt cold, even through Getts's expensive athletic shoes.

There were three soldiers working behind a long counter,

two lower grade officers and a grizzled sergeant. Getts's escort leaned over the counter and spoke a few words to the sergeant, then nodded toward Getts and left through the front door. The sergeant tried his best to smile, but the effort was weak, and he seemed ill at ease. He extended his hand toward a hard wooden bench, implying that Getts should sit, but Getts politely shook his head. He had been sitting long enough.

The sergeant dialed three digits on a desk phone, spoke a few words of Russian, and hung up. Within two minutes, a non-uniformed man appeared through yet another door, apparently coming from the innards of the building. He was taller than Getts, bigger across the shoulders, and had long arms and big hands with feet to match. His hair was reddish but thinning in front. He made no attempt to smile and managed to convey the impression that Getts was not there with his acquiescence.

"I am Captain Rudi Kubichenko," he said, hand extended. "You are Commander Getts?"

Kubichenko's English was quite effortless, Getts was relieved to hear. "That's right. You can call me Bob if you like."

"Not yet in my army, Commander. Please, sir, this way." Kubichenko did not speak again until he had led Getts down a corridor filled with administrative offices and staff. Captain Kubichenko made a left turn and stopped at a steel door. He knocked, then entered without approval from inside. Getts followed.

Kubichenko ignored a woman who sat at a desk operating a computer, walking past her and opening an inner door, then jerking his head at Getts. Getts entered the room, followed by Kubichenko. Behind a steel desk, in the full uniform of a general officer, was a man who looked exceptionally tall, even sitting down in a swivel chair. The man's hair was cut short and, despite his comparative youth, perhaps in his early forties, was almost completely gray. He drew slowly his long legs under him and, like a stork rising from the banks of a lake, stood behind his desk and extended an open hand to Getts. "I am Colonel General Nikolai Glavnoyi," he said in clear but heavily accented English.

"Commander Robert Getts," Getts said and took one

of two visitor chairs in the small office. Kubichenko took the other.

"It seems that we have a mutual problem, Commander," Glavnoyi said. "Are you familiar with our RN-14 biological artillery shell?" he asked.

"Yes. The weapons grade yield, I think." Getts said.

"That is correct. We seem to be missing twenty such rounds. We are doing an audit now in case there are more," the general said.

"Lost?" Getts asked. "Or stolen?"

"Sold. An officer in charge of one of our storage sites was approached by a man who offered to pay a large sum of money for the projectiles. I am embarrassed to say that our officer agreed," the general said.

"Do you know who the buyer was?" Getts asked.

General Glavnoyi turned his head slightly and nodded to Captain Kubichenko. "The officer at first denied everything but then told us that the man's name was Rául Vlatava, a Czech," Kubichenko said. "But as our officer considered more, under interrogation, he thought the man was German. A description by a number of lower ranks who helped in the crime brought up names. Some we knew." Captain Kubichenko glanced quickly in the general's direction, as though to ask for assurance to reveal more. He went on. "We have . . . extensive files, and this is the man they identified."

Kubichenko produced a photograph from his pocket and passed it to Getts. The photograph was of a youthful man with dark hair, intent eyes. A disdainful quality about his arched eyebrows imparted aloofness. He was wearing work clothes, on a waterfront loading dock with a cargo ship looming behind him. His face revealed displeasure at being the subject of a camera lens. Getts had never seen the man before, but there was no question in his mind that he was looking at Conrad. He spoke his name.

"Yes," Kubichenko said. "He currently goes by the name of Eisler."

Getts's heart hit his stomach.

"Do you know where he is in Germany?" Getts asked.

"No. We have no dealings with him now."

The Cold War was indeed ended, Getts absently thought.

"Did the anthrax rounds get out of the country?" Getts asked.

"Yes," Kubichenko said.

"I want to see the officer who sold them," Getts said.

"I'm afraid that is not possible," General Glavnoyi said, rubbing his eyes. "Major Valitnikov committed suicide in his cell. Out of shame, of course," the general said.

"And the others? The ones who helped him? There must have been a bunch of them," Getts said.

"There was, ah, great self-loathing among the criminals," Glavnoyi said without a hint of remorse. "But I can assure you that we know what they knew, and that you shall know it, too."

Peach had dressed in civilian clothes and was prepared to leave his bachelor NCO quarters when the telephone rang. "Peach," he said into the mouthpiece.

"Bobby here."

"I'm on my way out the door to fuck your girlfriend. Make it quick," he said.

"You better make it quick. You don't have much time," Getts said.

"That so?"

"Yeah. My mother called a few minutes ago. She doesn't know where Dad is," Getts said.

Peach knew that Getts would call from a safe phone and that the lines into McReynolds were secure, but their speech was still guarded. "Is she worried about him?" Peach asked, beginning to squeeze the handpiece tighter.

"Yeah, but I have a feeling he's going to turn up. If that happens, I'll need help. You know what a hassle he is. It's a lot to ask, but could you drop over?"

"Sure. I've got nothing better to do. Need any cigarettes?" Peach asked.

"Yeah. Ten packs ought to do it," Getts said.

"I'll call my travel agent right now," Peach said. Getts would know he was referring to Blacklight Transportation Services. BTS had at its command a dozen pilots and crew with transport aircraft configured for deep black work round the clock.

Peach would quickly put together a Blacklight team and, with their equipment, be airborne within four hours.

* * *

Armed with SVR route information about how the anthrax shells would be off-loaded from an aircraft and onto a train in Prague, Getts's brain was operating at high speed as he planned Blacklight's next move. He did not return to the state security building in Bonn, but flew directly to Frankfurt am Main to rendezvous with Peach and the Blacklight.

An L-1011 with civilian markings, part of SpecWarOps-Com, was parked inconspicuously on the airport ramp. Peach and the Blacklight, who were waiting in a hotel near the airport. Getts arrived at 0410 local time and, after one hour of sleep, used a house phone to rouse Peach. The chief gunner's mate was already up. "Message from Rabbi," Peach said when Getts walked into his room. "Razorback is dead. His body was found on an autobahn about fifty kilometers from Kronberg."

"How?" Getts said.

"Bullet in the back of the head. Rabbi said he and Razorback had interviewed a guy by the name of Erich von Eisler. Rabbi said Razorback was suspicious of the guy, and probably drove back there from Bonn. Rabbi feels like shit. Blames himself. Looks like Eisler could be Conrad. German police went to his house, but he was already gone. His woman, too."

"I know where he is." Getts produced the photograph of Conrad given to him by General Glavnoyi ten hours before. Getts was deeply sorry about Razorback. He would be entered on the rolls with pride and deference. But there were the living, to consider too. "Tell Rabbi when you talk to him that it could have happened to any one of us. Okay, let's call up the troopers." For a long moment, Getts felt a strong downward tug on his facial muscles as depression began to drain his heart and brain. He took two Desyrel, swallowing them without water. He forced himself to function beyond the paralyzing effects of melancholy.

They assembled in Getts's roomy suite for their briefing. Peach, Bartender, Crush, Busboy, Huck Finn, Valentino, Redskin, and Toni, as well as Carla and Sneezy, who had just arrived from Bonn, were dressed in athletic shoes, Gore-Tex jackets, and chinos, as though they were a hiking club or even tourists. They helped themselves to coffee and sweet rolls as Getts took center stage.

"Like to stop training for a while?" he asked.

"Not that I'm not having fun, man . . ." Valentino quipped.

"Why, is this going to be different, Bobby?" Sneezy asked.

"Dumb shit," Huck Finn said. "They brought us over here to start another super race."

"That's right," Peach added. "Government's renting us out for stud." After several moments of similar brief exchanges, Getts's face sobered.

"Razorback was shot in the head, behind the ear," he said. Suddenly the quiet in the room was complete. "We got a fix on who Conrad is. He's got a face, and he's the one that did the job on Razorback." Getts passed out copies of the photograph. "Get a very good look at it because you're going to be seeing it up close and personal." Each member studied the likeness intently.

"The situation is like this," Getts said. "Conrad has twenty anthrax weaponized artillery rounds that he bought in Russia. Doesn't take a systems engineer to figure out that he'll plant them like flowers if he gets them to the U.S.A." There were low murmurs among the Blacklight group.

"How big are the rounds?" Bartender asked.

"Ten kilograms, in powdered form," Getts said.

"Jesus," Huck Finn marveled. "He can take out a lot of people with that stuff."

"Tens of thousands," Getts said. "And it's a bad way to die." Weapons-grade anthrax spore, especially if it was a recombinant form, could take several days, if not weeks, to show clear symptoms in the victim. The spore would then attack the membranes of the lungs, creating a thick, globular, bloody sputum that foams out of the mouth. The pain would be so intense, the victims would plead to have death take their misery away. There was no known antibiotic vaccine.

"The shells were flown from Kursk, Russia, to Prague on an An-26," Getts went on. "They were put on a train in the Czech Republic. That was sixty hours ago. We think the train's destination is Marseilles. We're going to stop it."

"Silly me," Valentino said, "but why don't we have the railroad people stop it?"

"Because they may have a round wired to detonate. It's one thing to lose a train full of people, something else to lose a whole countryside," Getts said.

"The plan is to take over the engine, kill Conrad and anyone he might have with him, then stop the train and cut the baggage car," Getts said.

"What if they take hostages?" Bartender queried.

"We can't let hostages get in our way," Peach responded.

"Jesus," Busboy blurted, "we're going to kill hostages?"

"We're not there to negotiate deals," Getts said. "We're taking these fuckers out. Everybody got that? Collateral damage is not to be considered. All right, in a couple of minutes we're going to talk to the folks who run freight yards in Prague. If we find out where the train's going to be and when, we'll knock it over. Okay so far?" There were no questions. "Okay, Peach."

Peach punched in coded numbers on his PR-2000 and waited. Presently a connection was made. "Getts calling for Mr. Wallis, please." After the connection was established, Getts used his own portable phone to hook into the conversation.

"Wallis here," came the unmistakable voice of Carlisle's director.

"This is Getts. Peach is on with me. Who've you got for us?" the Blacklight leader said.

"Hello, Robert. Mr. Lacos Brzenislav is the freight manager for the Czech state railroad in Prague. He's standing by. He doesn't speak English, but he can get by in Italian. How's that with you?" Wallis said.

Getts exchanged looks with Peach, who nodded. "Peach can hack Italian," Getts said.

"Very well, hold on." There was a silence, followed by several clicks while the connections were made. Finally, a voice answered the other end of the line.

"Signore Brzenislav?" Peach said in Italian.

"*Si?*"

"My name is Peach. You know the train we are interested in? The one carrying metal ore?"

"Yes," the Czech said. "It is in the baggage car."

"It is not in a freight train?" Peach asked.

"No, a passenger train."

Getts and Peach exchanged looks of surprise. Then Getts

whispered to Peach: "Hostages." Peach nodded. He spoke again into the PR-2000. "Where is the train now?"

"It is gone."

"Yes, but when?" Peach asked.

"Last night. Ten o'clock."

"Where was its final destination?" Peach said.

"Marseilles."

"Where is the train right now?"

"Uno momento." There was silence for several minutes before the Czech's voice came back. "Innsbruck. *È là, ora.*"

"What is the train's exact route from there?"

"I can get the times of station arrivals and departures for this train. It will take an hour, perhaps two."

"Please obtain that schedule for us, Mr. Brzenislav," Peach said. "This is an emergency."

"So I have been told."

Carla stood on one foot with her back to a roof support in the Lyons train station platform. Peach leaned amorously over her, his face inches from hers. Each had a rucksack slung over a shoulder. They seemed deeply in love.

A few feet away were Valentino and Toni. Toni had cut her dark hair short and wore a cotton polo shirt and a colorful Gore-Tex loose-fitting jacket with several zippered pockets. She also had rubber-soled mountain boots that highlighted her athletically sculpted body. She was sitting on Valentino's lap who, in turn, rested easily on a four-wheeled baggage cart. Seated next to him was Redskin. All had their hands near rucksacks. They looked like they might be on spring vacation from college.

"I'm just thinking," Valentino said.

"About what?" Toni said, forcing herself to seem engrossed in her "lover."

"That bulletproof vest you're wearing makes your tits disappear."

Toni's eyes narrowed slightly as she pinched his cheek. Hard. "Pig," she said.

"I've never been out with a Jap before," he said.

"I'm Chinese, you turd," Toni said.

The two stopped their bantering as they noticed Alpine Train 1444 whine smartly into the passenger section of loading platform 5. The train was thirteen cars long, including the diesel locomotive, two baggage cars, a dining car, five second class cars, two first class cars, an observation car, and a crew car.

Getts materialized farther down the loading, a two-day stubble of beard on his otherwise boyish face. Mingling with an incoming crowd of French, Swiss, and German passengers were Crush, Bartender, Busboy, Sneezy, and Huck Finn. They all boarded the train separately.

The plan provided for Carla and Toni to do the first shooting, based on the assumption that women might have a better chance to get near the German without being suspected. So Carla and Toni packed additional firepower. In addition to the OICW gun that fired 5.56mm expander rounds with six 20mm HE each, they would carry Star .45 semiauto pistols with lightweight titanium frames that would fire steel ball bearing loads. The OICW gun would fit easily and unseen in slings under jackets and coats. If they were anywhere near the target, Conrad would die. As the train began to move out of the station heading south along the Rhone River, the Blacklight team were aboard at their assigned locations. Getts and Bartender took seats in a second class car near the end of the train. With them were Toni and Valentino.

On the opposite end of the train in the fourth car, also a second class accommodation directly behind the dining car, were Carla, Peach, and Redskin. Sneezy and Crush each sat at opposite ends of the observation car, which was the sixth car from the engine. Busboy and Huck Finn stepped aboard the fifth car in line and got set to move forward in order to neutralize the engine and crew.

As the train picked up speed, Busboy and Huck Finn got to their feet and moved casually down the aisle of the train. As they shuffled along, each took out a can that resembled a popular soft drink, but which was in fact a flash/bang grenade designed to explode with maximum noise and minimum damage. They were meant to be used as distractions in a firefight.

Toni and Valentino waited a full ten minutes for Busboy and Huck Finn to reach the engine, at which time they rose from their seats and began moving forward on the train, still playing the lovers. Valentino stayed a step behind Toni to give her the first and fullest field of fire. He would back her up.

They passed from car to car without spotting anyone suspicious. There were many of the same people they had seen on the platform in Lyons: tourists from neighboring countries, several business travelers, a few children.

Getts and Bartender had started forward from the ninth car. As Bartender moved back to the last passenger car, he saw two men in the rearmost seats who fit the profile. They had hard, weathered faces, and wore slightly oversized suits. Bartender guessed that their clothing covered flak vests. Others in the car included four elderly couples, a young woman and a French railroad employee no longer on duty. Bartender and Getts took an empty seat in the front of the car near a window.

"Did you see them?" Getts whispered.

"Yeah."

"Where do you carry? Did you see a sling?" Getts said.

"No. The weapons must be in their bags," Bartender said.

Busboy and Huck Finn continued through the dining car. There, Huck Finn spotted two men eating an early lunch. One was over six feet, in his late thirties, and had large scarred hands. A fighter, perhaps. The second man with him was under six feet and had an athletic physique, with brown hair, a moustache and wire-rimmed eyeglasses. As he and Busboy passed by, it seemed to him that the man with eyeglasses resembled the photograph of Conrad. Because he could not be certain and because it was not yet their priority, he and Busboy passed through the dining car into the kitchen. They were spoken to sharply by kitchen personnel, who told them that they were in an area off-limits to passengers. They ignored the staff's remarks and passed through connecting doors to the second baggage car.

They were quickly overtaken by a red-faced train conductor. *"Les messieurs, vous ne pouvez pas être dans cette partie du train. Revenez,"* he said, attempting to shoo them back to the passenger car.

Busboy opened his jacket slightly, revealing his OICW slung in a rig that allowed quick access. *"Déverrouillez la porte,"* Huck Finn snapped to the conductor. The railroad employee's eyes widened. He fumbled for his keys, then unlocked the passage door to the baggage car as he was ordered. Busboy shoved him through the door ahead. They stepped inside the baggage car and locked the door behind them. As they made their way down the length of the baggage car, Huck Finn saw the containers they had come for. They were crated and marked LES ÉCHANTILLONS DU MINERAI. Like the man in the dining car, however, there was nothing that they could do with them. He exchanged a knowing glance with Busboy. They arrived at another locked door. Busboy nudged the conductor who, knowing the drill by now, unlocked the door and stepped through the connecting deck and opened the door to the first baggage car.

Busboy pushed the train conductor through the pneumatic doors to the engineer's compartment. There were only two men on duty there. Huck Finn now had his OICW unholstered, and he pointed it at the crew members. All three raised their hands.

"Le prochain arrêt. Qu'est-ce qu'il est?" The next stop. What is it?

"La Vienne," the engineer answered.

"Allez à travers. N'arrêtez pas." Do not stop.

Huck Finn motioned for the Frenchmen to put their hands down. "I got 'em," he said to Busboy. Busboy replaced his weapon into the sling under his jacket and began to retrace his steps back toward the train cars.

Back in the sixth passenger car, Carla and Peach spotted two men, one sitting at the south end of the car, the second at the north, both appearing out of place. They were not dressed like the local French, nor did they seem to be tourists. They were hard of belly and wary of eye. When the man in the north seat met Peach's eyes his left hand moved almost involuntarily under his jacket. He turned slightly in his seat. There was no doubt in Peach's mind that the man was a target. He did not force the situation by looking back over his shoulder at the man. Instead, Peach kissed Carla lightly on the neck.

As Getts entered the observation car, he spotted two more potential targets. Redskin arrived at the base of the stairs leading up to the observation deck and spoke briefly with Getts. Then he continued up the stairs and took a seat in the rear of the car.

Getts continued through the train and entered the fifth

car in line, a second class accommodation. Getts recognized potentially fatal errors Conrad's men had made. They had become so spaced apart on the train that their collective firepower was diluted. And they were obvious, not practiced at the game of covert deception. They looked like thugs. And, perhaps worst, they carried their weapons in travel bags, not as easily accessible as Blacklight body slings. Getts, after conferring briefly with Redskin, who had by now traveled the length of the train, counted six.

There were eight.

Toni and Valentino suddenly came face to face with Conrad and Perkins Southwith. Before Toni could make her move, however, a woman rose to her feet and stepped into the aisle between them. Conrad showed not the slightest sign of interest in Toni as he opened a door to his left and entered the men's restroom. Toni and Valentino stood politely aside while Southwith continued down the aisle alone. Toni perched on the edge of an empty seat as though waiting for the ladies room to become vacant. Her wait stretched into several minutes. She was considering entering the adjacent ladies' room and firing her weapon through the thin metal walls separating the two lavatories when the men's door opened slightly.

Southwith abruptly rose from his table and walked through the door of the dining car toward the rear of the train. As he passed into the next car a hand appeared at a point near the floor of the dining car. Instinctively, Toni knew it was a hand grenade. "Grenade!" she shouted. Valentino saw it, too, and immediately leaped to his right and went to the floor. Whether out of training or prescience, Toni did precisely the right thing. She, too, went to the floor but placed her body against the bulkhead of the train car.

The grenade rolled down the aisle of the train, passing the crouching commandos. The weapon was an infantry fragmentation explosive designed to hurl pieces of steel in every direction. When the blast came, every window in the car was blown out, a gaping hole ripped in its side. Four civilians seated near the center of the explosion were killed outright, and seven more were injured seriously. Among one of the seriously injured passengers in the car was a mercenary in Conrad's employ. A second grenade exploded. This one was smoke.

The explosion could be heard in the tenth car, and two of Southwith's men seated in the rear jumped to their seat, their Skorpion machine guns now drawn from their bags, and they rushed toward the door of the car. As they sped passed Bartender, who was positioned in the second seat from the door, he moved quickly to retrieve his OICW from its sling. He fired the entire 30-round magazine into their heads and backs. Bartender rapidly slipped a fresh magazine into his gun and started forward among screams of passengers.

In the observation car, one of Southwith's men had suspected that Redskin could be a threat, and when he heard the explosion, he moved to his Skorpion. Redskin went for his own weapon. There was a point blank exchange of automatic gunfire. Redskin took three rounds in his face, but not before he had killed one man and critically wounded a second. One civilian, an attractive women in her middle thirties, was killed by a wild burst from the second Southwith man. Passengers screamed and fell to the floor.

The train's engineer, terrified by the unfolding events and acting before Huck Finn could stop him, hit the accident switch. The train's wheels locked as the emergency stop system went into operation.

In the fifth car, Carla had her .45 auto pulled and snapped two rounds at a man in the southeast corner of the car. The dispersing shot load took off the side of his head and blew out a window. A Southwith man was coming up with a Skorpion but was close enough to Peach for the big, fast commando to drive the web of his open hand deep into the mercenary's throat. His larynx broke instantly, and the mercenary dropped the assault gun in his hands and clutched at his throat, gurgling for air. Screams of innocent civilians, tossed forward over seats and into the aisle, competed with the squeal of the emergency braking system.

As the train ground to a halt, a second fragmentation grenade followed again by a smoke grenade, went off in the dining car. Getts, about to enter from the north end, was blown backward through the coupling doors and landed in the fourth car. He was considerably deafened by the blasts, and his weapon had been blown from his hands. His eyes watered, and he knew that several ribs were either cracked or broken. He staggered to his feet just as Valentino arrived from the north. "Get out of the train," he said through gritted teeth. "Tell everybody to get out and look for Conrad."

Getts exited on the west side of the train. Most of the Blacklight team were on the east side where grass grew high and the uneven topography of the land quickly was overcome by thick forest. Getts sensed rather than saw a form rolling out from under the stilled wheels of the train. He dived forward under the train, as dirt and rocks kicked up from the frenetic burst of fully automatic gunfire from a Skorpion. He felt something slam into his leg, but the pain was not debilitating. Getts believed it was caused by a loose rock. Though he had lost his OICW in the explosion, Getts still had his 9mm 15-round Glock, and as he rolled under a set of train wheels he snapped off two shots in the general direction of his assailant.

No hits.

Then, at wheel stations farther up the same car, Getts saw a form scooting between the wheels of the train. Getts moved his body slightly sideways and snapped off three more rounds, then dived out from under the carriage. He spied a culvert near the tracks, which he hoped led back under the tracks. He dived head first in a tuck and roll. The drain pipe seemed too small to risk getting caught in. He pressed his back against the shoulder of the track and waited for his antagonist to come into view, the Glock ready to shoot. He waited several ticks before he realized that there was no suppressing fire from the other side. Something must be preventing the other man from firing his Skorpion. It was possible that one of his Glock rounds had hit the man or his weapon. Getts crouched, looking for his prey. Suddenly, the full weight of a man fell upon him from above.

Getts could feel a garrote slip over his head. He immediately turned his head hard to one side so that the cutting edge of the wire was against the muscles of his neck rather than his windpipe. The pain quickly intensified as Getts strained to twist his hips perpendicular to his attacker's crotch. Slightly off balance, the attacker was unable to maintain his advantage and fell to the ground, the garrote no longer effective.

Getts immediately kicked the man in the temple, and as his attacker's body rolled, Getts recognized the figure of Perkins Southwith.

Southwith quickly recovered and established himself in a fighting stance. The two men moved in a small area, on the balls of their feet, hands ready, each man looking for an opening. Getts wore an ankle holster containing a 9mm PPK, but in close combat he had to wait for a chance to draw the weapon. Southwith shot a kick at Getts, who moved right, taking the blow on a shoulder. Getts feinted a kick, then threw a martial arts punch toward Southwith's face, shattering his nose. It was not the paralyzing blow that Getts had expected, however, and Southwith fought through teary-eyed pain to deliver by reflex a chop to Getts's neck.

Southwith then produced a knife from a sheath in the small of his back, snapped open the blade and moved toward Getts. Getts leaped backward, rolling away from the shoulders of the track, and retrieved the 9mm from his ankle holster and delivered three rounds into Southwith's throat framing the mercenary's surprised expression in red.

When it became obvious that Conrad had bolted from the train, the Blacklight searched for six hours for Conrad, but the man was at least as much at home in the rugged terrain as the Blacklight men. They came across a road that led to the town of St. Chamond, and it seemed obvious that Conrad had somehow found a vehicle to take him at least that far. Bartender and Huck Finn established a dialogue with the local gendarmerie, and a manhunt was initiated. Twenty-four hours later, there was no sign of the German terrorist, and it was assumed he had slipped out of town just as he had come in.

Back in the baggage car of the Lyons/Marseilles train, Getts, Peach, and Valentino tore open the crates that were labeled "Ore Samples." The crates were full not of artillery shells, but common rock. During the next thirty-six hours, Getts and Peach worked their way back along the train's route through France, Switzerland, Germany, and the Czech Republic. Further investigation with the freight superintendent in Prague revealed that the ore samples he described were indeed received from a Russian Air Force An-28 and that they answered Getts's description perfectly.

Getts and Peach then spent a day at the Prague International Airport and learned that a chartered DC-9 air freighter had received clearance to depart Prague for London that same afternoon in question. London Air Traffic

Control, however, showed no arrival for a DC-9 bearing those aircraft I.D. numbers. The range of the DC-9 was 6,000 miles and could have easily been configured to carry fuel for an additional 4,000 miles, thus enabling it to be virtually anywhere in the world.

Including the U.S.A.

Chapter Fifteen

An agricultural officer in the French Embassy in Beirut, Lebanon, was brought an envelope containing photographs from his communications office on the third floor of the building. The photograph had been sent by microwave on a KG-10 5000 imaging satellite, code worded *Capricorn*, an inter-intelligence service coordination designation. The French embassy was cooperating with the United States intelligence assets—including the H. P. Carlisle Foundation—in running down the whereabouts of the terrorist, Conrad. The agricultural officer, Robert-Pierre Roumelet, who in reality knew nothing about crops, studied the photograph briefly, then made a telephone call to a number in south Beirut.

Roumelet left the embassy and drove to his apartment in Bachoura off Rue Basta, got his own car out of a garage, and drove slightly over four kilometers to the Haret Hraik section of the city. He placed an iron bar, which ran from the steering wheel to the brake of the car, and locked it. He climbed three flights of stairs to the top of an apartment building that was missing one entire wall from artillery fire from a Christian Militia gun. The door that Roumelet knocked upon was answered immediately by a Semitic man who called himself Mehmet-Rauf. Roumelet handed Mehmet-Rauf a sealed envelope. "They left yesterday on Syrian Air for Damascus," he said. "We need to know where they are now." Then he turned, retraced his steps to his automobile.

Mehmet-Rauf opened the envelope and studied the photographs contained inside for several moments. He retrieved a black felt tip pen, drew various articles over one of the glossy photos including glasses, a mustache, hat. He studied each image until he believed he would recognize the face anywhere, then struck a match and held it under the pictures until they had burned completely.

Mehmet-Rauf put a few articles of clothing into a light cotton bag that he carried over his shoulder. He added a 10mm camera, binoculars, and a two-way miniature VHF radio to the pack. He strapped a money belt under his plain white cotton abayeh, and walked a few blocks to Avenue Jamal where he could catch a city bus going southeast out of town. In Baabda, he boarded yet another bus packed with people holding children, food baskets, sometimes small animals. The bus made slow progress climbing over the Jabal Lebanon mountains, wound its way down the other side, creating welcome air in the one hundred plus degree heat inside the bus.

Mehmet-Rauf left the passenger bus at Majdel Aanjar, ate rice and mutton wrapped in grape leaves, his only meal of the day, in the palm shade of an outdoor cafe. It had taken him five hours to travel less than fifty kilometers.

He walked through the streets of the city until he found a bicycle shop. He chose a used ten-speed Peugeot. Mehmet-Rauf paid the equivalent of two hundred French francs for the bike. He wasted no time in the city but began riding his bicycle at an even pace east by southeast across the Bekaa Valley where temperatures, even in the late afternoon, rose to one hundred twelve degrees. He crossed the border into Syria without challenge and did not stop for water or rest until Jdeide.

Despite the heat of the day, Mehmet-Rauf felt a shiver run slowly through his body from shoulders to toes. This was a country where spies were first tortured at length then put to death. A merciful death was simple beheading, with the head of the "traitor" put on a pike near the entrance of the town or city where he was caught.

Pedaling the bicycle uphill was tiring, and Mehmet-Rauf got off to push the Peugeot most of ten kilometers until he had reached the summit of the Al Jabal pass at about two thousand feet. He coasted down the other side of the mountains into the town of Oadsaya. It was midnight by the time he arrived there, some fifteen kilometers from Damascus. Not wanting to attract the attention of police or security soldiers, he found an inn and slept until dawn.

He rose at once, breakfasted on dates and bread, washed in a town fountain, then set out for Damascus on his bicycle. He assumed a trail from the airport to the city would be cold so Mehmet-Rauf pedaled toward the Palace of Assad.

He arrived near the palace, but realized that there was no way that he could watch every entrance to the multigated city. He went to the north side of the city and traded his bicycle to a peddler along with one Syrian pound, worth about twenty U.S. dollars, for a cart laden with coarse cotton thobes and keffiyehs. Mehmet-Rauf pushed the cart innocuously in a wide circle about the palace, talking with local businessmen, lauding Assad. He said Muslim prayers while performing required ablutions, then knelt on a prayer rug facing Mecca, the Holy House of Allah. These daily Muslim requirements were supremely inconvenient to an American Jew.

Within two days of praying, eating lightly, and talking with Arabs, Mehmet-Rauf learned of a black government car that several days prior had carried an important European family to an ancient castle. There were several castles in Syria, Mehmet-Rauf knew, among more than one hundred built in the Levant by European Crusaders between the eleventh and thirteenth centuries. One castle in particular nudged itself into Mehmet-Rauf's attention. It was the magnificent castle of Krak des Chevaliers, built for the Saracens by a Byzantine architect of the twelfth century. The French captured the fortress and reinforced its garrison to make it impregnable. Krak was located in Syria near the northern border of Iraq. Despite the distance involved, he traveled to Krak and watched its two main gates for a number of days. Several times, he saw important personages enter and leave the gates by limousine, but none resembled Conrad or his woman and none included children. Mehmet-Rauf returned to Damascus to begin all over.

One day Mehmet-Rauf shared coarse bread and goat cheese with a truck driver who delivered air-freighted foods from incoming flights originating from Europe and the Far East. Until recently, the driver said, his main customer was Assad's palace and the city's finest hotel. But in the past week he had added another stop to his regular itinerary: it was the Rudyah Castle, an eleventh-century monolith located on the Nahr Barada some thirty-five kilometers northwest of Damascus.

Mehmet-Rauf pushed his clothing cart along the road to Doummar and Oadsaya. After walking about twenty-eight kilometers, he left the main highway onto a road that wound through wadis and sparsely populated areas. After about five more kilometers, he saw Rudyah Castle at a distance of about one thousand meters. He felt it was as close as he could get without being challenged by security personnel mounted on armored carriers. He turned off of the road and found a wadi that offered enfilade on two sides. He felt reasonably safe for the time being.

He drew a piece of netting from under the clothing that he "sold" from his cart and placed it over the car, propped poles under two edges to provide shade for himself. Using a set of powerful binoculars and standing at the edge of the wadi, he could see the castle itself. The fortress stood on a mountain spur with ravines on three sides at an elevation of about fifteen hundred feet with mountains miles behind it rising at least another two thousand feet. Rudyah Castle's giant taluses made it appear an artificial mountain with facing walls of bossed masonry blocks. Rounded towers could provide flanking fire from well designed loopholes for trapping an assaulting force. There was no longer a moat in front of the castle, but the drawbridge remained. Several hundred years past, water had been diverted from the Nahr Barada. But with the advent of gunpowder, obviating catapult and longbow as the best weapons against castle walls, the Barada had been dammed near the castle to allow free-flowing irrigation water for cotton crops that now provided the largest part of Syria's textile exports.

Still, short of artillery put into place and used as direct fire against the Rudyah Castle, nothing would allow access to the town-sized grounds inside. Mehmet-Rauf retrieved dried lamb and figs from his cart and settled down for what might be a long wait. It could be days or even weeks. But sooner or later one of the Eislers, if they were inside, would emerge.

Mehmet-Rauf had been on station for five days, waking in the wadi before dawn, often packing his sleeping bag with an extra blanket at night to protect himself from bitter desert cold. He had used most of his week-long allotment for food and, as he boiled water for tea at sunrise, considered walking to the city for fresh provisions later rather than earlier. Within the hour, he was rewarded for his management of time when the outer gates of Rudyah opened. Two military vehicles rolled out of the private road, followed closely by a large Mercedes sedan and followed by yet another all-terrain military transport.

As the procession neared him, Mehmet-Rauf rose from his haunches for a better view. He exposed himself to the castle's security forces, but, he felt, the risk was worth it. As he peered at the tinted rear windows of the automobile, he could see a face press itself toward the glass to return his inquiring stare. It was Conrad.

Chapter Sixteen

Back at Camp McReynolds at the cramped Blacklight headquarters, was a briefing room that took up most of the building's space. Battle casualties from the operation in Europe—Redskin and Razorback—had been replaced in the ten-pack by a single trooper, Rick Heggstad. Peach, seated at the front of the assembly, made a mental note to talk privately with Heggstad.

Windows were shuttered on the inside and checked again by Bartender. Conversations were kept low key, muted as if the building was surrounded by enemy spies. The sound of the front door banging open prompted Peach to come to his feet and shout.

"Room, ten-HUT!"

He stood to one side of the room, shoulders back, at rigid attention. At once, every Blacklight trooper was on his or her feet, eyes straight ahead as Getts strode into the room at a quick pace. He mounted the two steps to an elevated stage, and stood before them.

"At ease. Sit down. No fun, was it?"

Murmurs of agreement could be heard through the assembled group. "We think we've found Conrad. If you think the last go-round with him was bad, this one is an absolute bitch. He's in a castle in Syria. The good news is that we know which one. The bad news is we don't have a floor plan. And after nine hundred years since the Crusades, we aren't likely to come up with one, either."

"You telling us we have to take the place without knowing what's inside?" Bartender blurted. He had been on assaults before and knew the crucial value of intelligence. He knew, as Getts and Peach did, that a whole assault team could be lost if they were surprised inside. Going in blind was the most dangerous game of all.

"We don't know anything about their defense system, either," Getts said. He nodded his head toward Busboy, who was standing by a projector. Overhead lights dimmed, and a picture of Conrad, dressed as Eisler, appeared on a screen. "We've got better pictures of him now. As you know, his latest guise is Erich von Eisler. He sometimes looks like this. . . ."

Busboy turned another slide that revealed Conrad digitally altered and wearing a hat and glasses.

"Or this. . . ."

Another shot of Conrad appeared with mustache, another with a beard.

"He has a woman," Getts said, again nodding toward Busboy. Immediately, a photograph appeared on the screen of Lisa Hohelganz. An appreciative murmur spread among the audience.

"The man's got good taste," a voice said from the darkened room.

"He's well-financed, protected by Lybia, Iran, and, in this case, Syria. After he got away from us in France, he arranged to meet Lisa Hohelganz in Rome. Right now he's in Syria. We want to get him—fast—before he can lick his wounds and get out of there. The hard part is getting to him there."

At a nod of Getts's head, a photograph of the Rudyah Castle flashed on the screen. The Blacklight battle group trained their eyes, studying the fortress in appreciation, looking for flaws in its nearly thousand-year-old design that might offer a small force a way in.

"Security forces are garrisoned there around the clock. I don't have specific intelligence yet, but somebody's working on it. Tough nut to crack, isn't it? Well, it was supposed to be impregnable nine hundred years ago and looks just about as mean now." Getts had the lights turned on and the projector turned off.

"Obviously, the United States can't land an army in Syria. We can't go to war over one man, even Conrad. But we have to get him and get him fast. We have reason to believe the anthrax shells are in the United States—or soon will be—and Conrad will move any day."

"Hell, Bobby," Heggstad thought aloud, "we don't look like Arabs. Except maybe Valentino, there."

Quiet laughter ensued.

"He's right. We can't just walk in. We'd look conspicuous wearing robes with one hundred fifty pounds of supplies and ammunition under them," Getts agreed.

"How about a HALO jump?" Carla asked.

"Thought about that," Getts said. "But Syria has damn good radar and fast interceptors. I'm thinking that we can do it with HAHO."

"How high?" somebody from the back of the room asked.

"Over forty thousand. Maybe as high as fifty," Getts said.

"Shit," Crush said. "Can't be done."

"Yes it can. I want you all to listen to a weather report," Getts said. He nodded toward Peach.

In an adjoining room, sitting at a small conference table poring through a thick briefing book was a slender man wearing heavy glasses and dressed in the khaki gabardine uniform of an air force officer. Gold oak leaves on his tunic collar indicated his rank of major.

Peach opened the door and stepped inside. "We're ready for you now, Major Truly."

"Right with you, Peach . . ."

Inside the briefing room Major Truly was introduced by Getts.

"This is Major Truly, Met. Officer for the 442nd Bomb Wing, Biggs Air Force Base. Major."

Major Truly picked up a pointer and stood near the screen. "Naturally, I don't know what you people plan on doing when you get there, but I can assure you that it's going to be hot where you're going. Slide, please."

Busboy placed a slide onto the machine, which illuminated the Mediterranean and Red Seas and surrounding countries. The areas were marked with meteorological notations, wind current patterns, pressures marked in millibars; isothermal lines contoured the projection.

"Mean temperature at 1,000 feet elevation in this five hundred kilometer corridor is officially 108°, but like they say in Death Valley, it's dry heat."

The major waited for appreciative laughter but received none. He continued. "Fact is that the temperature will be closer to one hundred twenty. For the next ten days, we'll see some cirrus formations at thirty to forty thousand feet with light winds two to four knots during daylight and late night hours, with only late afternoon increases into the ten to twelve knot range. Contrails will show up on radar at twenty-two thousand. If you're in the mountains here," Major Truly pointed to a few more locations on the chart, "and here, cloud cover won't drop below sixteen thousand feet. Water temperature will be a pleasant eighty-three degrees if you have to ditch, so take along a good book and enjoy."

Major Truly beamed at his little joke. He surveyed the sober faces of Blacklight people. "Air crews don't like that one, either."

"How about jet streams?" Getts asked Truly.

Major Truly called for another projection. He indicated two rivers of air, colored red, circling the entire globe and pointed to the Middle East in particular. "There are two major jet streams moving during this period," he said, "the first at 38,000 feet, the second at 49,000. The first will travel west to east at about fifty-one degrees north latitude, the other will move from west to east at latitude thirty-two degrees through this part, about longitude thirty-five."

"How precise can you get that?" Getts asked.

"Well, I can get it damn close, say within a few miles, but the projection won't hold for more than eighteen hours," Major Truly informed him.

"We're looking for something at thirty-three point thirty north latitude and about thirty-six point nineteen south longitude," Getts said. "What are the parameters on these streams?" Getts asked Truly.

"Stream two right now is about thirty-seven kilometers wide," the weather officer said. "One to three kilometers thick, velocity around two hundred fifty miles per hour, sometimes reaching three hundred."

"Could it decelerate?" Getts wanted to know.

"Sure," the major said. "They get down to around one-eighty. But this time of year we'll see sustained velocities. I'd say nothing under two-fifty or so." The major looked at the map again before speaking. He then pointed at a specific area on the screen. "This one will drift north, around here—Turkey—Rustavi—the southern tip of the Balkans, and Russia around Rustavi."

"And the other one?" Getts asked.

Major Truly considered for a moment, then nodded his head. "The winds there are moving around." The meteorological officer indicated a place on the map nearer the Levant. "I can get you briefed on short notice. . . ."

"Do that, Major. We'll have your stuff moved in here with us until we leave. Give Peach a list of what you want brought over."

"Now wait a minute, Commander, I . . ."

"I'll clear it with your commanding officer. You can call your family. Don't tell 'em where you are, just that you can't come home."

"Yes, sir," the major said. "I don't suppose you'll tell me the nature of your mission?"

"Nope," Getts responded.

"I didn't think so, sir." Major Truly saluted, turned and left the briefing room.

Getts addressed the Blacklight team, who were sitting ramrod straight in their chairs, excitement permeating the room.

"You've probably guessed it. We'll HAHO inside the jet stream that crosses our target. I expect we'll go out somewhere around here, maybe over the top of the Red Sea, maybe out here in the Med," he pointed to a wall map.

"Can't be done that way, Bob," Valentino said.

"Yes it can," Getts assured him. "We need to fly in our chutes, about one hundred fifty miles from about here, over the Jabal Mountains, and make a footprint here, in the desert north of Douma. We'll miss security forces there," he concluded.

Toni knitted her brow. "We've all done high altitude high opening, but not forty thousand feet."

"Yeah," Heggstad agreed. "That's what Valentino was trying to say, I think. Something like 2.9 millibars of air pressure, that high, man. You stream from there. You ain't gonna fly."

Getts nodded toward Peach. "Peach?"

Peach turned to face the group. "I've done more HAHOs than anybody in this room. We can use cargo chutes," he said, anticipating the problem. "We can inflate the chutes with charges. Blow 'em open. And they're steerable." Peach scanned the room, challenging objections. None came.

"Peach is right. We go out at forty-plus thousand inside the stream. If the stream is moving at two hundred and sixty miles per hour and we maintain a one to fifty fall ratio, we'll make a footprint here, at Hainjan Wadi."

Crush stood and sat on the backrest of his chair in order to see better. "What happens if we don't hit the stream? Hell, that thing isn't all that thick."

There was silence in the room for several moments. Getts simply said, "Any other questions?"

"Pressure suits?" Bartender ventured.

"Air force has 'em, and we're going to get 'em," Getts said.

"How about the cold, Bob?" Busboy asked. "We're gonna freeze our balls off."

"I'll risk it if you will," Carla deadpanned.

The room exploded in laughter.

"Research has a thermal wrap they've been dying to try on real people. We'll volunteer. Toni," he said, nodding toward the smallest trooper, "you and Carla get yourselves a couple bathing suits. Stuff that looks good. We need stand-by communications relay on the beach."

"You mean I don't jump?" Carla asked, incredulous.

"Not this time. The rest of you will exfiltrate by helo, so we might have to hold a hot LZ 'til the birds get there. Bartender, you and Sneezy are designated pistoleros. Use the OICWs."

"Allllll right!" Sneezy said, clearly glad to be included in the mission.

Getts surveyed the room. "Remember, all of you, we're there to get one man. We're not out to erase camel drivers." Getts retrieved a piece of paper from his pocket. "Okay, here's the list of jumpers. There's only room on the black plane for nine. On the target team, I want Peach, Bartender, Crush, Huck Finn, Valentino, Heggstad, Sneezy, and Busboy. I'll lead. Peach takes over if I catch a cold. Everybody carries subsonic ammunition suppressors. After we fire them off, it's going to get noisy anyway. We'll need climbing gear for a two-hundred-foot descent. We might have to get above the castle and work down."

"When do we draw up the assault plan?" Huck Finn wanted to know.

"Start on it tomorrow, Huck. We're still trying to get some sense of the inside of the castle. So far no joy."

"How about an ambush?" Toni asked.

Getts shook his head. "We could wait hours, days, or weeks. There's too much risk. We'll have to go in after him," Getts said without relish. He glanced over the group. "If we have to, we'll go over the walls. Just like crusaders. Knives in our teeth. Then we'll use Israeli extraction choppers. They're the best in the business, and they know the terrain better than the Arabs. Okay, everybody see the division personnel officer. Get your personal effects in order. Sign up for insurance. See a chaplain. Write letters if you need to. Say nothing about the mission. From now on, nobody leaves the post for any reason. We board the aircraft in twenty-four hours. Questions?"

"How 'bout phone calls, Bobby?" Valentino asked.

"The phones on post will be taped. Sorry, no calls. Anything else? Okay, move out. Heggstad," Getts said, "you and Crush hang around."

As the group broke up, Getts moved near the troopers where they wouldn't be overheard. Heggstad was tall, about 6' 2", and perfectly conditioned. He bore tattoos on his arms and chest that almost kept him out of Blacklight, indeed out of the army. But he had the reputation of being one of the fiercest fighters in the SEALs, clearly Peach's equal in martial arts. "Heggstad, that's your real name, isn't it?"

"That's right, Bobby."

"Change it," Getts said. "You know the kind of people we go after. They've got friends, and if you kill them, their friends will go after your family."

"I don't have a family. Nobody. Besides, I'm related to the Berserkers. Know who they were?" Heggstad said.

"I guess not."

"They were a family of the toughest goddamn Vikings in the history of the world. If you were really an avenging motherfucker and went crazy in battle, you might be honored enough to be called a berserker. I'm related," Heggstad said with a proud smile.

"Jesus," Getts mumbled. "Okay. It's your life, man."

"May I have a word, sir?" Carla said to Getts.

"Sure." He sat on the back of a chair while she stood, Crush waited patiently in his briefing chair.

"I want to go on that jump," she said.

"Nope."

"I earned it, goddamn it, Bobby."

Getts looked at her intensely. "There are going to be other missions," he said. "Ones people will come back from. This is dirty," he added.

"When I volunteered for Blacklight and you accepted me, you promised my sex wouldn't affect any decisions made. You better not turn that into a lie."

Getts turned to walk toward Crush.

"I'm the best qualified for this mission," she said to his back.

Getts stopped, thought for a moment, took a deep breath. She was right, after all. "Okay. I'll make the change in the order. Sneezy stays, you go."

After Carla left the room, Getts took a chair near Crush.

"How's it going, man?" Getts said.

"Okay. Not enough dances for the troops but . . ." he shrugged.

"Your mother still living?" Getts asked.

"Yes. Father, too," Crush said.

"How do you get along with them?"

"My father's a doctor, a pediatrician. When I joined up, he was upset. But I think he's still proud of me. Why?" Crush said.

"What are you going to do when you get out?" Getts asked.

"I'm not getting out, Bobby. I like my chances for advancement right here."

"Easy life here, huh?"

Crush laughed, then his face sobered. "This one's going to be a shitter, and if we make it out in one piece, there's going to be another one." Crush flashed another smile as Getts's frown deepened.

"I have the results of your Minnesota Multiphasic Personality Profile," Getts said. Crush did not blink. "Do you know what it says?"

"Not interested," Crush said, his eyes drifting to a window.

So Crush knew the test results. "It says you'd be better off working in a meat packing plant than . . ."

"Than where?" Crush interrupted harshly. "What the hell is this if it isn't a butcher shop? We going to the Middle East to sell Conrad insurance? If that's the case, maybe I better not go." Crush's jaw set, his eyes blinking rapidly.

Getts made a mental note to tear up the report on Crush. He just hoped that when the pressure got to critical mass, Crush wouldn't explode on him. And the others. "Okay. Draw your gear." Crush did not say thanks, but merely turned on his heel and left the briefing room.

Chapter Seventeen

Peach used heavy wire cutters to cut the cyclone fencing that surrounded the post. He pushed out enough space to squeeze through, then eased the bent wire back into place and knitted it closed with fine piano wire. He watched for any perimeter patrols, but it appeared that no more than routine military police activity would be scheduled for tonight. He wore civilian clothes; stylish trousers that were pegged slightly at the cuff, a white T-shirt under a "Members Only" jacket containing a number of zippered pockets.

He jogged a quarter of a mile to the main road, stopped by a civilian store's pay phone, and dialed a number.

"Hello?" came a foreign voice over the line.

"This is Wes Jones. I have a message for Magetz."

"Yes?"

"Tell him Blacklight moves out within forty-eight hours. Syria. Krak Castle. A U.S. Navy task force off As-Sarafand provides air cover and extraction. There's no way to stop us going in, but tell Magetz that he can have his people at the pick-up location. Got that?"

There was a brief pause at the other end. "Yes, thank you."

"Don't thank me, rag head, just put a check in the mail."

Peach used the same route going into the post as he used going out. When he had thrown away his cutting tool and brushed dirt from his civilian clothing, he was suddenly bathed in the glare of spotlights and a voice from the darkness said, "Don't move. You're under arrest."

Getts had not been in bed, despite the late hour, when Major Dennis Brae informed him that one of his men, Chief Gunner's Mate Peach, was in a stockade cell for violating base restriction. Getts was at the stockade five minutes after hanging up the telephone.

"Cut a hole through the wire," Major Brae said to Getts. "Bring Peach out here," the provost marshal ordered a uniformed corporal. "What's his rank, anyway?" the provost marshal asked Getts.

"Chief petty officer. Did he offer any resistance?" Getts asked.

"Nope. Good thing, too. I have some pretty damn tough troopers watching the perimeters of the post. One of your people tries to get rough with them, they're liable to wake up in the post hospital."

"Good thing Peach didn't know that," Getts said.

The major gave him a quizzical look.

"Would have scared him to death," Getts said.

"He'll have to pay for repairing the fence, too," the gray-haired Major Brae added while making notations on a detention report.

Peach was escorted from the rear of the provost building to the desk where Getts and Major Brae waited. "Hi, Bobby," he said.

"Say 'sir' when you speak to an officer, soldier," Major Brae snapped angrily. "Fact you're wearing civilian clothes doesn't mean you don't stand at attention, either."

Peach obligingly drew himself into a brace while Getts stood before him. "You broke restriction," Getts said.

"Yes, sir," Peach responded.

"Explain yourself," Getts ordered.

"I have no excuse, Commander, sir," Peach said, eyes dead ahead.

"Anybody ever tell you that you're a sorry sack of shit?" Getts demanded of the prisoner.

"Not to my face. No, sir," Peach said.

"Anybody ever say it to your back?" Getts said in mock seriousness.

"Yes, sir. I'm sure they have, sir."

"Well, you can put me on the list of people who have said it behind your back. Is that clear, Chief Gunner's Mate Peach?" Getts barked.

"Yes, sir. Very clear, sir."

Major Brae looked on in confusion. "Uh, Commander Getts, would you like to prefer charges against this, man? We can keep him right here in the stockade until you decide, sir."

"Frankly, Major, I think that's just what Peach would like. A nice soft rack here in your stockade. But I'm going to take him with me back to the barracks and bust him down to recruit, then work him to death, drive him until he can't stand it another minute. A little torture is good for enlisted men."

Major Brae's jaw jutted forward with undisguised satisfaction as he regarded a woeful-appearing Peach. "That's how we deal with his kind in the real army, Commander."

"Right. Got some kind of release form I can sign?"

Getts scribbled his name and rank at the bottom of a yellow form put before him by Major Brae's night clerk.

Outside the stockade entrance, Getts and Peach walked

together back to the Blacklight compound. "Where'd you go?" Getts asked.

"Just out. Guy with a dick as big as mine likes to have it admired once in a while. Know what I mean?"

"Why didn't you put a picture of it on the bulletin board at the BX?" Getts asked.

"Not the same thing as showing it around town," Peach said.

"So what *were* you doing off base tonight?" Getts asked.

"Had to call some Arabs in New York. Told 'em we were going to jump into Syria pretty soon and they better get ready for it," Peach said as they walked at a leisurely pace.

"That all you told 'em?"

"Well, I said that they couldn't stop us from going in, which was true, but that if they set up an ambush where the choppers are going to pick us up that ought to work out pretty well for them," Peach said.

"I suppose you told them that we're going to have off-shore navy cover, too."

"Yep," Peach said.

"Good man," he said, slapping the chief gunner's mate on his back.

Chapter Eighteen

Wallis was immaculately dressed in flannel trousers and club tie, but fatigue tugged at his already baggy eyes. He pushed his teacup carelessly across his desk as he pored over papers and photographs with a large magnifying glass. There was a knock on the door, and, without Wallis's acknowledgment, Colonel Barnes entered the room. Under his arm, he carried a fresh stack of photographs and data bank printouts in expandable manila envelopes. He placed them on Wallis's table where he was working.

"I have some new Keyhole photographs, sir," he said.

"Hmmm." Wallis began looking over the new batch at once.

"Our tendency people think they have the solution. Want to hear it?"

"I am your devoted audience," Wallis said without looking up. "Lay it on me."

"Force him out of the castle. There sure isn't any way inside. Use the Fanus signal system to put Conrad on the road. For example, suppose we use Fanus's call sign to advise Conrad that Assad is going to sell him out. Arab leaders consider him a liability. They're going to leave the gates open and let someone like Getts walk in. The tendency folks think that Conrad can't afford to sit and wait until that happens," Barnes concluded.

"Too complicated," Wallis mused, his hands behind his head, fingers interlaced. "I think Getts can get the job done his way. The problem, of course, is without knowing the castle's floor plan we're risking heavy casualties. I'm not sure they can get out after the first shot is fired. Thanks anyway, Adrian, it was a good try."

The selected Blacklight force was flown in a C-130 to Fort Bragg, North Carolina, where they were fitted out with HAHO suits and rendezvoused with a "black plane," in this case a B-1 bomber that was configured for special missions such as these. Each Blacklight trooper was responsible for stowing his or her own gear on board. One of the air crew marveled at the amount of material the relatively small force was taking along. He was tersely informed that ninety percent of it was ammunition. The old army axiom was that you can always eat your boot, but you can't shoot your enemy with one. Still, each Blacklight trooper would jump with virtual helmets, IR equipment, and force multipliers tied to their legs by tethers.

The B-1 received takeoff clearance from the tower at 0333 hours, and rolled down the runway, rotating at 120 knots. It retracted its gears, increased speed, then raised its nose in a steep angle of attack into a cobalt sky. The pilot radioed a special identifier code to NORAD, then dialed in a compass vector of fifty-one degrees for latitude thirty-two north, longitude thirty-five east, which would take them a distance of five thousand three hundred eighty miles.

A crew member, the ECM officer, rose from his panel near the pilot and made his way toward the midsection of the aircraft. He surveyed his passengers, who were quietly checking and rechecking their equipment, including life-support systems to be used when they exited the aircraft.

"Sorry about the cramped accommodations. We don't often carry passengers. But there's plenty of coffee on board and a lot of sandwiches. Let me know when you get hungry."

He received nods, nervous smiles, and a wave of a hand in response.

"Guard frequencies 319.1 through 321 on your single sideband. Okay? I'm expecting a call from home," Getts said.

The oficer smiled, patted Getts encouragingly on the shoulder. "No problem, Commander."

A late sinking sun darkened Wallis's office prematurely, it seemed. Wallis and Barnes had been sitting quietly for hours, sifting through intel data, trying to think of a way to deliver more information to Getts about the castle.

"Barnes," Wallis said suddenly, in a fit of inspiration.

"Yes, sir?" the colonel sat upright.

"Find E. H. Bollan in a telephone book somewhere in Maine. Tell him that you are the personal secretary for Doctor Bradley Wallis of the Carlisle Historical Society and that he has won our annual award . . . make that special award, for . . . for his contribution to the *Visual Reconstruction of History*. Tell him that the president of our society, Doctor Wallis himself, is arriving there today to present him with his prestigious recognition."

"Historical Society . . . ?"

"Yes. Quickly, man," Wallis said. He strode across his office toward the door. As he pulled it open, Cletis, his butler, stood with Wallis's coat, hat, and umbrella at the ready. Wallis, who seemed totally unsurprised at his servant's prescience, shrugged into his coat. "There are a pile of teacups behind my desk, Cletis. You might make yourself useful by picking them up."

"Yes, sir," Cletis responded.

"Who's E. H. Bollan?" Barnes called after his superior.

"He builds castles. Call me in the car when you find his address," the spymaster said as he hurried toward his ancient elevator.

E. H. Bollan lived on the Maine coast, twelve miles north of Cutler. Bollan had bought a small plot of ground ninety feet above crashing Atlantic breakers so that he could cogitate on the history of the world while being rhapsodized by nature's fullest instrument, joined by cries of gulls, terns, bass seals, alto and soprano winds. He never tired of looking at every color under the sun, never wearied of the ceaseless caressing sounds in his ears.

He had loaded ships in Boston Harbor all of his life, had read history, focused acutely on several centuries that he admired most, and had published a small book on the subject while still operating a forklift to move cargo skids. Few people had read his book. One who had was Bradley Wallis.

When Bollan retired from the longshoreman's union, he moved farther north, bought the small bit of land he could afford and continued his studies of castles.

Bollan's furnishings were from the late 1950s. Some of them, like an ornate baseplate standing lamp with a shade once yellow now green, were discolored by mold and sea air. The house was full of books. There were books in cases, stacked on the floor, piled in the kitchen. While Bollan sat reading one of his precious books, smoking a slow burning pipe tobacco called Escudo, the tranquillity of his existence was interrupted first with a distant humming, until the sound continued to increase as its source neared his house. The entire house was soon vibrating, shaking as though a massive excavation was taking place under its foundations.

Bollan leaped to his feet, stepped to the front door and, flinging it open, saw a huge helicopter descending onto his front yard. While the elderly man stared transfixed, a door opened on the helicopter's side and Bradley Wallis, holding his hat onto his head, stepped out. Wallis, gripping a briefcase in his free hand, motioned to the pilot of the helicopter, who switched off the engine of the rotor craft.

"Mr. Bollan? E. H. Bollan? I'm Bradley Wallis. How do you do?"

Bollan, still incredulous at the magnitude and suddenness of Wallis's arrival, took the offered hand. "Ah, a pleasure, Mr. Wallis." The two men moved toward Bollan's open front door and went inside. "Doctor . . . ah, Professor . . . ?" Bollan began.

"Call me Brad."

"Yes. Well, do you always travel that way?" Bollan nodded toward the giant helicopter that was as large as his small house.

"Car trouble. Well, this is quite a retreat you have here, Mr. Bollan. Very . . . out of the way." Wallis smiled.

"Care for a drink?" Bollan offered.

"Scotch, if you have it. No ice. I've come a long way to see your castles."

Bollan moved into the kitchen where he fetched a bottle of single malt scotch and two glasses from a cupboard. "How do you know about my castles, Mr. Wallis?"

"I subscribe to *Renaissance,*" Wallis said. "I remembered several years ago that one issue featured your enormously interesting castles. The Carlisle Society wasted no time in selecting you for our award."

Wallis accepted his glass of scotch gratefully. "Would you think me terribly rude if we looked at your castles now?" Wallis touched Bollan at the elbow as if propelling toward their common destination.

"Er, no. Back this way," Bollan said as he led Wallis through his small kitchen and out a rear door. A light rain had begun to fall, but Wallis and his host remained dry as they walked along wooden planks laid on the ground under a continuation of roofline toward a greenhouse less than twenty feet from the main house.

"That article appeared five years ago," Bollan said, still incredulous.

"That recently? How lucky for you. Most of our awards are posthumous," Wallis replied.

Bollan unlocked a door to the greenhouse and flicked on a light switch on a nearby wall. Wallis's reaction was unqualified surprise. He had marveled at colored photographs of Bollan's sand castles, but the view of a half acre of medieval castles and forests built to scale in the most realistic detail was breathtaking.

"Good heavens," Wallis marveled aloud. Each castle setting was built waist high upon its own raised dais and was topographically accurate. Some were manned by troops of knights in armor, some on horseback, some enduring siege with catapults and scaling towers as armies assaulted their enemies. Other castles displayed a more tranquil existence; many with entire villages within the outer ramparts while walled baileys formed second concentric rings around keeps. Lush gardens and groves grew inside the walls while miniature workers, artisans, and builders were engaged in their crafts. To Wallis, they appeared alive. Most of the castles had moats surrounding them, almost all with but a single drawbridge for access. Even small balustrades were cut through bartizans or turrets.

It was a fantasy land, made perfect by scale and diversity. One could lose oneself in the pristine times of knighthood's code of chivalry, Wallis felt. He said as much to Bollan.

Bollan was pleased. "Matter of fact, most knights were illiterate. Very few had interests outside of drinking, carousing, and fighting wars. And they didn't live all that well. See, here." Bollan drew Wallis toward a castle noticeably smaller than the others. "This was typical of the kind of castle most knights owned. They were often run down. No such things as individual rooms. Animals usually slept indoors along with the servants and masters. The places stank. Everyone slept on straw ticking, which was usually infested with insects of all kinds, including vermin. It's more romantic to look backward into the middle ages and imagine what it could have been like rather than what it was." He smiled as he sipped his drink.

"Yes, I suppose. But still, they were staunch men, eh? And dedicated. I admire that," Wallis said, unwilling to desert his dream of principled men loyal to their kings.

"Yes, they were staunch. Knights of these times were the most fearless fighters, the most effective killers in the world, bar none. Attila the Hun and his horde would have had no chance against an army of French or English knights, for example. But dedicated? Only to whatever prince that could afford their services. Wars are not fought out of love, Mr. Wallis. They are fought for only two reasons: first is a tribal philosophy, which includes religion. The second reason is greed. Those two dangerous ingredients were involved in the murder of so-called infidels over a period of hundreds of years in the Holy Lands."

"Fascinating," Wallis said as they strolled through myriad castles.

"This one is Pevensey Castle," Bollan said. "It was built in the third century by the Romans and captured by the Saxons in 491 A.D. It's crude compared with, say, Rochester Castle. . . ."

Wallis followed Bollan as they continued their tour.

"This is what it looked like in 1088 when it withstood the siege of Bishop Odo, the king's uncle. He loved war twice as much as Thomas à Becket, and when he was barred by the church from using a sword he continued to fight battles using a mace. But he couldn't dent these walls of rock."

"Astonishing," Wallis said, and meant it. "What about castles in the Middle East?"

"Ah, the Holy Lands," Bollan said. "Point of fact, it was the Byzantines to whom our European forebears owe gratitude for the improvements of castle design. At least from the twelfth century on. European castles became larger, and their fortified areas became more complex."

"And Syria? I understand there are castles there," Wallis said, not wanting to appear overanxious lest he give away his purpose.

"One of the finest surviving castles in the world is the Krak des Chevaliers, a Crusader fortress on the border of Syria and Lebanon. Over here." Bollan led Wallis toward another part of his huge kingdom. He stopped before an extraordinary replica of Krak Castle.

"Most people don't know that it was built by Saracens who were learning European warfare. The word Krak comes from the Levantine Arabic Karak, meaning 'fortress.' Crusaders took over the site in . . ."

"Yes, yes," Wallis interrupted, feeling the loss of precious time as Getts and his Blacklight force were even now somewhere high over the Atlantic Ocean. "This one," Wallis said, retrieving a photograph from a manila folder under his arm. "Are you familiar with this sort of castle?"

Bollan studied the aerial photograph. "Hmmmm. Do you have any other pictures?" he asked.

Wallis produced another satellite photo. Details of the castle were quite clear, very detailed.

"Interesting," Bollan said.

"Yes, isn't it? What can you tell me about it?"

"It's called the Towers of Fouquat," Bollan pronounced.

"No, it is Rudyah Castle," Wallis corrected.

"That is the Arab name for the edifice. When it was built, it was called the Towers of Fouquat, named after the family who built it," Bollan said.

"Then you know it?" Wallis could not contain his eagerness to hear more. "Is it . . . a strong castle?"

Bollan chuckled. "As a matter of fact, it's not a castle at all. It's actually a gate house. But don't feel badly about making that mistake. Back in the eleven hundreds, when Fouquat was built, the castle guard, including their horses and weaponry, were housed in a gate house. It was also the armory. Gate houses kept getting bigger and bigger until they reached this size. See how this one is set into the rocks? And the cliffs above? I imagine they slept soundly in this one." Bollan beamed at the photo.

"No way for attackers to get in, I suppose. That is, no way except over a wall."

"Probably, but if I wanted to get in, I think I would look at the castle drawings," Bollan said.

"I beg your pardon. You said drawings. What did you mean?" Wallis asked.

"I have blueprint drawings of most of the world's castles," Bollan said.

Wallis held his breath while Bollan rummaged through large, wide, filing cabinets that took up a good part of a wall nearest the house.

"Ha!" he said, triumphantly withdrawing from one of the drawers several sheets of architectural paper. "1947. The British did these . . ." he beamed.

"Uh, Mr. Bollan, I wonder if I could borrow those plans. It's very important."

"Sorry. I never let my . . ."

But Wallis had already rolled up the prints and stuffed them away. "You needn't fear about getting them back, Mr. Bollan. You have my guarantee," he said, holding out his hand. "Good-bye."

"Ah, good-bye, Mr. Wallis. Er, I suppose there's some sort of ceremony connected with the award . . . ?"

"Award? Oh, yes, yes. The award is usually sent by post. That's it. The award is in the mail."

The pilot of the helicopter had already begun turning over the three thousand horsepower engine when he saw Wallis hurrying from the house.

Senator Toby Johns had rejected his wife's not so subtle urgings to get a haircut. She did not share the vain senator's self-image of a man of the people, a country rustic who spoke simply and to the point, and that somehow overgrown gray hair covering much of the ears was central to that image. It was as though Senator Johns was advertising the fact that he was more concerned with long hours of thankless toil in the dank rooms of his senate office building rather than presenting a neatly coiffed image to his constituency. A constituency that he regarded, as a matter of fact, as national, not merely statewide.

Walking leisurely along a sidewalk near his office in the Israeli embassy was Julian Levi, a man who made a habit of enjoying the best of his good life as represented in kitchens and restaurants in America's capital. Despite his expanding waistline, Ambassador Levi, having served as a tank commander in the Six Day War and countless hand to hand conflicts with members of his opposite political party, understood combat.

"We could have discussed this over lunch. The fish at cid Rose is beyond belief," he said to Senator Johns.

"I don't have time for lunch," Senator Johns postured.

"Very well, the affairs of Israel don't follow after the needs of my gut, either, Senator. What can I do for you?"

"I'm worried about what my country might be getting itself into," Toby Johns drawled. "And yours. Remember, Julian, if we get punched in the nose some of the blood that comes out will be yours."

"We want it that way. We are comrades. We are committed to one another. The world knows that," Levi pontificated.

"Yeah, well, General Lathrop has intercepted several radio signals and telephone calls from a secret American Army operations group. Seems they're on their way to an action in the Middle East. You people know anything about that?" the senator asked.

The ambassador shook his head. "No. I'm sure I would have been told. Doesn't General Lathrop know what they're about?"

Without directly answering his question, Senator Johns reflected on repercussions. "It's some kind of damn secret group, bunch of mavericks who figure they're going to invade Libya or Syria or someplace like that. We can't afford to insult our allies, our, uh, good friends."

"Yes, they're lovable people. But how does that concern us?" Levi asked.

"I want your assurances that you won't help them," Senator Johns stated.

"Why don't you recall your men?"

"Isn't that easy," the aging senator exhaled. "Apparently they have the blessings of the President, that shithead. But their operation, whatever it is, is illegal. Certainly immoral. If your country does anything to involve itself in this matter I'll take it personally, Julian. I mean that. As chairman of the Armed Forces Committee, I'll see to it that Israel won't be able to buy, much less borrow, a damn staff car from the United States. Got me on that?"

Ambassador Levi flushed, raised himself to his full five feet six inches. "I will not be threatened, Senator. Israel will not be threatened. Not even by its best friend."

Toby Johns laughed, "Now that you got that off your goddamn chest, Julian, think about what I just said. When that turd sitting in the Oval Office is gone, I'm still going to be around."

Ambassador Levi turned his head away. "I'll look into it," he said.

"Do more than look into it, Julian." Senator Johns put his arm warmly around the shorter man's shoulders and gave him a friendly squeeze. "Neither one of us needs to be embarrassed."

Chapter Nineteen

The B-1 was flying at an altitude so high that no sound would reach the ground below. Its approach from central Egypt in a northeasterly direction, however, was detected by Saudi Arabian AWACS aircraft. A Capricorn transponder signal was sent, and the American air force liaison officer aboard the AWACS cleared the black plane through the Saudi air defense alert system. There were no other radar systems, save Israel's, capable of deciphering the B-1 track. If required, the B-1 could defeat search radar, but as it entered space over the Red Sea there was nothing to evade.

Getts and nine others inside the bomber were fully suited and were making last-minute equipment checks out of habit. The B-1 was equipped with bomb load ejection chambers similar to a pistol chamber that revolved with each shot. In this operation people, the Blacklight team, would be the bullets dropping from the bomb-bay cylinder.

"Commander Getts," the pilot squawked via his intercom, "we're coming up on the stream. When we drop in, it's going to be a little bumpy."

"Okay, we'll be ready when you are," Getts responded.

Several more minutes passed while Getts watched for a green jump light. In mild irritation, he punched the intercom switch. "What's the holdup?" he said to the pilot.

"Wait one, Commander. We got a signal from your people. They say to stand by in a holding pattern," the pilot responded.

"What for?" Getts demanded.

"I just drive this pig, I don't read minds, sir."

"Okay," Getts said.

The pilot put the B-1 into a shallow turn.

"What's happening, Bobby?" Peach asked.

"Don't know. Wallis has something on his mind."

There were all kinds of dangers in Getts's plans, he knew. Waiting in ambush with enough force to knock out Conrad and his escort was inviting discovery. Getting out alive was another a gamble unless the timing was of their own making, not Conrad's.

"Commander Getts," the pilot said over the intercom, "we can hold for about another thirty minutes before we have to refuel. We've got a KC-135 on its way from Turkey, but we'll have to leave this station to meet it. Your call."

"I'll take the thirty minutes," Getts said without hesitation.

"Like I say, Commander, it's your call, but what's your plan if we have to leave orbit to refuel?"

"We jump anyway."

In the cockpit, the pilot and crew, all listening to the conversation, exchanged glances. The copilot shook his head.

The pilot toggled his intercom to Getts. "We're two minutes to the HARP. I've got to get into the stream now, or it's no go."

Getts took only a moment to consider. He knew that once they reached the high altitude release point they would have to go or abort the mission. "Do it."

Getts put a listening device into his ear, which was attached to a small wire taped to the side of his jaw inside his helmet. This way, he would be able to stay in touch with all other members of the team. He passed his roll of surgical tape to Peach, who ripped off two pieces, then continued passing it around. Each member taped his or her earphone and mike wire to their heads. Over this, they pulled tight but porous masks similar to ski masks with holes for mouth, nose, and eyes. Then they donned their space helmets. Getts's work was interrupted by the ECM Officer.

"Traffic coming in for you on print."

Getts, moving with difficulty in his clumsy suit, plodded along the bomber's innards to a place where a FAX machine, was just finishing printing out two drawings. Getts studied them quickly.

"How much time do we have?" Getts asked the ECM Officer.

"Skipper's gonna make one more circuit before dropping

into the stream. We might have to paddle this son of a bitch through the Straits of Hormuz to get it home."

Getts showed his understanding and appreciation by quickly squeezing the crew man's arm. Then he returned to his Blacklight group, facsimile reproductions in hand.

"These are layouts of the castle," he said, simply. "Start your oxygen. We'll study the pictures on the ground."

Blacklight team members actuated their oxygen flow control valves, pulled on thermal glove liners, then outer gloves that locked onto hands and wrists with Velcro.

The aircraft suddenly began to buck violently, vibrating for several more seconds before settling into smooth flight once again.

"Commander Getts," the pilot said over his intercom, "I've got flaps down, power back, and we're still doing almost four hundred miles per hour over the ground. Apparent airspeed is under two hundred. Believe it or not, we're close to stall right now."

"Gotcha," Getts acknowledged.

"This is about as slow as we can make it, so watch for the green light and good luck to you."

"Roger. Thanks," Getts said.

Busboy occupied a launch space with Carla. As she went over her equipment once again, Busboy was having trouble adjusting his oxygen valve. To alleviate sticking, Busboy spat on the valve stem, manipulated it around once or twice, then spat on it again.

"Systems on line?" Getts asked all the members of the team. "Roll call," he said. One by one the remaining members of the Blacklight team answered as their names were called. Heggstad . . . Huck Finn . . . Carla . . . Bartender . . . Crush . . . Valentino . . . Peach . . . Busboy. . . .

All answered save Busboy. "Busboy, you on line?"

"Yes, sir," Busboy answered.

" 'Sir?' How do you know I'm really an officer and not just a smart corporal?" Getts's voice came over the intercom.

"That tears it, by god. I ain't goin'," Heggstad declared.

Nervous laughter was interrupted by the metallic voice of the pilot. "Thirty seconds and counting: Twenty-seven . . . twenty-six . . . twenty-five. . . ."

"Anybody misses the IZ, use your GPS to hook up.

You'll have one hour," Getts repeated an instruction they all knew well.

The large bomb-bay doors, driven by hydraulic rams, suddenly sprang open underneath the speeding aircraft. Immediately, the pod loaded with human cargo, dropped into jettison position. Within the instant, the first two Blacklight jumpers were released. The cylinder rotated, and two more forms, equipment attached to their bodies like an umbilical cord, were jettisoned into cobalt skies.

There were mild explosions as each parachute was fully deployed by small explosive charges. As each canopy blossomed, the jumper concentrated on flying his chute as closely as possible to their leader, Bob Getts. Even at this incredible altitude, Blacklight jumpers could discern that they were moving at a high rate of horizontal fall in relation to the ground. There had always a feeling of great exhilaration at the moment a chute opened and the descent was begun, a sense of freedom few people ever experience. But this time, Getts heard no cries of joy as they formed up behind him, guiding on the orange chemical light attached to his space suit.

Getts craned to see upward. "Last man in line. Are we all here?" he demanded into his lip mike.

"This is Crush," the voice said over the communications system. "I count only eight. Only eight chutes, Bobby!"

Another voice jumped in, calm, almost detached. "Count yourself, asshole."

"Oh, yeah. Nine."

From this altitude, Getts could see the curvature of the earth, the dawn spreading behind the Jabal Mountains.

Getts could see one of the chutes drifting off from the others. "Busboy," Getts ordered over his intercom, "tighten it up. Steer right."

But the parachute continued to drift away from the battle group.

"You're going out of the stream, Busboy. Shape your chute!" Heggstad called to his comrade.

Busboy's voice, when it came over the communication system, was weak, faltering. He could not reach his oxygen valve, now frozen closed in minus sixty degree temperature. "No . . . air . . . oxygen . . . sorry . . . Bobby. . . ."

The young Blacklighter's chute fell far behind as he

passed from the narrow band of fast-moving air. Getts knew, as did the others, that Busboy would be dead within minutes, his body falling lifelessly into the Red Sea. When Getts spoke again his voice was subdued. "Roll it in, Valentino. We don't want to lose you, too."

Conrad was returning from Damascus in his air-conditioned limousine when he happened to look out of his window to see the ragged Arab tending his peddler's cart at the side of the road. As they flashed, past something about the way the peddler watched the car bothered Conrad. The back of his neck tingled a bit. Limousines such as Conrad's were not common in this country so it was no wonder that the Arab would stare, Conrad thought. Still, something about the man seemed familiar. Was he not in the same area two days ago? And what could he sell this far from town?

Conrad was infected by strong feelings of paranoia. He was aware that his torments were abnormal, but Conrad understood that his chances of remaining alive were enhanced if he gave heed to threats against him, both real and imagined.

One of his bodyguards, Rezi, a short, muscular, regular army sergeant in the Syrian army, watched Conrad like a hawk. Conrad, for intuitive reasons, believed that Rezi was spying on him.

"Rezi," Conrad spoke sharply to the Arab security man.

"Yes, sir?"

Conrad, stood on a small balcony in the keep, and looked downward to the grounds below where Rezi sat with young Karl. "There is a man near the main road with a cart. Go look," Conrad ordered.

Rezi moved to stone steps leading up to the outer rampart wall to look.

"Not there, you fool," Conrad shouted, "I said go look. That means *go*. Do you understand English? I mean walk out of the gate and down to the road!"

At that moment, Conrad heard the screech of a pair of baboons from their lofty towers in one of the turrets along the castle wall. He looked up to see a pair of drills staring down at him, spying on him as they spied on everyone inside and outside of the castle. Though they were trained for guard duty, he knew they could never be disciplined like a dog. They were smarter than a dog, stronger, more violent, in fact. He watched Rezi as the simple soldier walked to the steps leading to the ground below.

Lisa appeared silently at Conrad's side. "I hate them," she said, her gaze directed at the castle walls, the baboons. "They are evil."

"They are neither good nor evil. They are here to protect us."

Mehmet-Rauf had traded the used cotton garments he had bought weeks before in Damascus for slats of wood and pieces of corrugated metal. The cart was substantially heavier than when he hauled clothing, and he found himself having to lean far forward to push his heavily laden cart up a long grade. It was midafternoon with temperatures more than 110°. He did not hear the voice that ordered him to stop until the second or third warning.

He turned to see a short, stout, Arab approaching. The Arab carried an assault rifle but wore no uniform. Mehmet-Rauf could not see behind the Arab's dark glasses, but he knew that no humor would be found there.

"Blessings of Allah," Mehmet-Rauf said, nodding toward Rezi.

"Hmm. What are you doing here?" Rezi asked.

"With respect, sir, every man must be somewhere." Mehmet-Rauf scratched his head as though the answer to the question was obvious.

"Yes, and you are here. My question is why are you here and not somewhere else." The security man began to push and poke among Mehmet-Rauf's cart.

"I am collecting material, as you can see," the disguised spy responded. "I am building a house for my wife and children. It is not easy to find what I need."

Rezi was struck with remembrance. The roof of his childhood home had been corrugated tin, its floor was dirt. They had no running water and food appeared irregularly. Had it not been for the army, Rezi himself might be pushing a cart down a lonely road scavenging for bare boards and pieces of tin. Rezi's tone and attitude seemed to change. He exhaled, his rifle muzzle drooping toward the ground. When he spoke his voice was softer than moments ago. "How many children do you have, Citizen?"

"Four," the spy lied with a twinge of regret.

Rezi reached into his pocket and came out with a few bills. He pressed them into Mehmet-Rauf's hand. "Take these." The spy was speechless. As Rezi turned back toward the castle Mehmet-Rauf could find no words to say in response to this singular act of kindness, especially from an armed man who was certainly his enemy.

"Well?" Conrad said to Rezi as he entered the castle gate. Standing next to Conrad was Captain Ahmmad.

"Nothing, Herr Eisler," Rezi reported.

"Nothing, what? Who was the man?" Conrad demanded.

"He was no one, Herr Eisler. A harmless brother who gathers pieces of wood to build shelter for his family," the security man explained.

"Yes, I am sure that is what he told you. Now you tell me, where was he from? Where was he going? Where does he live? Eh? Did you demand proof?"

Rezi said nothing.

"Herr Eisler . . ." Captain Ahmmad began.

"You shut up," Conrad snapped at Ahmmad. "Well?" he demanded of Rezi.

"I did not ask for documents, Herr Eisler. Poor people like him often carry no papers. Many cannot read. It was obvious. . . ."

"Obvious!" Conrad exploded. "Obvious? You are a mind reader, I am delighted to know. I feel so much safer knowing that you are on duty to read the minds of people who are trying to kill me. Do you realize who you have been assigned to protect?"

"Herr Eisler," Captain Ahmmad said firmly, "I will take responsibility for the performance of my own men. Please be kind enough to instruct me in your specific orders for protection. Rezi," he said, turning to the compact soldier in civilian clothes, "get about your duties."

White sands curled around a section of exclusive beach front hotels in northern Israel. Each hotel's marina had slips filled with yachts from around the world. Wealthy Europeans and Israelis were at play, well protected. In almost every direction were unobtrusive khaki-clad Israeli soldiers carrying automatic weapons.

Toni's richly tanned skin was beautifully showcased in a

minimal white bikini. Over one shoulder, she carried a canvas beach bag containing what looked like a walkman. She
wore a headset and a pair of designer sunglasses.

An Italian man in his early thirties stepped from the
cabin of his powerboat. He wore brief bathing trunks over
a hairy, yet well proportioned body. His bearing, his obviously expensive boat, and the way he wore his loosely tied
beach robe, reeked of indolence. He carried a gin and tonic
in one hand and a cigarette, held in the continental fashion,
in the other. His eyes arrested on the exquisite body of
Toni as she walked the slips.

"I am Adriano," he said as he approached her.

Toni lifted her sunglasses, squinted one eye, then allowed
her glasses to slip back into place. She said nothing in
response.

"You are a most beautiful lady," Adriano purred. "I
watch you come up the beach from my boat." He pointed
at his craft. "White with red trim. Lines beautiful, like
yours. I would be honored if you would join me aboard my
boat for a drink," he said.

"Fuck off," Toni said, moving nothing but her lips.

"Ah, an American," Adriano gushed. "I love Americans."

Ignoring the Italian, Toni adjusted her radio receiver to a
UHF band that only she could hear through her earphones.

"Trespasser two, we've got traffic on niner-one. . . .
Stand by for a burst transmission. . . . Pathfinder, this
is Burning Tree guarding your freq. . . . Roger, Burning
Tree. We have Magic on 4-level. Stand by please . . .
Coming on . . . Acknowledge. . . ."

At a desert airfield in central Israel, there was a flight of
fast attack helicopters, parked in a state of readiness. Camouflage netting had been placed over the helicopters while
they remained parked outside. Fighter aircraft and fighter
bombers were inside underground hangars.

Maas, who wore a crisp uniform of desert fatigues and
the rank designation of brigadier general, walked purpose-
fully along the flight line. None of the helicopters that Maas
stopped to inspect, unlike other aircraft on the base bearing
the Star of David, had identification anywhere on their
fuselages. A man sat inside the cockpit of a chopper.

Maas looked up at him. "Benjamin."

Benjamin Elkerbout, a pilot not yet twenty-four, looked down from the cockpit. "Hello there, General. Welcome home, sir."

"Thank you. We fly tomorrow, Benjamin. Two ships, two crew men besides the pilot. I will be in your crew."

"Where do I take my machine, sir?" the young pilot asked.

"A quick run through the mountain passes. About seventy-five kilometers each way. Could be nasty coming out."

"Then shouldn't we take an extra door gunner, sir?" the pilot wanted to know.

Instead of answering, Maas held up a finger and waggled it back and forth in a *no, no,* sign. His business with Benjamin finished, the general walked toward the operations offices.

Chapter Twenty

Within the inner walls of Fouquat castle, several gardeners worked six days a week to maintain the huge grounds, trimming cypress trees and searching relentlessly for weeds among the meticulously maintained lawns, exotic shrubbery, and countless flower beds. The castle drew its water from a deep well, not trusting the waters of the nearby Nahr Barada River where poisons or toxins could be added. There was an Olympic-size swimming pool located on the south side of the castle grounds. A second pool was inside the keep.

It was in the outdoor pool that Conrad's assigned head of household security, Captain Ahmmad, found Conrad and Lisa. They were swimming in the pool, naked. Captain Ahmmad had strict orders to keep his thoughts to himself and his tongue inside his head where European customs were concerned. Still, Captain Ahmmad found it enormously difficult to put from his mind the holy laws of Sharia. When the Eisler woman ignored Islamic law and removed her clothes in view of men, he thought about how such sinful women should have the skin flayed from their bodies or, at least, be stoned to death.

She would lie in the sun with nothing but a scant cloth covering her pubic region and often nothing whatever over her breasts. That she be allowed to marry again after the death of her husband was an affront to Allah and to the Prophet Muhammad.

Captain Ahmmad refrained in all cases from looking at the woman and privately warned his soldiers that they would be severely disciplined if they did not do the same. It caused him personal displeasure that the Arab people should employ such filthy infidels in resisting the power of the Western Satan, but he comforted himself with the certain knowledge that in a day not far away, the man called Conrad would have his throat cut and bled out as a sacrifice to Allah.

Now, as the Europeans touched each other inside the pool, the captain kept his eyes above and to the right of the women, reporting only to Herr Conrad. "A call from the President's house, Herr Eisler."

"The President? Is he on the telephone now?" Conrad said.

"No, sir. The call was from his secretary, sir. He wishes to extend an invitation to you and Frau Eisler for dinner on the second day of next week."

Captain Ahmmad's peripheral vision was betraying him as an outline of the European woman's bare backside became visible only inches under clear water. The captain moved his head slightly to the right to make blocking her body an easier task. Captain Ahmmad was not sure, but for a moment he believed that Conrad was amused at his discomfort.

"Ah, well, of course. Please tell the President's secretary that we would be delighted to come."

Conrad turned dismissively away from the captain and swam to Lisa's side in the pool. He put his arms around her, and they kissed. "Conrad," she said, enjoying the sensation of his naked body pressing against hers, "when do you work? I mean, don't you go visit oil wells or something? And do all petroleum engineers live in castles?"

He kissed her lightly on the mouth. She playfully flicked her tongue into his. "I will explain everything about my work very soon, my darling."

"Oh? You have secrets about your work? Tell me now," she insisted.

"I will, but not now."

"I want to know now, Conrad."

Conrad glanced around to ensure that no one was listening to their conversation. "Please, try to remember to call me Erich."

"But it is so stupid," Lisa laughed. "And these ridiculous laws about women. Why, they walk around covered up like mummies, the poor wretches."

"It's their custom," he said.

Lisa laughed and gently cupped his genitalia. "Since when did you ever care about custom?"

"Since I became employed by religious Arabs. They can be dangerous," he cautioned her.

"Do they pay you well?" she asked out of curiosity.

"Very well."

"Well," she kissed him lightly on the neck, "at least we can be together. And you were right. The desert has a kind of magic of its own. I may come to like it very much."

Three drill baboons screeched from atop the south wall as they disagreed over an unfathomable primate need. Lisa looked sharply up, shivered. "Can't you get rid of them?"

"Forget about them. Think about me."

The *Gottfried,* a shabby, weatherworn freighter was being loaded at dockside in the Rio de la Plata, Argentina. She flew the Swiss flag but was chartered to the Haing-Lee Ltd. Maritime Services out of Singapore. This was scheduled to be her last trip before the scrap yard and not a moment too soon for the Swiss government. She was a hag of the seas: overweight, overaged, and with little means of visible support.

Her skipper was Captain Kurt van Schlicker, a Dutchman who sold his first illegal cargo of ivory, and his soul along with it, at age twenty-two. Now at fifty, he wore a scruffy, dappled beard and paced the bridge of the *Gottfried* as he

waited impatiently for a tug and barge to arrive from the
east side of the channel. Having failed his skipper's physical, not once but three times, it was to be Schlicker's last
voyage for Haing-Lee. He had stashed considerable por-
tions of his contraband payroll in banks around the world,
owned property in San Francisco, and could have easily
turned a deaf ear to the two Arabs who contacted him five
days ago when he arrived in port. But the undeclared cargo,
to be integrated with casks of wine from Cyprus, would
provide a great deal of money for small risk.

The day was hot, surprisingly humid for these latitudes
at this time of year. Van Schlicker considered availing himself of the bottle of lager chilling for him in his cabin. While
the tug he was waiting for was even now making a small
turn to come alongside the *Gottfried,* there was still time
for a long, deep pull from the bottle. He sighed, reluctantly
rejected his refreshing idea, and leaned over the port rail
of the bridge deck.

"Ah del barco, en el Gottfried," the voice of the tug's
skipper hailed van Schlicker's ship. *"La carga."*

Van Schlicker responded with a flaccid wave of the
hand. *"Ja."*

Lightweight line was thrown from the stern of the tug
and the bow of its barge to temporarily secure the smaller
ship to the larger one. On deck, a bosun's mate and a
cargo-boom operator swung a heavy net over the side to
barge level. While ten casks—labeled inconspicuously as
wine—were loaded into the net for transfer, a dark complexioned man climbed the ship's ladder.

Van Schlicker, seldom in a good mood, was irascible as
the man, wearing a modest sport coat and cotton trousers—
his aquiline nose offset by a heavy beard and mustache—
stepped aboard. "Who are you?" van Schlicker demanded.

"I am Magetz," the Arabic man said, calmly. "I am to
accompany the wine to America."

"Hmmph. You were not part of the consignment," van
Schlicker said. "Go ashore."

Unfazed, Magetz withdrew from his pocket a large roll
of American $100 bills. "I was hoping you could make an
exception in my case, Captain. Naturally, you will require
a substantial price for your inconvenience." Magetz peeled

off a number of bills and handed them to Captain van
Schlicker.

"All right, Mr. Magetz," van Schlicker said, "you have
touched my heart. Welcome aboard."

Magetz did not repair to his assigned accommodations
immediately, but stayed on deck until he saw that the casks
containing anthrax biological warheads were secured in a
cargo hold.

The day had dawned in full glory. A solitary man, Mehmet-
Rauf, climbed around craggy rocks, keeping to narrow
trails made by goats that roamed the dry lands in search
of forage. The spy, pausing to find landmarks, sat atop a
large rock to rest and wipe his brow. There was very little
sweat, as moisture quickly dissipated in the furnace that
was Syria.

After resting several minutes, the spy rose from his place
of repose. He took only a few steps before what seemed
like a rock suddenly rose from the ground and took on the
grotesque shape of a man. The "rock" held one arm around
Mehmet-Rauf's neck, and placed a knife just below his ear.

"Southpaw," Crush said.

Moving with difficulty, the spy raised his right arm. At
the end of his struggling arm, he extended three fingers.

The big man rumbled a chuckle from deep within his chest.
"One is a fast ball, two is a curve. Three ain't nothin',"
he said.

"Who comes up with these idiotic passwords?" Mehmet-
Rauf choked in disgust. "Where are the others?" he wanted
to know.

Mehmet-Rauf could only now make out the forms hidden
among nearby rocks, men who blended so perfectly with
their surroundings that they were all but invisible. They
materialized into a semicircle around the spy.

"I'm Getts," one of them said.

"I was told to expect nine," Mehmet-Rauf said.

"We lost a man over the Red Sea," Getts said.

"I'm sorry," Mehmet-Rauf said.

"So are we," Peach said.

"Anybody here from Chicago? That's where I'm from,"
the spy said.

"I am," Carla said, hoisting her OICW over her shoulder.

The spy's tired eyes rekindled. "Yeah? Well, what do you know? Actually, I lived outside the city. Niles. Ever go to a place in town called the Faucet Tavern? Used to drink beer there while I was going to graduate school. Not a real big place, but they pumped a hundred kegs a month. Everybody showed up there sooner or later. That's where turtle races started, you know."

Carla nodded her head. "Couldn't be in town twenty minutes without going to the Faucet," she agreed.

"Yeah! What I wouldn't give for one of those chili dogs and a cold draft, right now," the spy raptured.

The Blacklight team waited patiently for the spy to complete his reverie. He was doing a dangerous job under difficult conditions, and they would not rush him.

"I've got some photographs of the castle. Don't know how much good they'll do you," Mehmet-Rauf said. "I've been watching the place for over a week."

"You've done your job well," Getts said, glancing at the glossy photos. "How many men do they have inside? Any way to estimate?"

"I'm not sure, but if I had to guess I'd say there's a detail of about eight to ten plainclothes security inside the castle grounds. Probably ten or twelve more uniformed people who live in the garrison building. Then, there's a regular Syrian Army battle group posted on the north side of Damascus. Maybe two hundred men. They'd probably get here fast when the balloon goes up."

"How fast?" Getts asked.

"Thirty minutes, at most. They're mobile, naturally."

Getts knelt to the ground and spread out a map. "We want you to take us to the castle, but we want to avoid all contacts with locals. The whole mission blows up if we don't get to the castle unseen."

"I understand," the Chicagoan said.

"So we'll loop around, up here," Getts said indicating with his finger on his area map, "avoiding the roads so we come out on the northeast side of the castle. Okay with you?"

"Sure. It'd be a lot easier to follow this wadi, but we can cross these hills, if that's what you want."

Each man shouldered a hundred pounds of gear, including weapons, explosives, ammunition, camouflage suits, and communications equipment. Carla carried less, only 70 pounds. She was strong for a woman, but her body frame could not support the same load as Rick Heggstad who stood over six-two and weighed over two hundred pounds, most of it solid muscle mass. But the Blacklight knew Carla would deliver the difference of 30 pounds in performance. They set off marching in single file, Crush walking point, Getts number two, Peach taking the rear, assuring that the unit was not surprised from behind.

The terrain was rugged, the soft sand shifting first to hard, coarse, grated rock, then to slick rock. Steep trails, cutbacks, and cracks were carefully traversed. The sun beat down on their floppy camo hats and raised the ambient temperature well above 110°. Getts and his men would have preferred to move at night, when it was cooler and there was less risk of discovery, but time was of the essence if they were to get to Conrad before he could get to the warheads.

By 1410 hours Zulu, the Blacklight team had traveled eight kilometers over difficult terrain. As they rounded the base of a hill where a dirt road could be seen far below, they were halted by an emphatic hand signal from Crush, who kept low as he crept back to the team. Getts moved forward to meet him. Crush pointed up the hill toward a ridge. Getts followed Crush's finger with his eyes. Above the team's line of march were five people, two of whom were women. They appeared to be a family. Surrounding them were goats roaming the hill, picking at the sparse vegetation among the rocks.

"Have they seen us?" Getts asked.

Crush nodded.

Getts looked upward again. The herders made no move to pick up their slow pace, no faster than the slowest goat. They did not look down, either. Peach kneeled by Getts. "I'll go with Crush. We can take 'em out," the chief gunner's mate said.

Getts did not issue an order. He continued to watch the goat herders for several moments. The small nomadic family continued to move slowly across the ridge.

"We got to move, Bobby," Peach said. Crush was almost vibrating with energy, sensing a kill, his pulse racing in anticipation of taking out a potential threat to the mission.

Getts loathed the notion of killing people whose lives

were hard, who were forced to scrabble upon this hard, arid land to maintain a hand-to-mouth existence. "Let 'em go," Getts said.

Crush's head snapped toward Getts in disbelief. But if Peach was disappointed, he did not show it. The order was given, and it was time to move. Peach motioned Crush back to the point, gave another hand signal to the team, and almost as one, weapons were put on safe and the trek resumed.

At 1833 hours, Getts signaled a break. As the team settled into sand and rock, picking out fragments of shade wherever it could be found and drinking water, Getts raised his binoculars to get his first sight of the Towers of Fouquat some thousand meters distant. His view was almost level with the base of the massive walls. But he noted that as the team neared the castle, they would be moving downhill, and that when they were within three hundred meters, they would be slightly below the stone walls.

Mehmet-Rauf moved to Getts's elbow. "How will you get out?"

"Israeli helicopters," Getts said. "They'll land about here," he said, pointing to a location on his map.

"That's very close to the castle, Commander. Won't they come under fire? And what about the Syrian battle group?" They'll have heavy weapons, maybe even ground-to-air missiles. I don't know."

"I don't know either, but after we go in, we'll send the signal to the choppers. Either way, we'll be finished in thirty minutes. They're only one hundred and fifteen miles from here. The code word is *rascal,* sent in the clear on international emergency frequency. It'll take them forty minutes to arrive from the time they get our signal. They'll drop in before the battle group shows up and, as we say in the biz, we be gone."

"Of course, we'll have air cover from the navy task force offshore. Right?" Mehmet-Rauf suggested.

Getts shook his head. "There ain't no ships. No canoes. No rubber ducks."

"But I thought . . ."

"We had a rat sharing our table, so Peach set out some cheese of his own. We're hoping the Syrians are spending their time looking for a naval force instead of us."

He produced the satellite photos relayed to him from

Wallis at Carlisle and compared them with his visual scan. Peach moved to his side, seeing what Getts saw. "I don't see anybody on the walls," Getts said, passing his binoculars to Peach, who studied the fortress.

"Nothing moving," Peach said.

"I can get close," Mehmet-Rauf said. "They have already talked with me today. They think I'm a poor local man picking up junk from the road. Tell me what you need."

Getts looked at Peach, considering the spy's plan. Then he reached into a pocket of his pack and came up with three items that looked like ordinary rocks. "Passive mini-agents," he said to the spy. He also removed the small battery-powered transceiver that controlled the mini-agents. "If you can you get close enough to throw them over the walls, we might be able to see what's going on inside. Can you do that?"

"Sure."

Getts regarded the spy a bit longer, then nodded his head. "All right. If you get caught, try to walk away. If they take you inside the castle, hold out for as long as you can. Tell them any kind of story you can think of. The longer the better. We won't be long behind you."

"Got it," the spy said, placing the "rocks" into his pockets.

"Good luck," Getts said.

Getts and Peach watched as the spy began walking down the goat trail toward the imposing Towers of Fouquat, his loping gait unhurried.

The Blacklight team scanned the castle, making personal notes, comparing what they saw with the satellite pictures. "Let's move up to five hundred meters," Getts said, pointing to the last line of rocks near the towers. "We'll rest up until it gets darker, then put on the camo prism suits."

"I'll do the recon," Peach volunteered.

"That's my job, Peachy," Getts said. "We'll go in at 0300. Give 'em some real fucking nightmares."

As Mehmet-Rauf reached the base of the castle walls, he fumbled in his sack cloth bag for the mini-agents. He found the first, roughly the size of a baseball, and threw it in an arching path over the wall. He then threw over a second; as he was looking for the third and last "rock," a solid blow hit him on the top of the head. Stunned, he fell heavily to his knees. As he struggled to get to his feet, he felt excruciating pain in his left arm. The scream that came to his lips was drowned out by still another scream, this one near his ear. He was struck again, and he went down once more. Incredible pain shot from one side of his head to the other, the shrieks around mounting in a crescendo. He tried to pull himself free from what he believed at first were attacking Syrian guards, but he was unable to move his arms and legs. It was as though they were weighted down. So concerned was he with unendurable pain, he did not realize that his attackers were drill baboons, gripping at his limbs with the strength of ten men, tearing at his flesh and hair with their razor-sharp fangs. Terrified, Mehmet-Rauf screamed for help at the top of his lungs, but his wail had hardly escaped his lips when his throat was ripped out by huge incisor teeth.

Chapter Twenty-one

Inside the castle, Captain Ahmmad walked as quietly and unobtrusively as possible from the kitchen on the first floor of the keep to another small security room located on the same floor. As he walked along the south side of the huge main floor of the house, he was conscious of the opulent furnishings and artwork that had been restored to their original luster almost one hundred years ago.

To him, the building resembled more a museum than a domicile. Suits of medieval armor stood at either end of the great hall, their crossed broadswords poised above the main fireplace. Tapestries of coats of arms in royal blue and gold thread graced vaulted windows. Battle flags, once carried by the troops of anointed houses of Europe and the Levant, hung from staffs near the study at the east wall. One doorway from the study fronted a ballroom and cinema, including a stage that rivaled theaters in London or New York.

Objects of art, including paintings by European masters as well as Middle Eastern artists, were placed with careful consideration. Graceful sculptures, especially those that traced the artistic history of the Levant, were placed in strategic locations throughout the house. Captain Ahmmad, always impressed with the castle's grandeur, strode toward the security room. Unmarked, its heavy door was, like the others in the keep, made of thick mahogany, its doorknob ornate. He opened the door and entered.

He did not immediately speak to the man inside the room, whose task it was to monitor the many screens that were arrayed around a central terminal. Their sweep offered unobstructed views of the outer walls, including underneath each of the four corners on the turrets, while another set of moving cameras was placed inside the keep itself. However, by the direct order of Herr Eisler cameras on the upper levels, where the living quarters were, had been deactivated. Captain Ahmmad understood the privacy issues, even if he disagreed with it from a security point of view. Other screens showed not pictures but electronic flatlines and spikes responding to heat sensors and motion devices placed upon the outer stone walls.

In addition to Captain Ahmmad, there were twenty security men in all, the majority assigned to the four walls, with two men outside the castle. The balance were stationed at the castle's main gate to monitor vehicle and foot traffic.

"Sir, a man outside the walls was attacked by the baboons," a communications technician reported to Ahmmad.

"Is he alive?"

"No, sir. He was, well . . ."

"Never mind. I know what the corpse must look like," Ahmmad said. "Have him buried when it gets light."

"And a call from Four Army, Captain," the technician said, referring to a designation for the palace guard in Damascus. "Goatherders report men with guns in the mountains."

"How many? Where in the mountains?" Ahmmad said, not particularly alarmed. Men with guns in this country were not unheard of, but it was unwise not to know who they are.

"Less than a dozen. South of El Fal road."

"Is Damascus sending out a patrol?" Ahmmad asked.

"It did not sound like it, sir."

No, of course not, Ahmmad thought. *It is our sector. Why should they care?* "All right. Call the barracks. I want five men for a patrol. Tell the others to stand by to move on a moment's notice. I'll take an AFV," Ahmmad said, using shorthand for the Russian made BRDM-1 reconnaissance vehicle.

The Blacklight team had rested an hour when the gates of the castle swung open. The sun was settling behind the jagged peaks of the mountains as a recon carrier with a machine gun mount over the cab raised a cloud of dust, moving at good speed in their direction. "Recce vehicle coming out," Heggstad reported. "Two kilometers." He peered hard through his ambient-light binoculars as Getts joined him at their perimeter. "Counting four, maybe five in the back, the driver and . . . another man up front. They have a radio on board," he added.

As Peach joined Getts, other troopers heightened their readiness, checking their flanks and rear. "Think they're looking for us?" Peach asked Getts.

"Maybe. But they're not sure we're here, or they would have brought out all their folks. Anything coming from Damascus?" he said.

Peach glanced in Bartender's direction, who was responsible for their right quarter flank and the road leading from the city. Bartender shook his head in the negative.

"Nothing so far," Peach said.

They watched for a full minute in silence as the BRDM-1 car wended its way farther from the castle. Then, abruptly, the vehicle made a right turn from the road and started climbing the long slope toward Blacklight's area. "Okay," Getts said, softly. "They're looking for us." Getts thought for a moment. The AFV was really no threat to them. They could take it out without raising a sweat, but not without making noise in the process. Even if they could dispose of the track and its crew silently, the recon vehicle would be expected back at the castle. Certainly, they were in radio communication. The team would lose the element of surprise. Dying in pursuit of the objective was one thing, but not being able to even carry it out was another. Getts made up his mind. "Let's put on the suits."

Within minutes, the Blacklight had donned their camouflage prism suits, covered their gear, then found declivities among the rocks in which to sit or lie. Guns loaded and off safety, they waited for the scout vehicle to approach. A rising full moon would assist the commandos very well, their prism suits reflecting its light while outlining the enemy in its glow.

When they were twelve hundred meters away, Captain Ahmmad ordered his driver to halt once again. Ahmmad rose from his seat, raised binoculars to his eyes and began to sweep the surrounding hillside. Behind him, his sergeant swept a different quadrant. "Up there," Ahmmad said, pointing his fingers at the line of large rocks set back from the road several hundred meters. It seemed to Ahmmad a likely place from which to operate if he were leading a raiding party. A slight chill swept over Ahmmad's body, and he was suddenly afraid of the coming dark.

Getts watched as the AFV slowly advanced up the steep hill, then stopped a scant hundred meters from the Blacklight team. Captain Ahmmad got out of the recon vehicle and began to examine the mountainside with binoculars. For a long moment, the binoculars, fixed upon the very spot where Getts and the others lay hiding. Getts gripped the butt of his OICW tighter, ready to leap into action. In his mind, he had begun a countdown. If the glasses remained fixed on Getts's position, he would have to kill the Syrian.

But they eventually moved. Ahmmad had not seen Getts's men, who, though inert, were directly in front of him. The Syrian army officer stepped back into his scout vehicle and drove back toward the main road. Inside the car, Ahmmad used the VHF radio to contact the castle security room. "Jamal," he said, "we have no enemy in sight, but that does not mean no one is out here. Understand?"

"Yes, sir," the radio crackled. "Shall I notify Damascus?"

"Yes. And tell them to send out patrols. We should not have to do all the work. Lazy bastards."

"Shall I say all of that, Captain?"

"Yes, if you like. They will probably execute you, as well."

*   *   *

At 0245, the Blacklight team had moved within three hundred meters of the castle walls. Huck Finn and Valentino had finished a 360° circumnavigation of the castle. "We found Mehmet-Rauf," Valentino said to Getts.

"Is he dead?"

"Ripped to shreds. Like a pile of bloody rags. Look, up on the walls."

Getts, Peach, and the others used ambient-light glasses to scan the walls again. "Looks like monkeys," Getts said. "Looks like they have a private zoo behind the walls."

"They're drill baboons," Peach said.

"Ever run into them, before?" Getts asked.

"Nope," Peach shook his head. "But I heard about the French *Lance Pointe* in Pakistan. They lost four men to those fuckers. Faces ripped up, arms pulled off."

"Better than guard dogs?" Getts asked.

"Their hearing's just as good. Plus they fight in packs."

"Well, we'll see how they handle u-audio when the time comes." Getts referred to ultrasonic noise sources that they carried in case they ran up against canines.

The light intensifiers each trooper wore inside his helmet turned the night into a kind of eerie green day. "Infrared at the walls," Huck Finn whispered, his glasses examining small optical detectors retrofitted into the stone walls of the castle.

"See any motion sensors?" Getts asked.

"Negative," Valentino said from his observation point.

"Agree," Huck Finn said. Getts therefore knew that the security guard was using heat detectors in the same role as motion detection. "Cameras?" he said.

"Four corners, full view," Huck Finn said referring to the cameras that swept each wall at its four corners, mounted under the turrets of the stone edifice. As Getts considered how to neutralize the electronic sensing system, periodic screeches from the baboons set his teeth grinding. Others felt the same way. If they had to fight baboons, the battle would become an unknown quantity. "Fuckers," Peach said to no one. As if to respond to his discomfort, there were two more cries from the drills.

Carla, squatting next to Bartender, met his eyes. "I'll kill 'em all," she said, clenching her jaw.

Bartender nodded. "Ugly sons of bitches."

"We'll try the audio busters," Getts said. "If it works, Heggstad and Peach will knock out the north and south cameras, while Valentino and I get the infrareds. Carla, you and Bartender zero in on the west side. If the drills come that way, burn 'em."

"With pleasure, Bobby," she said and moved off to find a shooting position that would maximize her field of fire. Bartender moved in the opposite direction.

At 0310, Heggstad and Peach waited patiently at their stations one hundred meters from the walls, barely out of range of the infrared heat sensors.

Crush withdrew a small VHF transmitter from his cargo bag, designed to emit high frequency waves that were audible only to animals. The preset wave length was designed to strike at dogs and other animals that had similar inner ear construction. Drill baboons were not on the tested list, but the commandos would know their effect soon enough.

Getts closely watched the drills occupying the walls and turrets as Crush began to work the frequency ranges at the end of the TM's power pack. The baboons increased their pitch and rate of screeches, but Getts thought it was not because of the audio buster, but because the animals sensed their presence. "What have you got left, Crush?" he said.

"Have to get closer," the trooper said.

"Okay, let's move up."

Getts and Crush moved slowly, quietly, to approximately the same area occupied by Peach and Heggstad.

"My God, those filthy things never shut up," Lisa complained.

Conrad, despite the early morning hours, had not been asleep. He, too, had been awakened by the agitated drills. "Remember that they are on our side," he said. "They are our lookouts."

"But who would come after you in Syria? We are in the middle of a desert," she said, angrily fluffing her pillow.

Indeed, Conrad thought, who would come for him here? There was hundreds of miles of desert to cross, mountains to traverse . . . not to mention those goddamn monkeys. Impossible, he thought.

Down in the security room Captain Ahmmad had yet to close his eyes since opening them nineteen hours before. He was watching the monitors intently, as though he might see something that his technicians had missed. "Turn up the brightness on the cameras, Feyed," he ordered.

"They are up as high as they will go, Captain," the soldier replied.

Ahmmad began to pace the room, constantly swiveling his head between the monitors. He had changed the sound sensors from clear audio to baseline graphs on the electronic impulse scale, and he watched as spikes appeared on the otherwise black screen. God, the drills were making noise. Not once, but four times, Ahmmad had left the keep to accompany patrols outside, as well as inside, the castle walls, only to find nothing. Yet the drills continued their excited howls.

"Contact Damascus again," he said. But before the technician could dial the number for the Fourth Army, Ahmmad countermanded himself. "Never mind," he said. He had already alerted them twice. Calling again might make him sound like he was losing his nerve. He was not frightened, of course, but he was afraid of failing his assignment. Something was out there. But he couldn't see it. He just knew.

Then it happened. The drills went mad. They howled, screaming at a feverishly high pitch, and as Ahmmad and his household troops ran outside, the beasts leaped high into the air, crashing into each other in desperate attempts to move from one place to another, rolling and running.

"What is wrong with them?" Ahmmad demanded, but received no answer.

Inside the control room, the monitors began to reflect the chaos on the outside. Infrared and heat indicators blurred the screens, the audio spiked, and cameras showed drill baboons gone mad, running aimlessly through desert sands and rocks away from the castle.

Outside the walls, Peach and Heggstad moved quickly in on the infrared sensors, knocking each out with the haft of their commando knives. As they each reached opposite ends of the walls, they used their silenced OICWs, firing upward to disable the sweep cameras. Then, they reached into cargo bags strapped to theirs waists coming up with the walnut-sized mini-agents. The entire team began tossing them over the walls, at strategic locations, adding to those already in place thanks to Mehmet-Rauf. The agents were distributed about 30 meters apart, well inside the grounds of the castle. They covered the courtyard, the inner woods, stables, the garage, the barracks, and two turrets of the keep.

At Peach's signal, the team moved forward until they were flat against the wall. As the rear guards, Carla and Bartender moved into position to cover the El Fal road leading from Damascus. Their heavy 20mm rounds were loaded into their OICW rifles.

Like Carla and Bartender, Peach and Heggstad continued to wear the prism suits and were nearly invisible in the night, even to other Blacklight teammates who stood only a few feet away. Getts, Crush, Huck Finn, and Valentino had shed the heavier prism covering for their regular dark brown and black commando camo uniform.

Getts and the others switched on their power packs that would support the communication equipment built into their helmets, including the data and pictures that would funnel into screens from sensors from the mini-agents.

Getts retrieved a burst transmitter from a cargo pocket and switched the UHF channel to an airfield in Israel. "Rascal, Rascal, this is Blacklight, this is Blacklight. Night into day. I say again, night into day." Getts had given the signal to General Maas that the assault had begun. It would finish in exactly 45 minutes, one way or another. Pickup rotor craft would leave Israel in mere minutes.

Getts and the others selected back and forth from the views the mini-agents afforded them. They watched their screens while Syrian soldiers raced from their barracks located near the north wall, pulling at shirts, pants, equipment, and guns as they trotted toward assigned defensive positions. Getts counted as six of them entered through the main door of the keep. He glanced at Huck Finn who held up six fingers. Getts nodded. Valentino pointed in three directions and held up ten fingers, then adding another one to indicate his count of eleven soldiers dispersed to various locations about the grounds. Getts nodded his receipt of the information while Valentino turned and repeated his gestures to Crush and Huck Finn.

"Hack coming for twenty minutes," Getts spoke into his mouthpiece alerting the team to synchronize their watches. "Ready . . . hack." Each trooper was then on the same time frame. They had no more than twenty minutes to finish the job of getting over the wall, killing all resistance inside, and killing Conrad with certainty.

And making their escape.

At the Israeli helicopter base, an NCO using a sophisticated radio monitoring receiver had no trouble in hearing Getts's radio call. Even if he had not heard it with his own ears, the signal had been recorded automatically, and the code word tripped a blinking warning light within the system. The Officer in Charge of the communications room took the printed form of the message directly to the office of Brigadier General Maas. The OIC entered the general's office without knocking, even though he could hear raised voices on the other side of the door. The officer was surprised to see two men in General Maas's office whom he recognized immediately. One was a very high ranking military commander, the other an important government minister. Each of the three faces in the room was red with emotion, brows knit.

"Oh, excuse me, General. The Rascal signal just came in, sir."

"Give it to me," Maas snapped, as though he wanted the other two not to see it.

The communications officer retired without a word.

Outside on the tarmac, the army helicopter pilot named Benjamin was sitting in his cockpit with his engine turning at medium revolutions. Ready at the doors of his assault helicopter were gunners. Behind their helicopter were three more in a row, all awaiting the emergence of their general, who would lead them to their rendezvous point with the American commando unit known as Blacklight.

Benjamin saw Maas and two other men appear from their hangar area some sixty meters away. The government minister seemed to be tugging at the general's sleeve.

"Stand out of my way, Minister," Maas was saying to the civilian. "We must leave this very minute."

"You will not. That is a direct order from the prime minister."

"Then, sir, the prime minister can court martial me when I return." Maas walked around the minister but, at a nod from the minister, was halted by two armed and uniformed guards. Maas turned back toward the ranking civilian.

"You are sending brave men to their deaths," he seethed.

"I have sent men to their deaths before, General."

"This is an execution. Betrayal!" Maas's eyes narrowed as he spit out the words.

"The decision is not ours, General Maas. It was the Americans," the minister said.

"I don't believe it," Maas said.

The minister turned to the ranking general, who had stood to one side watching and listening.

"You give me no choice, General Maas. You are relieved of your command, effective immediately," the senior general stated.

As the three men walked back toward a waiting staff car, Benjamin could see a junior officer trot out to the helicopter flight line and draw his finger across his throat.

It was the signal to cut his engine.

Defending the castle was a difficult exercise as the Syrian forces could not split their exterior fighters and concentrate firepower on the two doors, because of the risk that the Blacklight team would scale walls no longer covered with sensing devices, cameras, and monkeys. Captain Ahmmad forced himself to stay inside the keep where he could direct a battle that seemed to him an imminently losing proposition. "Omar, stay on the north gate, but send two men halfway down the wall and two along the east wall," he said into a radio attached to his fatigue uniform.

"I have only four," Omar responded.

"So," the captain said, gruffly, "do it with four. Just do it."

Their transmissions, of course, were monitored by Blacklight, who wordlessly listened outside.

"Feyed, are you ready at the west wall?" Ahmmad said.

"Yes, sir."

"Keep watching the walls."

"Yes, sir."

An eerie silence descended over the keep. Conrad left his bed, pulled on dark clothing, and opened a closet in the master suite. Inside was an armory of several assault rifles, submachine guns and pistols. He armed himself with a Glock 9mm, and inserted a drum magazine into an AK-47.

"Conrad," Lisa said, "what is it?"

"Nothing. I am going for a walk. Don't be frightened."

"The monkeys have stopped screeching. What does it mean?"

"It means nothing, Lisa. Stay here," he said.

"I am going to get the children," she said, swinging her legs out of bed.

"The children are fine. Leave them." Conrad exited the suite, and, as he stepped onto the balcony he heard an explosion. He could not immediately tell its location, but he thought it came from the north. There followed another concussive explosion, this one larger than the last. Lisa, clad only in light lingerie, emerged from the door behind him. The lights flickered and went off. She began to scream until Conrad clapped his hand firmly over her mouth. "Shut up! Do you want to signal them where we are?"

He waited several moments for the emergency generator to operate, but it did not. As his eyes adjusted, he made his way back to the master suite, passing through two more sets of doors until he found the back stairway leading down to the ballroom and cinema.

When the main gate was blown into splinters by a combination of C-4 plastique and smoke grenades, Getts, Valentino, Crush, and Huck Finn, only 20 meters down the same wall, tossed titanium grapnels over the west wall. Using sliding hand-locking ascenders, they quickly began scaling the 25-foot stone walls. Each man hauled up his OICW, ammunition, communication gear, as well as a 40-pound bag of special explosives and highly compressed containers of atomized nitro-gas. The exertion called for an extreme anaerobic expenditure of energy, but the Blacklight team were trained in this very exercise, and the four troopers completed the climb in less than a minute.

At the moment the second blast removed the north gate from its hinges, sending large slabs of steel and wood hundreds of feet into the air, Heggstad and Peach dove through the breach before the dust and smoke could clear and crouched motionless against the inside of the wall, unseen beneath the cover of their prism suits. They could clearly see their enemy with light-intensifying glasses. Heggstad found himself scarcely twelve feet from a Syrian soldier who rubbed at his eyes, trying to clear them of dust and debris. Heggstad gunned the man down with a three-round burst from his silenced OICW.

A second soldier appeared around the side door of the barracks, looked directly at Heggstad without seeing him, then turned to look beyond the inner courtyard at the west gate. Heggstad fired another short burst into the soldier's torso, then moved forward to take up station near the barracks door before the men hit the floor.

Peach spotted three soldiers among the trees around the stable building. They were not an immediate threat to him. Their assignment, as near as Peach could tell, was to defend against forced entry at the main gate along the west wall. He debated between taking them out or proceeding directly the team's goal: the main door of the keep. At the last moment, he decided to eliminate the Syrians so that they could not possibly interfere with their withdrawal. Peach began walking toward the soldiers from their rear quarter. As the two continued looking toward the main gate, the third turned his head, his gaze sweeping the inner courtyard and the shrubbery beyond the trees. Peach froze. The soldier continued to look in Peach's direction but then again looked away, not discerning Peach inside his prism suit, which had taken on the hue of the foliage around him. Peach continued to advance until he was within ten feet of them. Guns barked out beyond the west gate. The Syrians half rose, raised their guns to fire in that direction. Peach calmly depressed his trigger, and the OICW hosed the Syrians into the next world.

Now safely over the wall, Getts raced to the single side door of the keep, stopping long enough to booby trap it with a mine, attaching a detonation line to its external door handle. Opening the door from within would automatically trigger the mine spraying everyone within a twenty-foot radius with hot shrapnel. Getts then ran on the rear of the keep, silently followed by Huck Finn, Crush, and Valentino.

Getts stopped at the main rear entrance to the keep and helped Huck Finn squeeze plastique into several locations on the door jamb. He then stuck a det cord and a detonator into it and stepped back into the shelter of the wall.

They waited while Valentino and Crush positioned themselves on the opposite side of the door against the wall. At Getts's signal, Huck Finn blew the door. The four Blacklight leaped through the opening and began a room-by-room search of the keep. Getts raced down a hallway that opened to a number of rooms below the balcony. He kicked open one door, only to find it empty of humans but full of linen and household maintenance items. Huck Finn tried the handle of the next room. It was locked, and it was too heavy to kick in. Using hand signals, Huck Finn motioned Getts to flatten himself against a wall while Huck Finn pulled the pin on a grenade and placed it on the floor at the base of the door. In seconds, the hand grenade exploded, leaving pieces of wood hanging to the sides of the jamb, still attached to hinges. As soon as the first grenade exploded, Getts tossed a second one inside. This grenade, a specially constructed device to uniformly scatter 12-gauge buckshot at high velocity, devastated the room and left two bodies on the floor. Neither was Conrad nor Captain Ahmmad. The monitoring equipment in the room was destroyed, the hardware shredded and sparking.

Crush and Valentino, meanwhile, had rushed to the main staircase and sprinted to the top. Valentino went right, Crush to the left. Each trooper could examine one of his small BSI (battle situation indicator) screens on his helmet display and know by colored IFR dots where his comrades were during the entire assault on the building. Valentino saw dots representing Getts and Huck Finn exit from the security room and into the reception hall. Likewise, he could see Peach and Heggstad positioned outside the keep in the courtyard. Working rapidly, Valentino moved from apartment to apartment along the balcony. He reached the master suite, threw open the door, and waited a second to make sure no lights were on inside. He then moved inside, searching the darkness through his night-vision glasses. Two Syrian soldiers armed with automatic weapons sprayed the doorway where Valentino had been a moment before. They were reacting to motion, unable to clearly see the Blacklight trooper. Valentino cut them down with three rounds stitched neatly into each soldier's chest. He then moved to the inner bedrooms.

He carefully but quickly opened closets and bathroom doors. They were all empty.

At the west end of the balcony, Heggstad was about to open a third door leading to the children's rooms, when a fusillade of fire hailed from inside. The rounds penetrated through the heavy door, and one of them caught Heggstad squarely in the chest. He went down backward, feeling a heavy pain to his solar plexus, but raised himself quickly to his feet. The rounds that had come from behind the door were not capable of piercing the body armor worn by Blacklight troopers. Heggstad would have a very sore chest but would lose no blood nor suffer an open wound.

He pulled the pin on a hand grenade, placed it into the cleft of the door, and stepped back. The explosion disintegrated the door, and when he leaped through the opening, the severely wounded body of Lisa Eisler was lying against one of the walls, an assault rifle nearby. Her children were crying. But the sight of the once beautiful young woman stopped Heggstad in his tracks. She was not dead but was bleeding heavily from her nose and ears. The concussion also seemed to have torn the flesh below her left breast. Slowly but resolutely, she grasped at the stock of the assault rifle.

"No, no . . ." Heggstad said, even while he was raising the muzzle of his OICW. Clearly, she was protecting her children. Heggstad desperately wanted to reassure her that her children were in no danger, but the words had hardly formed in his head when the woman's assault rifle was nearly ready to fire at him. He pulled the trigger first. Lisa's lingerie offered none of the protection of a bulletproof vest. Her body was blown open by bullets designed to make an incisive entry then tumble inside, gathering up flesh as they tore through the body and continuing out the other side, leaving terrifying gaping wounds. Lisa was dead from the first round almost before the third had ripped through her heart.

The children were shocked into utter silence. Their eyes were wide at the specter before them—a monster far more fearful than the drooling gargoyles of their worst nightmares, a helmeted creature with a fire stick in his hand. He stood before them ready, they were certain, to strike them dead and carry them off to Hell. "Come with me," Heggstad said, extending his hand. They did not dare to move.

"Nobody's going to hurt you," he said. "Come on, I'll get you out of here." There was a huge explosion downstairs. Heggstad's BSI showed that a Blacklight trooper was engaged in a firefight on the main floor. He heard the unmistakable sound of a Russian-made F1 hand grenade. Several automatic weapons fired at the same time. Outside the keep, on the corner of the outer castle wall, he heard the snarl of a Swedish-made MAG machine gun. He had no more time to give to these stricken children. He had to leave them and assist his teammates. But still he slung his OICW over his shoulder, scooped little Lucille up in one arm and Karl in the other, and raced back along the balcony to the master suite, where he knew there was a back stairway out of the house. Heggstad's only thought was to get them outside, away from the certain maelstrom that would soon engulf the ancient keep.

Hardly conscious of the weight of the small children in his arms, he descended the stairs toward the ballroom. Halfway down, he was suddenly confronted by a man with a gun. There was not the slightest question in Heggstad's mind that the man he faced only a few meters away was Conrad. And he knew that he had committed a fatal mistake. There was no way he could get to his weapon.

Conrad smiled, raised the barrel of his submachine gun and fired a long burst. The rounds hit Heggstad's left breast and took off the upper half of young Karl's head. The second and third bursts struck Heggstad in the throat and in the face. As he fell sideways, his arm curled protectively around Lucille for as long as possible. Still, she tumbled to the bottom of the stairs. Conrad hardly gave her a second glance as he rushed up the stairs and into the master suite.

Lisa was not there. Conrad did not expect that she would be. Without pausing, the terrorist loped down the long upper balcony until he reached the children's room at the west side of the keep. And Lisa's body. He knelt by her, setting aside his machine gun so that he could touch the only person in the world he had ever loved. He caressed her hair, then leaned forward and kissed her bloody lips. He could not bear to think that her once warm, firm breasts were now pulverized by military ammunition. She deserved much better. She deserved a long life, a life with him. A cry arose from Conrad's breast as his eyes turned cold.

Captain Ahmmad had reached a small upper-level balcony located between the main door of the keep and the west wall of the study. When Getts came into view below him, Ahmmad fired all of what was left in the banana clip of his AK-47. Getts's body armor saved his life, but one of the rounds struck his helmet, knocking out his BSI capability and shattering his right cheekbone. The pain was immediate and intense.

Peach, now shed of his prism camouflage suit, had just entered the main door, saw the gun burst from the balcony, and aimed upward to squeeze off a three-round burst. One of the bullets caught Ahmmad in the left arm just above the elbow, but the bullet continued driving until it had torn almost all the muscle and flesh from his arm and part of his shoulder. Ahmmad fell against the edge of the balcony box.

"You okay, Bobby?" Peach said as he reached Getts's side. He only glanced at Getts, however, so that he could continue to sweep the interior of the keep for more enemy soldiers.

"Yeah, I'm okay," Getts said, painfully. His lower jaw was intact, but he could speak only with great effort. "Conrad . . ." As Getts spoke, he pointed toward the west wall of the keep. The two men then moved together across the great reception hall, keeping back to back so that they could see and fire 360 degrees. Conrad was not in the hallway, not in the dining room. The two commandos spied swinging doors leading to the kitchen. There was a bloody handprint on one of the doors. They dove inside.

"Heads up, Blacklight!" Carla's voice crackled over the communication band. "Army's on their way."

They had expected reinforcements from Damascus. Only scant minutes remained. There was no time for a room-by-room search for Conrad. Peach and Getts moved toward a flight of stairs that led from the end of the massive kitchen. They passed several large butcher blocks. Knives, pots, and utensils were hanging from overhead racks. There was also a large walk-in refrigerator. Getts pointed toward an iron gate that led to a wine storage room. There was blood on the gate latch.

"Go, people, go. . . ." Carla's voice came over their earphones.

"Valentino, Crush," Peach snapped over the com band. "In the kitchen. Bring the bomb."

Within seconds, Valentino arrived in the kitchen, while Crush kept watch at the door, his shotgun ready.

Highly compressed gasoline, when atomized with oxygen, sprayed into an area, and then ignited, creates catastrophic explosions, second only to thermonuclear detonations. Fuel-air bombs could be made to achieve the same effect with a special nitro-gas mixture, which Valentino carried on his back. Valentino deposited the twin compressed tanks in the middle of the kitchen, and with Peach's help he set up the dispersal and automatic ignition system on the bomb.

"Getts, I know you're out there." Conrad's voice came from within the darkened bowels of the wine room. A slight smile crossed Getts's pained face. Peach gave a silent thumbs-up. "You're a fucking coward, Getts. You always have been. If you had an ounce of pride in your diseased heart, you would face me like a man."

Rather than answer, Getts removed a meat clever from a butcher's block and slid the handle through the latch of the gate so that the door could not be opened from the inside.

"Do you hear me, Getts?" Conrad roared. "You have no insides, no balls, no honor. You turned to jelly when you knew it was me you were after. Isn't that right, Getts?"

Getts did not answer.

Compelled to find out what Getts and his team were up to, Conrad adjusted his position so that he could see through the grated door. When he saw the canisters being attached to the fuel-air bomb he screamed, in a long, animalistic howl. Then he rushed the door, no longer caring that he was exposing himself to a bullet. Better a bullet than the fate he saw awaiting him. "Getts, let me out. You cannot do it like this! Getts, please!"

Valentino snapped his fingers to get their attention. He then twisted the starter valve to the bomb. "Two minutes," he said into his com phone. "Blacklight, clear the castle. Two minutes to fuel-air explosion."

Peach, Valentino, and Crush moved rapidly for the main exit. Getts hesitated only long enough to answer Conrad's cries for mercy. "All of this, Conrad, has been brought to you by the United States of America, with whom you will no longer fuck." Getts glanced at the ticking fuel-air bomb. "Don't light a match 'til I'm gone. Okay?"

Getts ran to join the others, racing toward Carla and Bartender's position in the rocks two hundred meters from the castle. There were only seconds left on the fuse of the fuel-air bomb.

"Troops are here," Carla said. "I count five APCs, four trucks, a couple field guns, four mounted heavy machine . . ."

The explosion rent the night.

Even though the Blacklight were well away from the blast, there was a vortex created by all of the oxygen suddenly sucked out of the air. It made trees and shrubs move, flapped fatigue uniforms wildly, and whipped field glasses away from eyes. Then the entire roof of the keep rose upward into the sky, pushed higher by a giant sheet of red flame, as though from the bowels of Hell had opened. Ancient stone was catapulted outward; the vegetation was seared; and the keep was flattened down to its foundation. The Blacklight team could not take their eyes from the devastation. Even the approaching forces from Damascus stopped in their tracks as the horrific explosion rocked the earth.

Carla zeroed in her OICW rifle for a shot on the lead troop carrier. Getts could see the laser dot on the windshield of the vehicle. Carla pulled the trigger. The windshield disappeared, and a split second later the carrier exploded with the impact of the delayed action 20mm round. The APC remained motionless, burning, while others pulled around it. Bartender sighted in and began squeezing off rounds, causing Syrian gunners to fall, hide behind their armored shields, or simply abandon their gun positions.

Getts and the others searched the sky for helicopters, listening for the sound of overdue Israeli rotors.

"We can't wait. They're not coming," Getts said. "Peach, call these coordinates in to Toni." Getts handed his chief gunner's mate a slip of paper from a one-time pad. Peach read it. ". . . Yankee. Whiskey, hotel, five, niner, six, two eight, eight, niner." He looked sharply up at Getts. "That's on the coast, Bobby. We can't get there."

"We haven't tried yet." Getts said.

"I don't have to try. I can read a map. There's a range

of mountains to go over, and we have to cross a desert just to get there," Peach said.

"If it's a bitch for us, it's going to be a bitch for them, too. Send Toni the message."

Peach shook his head. "I can't wait 'til she gets this one." Then he began coding the message on his one-time pad.

"Listen up, now," Getts said to the rest of the Blacklight force, who gathered around his map. "Don't mark your map in case you lose it." The group knew, of course, that Getts meant that if a Blacklight was killed and his map found by the enemy, it had better not point out their escape route.

"We're going from here to the Lebanon border, south of Aita el Foukhar. We'll cross the Mazar mountains, then four miles through the Bekka Valley. We go north of this lake, Qaraaoun, and past the village of Ain Zebde. The big hike is over the Jabal el Barouk mountains. They're seven thousand feet, but there's a pass at six thousand. We'll have covered about fifty miles as the crow flies. We can make that in a couple of days, if we get lucky." Getts looked around at the group for signs of dispute. There were none.

"It's all downhill from there. Over the Barquk River, low mountains, fifteen hundred feet down past a little town called Gharifah. We can see the ocean at Barja. Total hike from here is about fifty-three miles, or eighty-two klicks."

"Where do we come out?" Valentino asked, peering at the map.

"Here, about a mile above the main highway. We'll use a squeaker for Toni to home on."

"Sounds like fun," Crush said without a sign of enthusiasm.

"We move at night," Getts said. "They fuck with us in the dark, we tear 'em up."

The Blacklight team walked three more miles through rocks and almost invisible goat trails while Syrian helicopters beat the air searching for them. Peach sent the transmission to Toni in Israel, advised her of their intentions, and told her they would send revised ETAs as necessary.

Then they dug under rocks, covered themselves with camouflage netting, having left behind their heavy prism suits, posted a single guard, and tried to sleep.

That night, they were making steady time along the ridge

of elevated land in the lower Jabal Mazar range. They were moving silently at a double-time pace following paths made by animals, occasionally crossing man-made trails that paralleled their own direction. They all heard the familiar hammering sounds of propeller blades and the roaring of helicopter engines. Like fingers of death, powerful lights stabbed intermittently through the blackness. The Blacklight force concealed itself as well as possible, weapons ready.

As the searchlight moved nearer the group, its brilliant arc crept over Crush's leg, stopped, then returned. Crush, who had hidden himself by an outcropping of boulders, could not move any closer to the rock. All at once there was a burst from a machine gun as the chopper poured fire below. Getts heard sounds of stifled screams as someone was hit with a tracer round.

"Knock out the light," Getts ordered.

Blacklight opened up a torrent of ground fire as the helicopter twisted and wheeled for the door gunner to maximize his field of fire. Crush rose, purposely exposing himself to the glare of the light, as he set himself for a clean shot at the helo. He squeezed off a burst just as the helicopter wheeled overhead. As Crush was hit with heavy rounds in the chest, the helicopter's arc light disintegrated.

Even without the light, the pilot would not slacken his concentration of fire into the group. He dropped lower, the machine guns hammering wildly into the surrounding rocks.

Peach crawled to Crush's fallen body and retrieved his LAWs, a wire-guided missile designed for use against tanks and other ground-based armored vehicles. Peach waited until the helicopter swooped low for another strafing pass. Then he pulled the trigger. After a short flight, the rocket struck one of the rotors of the chopper. With a tip blown away, the helicopter dipped upwards, rolled over onto its back, and plummetted straight down, smashing against the rugged terrain below.

"Hell of an idea, Peachie," Getts said after the helo went up in flames. "I didn't know you were that smart."

"If officers had any brains, they'd be chiefs, too," Peach rejoined.

"Who's hit?" Getts asked.

"Crush bought it," Carla said.

Huck Finn lay on the hard ground, trying not to wince at the pain caused by a tracer round that had burned right through his upper body.

Valentino got to him first. "Huck, man, you okay?"

"I think I'm gonna cry," Huck Finn said.

The others smiled at his flip courage. Peach moved to the wounded trooper's aid. He applied a compress, then taped a bandage over it.

"You'll be okay, Huck. We'll get you out of here, man," Valentino said.

Huck Finn tried to rise but could not.

"He can walk," Valentino said, knowing Huck would certainly try.

"No, he can't," Getts said. Getts knew that loss of blood would soon be fatal. He had seen many of these wounds.

"Then I'll carry him," Valentino said.

"Hey, Bobby's right," Huck Finn said, his strength ebbing. "I wouldn't make it. Leave me, man. I'll be okay."

Getts spoke to the others. "Grab your gear. We've got a lot of miles to make up. Peach, move 'em out."

Getts moved to Huck Finn's side and knelt down. "Huck Finn," he said. "What's your real name?"

"Bowers. Ron Bowers."

"Where're you from, Ron?" Getts asked gently. "Wouldn't be Montana, would it?"

"No, sir. Hoquium, Washington."

"I know where it is. It rains a lot there."

Huck Finn smiled, closing his eyes as though he was terribly tired, then struggled to open them again. "All the time. Seems like every day."

Getts took a syringe of morphine from his own medical kit and injected the spring-loaded needle into the wounded man's arm. "It'll take away some of the pain," he said.

"Doesn't hurt much now, anyway," Huck Finn said, his speech slurred.

"Family still there? In Hoquium?" he asked.

Huck Finn nodded his head.

"I'll look 'em up," Getts said.

"Been a blast," Huck said, just before his eyes closed forever.

*   *   *

Toni was wearing a smart cotton beach suit as she walked languidly down a concrete sidewalk at the marina. On her arm was Adriano, the Italian who had tried without success, until today, to make a date with her. Adriano was wearing a white linen jacket, powder blue slacks, white shoes, and a red scarf tied loosely around his neck. In his free hand, he held a tall frosted drink.

"I knew, of course," he said, "that you would come back to me. Who else is there? We are the only two beautiful people in this . . ." He waved an arm.

"You say your boat is fast?" Toni asked.

"Yes, it is. You see, I am a fast man. It is only correct that my boat match my—"

"What about its fuel range?" she interrupted.

"Fuel? It is fine for cruising. I thought we were going only for a little ride, my darling," he said as he took another sip from his drink. He massaged Toni's buttocks and was pleased that she did not in the least mind his advance.

"I don't like to run out of gas," she said simply.

"But of course not. Well, I suppose it would be . . . about two fifty, three hundred fifty kilometers."

"Big difference between two fifty and three fifty," Toni said. "Got any extra tanks aboard?"

Adriano laughed. "My, but are we not cautious?"

"I want spare gas cans on any boat I go riding in. Just for emergencies," she insisted.

Adriano looked at the superb, well-toned muscles of the Oriental beauty before him and decided that extra gas cans were a small price to pay for his fantasy to become a reality.

As Toni looked quickly and efficiently about the boat, she was pleased to see that besides being as beautiful and as expensive as Adriano promised, it was solid in construction. It had not been designed for water sports, and likely had a top speed of under thirty knots, but the cabin section had been constructed to sleep four; eight if they were good friends.

"You have captured my soul. I desire you . . ." the Italian was crooning as he placed his arms around her.

"You're kind of a knockout yourself, Adriano, but the deal was a boat ride. Let's do it," she said.

"But, my love, there is really no reason to leave the dock," he whispered passionately into her ear.

"Yeah, that's what I figured." Toni reached into her purse and came up with a 9mm Walther pistol and placed it solidly behind the Italian's ear. "Now, listen up, Adriano. You're going to be confused about a lot of things for a while, so don't waste my time by asking questions."

"Surely this is a joke," he sputtered.

"Start your engines. I'll cast off the lines. When you get to the harbor entrance, steer eighteen degrees magnetic. We're going right up the coast."

Adriano had turned on the ignition and started the engine, turning toward Toni with a last plea to be reasonable.

"Toni, my darling, can we not have one little drink and talk about . . ."

"Shut up and drive, Adriano. I can run this boat damn fine without you, and if I have to blow your fucking brains all over your teak deck to shut your mouth, I'll do it. Now move your ass," Toni snapped.

The pleasure craft went to full power as it passed the last speed warning buoy. Wind made sea swells deep enough for a full speed run to be hard on the boat. Never lowering the muzzle of her Walther, Toni ordered Adriano to throttle back. She estimated that their true speed was close enough to arrive at her map coordinates in time.

The Bekka Valley was only six miles across, and despite the harsh terrain, the immense burden of fatigue, and the sting of battle wounds, the Blacklight force still trotted at double time, their heavy packs on their backs and weapons slung over their shoulders. Getts kept his eye on Carla, who never complained or asked for help in carrying her share of ammunition, grenades, and her own OICW. They stopped to rest each hour for ten minutes. It took little more than three hours to traverse the Bekka. When they reached the foothills of the Jabal el Barouk mountains, there were already streaks of light in the sky to the east. They found a wadi two kilometers from the village of Ain Zebdé and dug in, spreading their ghilly netting to camouflage their position.

They listened throughout the day to the engines of fixed-wing aircraft and helicopters, and vehicles grinding their gears over roads and up and down hills within a twenty-mile radius. The Syrians did not know the Blacklight's route and tried to cover all possible paths that led to the sea. Blacklight had no intention of exposing themselves during a daylight march and dug into the ground. With effective netting covering them from both the sun and aerial observation, it would be a stroke of luck if a Syrian soldier stumbled into their midst.

They waited until the sun had set before beginning the climb over Jabal el Barouk mountains. Enemy patrols were numerous in the mountain passes, and long detours were necessary to circumvent them. Before reaching the chain's summits, they found themselves critically low on water, even having rationed themselves to a single cup per day.

"Drink the rest of it," Getts ordered them. "We're not going to find a streetcar between here and the Med." They had eleven miles to go until reaching the Barquk River, but Getts had no illusions about drinking its waters. Nor did he have any intention of taking the time and the risk of boiling it.

Moving out after sunset, two thousand feet down the Jabal el Barouk, Peach spotted a roadblock several hundred yards ahead on a tertiary road, hardly more than a trail. They made plans to go wide of the roadblock and moved out silently, in single file. It was not possible to pass safely to the right, so Getts motioned the team left. Still following Getts's hand signals, the Blacklight team moved with ultra silence, in slow motion, until they had positioned themselves to put their enemy in a cross fire. The Syrian soldiers were sipping tea and eating bread—their attention on anything but the danger surrounding them—when Getts opened up with his own OICW. The other Blacklight troopers quickly depressed their triggers. Most of the Syrians were killed in the first volley of rounds, but one brave soul made it to his personnel carrier and turned the machine gun toward the darkness around him and began spraying wildly. While Getts and the other troopers put their heads down, the courageous Syrian managed to start the engine of the APC and drive away, taking with him the knowledge of exactly where the action had taken place.

*   *   *

Bobbing up and down in the pitching boat left Adriano hanging over the side of the rail expelling his meal and the bile that lingered in the lining of his stomach into the Mediterranean. Toni continually swept the shoreline with binoculars, referring to her hand-held GPS, keeping the boat churning ahead. This part of the coast was remote and sparsely populated. She checked and rechecked her map coordinates countless times, watching carefully for the water cistern that was the assigned meeting place relayed to her by Peach.

"I can do nothing more," Adriano whined. "I must slip over the side and die. You may have the boat. It is yours."

"We'll be moving soon. Hang in there, *paisan,*" Toni said, not removing her field glasses from her eyes. She could see a few small houses, a distant village of rock or stone, few lights.

"Your comrades are very late," the Italian moaned.

"They'll be there," Toni said.

In the middle of the village, an armored personnel carrier with troops crowded into the back was moving slowly through the town. It was early, not yet fully light. Pressed against the walls of two small buildings, scarcely two hundred meters from the beach, were the tortured survivors of the Syrian desert and mountains. The Blacklight team moved stealthily away from probing soldiers as the Arabs, one small group among thousands strung out along the coast, were making their uninspired reconnaissance.

Peach slumped to the ground and allowed Getts to lie partially concealed against the rear of a tiny store. Every muscle in Peach's body raged afire, his back felt as though it were broken. It was several minutes before he could straighten up. When a soldier wandered in his direction, Peach grasped his commando knife from a sheath strapped to his boot and waited. He prayed the Syrian would not continue wandering in a straight line. But, at the direction of an officer shouting from a block away, the soldier continued searching toward Peach's and Getts's position. As the soldier passed a shadowed doorway, a strong arm quickly circled his neck, choking off his windpipe, as cold steel drove into his ribs. Peach let the man slip silently to the dust at his feet.

Gunfire broke out in the street. Valentino coolly returned fire at Syrian soldiers taking cover behind the APC. The carrier opened up with rapid fire machine gun rounds strafing the street, with no regard for the civilians, including children, who scurried for cover.

Carla, always calm, took a position at the edge of the beach behind a crude boat launching ramp made of timber. "Bartender! Peach! This way," she called out. She began placing her laser sights on strategic targets and pulled the trigger. Her first two rounds blew out steering tires on the APC. Its driver wisely remained inside the vehicle. Her third round penetrated the gunsight slit. While Carla turned her attention to individual soldiers running to and fro, trying to find cover, Peach staggered to her position with Getts on his back. The two men fell in a single heap behind the wooden boat launch ramp.

Gunfire from shore attracted Toni's attention. She quickly shifted her binoculars and saw the defensive position taken up by Carla near the launch ramp. The tide was not high enough to use the ramp, but Toni fire-walled the boat's throttles. Gathering speed, she spun the wheel to point her bow at the action.

Valentino and Bartender were less than fifty yards from Carla's covering fire. They silently counted to three, then dashed for the beach. Bartender went down. Valentino stopped, picked up the ex-Alabama football player, and dragged him to cover behind the ramp.

"Where you hit, man?" Valentino wanted to know.

"In the butt," Bartender said.

"We'll make the boat," she assured Bartender. "Peach first," Carla said, "then you two."

"Ladies first," Valentino said.

"It's my rifle that's covering your ass. Get moving," she said.

They could clearly see Toni standing near the rail while Adriano, sufficiently recovered from nausea to handle the wheel, kept the boat moving a few yards off shore.

"Ready," Peach said, once more placing Getts on his shoulders. They had shed their packs but kept their guns and a few clips of ammunition.

"Let's do it!" Valentino said, and the four men ran, limping, toward the surf.

Changing her fire-selection switch to 20mm rounds, Carla increased her rate of fire. For twenty seconds, she put out a wall of fire, each round pulverizing bricks and mortar, so that there was not a single shot of return fire. As she glanced over her shoulder, she could see that the four men had reached the boat and were aboard. Peach, Valentino, and Bartender immediately poured the remains of their ammunition into the few Syrian targets that were left. Carla then began running toward the boat. She was into the water, then knee-high in gentle surf.

"Drop the piece!" Peach yelled at her, her equipment slowing her down. She slipped out of her pack and ammunition carrier, and held her hand out. Valentino grasped it while Toni, seeing that the connection had been made, pushed the boat's throttles forward.

"We got her," Valentino shouted to Toni. "Go, go, go!"

Small arms fire had sprung up from shore, but nothing had come close to hitting them. As Peach was helped Valentino pull Carla aboard, her eyes suddenly rolled upward into her head. When they brought her over the rail and laid her on the deck, they could see the small bit of blood spreading over her tunic.

Peach turned her over with care while Toni ran for a blanket and medical kit inside the cabin.

Peach knelt close to her face, feeling for a pulse. Valentino, dripping wet, did the same thing in feeling her carotid artery. "Carla, wake up," the Italian said. "Damnit, Carla. Carla . . ."

Valentino looked up helplessly, then slumped against the highboard of the boat. His head bent slowly forward, and he began to cry. All on board had tears that blinded their eyes, but worst was Getts. He had loved the courageous woman as a comrade and had allowed her to be killed.

Chapter Twenty-two

However breathtakingly beautiful men found Kathleen Sawyer, she felt extraordinarily lucky that she had met a very attractive, intelligent man out of the incredible competition for eligible men unique to southern California. He was not yet forty, seven years older than Kathleen, but packaged in a perfect body that bore interesting scars about which he was fascinatingly reluctant to talk about. There were lots of things about Bobby Rawling that Kathleen was dying to know, but Bobby deflected her questions without effort while she, aware that their relationship was only months old, hesitated to push.

She knew that he worked for the government and that he was on some kind of medical leave. She knew that he had graduated from Stanford and that his major was psychology. Kathleen had finished only two years of community college and, because she was awed by Stanford's vaunted faculty, didn't feel entirely comfortable trying to chat about things intellectual. Kathleen had fallen into international modeling almost by accident, but in the ten years that she had worked at her meteoric and highly successful career, she had amassed more than enough money to maintain her present lifestyle in the company of her daughter, Allison.

While there had been a number of men in her life, none had held Kathleen's interest for very long, and that included Allison's father. Marriage had never been a serious consideration for her until Bobby came along. Now, however, though she still resisted the idea of a long-term commitment to a man, she believed Bobby Rawlings might be the exception. While she and Allison played on the beach at Pacific Palisades, Kathleen's thoughts continually produced the image of the brown-haired, brightly smiling guy waiting for her at her home.

On this midsummer day, it was almost 80 degrees, and the beach was crowded. Allison, at the age of six was not nimble, but she had no fear of the frisbee, and if she missed one of Kathleen's tosses, she would leap to retrieve the spinning disc from the sand and toss it back. She wanted the game to continue. They were near the water line, and Allison giggled with great excitement when she needed to chase it into the ocean. Her return throws were always an adventure, never spinning quite right, infrequently on target but thrown with all of her strength and enthusiasm.

To ensure that this throw flew all of the way to her mother, Allison spun herself around like a discus thrower and flung the plastic plate blindly into the sun. It soared in the general direction of Kathleen but, again, off course. As Kathleen turned her body to chase the gliding disc, a hand appeared out of the ether and easily caught it. Near-blinded by the sun, she tried to adjust her position so that she could see the man's face. The first thing she noticed was that he wore gloves. They were white, thin cotton material, and they disappeared up a sleeve that was part of an equally light shirt. The man wore a pith helmet to shade himself from the sun, and it was only when she took the frisbee from his outstretched hand that she could see his face. It was horribly burned, part of a once prominent nose missing, ears seared and shrunken against the side of his head. He wore dark glasses, and Kathleen felt momentary shame as she realized that she was glad his eyes were covered. She did not want to see into his pain. She shuddered involuntarily but forced herself to smile. "Thank you," she said.

"You are welcome," he said in a distinct foreign accent, his bloodless, scarred lips twisted into what might have been a smile. "I admire your beautiful little girl," he said.

Kathleen's first instinct was to back away, scoop up Allison, and get away from the apparition in front of her, but another wave of shame immediately washed over her. How selfish she was. This poor wretch must continually experience revulsion from everyone he meets for a condition that was certainly none of his own making. He was, after all, gentlemanly and probably starved for normal, human conversation. "Thank you," she said. Then, probably out of her sense of guilt, added, "Allison is starting school in a few weeks, so she wants to spend all of her time playing on the beach."

"Yes," the man said, "water is soothing. I had a child like Allison, once."

"Oh . . ." Kathleen was suddenly struck with a sense of dread. The man's reference to his daughter in the past tense distressed her and made her determined to end contact with him at once. "Well," she said awkwardly, "good-bye." Without waiting for a response, she stepped over to where Allison stooped near the water, took her by the hand, and walked up the beach without a backward glance. She slipped her sandy feet into rubber beach shoes, pulled their blanket together without folding it, picked up scattered articles of clothing, and began walking toward their parked car. As she trudged up the sand holding Allison's hand, Kathleen was again attacked by pangs of guilt over her reaction to the tortured man's plight. What a perfectly natural thing for him to say, that he had once had a girl like Allison, spoken by a soul who had doubtless loved his child with the same deep emotion that she loved Allison. And Kathleen's reaction was to turn her back and flee. How selfish of her. How many times had she seen a crippled man or woman, bound for life to a wheelchair, or a blind person who struggled with life in perpetual darkness, and tried to imagine how she would respond to a similar challenge? It was beyond her. She was not a religious person but thanked whatever deity was in charge of the cosmos for leaving her in good health and pleasant appearance. Embarrassed and confused with her chaotic state of anxiety, she attempted to put out of her mind the entire incident.

As she prepared dinner that evening, the recollection of the uncomfortable meeting began to fade.

They had hors d'oeuvres for an entire meal. Kathleen partially steamed three artichokes, then cut each in half, added spices, oil, and placed them on the barbecue grill to finish cooking. She had made a fresh bleu cheese dressing with plenty of garlic powder and pepper mixed with buttermilk and mayonnaise to dip an assortment of fresh vegetables into. She broiled brie cheese on Italian bread and completed the table setting with plump strawberries with sour cream and brown sugar nearby. Getts enjoyed adding bottles to Kathleen's stock of wine at her home on Riviera Ranch Road, and he had chosen a rich, ice-cold chardonnay that had a lusty oak flavor.

Getts had drunk two glasses of wine to Kathleen's one, partly as a function of thirst, partly as a perfect taste complement to the succulent plates of cold food Kathleen had served. They were eating in the kitchen with both French doors open wide so that the effect created the feeling of eating outdoors. Well before the meal was finished, Allison had insisted on watching television in the den of the large house. Kathleen was firm about which programs Allison could watch and did not simply let the child park herself in front of the video machine and subject herself to the mercies of mindless studio programming. Thus, Kathleen took it upon herself to dial in the local public television channel, KCET in Los Angeles, which she was confident that her daughter could watch.

When Kathleen returned to the kitchen, Getts was turning off the gas on the outside barbecue pit. The house was built in the late 1930s by a then-famous Hollywood actor. It was known as a California ranch-style home, single level, stucco, with a Spanish tile roof. It was built in a U shape with living room, bedrooms, dining room and den opening up on a large patio that was built around a huge oak tree and festooned on its borders with Canterbury bell flowers, sweet william, carnation, Easter cactus, and jasmine among other fauna. The house was situated on an acre of ground, virtually all lawn, with fruit trees that had to be maintained by a gardener who worked two full days each week. A swimming pool of Olympic dimensions was located conveniently near the master bedroom. Bobby swam every day, and Kathleen never tired of watching him flash through the water, more like a fish than a man.

They moved from their location in the kitchen to chaise lounge chairs on the patio. Daylight had given way to darkness, but in the warmth of heat still radiating from the earth, neither suggested turning on an outdoor light. As a consequence, lights inside the house were still off.

As his head rested comfortably against the soft plastic mattress of the lounge chair, Getts could feel the slight soreness of his body muscles, the result of a ten-mile round trip jog on the beach from the El Segundo power plant to a place beyond the Redondo Beach pier. He worked out on weight machines in the afternoon, careful to keep his upper body strong and elastic. The workouts had felt good. He only wished he could have done them in the company of Peach. His drowsy mind had almost missed Kathleen's telling of an incident that had bothered her on the beach today.

". . . because I think we all have our comfort zones that we're too damn unwilling to get out of," she said. "But even now I'm not sure what I would do differently, you know what I mean?"

"Hmm?"

"It was so hard to speak normally, to feel relaxed. I felt like a nerd. The poor man was probably dying to talk to somebody. Anybody."

"What man?" Getts said.

"Never mind."

"No, tell me again. I wasn't listening," he said.

"He was burned. That's all I said."

"A burned man. You mean sunburned? What was he doing on the beach if he was burned?" Getts asked.

Kathleen considered his question. "I don't know. He wore long sleeves and light cotton gloves. Long pants and a hat the blocked the sun. And he wore dark glasses, of course."

For a long moment Getts stared passed the large oak tree in the yard, squinting, not to adjust his eyesight but to refocus his mind. He felt the prickly heat of danger on the back of his neck but for an instant's eternity its form would not take shape.

". . . and his little girl. I suppose she was dead. I mean, he wouldn't have talked that way about a girl that he lost in a divorce or something. He might have lost his wife, too, but by then I was busy running. Good old Kathleen, when something unpleasant happens run away from it. That's what . . ."

"He was German."

"What? German?"

"The man on the beach. He was German, wasn't he?"

"He spoke with an accent . . . I guess he was. . . . How did you know? Have you seen him . . . ?" Kathleen almost gasped in pain as Getts's strong fingers squeezed her wrist.

He turned slowly toward her. "He's in the house."

She neither understood the meaning or the impact of his words. "Who?" she said.

Getts thought quickly. He needed a gun. His had come in his car, which was parked around the corner of the house near the front garage. "Do you have a gun?" he said.

"No. I don't want them in the house. Robert, what's wrong?"

He did not believe Allison was in immediate danger. He had to get to the gun, and he did not want Kathleen out of his sight while he got it. "Let's go for a walk," he said. He took her firmly by one hand and, staying between her and the house, began walking at a leisurely pace around the stone pathway near around the east side of the house. His car was still sitting where he had parked it. As he opened the car door, he pulled Kathleen down low. He felt under the dashboard where he kept a .45 cal. Star automatic with extra clips of ammunition.

It was gone.

And Getts felt, with only a glance to confirm, that his right rear and right front tires were flat. He did not have to inspect Kathleen's car to know that it, too, would have flat tires.

Like an athlete waiting for the kickoff in a football game, Getts was aware of butterflies in his gut. He had no choice but to go inside the house. Unarmed. "Go to the neighbors," he said. "Call the police."

"I've got to get Allison," Kathleen said, her chin trembling.

"Kathleen . . ."

"Don't tell me what to do, goddamn it." Kathleen rose and dashed toward the open garage door which, inside, gave entrance to the laundry room.

Getts caught up with her before she entered the house. "Let me go in first." He stepped in front of her, kept very low, made his way into the utility room and paused by the entrance to the dining room. He waited in the dark, his senses straining to hear any sound, detect any motion. An evening news television report could clearly be heard coming from the den. Moving silently, his rubber-soled athletic shoes making little or no noise on the hardwood floors, Getts moved in the direction of the den. As he stepped inside the room, he sensed movement in a far corner. A swinging motion. Not a weapon. Not the form of a man. A tall woman, perhaps. As he inched his way along the south wall Getts could now make out the shape. It was not a woman, nor was she tall.

He saw Allison, and she was hanging by her neck.

The rope was fastened to a hook that was also supporting the decorative chain of a light fixture in the ceiling. Getts again sensed movement, and he turned to confront the intruder. But there was no time to face this new threat as he rushed to lift the small child from her gallows. Ripping duct tape from her mouth, he placed his lips to hers and blew his breath into her lungs. Then Kathleen was at his side. She stifled a scream, quickly gained control, took over the mouth-to-mouth treatment of her daughter.

The television screen suddenly winked out, its glowing light disappearing and plunging the room into total darkness. "Keep down," he whispered into Kathleen's ear. Getts crawled, then rolled smoothly across the room to a telephone. He picked it up and listened. There was no dial tone. In another roll, he got near a light switch and flicked it to the "on" position. The room remained dark.

A round from a large-caliber handgun hit inches from his head. The muzzle flash came from a wide hallway that led to the largest sections of the house. Included in that part was the kitchen, where, Getts knew, were any number of culinary knives that would make lethal weapons in his experienced hands. But Conrad knew this, too.

Then Getts smelled it behind him. Fire.

He retraced his steps quickly to find Kathleen cradling Allison, the little girl now with her eyes open but staring blankly. "My God," Kathleen said, "the house is on fire." The back door was a wall of flames.

Getts returned to the long hallway guarded by Conrad. He dived head first into the living room, rolled. A shot struck the floor behind him, but he arrived behind the relative safety of a large overstuffed couch. At arm's reach, on the mantle near the fireplace, was a hurricane lamp. It was full of oil. Getts pulled the lamp from its resting place, discarded the chimney and readied a match. He raised his head up for a moment, then ducked down as another shot was fired inches from his head. Conrad, knowing Getts was unarmed, rose from concealment and took a step toward the sofa. Getts touched a match to the lamp wick. He started his arm movement while still crouched, rose slightly to guide the fiery missile and flung it hard toward Conrad's feet.

Conrad fired another shot, but this time Getts felt the bullet strike his chest. He thought it felt like being crushed by a sledgehammer. The force of it sent him sprawling backward. As he fell he heard a shout. Getts did not wait to judge the results of his Molotov cocktail. It had either done damage or, if it had not, Conrad would kill him. Ignoring his pain, Getts leaped over the stuffed sofa and dove headlong toward a figure who was fighting flame burning around his legs.

As Getts hurtled toward him, Conrad snapped off another shot, but his attention was on his flaming trousers, and the shot went wide. Getts hit him midsection, and the two men fell heavily to the tile floor. Conrad gurgled from pain. It could not have been caused by the impact Getts delivered, but from the hurricane lamp fire upon the man's already scarred body. It was fire upon fire, and Getts knew the pain would be unbearable.

Their struggle was ungainly, a matter of brute force, with each man injured and weakened from his wounds. The gun was lost to the German terrorist, but his fingers searched for Getts's face, his eyes, anything that he could rip and gouge. Getts's body was almost useless on its left side. He was unable to raise his left arm or use his hand. Pain tore at his insides. While still in a kneeling position, he threw a hard elbow into Conrad's face feeling, with satisfaction, bone breaking. Conrad made a sucking sound, then pulled away from Getts slightly, his hand retrieving a switchblade from a pocket.

Conrad was on his feet now, the knife held low in attack position. He lunged toward Getts, but the move was only to gain position and Getts moved back. He was losing blood quickly, and he felt bile in his throat from exertion, his backward step a stumble more than a light foot movement. Conrad made another movement, leading with the knife, and this time it was for a killing thrust, aimed at the wounded side of Getts's body.

Anticipating the action, Getts struck hard with a leg kick

into Conrad's midsection. Getts could feel the knife slice along his lower shinbone of his leg, but the cut was not disabling. While Conrad was staggering Getts pressed his advantage by driving close to Conrad's body and thrusting hard upward with his head to Conrad's chin. The blow snapped the German's head smartly backward, and the terrorist was stunned.

The fire in the rear of the house had progressed rapidly toward the battling men. Kathleen, carrying Allison in her arms, scuttled past Conrad and Getts to the relative safety of the south end of the house, where the fire had not yet reached.

Getts used all of his willpower to maintain his hold on a reeling Conrad and smashed his head once again into Conrad's jaw. He could feel teeth snapping inside his foe's mouth. Conrad made another feeble swing with his arm, but this time there was no blade in his hand and no strength in the effort. Getts positioned himself behind the German, locked his arm around Conrad's head and began dragging him toward the raging fire. He could now hear the distant sound of sirens, which he assumed came from fire equipment. They would not arrive in time.

Conrad was sufficiently alert to realize what was happening to him. He struggled mightily, but he was in no position to overcome Getts's grip around his neck. He could not get his feet under him. At the edge of the fire, Getts used almost all of his reserve strength to ram the terrorist's head into the stucco wall. Then he pushed Conrad fully into the roaring fire.

Conrad screamed.

Getts shut his ears to the man's howling agony.

Conrad staggered forward toward Getts and away from the fire, but Getts used his fist to slug Conrad squarely on the face and backward into the flames. This time for good. He stood and watched the terrorist's body as flames overcame him and he slowly charred into a pile of burning flesh.

This time he would not come back.

Epilogue

In a private ceremony in the White House conducted by the President of the United States and attended by the Secretary of Defense and the Chairman of the Joint Chiefs of Staff as well as Carla Henry's family, Carla was posthumously awarded the Congressional Medal of Honor. The citation, describing her action holding off an overwhelming force while allowing her comrades to retreat to safety, was classified top secret as others have been in the history of covert military operations. Carla Henry's mother and father accepted the award and were thanked most profoundly on behalf of the nation for their daughter's heroic sacrifice for world peace.

Peach remains in the United States Navy where he still serves on active duty. He was promoted to W-4, against his better judgment and personal wishes. Among his many decorations was the Navy Cross for gallantry, which was presented to him by the President at the same secret ceremony cited above.

Bradley Wallis served two more years as director of the Carlisle Foundation after the end of Conrad was brought about. He retired to Coventry, England, where he has written extensively of his forty-plus years in espionage. He is often consulted in matters of counterinsurgency policy by both political parties in Britain.

General Maas was promoted over the heads of other general officers to the rank of Colonel General. He was then made deputy director of the Israeli Mossad.

Major General Cornelius R. Lathrop was passed over for promotion and retired less than a year after the battle at the Towers of Fouquat. General Lathrop was then hired as president and chief executive officer of Cravelle Electronics, a field he knew nothing about but whose defense contracts he could secure. General Lathrop was found sitting behind the wheel of his Lincoln Continental automobile at four A.M. in front of the Hyatt Regency Hotel in San Francisco, a bullet hole in the side of his head. Police were at a loss to find motive in the case, robbery having been ruled out. The San Francisco Homicide Division believes that because the general's window was rolled partially down and there were no fingerprints, no signs of a struggle, that the general had known his killer. The case remains unsolved.

Rabbi, stricken with lung cancer, made a complete recovery and retired from the Mossad with high honors. He lives in Tel Aviv and in Monaco. He speaks with lessening frequency to Getts, who remains to this day unaware that Rabbi was Fanus or that he murdered Razorback. In 1947, he had indeed denounced his brother, Rudyeh, to the authorities as an Arab spy but it was Rabbi, not his brother, who was the spy in the pay of the Arabs.

Toni, now a captain in the U.S. Air Force, flies B-2 bombers.

Robert Getts was promoted to the rank of captain by presidential order. Awaiting further assignment he is currently a "fellow" at the Carlisle Foundation.

Kathleen Sawyer lives in Galveston, Texas, and is engaged to marry a yacht builder.

Bartender accepted a discharge from the U.S. Army when his tour of duty was up. He lost his battle with alcoholism and recently died of cirrhosis of the liver.

Getts traveled to Hoquium, Washington, and met Ron Bowers's family. Ron's father, a logger to whom his son had borne a strong resemblance, was rugged of body and mind. The senior Bowers, of German descent, had a wife of thirty-six years of Finnish extraction. Ron was one of two sons, Ron being the younger. Both boys had been outstanding athletes in high school and regarded as rambunctious, honest, and fun.

Getts spent two days visiting the town and the family. There were several cousins, aunts and uncles. He told them, truthfully, that Ron had been an outstanding patriot and friend, a man of unusual bravery. Mr. Bowers wrote to Getts several months later that their oldest son had just died from a brain aneurism.

E. H. Bollan is still waiting for his award to arrive in the mail.